Jewel
of
Innana

To Even & Jenna
Brightyest Blessings
always

Hannah
Gesnord

AUTHOR:
Hannah Desmond

EDITOR:
Roberta Binder
RobertaEdits.com

COVER ARTIST:
Rachel Clearfield

ART DIRECTOR:
Dana Irwin
irwindesignasheville.com

JEWEL OF INANNA

First Printing: 2017

Printed in the United States of America

This is a work of fiction. Names, characters, places, and incidents either are the product of the author's imagination or are used fictitiously, and any resemblance to actual persons, living or dead or storied events is entirely coincidental.

ISBN: 978-0-692-91302-4

Additional copies for this title can be ordered through:

Hannahdesmond.com

Jewel of Inanna

Hannah Desmond

Contents

PROLOGUE

Vernal Equinox, March 21, 1972

The first light of spring warmed the slate roofs and gilded the damp bricks of the New Orleans French Quarter. Silver flute notes hung in the humid air of a private courtyard. Lilly took the silver flute from her lips as James and Jolene came out of their apartment. Gently, putting her flute aside, she joined them by the fountain in the center of the courtyard.

Jolene opened her arms and gently pulled Lilly into an embrace, "Blessings on the equinox, dear child."

Lilly spoke a simple, "Thank you."

Turning, Lilly saw James open his arms; he gave her a quick hug, stood back and looked into her eyes questioning, "Have you had any sleep?"

"I slept a little. Since my trip through the portal, I haven't needed much sleep." Her friends nodded in understanding. Picking up her flute, Lilly headed up the spiral stairs to her apartment.

A swirl of psychedelic rainbows greeted her as hundreds of crystals, hanging in her bedroom window, caught the light of the early morning sun. Lilly smiled as she looked at the sleeping form of her lover, snoring quietly. Pulling the window shade down, she reached up and turned the ceiling fan to a lazy circulation. The comfort of the cool cotton sheets, the steady thrum of the fan, and the warmth of her lover calmed Lilly's mind. Cocooned in her safe haven, she allowed visions of her past to arise...

Part I

Captive

"Fear is static that prevents me from hearing myself."

Samuel Butler

CHAPTER 1

THE DARK CUPBOARD OPENS

Lilly closed her eyes, massaged her temples and tried to relax. The silence in the car was deafening. It hung in the air like a time bomb. With her eyes closed, the bundle of dynamite tied to the leaden weight between her and Alex appeared real. Shrinking inside of herself, she took tiny breaths of air and tried to disappear into the leather seat of the Mercedes.

The tension had been increasing for several days. As they traveled in silence, Lilly's anxiety grew. She rubbed the sweat from her fingers and hands on her skirt. Her heart pounded and tears burned behind her eyelids as her mind sped through the previous week. She couldn't pinpoint any transgression on her part. As far as she could recall, she hadn't spoken an irritating word to Alex. She had not whined or complained. She didn't want to give Alex an excuse to cancel the Thanksgiving trip to LaPoint for dinner with her mother and stepfather.

When they turned into the dirt road to her Mama's house, Lilly took a deep breath and pulled her lips into a smile. She stepped out of the car in front of the big old wood framed house that had been her childhood home. The cold, moist air of the bayou town was welcomed, it allowed her to cover her bruises with a turtle neck sweater.

By late afternoon, her facial muscles ached from forcing a smile. She couldn't fake it much longer. *'I need to talk to Mama,'* she thought. *'Maybe, this time, she will understand. Maybe Mama could tell me what to do.'*

After dinner, when mama headed to the back porch for a cigarette, Lilly joined her for a private moment. She didn't know how to approach the topic, so she blurted out with a sob, "I don't know what to do, Mama! No matter how hard I try, nothing I do pleases Alex."

Her mother grimaced, grabbed Lilly's arm and spoke harshly in her face, "You have always been headstrong. When you're married, you have to listen to what your husband says. Are you keeping the house clean? Do you cook decent meals for him? Do you open your legs willingly?"

Lilly leaned away from her mother's grip and spoke softly, "Of course I do, Ma. I want to have a good marriage. I don't know what I have done to change his love for me into hate."

"I find that hard to believe, Lilly. You never wanted to cooperate or do a damn thing to help out when you were living here."

Lilly ignored the tears burning her eyes and spoke in a hushed voice, "You don't understand, Mama, Alex is scaring me. One minute he's whispering sweetly in my ear, the next he is backhanding me and throwing me around the room. I'm scared."

Her Mother took a long drag from her cigarette, flicked the ash off and quietly commented, "If you ask me, he has good cause to try to knock some sense into you, God knows we never could."

Lilly ignored the mocking tone in her Mama's voice and tried to get through to her. "Do you remember how daddy could see the colored light around people and animals? I could see them too. The brightness around Alex was what attracted me to him. He shone like a gemstone with yellow and ruby red light all around him. The last time I saw his colors, they swirled wildly, muddy colored and filled with holes. I don't know what's happened. I'm worried about him, and I am afraid."

"Oh, Lilly, are you still talking that craziness about the colors around people? Your dad was nuts, and so are you."

"Mama, you remember the long talks we had about the people in town and the colors around them. You were there. Why do you think I'm crazy all of a sudden?"

"Oh, it's not all of a sudden. I thought your dad was nuts and, sadly, you inherited his peculiarity."

CAPTIVE

"You never said anything like that when he was with us. We use to laugh and share and…."

"Lilly, he was a good man. He was paying the bills. His wood carvings brought in good money, and his fishing skills were legendary. He treated us good. I didn't want to mess that up. I always thought he was nuts. It was a disappointment when you turned out as crazy as he was."

"His family was a real doozy too. I met them once, when I was pregnant with you. After I met them and saw what they were, I was worried about having a child with him."

"You met his family? I never knew!"

"Oh, yeah! He took me out to the bayou bungalows. I have never met a stranger bunch of bayou trash in my whole life. Your daddy and his sister, Pearl, were the only members of the family anywhere near normal. That should tell you something."

Salty rivulets seeped out of Lilly's eyes, burning her cheeks. She hung her head, her hair falling over her face.

"Don't go getting all sulky on me. Thank God you never met the rest of the relatives."

"I did meet them, Mama. We visited them several times when daddy and I were out fishing. I thought they were magical."

"There you go with the magic nonsense. They were trash, crazy trash. Some of them were downright mean, crazy trash. Don't be fooled by their sweet smiles and shining eyes. They have no scruples. Their hearts and minds are foreign, lacking humanity."

"Once your daddy was dead, I thought I could knock that nonsense out of you. Bring you into some sort of, I don't know, regular sense about things. It looks like blood won out. It seems I failed because you are as looney as he was. Messing up your good marriage cause Alex's colors are off.' Chances are, you're sick in the head?"

"No need to worry Ma, Alex has accomplished what you and Rex couldn't. I don't see the colors anymore. I am blind to them."

Her mother smiled, "I told you he would be good for you. There is hope yet."

Lilly's hand flew to her chest. She stepped away from her Mother, her mind opening like an old cupboard door. Childhood memories poured from the dark, dusty shelves in the recesses of her mind. Scenes of violence surfaced. Images of her stepfather, Rex, surfaced, a dark red cloud of fire swirling around him, as he cursed and beat her with a leather strap. Mama stood beside him, her shrieking accusations, providing lightning sharp strikes to the thunderous blows. Lilly's body flinched as the vivid memories bore down on her.

How could she confide in this woman? How could she believe there would be any help from a mother who encouraged beating and abuse? Understanding wouldn't come from this woman who denied the essence of who she was. "Okay," Lilly whispered and turned away as her mother lit another cigarette.

Opening the screen door to the house, Lilly stopped and called out to her mama, "Where are daddy's wood carvings?"

Her mother gave an exaggerated shrug, "Gone. They were stolen while Rex and I were on our honeymoon."

'Those carvings probably paid for your honeymoon,' Lilly thought as the screen door slammed behind her.

Chapter 2

I Will Not Always Hold You in My Heart

cenes of that Thanksgiving trip, the hugs and tepid goodbye's from her Mother drifted into her equinox dream.

She and Alex left early the day after Thanksgiving. Determined not to ride the two hours back to New Orleans in tense silence, Lilly turned the radio on as soon as Alex started the car. It was tuned to her favorite radio station. "Sometimes I feel like a motherless child," Richie Haven's voice proclaimed through the radio speakers. "Freedom, freedom, freedom," the refrain of the song filled Lilly's mind. Tears crept out of the corners of her eyes.

Alex switched off the music. "Enough nonsense!"

Lilly's hands curled into fists. She stared out of the car window and remained silent. The question she couldn't answer played over and over in her mind, *"What has happened to Alex, to our marriage, how have I failed?"*

The happiest day of her life, her wedding day, came vividly to mind. She remembered the vows she and Alex had spoken, surprising the magistrate, who offered a sterile civil service.

Lilly had spoken vows from her heart, "I will always think well of you, I will speak well of you, and I will always hold you in my heart. I will love you forever." Alex had repeated the same vows as he looked lovingly into her eyes.

Their honeymoon in New York was thrilling. Lilly, raised in the little bayou town of LaPoint Louisiana, was excited by everything in New York. Alex took her to the theater. He introduced her to fine dining and showed her the city from the top of the Empire State Building.

One night, after dinner at Tavern on the Green, they cuddled under a blanket as a horse-drawn carriage drove them through

Central Park under the full moon. The carriage was gently rocking through the park when Alex pulled her onto his lap. She straddled him, and they made love slowly and deeply. It was the first time she experienced an intense orgasm.

Her memory was so vivid there was moistness between her stiffened legs.

"Stop!" Alex yelled.

Lilly jumped, "Stop what?"

"Stop the finger jiggling, finger rubbing, whatever it is you do. I've told you before, it is beyond irritating."

A sob caught in her throat as she whispered an apology, "I am not aware I'm doing it, my hands tingle and I..."

"OK, stop doing it," Alex growled and resumed his stony silence.

Looking at him from the corner of her eye, Lilly's heart ached for the man she had fallen in love with. *'Where was the Alex who had introduced her to a new, exciting way of life, thrilled her with his attention and love? He had disappeared.'* She didn't know the heartless man who had crawled into his skin.

Lilly headed straight to the shower when they arrived home. The hot water relaxed her muscles. She felt the tension washing away, as a deep breath turned into a yawn. She wrapped herself in a towel and walked into the bedroom.

She was pulling the covers over her, when Alex came in, took off his clothes and climbed into bed. Lilly sighed as he reached for her. Their lovemaking was quick as he turned her on her stomach, pulled her to her knees and entered her quickly.

She collapsed onto her pillow when he was done, glad it was over, and she could get some sleep. Before she could take a breath, Alex lifted her head up by her hair "What do you think you are doing?"

"I...I...I'm going to sleep, Alex, I'm tired."

"No, no, you're not" he growled. "Do you think we are going to spend Thanksgiving with your parents and ignore my family?"

Lilly's head ached with weariness, "Alex, we had dinner with them last weekend. They knew we were going to visit my folks for Thanksgiving." This simple statement sent him into a fury.

He tugged cruelly on her hair again and spoke fiercely in her ear, "I just spoke with my mother. My sister and her husband are in from New Jersey. They are coming for dinner tonight, so get up and get busy."

Wrapped in her bathrobe, Lilly stood in front of the open refrigerator. There was a shriveled andouille sausage rolling around in the meat tray, wilted lettuce and a block of dry cheese. "I don't have anything to cook for dinner, why don't we order something from Becnel's Deli?"

Alex's jaw tightened, his eyes bulged from his head. His voice was as hard as nails as he spoke, "I would never disrespect my mother by serving her deli food. You get your lazy ass to the supermarket and put together a home cooked meal for my family!"

Lilly struggled to calm herself. She turned her back on Alex and bit back an acidic remark. Alex's hand darted quickly from behind her, popping her hard on the ear. The assault threw her into a spin, she grabbed her ear and screamed.

Alex caught her long silvery hair, again, and stuck a $50 bill in her hand. "Get your scrawny Cajun ass dressed," he yelled in her throbbing ear. The minute he released his hold on her hair, Lilly rushed into the bedroom and dressed, the cause of the leaden silence between them clear to her now.

She walked quickly to the front door, but not fast enough. Alex grabbed her arm and drew her to him. Kissing her neck gently, he cooed in her ear, "You know I love you. I want my family to love you as much as I do."

Lilly nodded her head, "I know, I want them to love me too."

Alex squeezed her arm as she slipped from his embrace. As soon as he unlocked the front door, she ran to the car. "Hurry back" he called after her.

Her ear was throbbing, and she screamed with rage, as she

16

sped out of the driveway. Different scenarios for escape played in her head. She always arrived at the same question, *'How far can I get in thirty minutes with $50 dollars?'* Hot tears of frustration blinded her.

The belated Thanksgiving feast was on the dining room table. Alex's mother, Fatima, sat across from her son. Lilly watched her look adoringly at Alex, admiring his fine high forehead, thick wavy brown hair, deep-set hazel eyes and the beautiful smile he was beaming in her direction.

Fatima never hesitated to sing her son's praises. Lilly could still hear her bragging, "My son was raised well, bred for success. He is a fine upstanding man with great potential. Everyone knows Alex is a hero. He survived three tours of duty flying missions over Vietnam. He finished his career in the service as a decorated officer and came home to be the private pilot of a powerful international businessman. There is nothing he cannot achieve in his life."

Her mother-in-law's gaze fell on Lilly once or twice during dinner. Her thick mouth puckered when she looked at her. Lilly could read her thoughts by the sour look on her face, *'This pitiful creature has tied herself to my Alex. She is so pale and sickly looking. What does he see in this weird girl?'*

Lilly and Alex were married at the courthouse in New Orleans before she met his mother. This was an ongoing sore point with Fatima and the whole family.

Not long after their marriage, Lilly overheard his mother berating Alex, "You've only known her for four months! She is a nobody, some sort of Cajun half-breed from the bayou. She wasn't a guest at the Gambino wedding, but part of the hired help. Further more, she is not one of us. She is not Italian and...is she Catholic?"

The thought that Alex's wife was not a believer in the Holy Mother Church distressed Fatima even more. "I thought you were

17

smarter than this, Alex. I'm terribly disappointed."

Alex had tried to defend her, "She wasn't hired help, she was a musician at the Gambino wedding. You have to get to know her mother, she is a sweet girl and of course she's Catholic."

"You are lying. A good Catholic girl would demand a wedding before the priest." Striding to the door, Fatima made a rude noise with her mouth and slammed out of the house. Lilly overheard the interchange from the hallway. She knew it would take a lot to win over her new mother-in-law. She soon discovered there was no chance of winning her over, Fatima's mind was made-up and her heart was closed.

After the awkward post-Thanksgiving dinner, Lilly stood at the kitchen sink and stared at the sticky pots and pans, the stacks of dirty dishes and delicate wine glasses. She ran hot, soapy water into the sink and stared at the pink and blue light reflecting on the soap bubbles. She closed her eyes and swayed on her feet. To hell with this, she thought, as she threw the dishcloth in the sink, left the dishes soaking and went to bed.

Fatima rode home in the back seat of the Mercury. She shook her head back and forth as she spoke in low tones to her daughter, Angelina, "I hope this Lilly creature is not now and never will get pregnant. I think she is slightly retarded. It is so sad, my heart is breaking for Alex."

"Momma I thought you spent a lot of time with her. You two barely spoke tonight."

Fatima heaved a sigh, "Speak? You think I want to speak to her? I spend time watching over her while Alex is away on his flights. I am telling you she is not right in the head. She mopes about the house, never even brushes her hair. I try to talk to her. I have invited her to watch my afternoon stories on TV with me. She mumbles incoherently and locks herself in the bedroom. Thank God Alex had the doors removed, at least I can keep an eye on her. I was afraid she would lock herself in a room and intentionally harm herself."

Angelina looked thoughtful, "What do you mean you watch over her, she is a grown woman. Are you babysitting her?"

"Angelina, Alex is worried about his little Cajun nincompoop. I have to sit with her every time he is flying out of town overnight. Sometimes he is gone for several days. It is awful, I'm telling you!"

"Momma, does she want you to be there?"

"I don't know, she mostly snivels around, doesn't say much, doesn't do much."

"You're right Momma, there could be something wrong with her. I hope Alex doesn't have any children with her. You will end up raising them."

Staring out of the window for a minute, Angelina took a deep breath and spoke quietly, "Is there anyway we can have her taken care of?"

Fatima inhaled sharply, "I've told you that life is over. Remember where revenge, secrets, and underhanded business got your father? He thought he was respected, the big important head of the Cosa Nostra. In the end, it made no difference. A gun to the back of his head blew his brains all over his birthday cake. You know this! Your older brother became a soldier for the Gambino family. Look how he turned out! He is in prison for the rest of his life. Alex was a child when we left the families. I walked away with you and my baby boy and I never looked back. I raised Alex to be a legitimate businessman, to have a safe life. I know Giuseppe's boys taunted him and tried to pull him into thievery and God knows what else. I always took a stand and made sure my Alex did not get involved with the thugs Giuseppe raised."

Angelina's eye's widened, "But momma, he did…"

Fatima cut her off in mid-sentence, "What you and your husband do in New Jersey is your business. Don't bring your dirty business here."

Angelina clasped her hands in her lap, shrugged her shoulders and reluctantly agreed.

Fatima made the sign of the cross, "I pray to the Blessed Virgin to protect Alex and send me no grandchildren from my retarded daughter-in-law. I hope the Virgin understands and it is not a sin."

Chapter 3

SECRET STASH

L illy jolted awake when the closet door slammed. She peeked through one eye and saw Alex putting on his pilot uniform. For a moment, a swirl of muddy color surrounded him. Sighing, Lilly closed her eyes. Alex walked over to the bed and shook her shoulder. She kept her eyes closed as he explained, "I've had a call and I've got to fly. My momma will be here by 8 o'clock. You make damn sure you clean up the mess you left in the kitchen last night before she gets here. I will be back in three or four days. You make my Momma feel at home."

Lilly gave silent thanks he was leaving.

He was still standing over her shaking her shoulder, "Do you hear me, Lilly? Answer me!"

Lilly opened her eyes and nodded her head. He was about to say something else, when he glanced at the clock and exclaimed, "Damn, I've got to go."

She lay perfectly still until she heard the car pull out of the driveway. When she lifted her head to read the glowing digits of the clock, it read 5:12 AM. Her head slumped to the pillow, and she curled onto her side and slid into oblivion.

A crashing noise woke her. She jumped out of bed, heart pounding, adrenaline rushing through her body. It took her a moment to remember Alex was gone. She peeked out the window and watched the sanitation crew toss empty metal garbage cans onto the cement driveway.

Her eyes flew to the clock. It was 6:45. She went into the doorless bathroom and tried to run her hands through the matted mass of her hair. She dropped her hands and grasped the sides of the porcelain sink. The familiar tingle in her fingers began moving into her hands. Bitterly, she mumbled to herself in the mirror,

"The tingling is getting worse. It may be nerve damage from Alex jerking me around. I've got to get away from him!"

Resolve and regret battled in her heart and mind, as it did every time Alex left town. She needed and wanted the resolve to leave, yet feared she would regret ending her marriage. A tiny flame of hope had burned in her heart, hope that the loving Alex she had married would reappear.

Turning the water on, she brushed her teeth, splashed water on her gaunt face and stared at herself in the mirror. A fit of shivering began and a moan escaped her lips. The purple bruise on her ear deepened to a darker shade beneath one eye. Gasping, she watched the red, raw finger marks on her neck crawl to her cheek. With bulging eyes she saw her small nose grow to twice its size. Blood poured from her nose mingling with blood oozing from a busted lip.

The tingling in her fingers grew in intensity, becoming painful buzzing electrical shocks. The strong sensation moved from her fingers into her hands and wrists. A rumbling deep in her throat, rolled into the back of her mouth and escaped as a roar of pain and anger. "This is not my future!" she screamed. A wave of energy propelled her out of the bathroom. Teetering between elation and insanity, she ran to the laundry room and grabbed a large wrench from the tool box. Returning to the bedroom, she went to work on the locked door of Alex's forbidden closet. She held the wrench with both hands, lifted it over her head and slammed it down. The brass doorknob clattered to the floor as the door swung slightly open. She opened the door and crept into the dark closet; the miasma of Old English after shave, tobacco and a hint of jet fuel assaulted her senses. The combined odors, the ever present companion to her pain and humiliation, paralyzed her. Tears sprang to her eyes, her throat closed and a thudding pain filled her chest.

Backing away from the closet door, she stood in the bedroom, took a deep breath, rubbed her tingling hands together, and momentarily freed herself from fear. Prepared for the olfactory assault, she stuck her arm in the closet and switched on the light before she entered. Breathing through her mouth, she searched the pockets of his clothes.

There was nothing, no money, no change. She collapsed onto the floor, defeated and spied the pair of red high top tennis shoes in the back corner of the closet. How unlike Alex to have old tennis shoes in his closet, she thought. I've never seen him wear high tops. She inched her hand slowly toward the red shoes and drew them to her.

She sat with the shoes in her lap, a frown furrowing her brow. The initials, A.D.C., Alex David Castiglio were written in black marker on the rubberized toes of the sneakers. Slowly, she loosened the shoestrings, pulled aside the tongues and found a thick white sock in each shoe.

With shaking hands she pulled the socks out. The sock from the right shoe was filled with rolls of fifty dollar bills. The sock in the left shoe held thick rolls of hundred dollar bills. "Yes, Yes, Yes!" Lilly threw the empty red shoes into the back of the closet.

With the wrench in her hand, she ran to the front door and went to work on the lock. Splintered wood flew as she beat violently at the last barricade to her freedom. She heard the outside knob hit the cement of the front porch. The inside knob fell into her hand. She held it for a moment, turned and threw it across the living room. A satisfied cackle escaped her lips as the door knob smashed a hideous lamp, a wedding gift from Angelina.

Sweat ran into her eyes. She stared at the lock mechanism, screws askew, but still in place. She stuck the end of the wrench into the lock and jiggled it forcefully. The door opened. Lilly's hand covered her mouth, *"Oh my, God, Alex is going to be so angry. He will kill me for this. There is no turning back; I have to get out of here."*

Her body trembled and her mind raced as she made one phone call, slipped her feet into a pair of loafers, and buttoned her coat over her pajamas. Focused only on escaping, she grabbed a big black garbage bag from the kitchen and ran through the house. The two money filled socks went into the bag first, underwear, makeup, deodorant, her toothbrush, a pair of shoes, a dress, and random bits of clothing followed. The tingling in her fingers ran up into her hands and arms. The sensation moved through her body, down her back and into her feet. Her body vibrated and her heart beat wildly. She hefted the garbage bag over her shoulder, sprinted through the front door and down the driveway.

Shivering in the early morning chill, she waited for her cab. A slit appeared in the window blinds of her nearest neighbor. She knew the neighbors whispered and gossiped about her, averting their eyes when they saw her bruises, closing their windows when they heard her screams. *'Let them stare, this is the last they will see of me.'*

Fatima arrived and found the front door open at 8 AM. The house was a mess and her nincompoop daughter-in-law was gone. She roamed through the house, instinctively knowing this was not a robbery. The stupid girl had run off. She made the sign of the cross and kissed her hand, thanking the Blessed Virgin for her intercession. "Maybe my Alex will have a chance for a happy life with a loving wife and beautiful children." Fatima called her brother-in-law, Giuseppe to come secure the front door. Her second call was to Angelina, to tell her the good news.

Chapter 4

THE POWER OF THREE

Hunching her shoulders, Lilly clutched her garbage bag of possessions close to her body and watched the hands of the black and white clock on the wall of the Greyhound bus station. Her panic grew as the minute hand jerked its way to 8 AM. Alex's mother, Fatima, would be arriving at the house any moment. The hateful old bitch would call Giuseppe and his thugs to look for her. The bus station was the first place they would check.

There were three people ahead of her in the ticket line. She had no idea where she could go. Her first thought was to return to LaPoint to seek refuge with her family. She quickly vetoed the idea, knowing there would be no support from them. Rex would call Alex's family and have them pick her up.

Panic paralyzed her as a shiny black Cadillac cruised slowly past the bus terminal and stopped at the red light. She couldn't see who was inside, but it looked like Alex's Uncle Giuseppe's vehicle. The traffic light turned green; the Cadillac drove away, and Lilly sighed with momentary relief.

The stench of sweaty bodies and stale cigarettes in the bus station made her stomach heave. She rushed out the door of the terminal, crossed Tulane Ave through a wave of exhaust fumes and entered the University Hospital. It was quiet in the lobby of the hospital. She breathed in the crisp, clean air, hoping to find temporary refuge.

The volunteer behind the information desk directed her to a pay phone. Lilly stood, phone in hand, trying to think of someone to call; *'Who would care about her? Who would help her?'* Suddenly the damn burst. She dropped the receiver and leaned against the wall, her head in her hands, sobbing.

A hand was on her shoulder, and someone was speaking quietly to her, "Miss, Miss, can I help you?"

Lilly turned around to see a middle-aged nurse with a halo of fuzzy blond hair and kindness in her eyes. "No, no I'm okay, sorry," Lilly stammered.

"You don't look okay, honey. My name is Trudy. I'm a nurse here in the hospital. I'm on my way to the cafeteria. Would you like to join me for some coffee?"

Coffee sounded good. Lilly nodded her head and followed the nurse to the cafeteria. Her rapid heart beat calmed once she was settled at a cafeteria table with coffee and a banana muffin. A few sips of the hot, dark brew relaxed her chest and she was able to take a deep breath. The safety of the hospital cafeteria soothed the cacophony in her mind, *'I'm safe, sitting like an average person, talking to another woman.'* Sipping her coffee, she looked up into the concerned eyes of the nurse and remembered her manners. "Thank you for the coffee. My name is Lilly."

Trudy smiled and said, "Happy to meet you, Lilly, Do you have family here in the hospital?"

"No, I walked over from the bus station to use the phone."

Trudy nodded her head, "The way you were sobbing, I thought maybe you had family in the emergency room or a seriously ill friend."

"No, I don't have any friends."

Trudy reached across the table and touched Lilly's hand. "I have had days when I felt alone with no friends. I know it is scary. Usually, it is not true. There are people willing to know and love us. Our work is to reach out, connect and trust."

Lilly stared into her coffee cup. It had been so long since she chatted with another woman, she had no idea what to say. The benevolent nurse's eyes were filled with compassion as she studied Lilly's pale face, and matted hair.

Lilly blinked away tears, "I'm sorry, I am a mess today. I don't seem to be able to stop crying. I am sorry to disturb your coffee break."

"No, no," Trudy said calmly, "You are not disturbing anything. It looks to me like you're in trouble, and I want to help."

"Why? Why would you want to help me? You don't know me. I could be a dangerous person."

Trudy gave a short laugh. "I don't think you're a dangerous person, but it appears you have run into one. You want to talk about it?" The nurse's kind face smiled with understanding. A deep sob rose from the pit of Lilly's stomach. Trudy gave her a napkin and patiently waited for her to speak.

Lilly blew her nose and raised her head, "I haven't run into a dangerous person, I married one." Trudy reached across the table and took Lilly's hand. Her eyes were kind as she listened to Lilly pour out a brief version of her disastrous marriage. "Today I escaped. He is out of town, but when he returns he will hunt me down. When he finds me, he will kill me. The problem is, I don't know where to go or what to do. I wanted to escape, but I didn't think it through."

The nurse nodded sympathetically, "Sometimes, we can look to the past to give us a direction for the future."

Lilly was confused, "What do you mean?"

"Well, what were you doing before you met Alex?"

"I had graduated from college and was playing flute with the Carrollton Baroque Quartet."

"You're a musician?"

Lilly nodded sadly, "I used to be, before..."

Trudy smiled and explained, "Whatever you have done in the past, you can do again. How long have you been playing the flute?"

Lilly's face lit up as she explained, "I played in the high school band in LaPoint, majored in music at USL in Lafayette and auditioned for the quartet two months after I graduated. I was thrilled when they asked me to be a part of their group."

"How long did you play with the ensemble?"

Unconsciously, Lilly looked up at the ceiling, searching for a remnant of her life. Unable to connect to her memories, she let her head fall forward as her hands covered her stomach. A flutter in her abdomen moved up to her chest and triggered the tingling excitement and anticipation she had experienced when she was working with talented musicians. Her memories were vague and confused, but the visceral excitement she experienced as a professional musician was still there. Three years ago she had owned her life, but the details of that time eluded her. Alex had thoroughly consumed her life, her own thoughts became drifting clouds.

"I didn't play with the Baroque for very long. Alex didn't like me being away from home so much. He said the rehearsals took too much of my time. I was tired of his complaints and guilty for disappointing him. I quit playing with the quartet. Alex put my flute away. I searched the house and the attic for months. I couldn't find it. I haven't played in over two years."

"Nevertheless, Lilly, you are lucky."

"How do you figure I am lucky, Trudy?"

"Because you have a talent. You are young, beautiful and smart. It won't take long to build a good life for yourself, sans Alex the asshole."

Lilly sat back in her chair, blown away by Trudy's assessment. Her head shook in vigorous denial. "I'm not lucky; I'm scared to death. I want to hide and make sure Alex can't find me. If he finds me, he will kill me."

"Do you believe he has it in him to commit murder? What would he gain by murdering you?"

Lilly thought for a moment, "He may not actually kill me, but he will make me wish I was dead."

Trudy's back straightened as she leaned toward Lilly, "Okay," she said in a matter of fact tone. Holding up three fingers on her left hand, she tapped each finger as she counted the steps to freedom: "Get a place to live, get a job, and hire a divorce lawyer."

"Wherever I live, Alex will find me."

Shaking her head no, the nurse explained, "Don't be so sure. If I were you, I would go to the French Quarter. Rent is cheap and the people living in the Quarter know how to be discreet. If you don't want Alex to find you, don't use your real name."

"What? Don't use my real name?"

"Right. How much time have you spent in the French Quarter?"

Lilly looked up to the ceiling again, trying to locate a memory, something normal she and Alex had done. "Let's see; Alex brought me to Al Hirt's Club once and to Antoine's for our first anniversary dinner. He forbade me going to the French Quarter by myself. He filled my head with horror stories of muggings and murders."

Trudy smiled, "That's good, the French Quarter won't be the first place he looks." Leaning closer across the formica table, Trudy spoke in a low voice, "The French Quarter conceals a subterranean world. You can become someone else. Use a pseudonym for a while, nobody cares. Pay your rent in cash. Most of the businesses owners will pay you in cash. Don't get involved with the strip clubs! That is an area of the subterranean world you don't want to visit."

Lilly grimaced, and entwined her fingers tightly on the table in front of her.

Trudy gave Lilly's hands a gentle squeeze. "Relax, take a deep breath, let your shoulders relax down from your ears."

Lilly followed her instructions and felt a little better.

"You will be fine. Get a place to live, get a divorce, get back to playing your flute. Pursue the life you want to live. Focus on the things that bring you joy. You can create a life that makes you happy to be alive. New opportunities lay ahead. Stay calm, keep your wits about you, new opportunities will present themselves."

A spark ignited in Lilly's heart. Maybe there was a way out of the mess she had made of her life. This ER nurse made it sound simple, three steps to freedom. Trudy stood up, "I have to get back to work, Lilly. Remember, you have a lot going for you."

"Thanks so much for talking with me, Trudy." Lilly watched her walk away in awe. Her hands tingled, and an unusual thought entered her mind, '*I may have met an angel.*'

With a new sense of resolve, Lilly looked around and grabbed the abandoned newspaper on the table next to her. Studying the classified section, she dug a pen from her bag and circled several places for rent in the French Quarter. She folded the newspaper, put it under her arm, picked up her bag of possessions and headed for the ladies room. '*It is time to get out of my pajamas, get dressed and find myself an apartment.*'

PART II

PANTHEA'S PANTRY

"BOUND IN A HOLLOW OF SPACE AND TIME,
ONLY THOSE TRULY IN NEED,
WITHOUT HARM IN THEIR HEARTS,
COULD FIND THEIR WAY TO ITS SANCTUARY."

Cate Morgan,
from "Brighid's Cross"

Chapter 5

SANCTUARY

Lilly stepped out of a taxi in front of 106 Rue Dumaine in the French Quarter. According to the newspaper, the apartment was available immediately. The rent was $35 a month. She stood shuffling her feet on the uneven bricks of the banquette for a minute, took a deep breath and pushed the buzzer with resolve. A gravelly voice startled her as it spoke through the metal grate in the door. "You here to see the apartment?" Lilly nodded. The door opened on rusty hinges.

A whiff of body odor and a corpulent belly covered by a grease-stained T-shirt assaulted several of her senses before she looked up at the man's face. His smile did not reach his eyes as he turned and signaled Lilly to follow him. They walked down a narrow brick alley which opened into a courtyard filled with bags of stinky garbage on one side and motorcycle parts on the other.

"The apartment's right up there," the man said, pointing to the second floor. "This is a historic building. The apartment is an old slave quarter. You can take a look. I've got a bad knee, can't make those stairs. I'll wait down here."

Lilly took the key and walked up the worn wooden stairs. Her heart sank when she walked into the tiny apartment. The stench of cat urine was overwhelming. Whoever had lived here previously had a cat, possibly many cats. The floor, covered with a muddy looking brown rug, creaked as she walked through the apartment. The walls were covered with dark paneling except for the bedroom which was painted Pepto-Bismol pink. Her stomach heaved, she shuddered walked swiftly down the stairs and returned the key. "It's not exactly what I'm looking for, but thanks."

"Okay, if you change your mind, come back. It may be available for a couple of days."

Out on the sidewalk, Lilly looked up and down Rue Du-maine. She took the folded newspaper from under her arm and checked the classifieds. The next apartment she had circled was at 607 Rue Saint Ann. She wasn't sure how to get to Rue Saint Ann. 'I'm not going to find it standing here,' she thought and began to walk. She had walked a block or two when the sound of a ship's horn told her the Mississippi River was straight ahead. Arriving at the corner of Dumaine and Rue Bourbon, she stopped to take in the unexpected scene. The sidewalks were filled with young men sporting full beards, long braids or halos of black hair. The women shown like butterflies, colorful skirts swishing around knee high boots and shoulders covered by silky, fringed shawls dancing in the breeze.

'Oh!' Lilly exclaimed to herself, 'this is where the hippies live.' The idea of living in the atmosphere of freedom the hippies cre-ated lifted Lilly's heart. She gave silent thanks to nurse Trudy as she stepped into an alternate world.

Turning onto Bourbon Street, she passed a young woman sitting on the steps of an old shotgun house. She took a few steps past her, stopped and turned back. "Do you know how to get to Rue Saint Ann?" The young woman nodded, "I do. Where are you going on St. Ann?"

Lilly looked at the newspaper, "607 Rue Saint Ann."

The young woman smiled and stood, "I know where that is, I'll walk with you, that will be easiest." A few blocks up, the young woman lead her across Bourbon Street and down one block. They stood on the corner of Rue Royal and Rue Saint Ann. "It's in the middle of the block" the girl said pointing down the street. "You can't miss it."

"Thanks," Lilly said as the young woman smiled and contin-ued on her way. Lilly easily found 607 Rue Saint Ann located one-half block from Jackson Square. She was surprised to find it was a shop, Panthea's Pantry. She opened one of the tall French doors, stepped inside and stopped in her tracks.

PANTHEA'S PANTRY

The strong, pungent scent of herbs filled the air of Panthea's transporting Lilly to childhood summers in her Aunt Pearl's country kitchen. Lilly, recalled happy childhood days spent in her Aunt's century-old home. Built of heart-pine, the house nestled in the forest near the banks of the Abita River. Lilly had sensed the magic in the nooks and crannies of the old house and flourished under the gentle care of her Aunt.

Those same olfactory stimulants floating through the air of Panthea's Pantry worked a bit of magic on Lilly's taught muscles and anxious mind. Her shoulders relaxed as she took a moment to cherish childhood memories of summer mornings swaying gently on the porch swing, dashes into the cool Abita River in the heat of the day and late afternoon with Aunt Pearl in the garden, harvesting ripe vegetables and snipping herbs.

The year Lilly turned ten the unthinkable happened, her father disappeared while fishing in the Dark Bayou. Aunt Pearl was the only person who understood the depths of Lilly's grief. She was the only one who could console her as she shared the grief of losing her youngest brother, Lilly's dad, Avery. When summer vacation and holidays came around, Lilly fled to the sanctuary of Aunt Pearl's arms. The scent of herbs filling the old house assured safety and acceptance, love, understanding, and guidance. The year Lilly turned sixteen, Aunt Pearl disappeared.

A pointed, "Can I help you find something?" interrupted Lilly's memories. Glancing at the woman with curly salt and pepper hair, Lilly realized it was not the first time the woman had spoken. Her round, black eyes sparkled and crinkled around the edges as she smiled at Lilly.

"No, I mean yes, I am, uh, looking for, I mean do you have an apartment for rent?

The curly haired woman smiled. "Yes, I do. Number 4 is available," she said as she rummaged through a cigar box full of keys. Picking out two keys she explained, "I am expecting a client any minute and my assistant is not here. Can you go up and take a look at the apartment by yourself, ma chérie? It's Number 4 upstairs on the right. The one with the green ribbon is the key to the gate, and the other key opens the apartment."

Lilly took the keys and stood still, unsure of which way to go. The woman saw her hesitation, "Oh mais non, you have no idea where it is. Go out the front door, take a right and open the wooden gate, go down the carriageway into the courtyard and up the stairs on the right."

Lilly closed her hand over the keys, nodded understanding, opened one of the tall French doors and stepped out onto the sidewalk. The gate was a wooden door cut into a larger, taller wooden gate. An intricate circle of wrought iron decorated the center of the door, allowing a peak into the courtyard beyond. Lilly opened the door in the gate slowly, peeked in then walked through the high vaulted carriageway and stopped under the curved arch at the end.

Water sparkled in the morning sun and splashed down a three-tiered cast iron fountain. Banana trees, turning brown in the November chill, rustled slightly as a breeze found its way into the courtyard. Delicate cast iron stairways spiraled up to the second floor.

A tiny smile lifted the corners of Lilly's mouth for a moment. She turned and ran up the spiral stairs. The front door of Apartment 4 faced the gallery and mirrored the front door at the opposite end. Two apartment doors lined up in between and faced out into the courtyard. The same pattern repeated on the opposite side of the courtyard. The connecting section, at the far end, was different. There were two apartment doors downstairs and a wrought iron balcony on the second floor, accessible from the inside by tall French doors.

Turning back to Number 4, Lilly opened the heavy oak door. She stood in the center of the sitting room and exhaled a huge whoosh of air. Her shoulders softened, and her stomach uncoiled as her eyes took in the room. An overstuffed sofa, sturdy coffee table, old wooden rocking chair, empty bookcase and an end table with a bright yellow lamp, created an inviting living space. Sunlight filtered through the narrow transom window over the front door. An intercom was installed next to the door. Lilly put her hand on the buttons of the intercom, 'No one can come in from the outside unless I buzz them in. Perfect.'

The late morning sun poured through the large window in the bedroom. Looking out, Lilly could see a corner of the courtyard and nearby rooftops. Making sure the window was inaccessible to any outside intruders, she sighed in relief and plopped onto the double bed. The mattress was perfect, but the springs were squeaky.

Across from the bed, stood an antique mahogany dresser with a beveled mirror mounted on top. A bedside table with a reading lamp completed the furnishings. *It's a good thing I don't have many clothes,'* she thought, opening the tiny bedroom closet.

The bathroom was classic black and white tile with a claw footed tub, a shower head, and a pedestal sink. A round window with frosted glass opened outward on a hinge. A narrow closet in the corner was perfect for towels and toiletries.

What a delightful surprise to find the kitchen when she opened the folding doors of a closet in the hallway. There was a two burner stove, a half sized sink, and a refrigerator under the tiny counter. Shelves lined the back wall filled with a collection of mismatched plates, cups, glasses, pots, and pans, all stacked neatly.

The apartment was cozy. The natural light from the transom window over the front door, the round window in the bathroom and the large window in the bedroom, provided enough light to make it cheerful. Sitting in the rocking chair for a few minutes and imagining herself living in the apartment, her fingers tingled as they moved over the smooth wood of the old rocking chair. "Yes, this is it," she declared out loud.

Running down the stairs and up the carriageway, she burst into Panthea's Pantry surprising a different woman behind the counter. This woman had long gray braids and a pointy nose.

"Can I help you?"

"I want to rent the apartment upstairs, Number 4."

"Oh, the apartments are Jolene's domain. She is with a client right now. Can you wait?"

"Yes, of course, I can," Lilly said breathlessly.

"Wonderful, make yourself at home. Have a look around, if you need anything, my name's Sabine." She smiled and Lilly noticed her severe face, with its long pointy nose transformed, revealing a gentle soul whose eyes shown with friendliness.

Lilly wandered over to shelves lined with jars filled with a variety of herbs. She read the names of the herbs and tried to remember their uses. She found Basil on the shelf. Aunt Pearl always had at least half dozen basil plants in her garden. Lilly loved the smell and taste of it. She and her Aunt spent hours harvesting and drying the herbs. As they worked together, Lilly learned the healing properties and the more esoteric uses of the herbs.

Lilly's lips parted as she closed her eyes and remembered a rainy summer afternoon in her Aunt's kitchen. They were making basil pesto. She could still smell the delicious aroma as her Aunt explained one of the healing properties of basil.

"When a person finds themselves at a crossroad in life," Aunt Pearl explained. "Basil will help with the anxiety and doubt accompanying their arrival. Decisions, sometimes hard decisions, must be made at the crossroad. Basil will stimulate the spiritual energy of trust. Smelling basil, putting it on the tongue and savoring it, activates the revival of zest and enthusiasm for life, easing doubt and fear."

Lilly took the jar of basil from the shelf, opened it, stuck her nose in and inhaled deeply. She slipped a tiny bit on her tongue, willing the magic of the basil to ease her recent arrival at the crossroads. Next a jar of nettles drew her attention. She remembered

Aunt Pearl suggesting it to a client. Her Aunt assured the stern looking woman the herb would ease her digestive upset, then once the woman was gone, Lilly heard Aunt Pearl mutter, "The nettle will also hold your tongue. You are going to have a harder time spreading your lies and gossip."

Lilly smiled and blinked back tears. The herbs and spices brought memories of Aunt Pearl to the forefront of her mind. She wiped the tears gathering in the corners of her eyes and allowed memories of Aunt Pearl to come.

Before her years with Alex, Lilly saw clouds of color surrounding all living things. The colors were something she took for granted. Her father and Aunt Pearl shared her ability. They often discussed the meaning of the colors, shapes and energy they saw. In her mind's eye, Lilly could see the bright pink light glowing around Aunt Pearl. Wisps of bright yellow and emerald green swirled through the pink encircling her head, hands, and heart. She was a joy to be near.

Lilly pressed her lips together, swallowed the lump in her throat and continued to explore Panthea's Pantry. She stood in front of a shelf lined with a variety of round cast iron pots. 'These would be perfect for gumbo,' she thought.

As she approached a shelf of cookbooks, the curly haired lady came back into the shop. A man wearing a white silk shirt, gold vest and baggy brown pants accompanied her. "Mack, ma chérie, it is always a pleasure to see you," she said as the man gave her a hug.

Stepping away from the embrace, Mack said, "It is always wonderful to see you. Your psychic gifts never cease to amaze me. I am in town this week, and I will be here Friday night for your salon."

Jolene smiled and said, "C'est bien! Afterward, we'll walk to Bourbon Street to hear your music."

"Splendid," the gentleman drawled. Rings flashed on his fingers as he placed a top hat on his head and sauntered out the door.

Squelching a desire to ask, "Who was that?" Lilly turned to the ladies behind the counter.

Jolene sighed, "It is always a pleasure to see Mack, but I'm afraid I have over booked myself for readings today. With Carnival approaching, I need to be opening crates of new inventory and stocking the shelves.

Sabine cleared her throat, "Jolene there is someone here to see you about the apartment."

"Oh mon oui," she said looking up at Lilly. "Did you like it?"

"I love it!" Lilly exclaimed.

"C'est, bien, I don't think I've ever heard anyone express such a sentiment over the little place. I am glad you love it. It must be yours."

"When can I move in?"

"Do you have the first month's rent?"

"How much is it? The newspaper didn't say." Lilly quaked inside, hoping the rent was something her money supply from Alex's socks would cover for a few months.

"The rent is fifty dollars a month."

Lilly's eyes widened, wondering if she had heard her right. "Fifty dollars a month?"

"Yes, fifty dollars. That includes water and electricity. Do you think you can pay that amount each month?"

"Yes, yes, of course, I can," Lilly said. She dug around in her garbage bag and slipped a fifty dollar bill from Alex's sock.

"My name is Jolene, and I suppose if you're going to be living here, I'll need to know your name." Lilly almost blurted our her name, but quickly recalled Trudy's advice to adopt an alias. Seeing her hesitation, Jolene spoke quietly, "It's okay, we can get to that later."

Tossing a wayward curl off her forehead, Jolene plopped onto the stool behind the counter. "Sabine, tomorrow I will run the register, you work with the clients. I need to put my attention on the store."

"Okay, Jo, we can trade places every day until I leave."

Jolene looked surprised, "Leave?"

Sabine sighed, "Yes, remember? I am going to Gulfport. My baby girl is having a baby in a few weeks."

"Oh, my stars! When are you leaving, Sabine?"

"We talked about this last month, Jolene. I'm leaving on December first"

"Next week? What am I going to do? I have no one to help me in the shop?"

Lilly, one hand on the door knob, the other clutching her garbage bag of belongings, stopped and turned around. "Jolene, I am looking for a job. I know how to cook. I know a lot about cooking."

Jolene and Sabine stared at her blankly for a moment. Jolene grabbed the newspaper from behind the counter. "Let's see if there are any openings for a cook in the paper."

"No, no, I thought I could work here for you since Sabine is going out of town. Nothing permanent, I understand, but I could pitch in for her. I could help out while she is gone."

"Yes, I will need assistance, but Sabine is not a cook."

Embarrassed, Lilly stammered an apology, "I'm sorry; I thought you might need some help in the pantry and I..."

Jolene and Sabine cut Lilly's explanation short as together they toned a compassionate, "Aww." Jolene came over and put her arms around Lilly's shoulders, "My dear this is not a cooking school. Is that what you thought?"

"Seeing the name Panthea's Pantry, I thought it was a culinary shop or cooking school. I saw all the herbs along the wall, I thought..." A flush crept up her neck and across her cheeks as she blinked back tears.

"Non, non, my dear, you are not the first person to mistake our little shop for a culinary school. Let me assure you we are not chefs."

Lilly looked up, "What are you? Jolene and Sabine exchanged quick glances. Sabine nodded, and Jolene said firmly, "We are witches."

Chapter 6

A WITCHY WELCOME

olene opened the door in the back of the shop and invited Lilly into the spacious kitchen of her apartment. The warm room, painted bright yellow, boasted a big window with a view of the fountain in the courtyard. Plants hung high in the window in beaded macrame holders. Lilly sat at the round oak table and swallowed a yelp when a large house cat pounced onto her lap.

Jolene spun around from the stove, "Meet Topaz, he is a long time member of our family. He didn't mean to frighten. He is welcoming you."

Lilly stroked the furry orange and white cat. She whispered in his ear "Hello Topaz; I'm Lilly," in a voice only the cat could hear. Topaz purred and curled up on her lap.

Jolene busied herself at the stove preparing tea while Lilly stroked Topaz and rested her eyes on the flowing fountain in the courtyard.

A cup of steaming tea and a jar of honey appeared on the table. Lilly breathed in the sweet aroma. She and Jolene sipped tea in comfortable silence for a few minutes. Topaz stirred, jumped onto the wide window sill, licked his paws, wiped his face and settled down for a nap in the sunshine.

"Jolene broke the silence with a question, I hope knowing we are witches won't change your mind about renting the apartment. Do you know anything about witchcraft?"

Lilly shrugged her shoulders and haltingly listed her ideas about witchcraft, "Not much. Witches cast evil spells, curses, fly on brooms, make love potions. All the things I heard growing up watching movies about magic and witches. I never thought there were real witches."

Jolene sighed, "Yes, sadly that is the archetype presented by Hollywood and hack writers. If that is all you know I imagine the idea of moving in with witches may be scary." Lilly pressed her lips together and closed her eyes as Jolene continued, "I assure you there is no reason to be upset or frightened. Most people don't know a lot about the craft. They are misinformed and have no concept about the practice other than what they have seen in movies. They think witchcraft is about devil worship, curses, and some even believe we practice human sacrifice. Nothing could be further from the truth. Of course, those people who covet power and control over others form covens focused on destruction and manipulation. That focus is called the left hand path. Misusing the power of the left hand path leads to a downward spiral into conflict, illness, depression and even violence. One of the principal tenents of Witchcraft is, 'What you put into the world returns to you threefold.' You can see it is foolish to manipulate and wish pain, grief or loss on others. That mess would come back and wreak havoc in our lives."

Lilly nodded as she sipped her tea and watched the sun sparkling on the fountain. "At Panthea's, we practice Witchcraft as a spiritual path. We begin our studies with the practice of Magic and travel through magic to a deeper understanding called mysticism.

"Those who follow the right hand path, the mystical path of the white witch, focus on knowing themselves and connecting to their inner power. By recognizing and honoring the elements of the earth and embracing them as a part of our selves, we become conscious of our oneness with the earth, each other and the greater universe. Developing the ability to know ourselves as a vital part of all that is, we touch power and focus intention to create our lives. This awareness and power is within the reach of every human being. The power to create and manifest our world is something we all share."

Lilly perked up as Jolene spoke of the power inherent in everyone. A seed took root in her mind, a seed that could grow

43

and lead her to a new reality, a place where her sad, fearful life did not exist. Shaking her head slightly; fear leached away the seed. *'I'm grasping at straws,'* a voice in her head spoke firmly, denying the existence of her own power. With shoulders slumped and head hanging, she listened as Jolene went on.

"The first law of witchcraft is Do No Harm," Jolene continued. "You will find many who practice the Craft are in the healing professions."

Lilly sat up a bit at the mention of witches as healers.

Jolene stood, stopped and turned around, "One quick question. Do you feel better knowing we are not evil?"

Lilly nodded, "Yes, something you just said made me think of my Aunt Pearl. I spent a lot of time with her as a child in Abita Springs. When I walked in the door of your shop and smelled the herbs, Aunt Pearl came to my mind immediately. I never thought about her being a witch, but she was magical. She had a huge herb garden, and people would come to her when they were sick or distressed. Her healing touch was well known throughout the North Shore communities."

Jolene smiled, "How wonderful to have a wise Aunt to guide you." Lilly nodded and sighed. "Ma cherie, do you have any more questions?"

Lilly nodded, "What exactly is Panthea's Pantry?"

"Excellent question! We offer many things at Panthea's. We sell supplies; Eye of newt, and toe of frog, wool of bat, and tongue of dog, lizard's leg, and howlet's wing."

A look of surprise and disgust passed over Lilly's face, followed by a smile as she realized Jolene was jesting.

Jolene was glad to see the young woman's face brighten. "Non, seriously, we do sell ritual supplies, incense, candles, a variety of herbs, stones, crystals, magic books, and jewelry. We offer psychic readings, teach classes in various aspects of the craft: tarot, palmistry, astrology and some classes on an individual basis. I host a metaphysical salon one Friday of every month.

A puzzled look crossed Lilly's face, "What is a salon?"

"Our salon at Panthea's is a gathering of people interested in esoteric studies, mysticism and powerful ritual. We get together to discuss the latest astrological influences, practice rituals, and magical workings. We share our knowledge and experiences with one another. You are welcome to join us if you are interested.

"We are also a practicing coven. Private rituals and group ceremonies are elements of our life at Panthea's. Not everyone who attends the salon is part of our coven. There are many folks in the Quarter who have interests in the ancient ways."

Jolene paused a moment and took a close look at Lilly. The young woman was exhausted. She noticed there were not only dark circles under Lilly's eyes, but red splotches on her neck and one of her ears was bright purple. The poor child sat, shoulders slumped, wiggling her fingers on the table.

Lilly noticed Jolene staring at her hands and immediately jerked them into her lap. "I'm sorry, my fingers tingle, and I move them unconsciously. I didn't mean to annoy you."

Jolene smiled as she reached her hands, palm up across the table. "May I see them?" Slowly, Lilly brought her hands to the table top. Jolene took them gently in her hands and stared at the back of the hands for a moment before asking quietly, "May I look at your palms?" Lilly nodded assent as Jolene turned her hands over and studied the lines across the palms.

An involuntary sharp intake of breath escaped from Jolene. The young woman's palms spoke of powerful potential. There was great love in her future, magical workings and a bright energy Jolene didn't recognize immediately.

"Well, am I going to die soon?"

Jolene smiled reassuringly, "Non, I am positive you are not going to die soon, ma chérie. I can confidently say your life is

PANTHEA'S PANTRY

beginning anew."

Lilly released a sigh and tried to smile.

"So my dear, I have revealed myself to you, would you like to tell me what circumstances have brought you here? You may confide your name to me. I promise it will be safe; I have lived in the French Quarter for over twenty-five years. You can rest assured; I have seen and heard it all."

Sitting in Jolene's kitchen, it was easier for Lilly to tell her story in greater depth than she had in the hospital cafeteria.

Jolene held her hand, gave her a box of tissues, reminded her to breathe and filled her cup with a soothing mixture of chamomile, hops, and skullcap tea.

Topaz awoke as Lilly finished telling her story. Leaning over, she stroked the big cats head. She was bone tired and hungry. A turkey sandwich oozing cranberry sauce and a scoop of New Orleans style oyster dressing appeared in front of her. "Left over from Thanksgiving dinner," Jolene explained. Lilly devoured every bite.

Resisting the urge to counsel the young woman at her table, Jolene asked, "What time can you come in for work tomorrow?"

In a daze from the overwhelming events of her day, Lilly blurted "I thought you didn't need a cook."

"I don't need a cook. I need someone I can trust to watch the shop while I am doing my tarot readings, someone to help me put up stock and, if you are interested..., well we will wait and see what else."

"Sabine can show you the ropes over the next few days. She will be leaving next week. We need to get you familiar with the shop so you will know your way around when she leaves. The pay is $5.00 an hour, 10% commission on the jewelry you sell and 25% off on any purchases you make."

Lilly's mouth dropped open, "There is jewelry in the shop?"

"Yes, a whole case. You didn't notice it; you were looking for pots and pans."

PANTHEA'S PANTRY

Lilly's eyelids drooped as Jolene opened the kitchen door and led her into the courtyard and up the winding stairs to her new apartment. Jolene handed her a set of clean sheets, a blanket, and towels. Lilly made the bed while Jolene emptied a bag of provisions into the tiny refrigerator.

"Get some rest; I'll see you around 10 AM tomorrow." Lilly nodded. Jolene slipped out the front door whispering, "All will be well. Blessed be."

Sabine was unloading a box of books when Jolene returned to the shop. "Are things okay with your new tenant?"

"Yes and no, you are going to train her tomorrow; she will be helping out in the shop."

"Thank the Goddess," Sabine sighed. "With Mardi Gras coming, we are going to need the extra help. She arrived at the perfect time."

Jolene raised her arms, her hands closed and opened in a swift poof, "Of course she did. The universe is always unfolding the way it is supposed to." Sabine nodded in agreement.

"The poor girl has been through hell, Sabine. I sense powerful energy within her, although she has been playing the role of victim for most of this lifetime. I can tell you priestess to priestess in strict confidence, she has the markings of a wise, old soul. There is some sparkly energy within her I have never seen. I think she may have Faery blood."

Sabine's head popped up from the box of books, "Faery blood! I've heard tales of a band of fairies living in the Deep Bayou. I thought they were just that, Faery tales. Where is she from?"

Jolene shrugged slightly, "Somewhere in the bayou, a little town called, LaPoint."

"I'm not sure what I was sensing within her. The energy she carries is something I've never seen. Possibly it is Faery energy.

James will want to look into it. I will need his educated opinion."

"One thing I am sure of, it is no accident she came here. I knew my advertisement would attract the right person. She has been lead here to heal and learn new ways of being. Once she finds her strength, she can connect with her latent power."

"Even in the mundane world, she has a lot going for her. She has come to us naive, beaten and afraid. Underneath those dark circled eyes, matted hair and terrified demeanor, she is a beautiful, sensitive woman and a trained musician. I am going to help her, and I hope you will do the same."

Sabine nodded in agreement. "I will do all I can to be a part of her healing."

Jolene headed for the storage room, stopped and turned around, "Sabine, some of your family lives across the lake. Have you heard of a healer named Pearl in Abita Springs?

Sabine thought for a moment. "My Aunt Clotilde had a friend named Pearl. They were both avid gardeners, herbalist, I think. Why?"

"Our new tenant told me she spent a lot of time growing up with an aunt who was an herbalist on the North Shore. She was a healer of some renown in the Abita Springs area. Living at Panthea's may spark memories of the teachings she received from her aunt."

Chapter 7

MORNING TERROR

Lilly awoke in the dark. She lay back, closed her eyes and listened for Alex's location in the house. She hoped he was in the shower so she could get into the kitchen and have some coffee before she had to deal with him.

Her body shot up into a sitting position. Her heart beat wildly, as she gasped for air. The memory of what she had done flooded her mind and body. Alarm blazed through her, waves of fear washed over her. Trembling, she burrowed under the covers and curled into a fetal position.

Dawn light was creeping over the horizon when she opened her eyes. The air was filled with the sweet aroma of strong coffee wafting through her floor boards from Jolene's kitchen below.

She swung her legs over the side of the bed, put her feet on the floor and walked to her tiny kitchen to make a pot of coffee. Sitting on the couch sipping her coffee, her eyes wandered over her new apartment. She blinked, her apartment disappeared and the sight of Alex's opened closet door, the shattered lock on the front door, the sink full of dishes she had left unwashed, and the pieces of broken lamp littering the living room floor flashed before her eyes. The enormity of what she had done fell on her. Tears welled in her eyes, sobs shook her body. She put her coffee cup on the battered coffee table, curled into a ball and surrendered to the racking fear.

'Why did I tell Jolene I would work in the shop? I need to stay inside. I need to hide. Alex's family will be looking for me and he will kill me.' Nausea overcame her and she ran to the bathroom. When the retching stopped, she stared in the mirror at her red, swollen eyes. She splashed cold water on her face and went back in her bedroom. Throwing herself on the bed, she pulled the cov-

ers over her head, and escaped into the oblivion of sleep.

The knocking woke her. Terrified, she ran to the door and looked through the peep hole. Sabine was standing there knocking loudly. Cracking the door an inch, she peered out, "Yes?"

"Hi, Are you coming to the shop? I wanted to show you around today. I was expecting you around ten. It's almost noon. I thought I'd check on you."

Lilly's lips tightened, she closed her eyes, "I'm terribly sorry I promised to work in the shop. I don't think it will be safe for me. I am going to stay in the apartment today."

"Okay, I can understand that, but I smell coffee and I could sure use a cup," Sabine said putting her hand on the door.

Lilly stepped back unable to stop the gentle invasion. Sabine closed the door and flipped the lock. They stood in the middle of the tiny living room staring at one another. Lilly remembered her manners, motioned for Sabine to sit down and went to pour her a cup of coffee.

Sabine sat in the rocking chair, a mug of hot coffee in her hand. She watched as Lilly's face contorted into a grimace. Lilly stared at Sabine and began to babble, "No, no I can't go out. It is too dangerous. I'm blind to the colors now, I can't see who to trust. The thugs will find me. I can't even imagine what they will do to me."

Sabine rose from the rocking chair and sat next to Lilly on the couch, "Everything is going to be fine. We will not let anything bad happen to you. I promise. Once you calm down, reclaim your balance and personal power, your ability to see the colors, I believe you are speaking of auras, will return three fold. Where better to learn how to use your innate power than working in a witchcraft shop. The shop is strongly warded, no evil energy can cross the threshold."

Wide eyed, Lilly asked, "How?"

"Its simple," Sabine explained, "magic wards."

Lilly stared at her, speechless. She had not said a word when

Sabine grabbed her by the hand and said, "Quick, get dressed, I know part of the answer."

"But..." Lilly began.

"Go, get dressed, all will be well,"

Reluctantly, Lilly threw on a pair of jeans and a t-shirt. Sabine took her firmly by the elbow and lead her out the front door.

They stood in front of the door of Lilly's closest neighbor. This apartment faced the courtyard. Sabine knocked and a beautiful young woman with a long blond pony tail, opened the door.

"Hi Madeline, you have a new neighbor."

"Hi, welcome to Panthea's," Madeline said.

Sabine turned to Lilly, "One of Madeline's many talents is hairdressing. I hope you will let her give you a new look." Turning to Madeline, Sabine explained, "Our new tenant is in need of a disguise."

Madeline looked at Sabine, raised a perfectly arched eyebrow, gave Lilly a close look and nodded in agreement. Lilly followed Madeline into the bathroom and took a seat on a high stool. Madeline tugged and combed through her snarled hair while Lilly chewed on her bottom lip and tried not to shriek. "Do you want me to cut your hair short?" Madeline asked.

Lilly reached around to the back of her waist and felt her hair. "Do you want to cut it to your shoulders or shorter?" Madeline asked.

Lilly inspected her face and hair in the mirror Madeline put in her hand. She stared at her reflection, pressed her lips together, tossed her head and said, "What the hell, cut it short." Madeline began to cut. The weight of Lilly's hair fell to the floor. Looking into the hand mirror, Lilly was surprised to see the silver blond curls of her childhood, framing her face.

Madeline stepped back and looked at Lilly. After a moment she said, "Your light hair will take color easily. Since you are wanting a new look, how about auburn?"

Lilly shrugged slightly and mumbled, "Sure."

As Madeline worked the color into her hair, she chatted about life at Panthea's, her lover, her job and how much she wanted and needed a car. Lilly listened patiently, managing to reveal very little about herself. A couple of hours had passed when Madeline, once again, placed the mirror in her hand. Lilly looked into the mirror and didn't recognize the girl staring out at her. She gasped and ran her hands through her short auburn curls.

Madeline smiled. "What do you think? Do you like it?"

Lilly continued to stare into the mirror. Noticing her mouth hanging open, she quickly snapped it shut, turned to Madeline and smiled. "Yea, I like it. I don't recognize myself."

"Exactly the effect we were going for," Madeline said with a laugh."Oh, wait I have one more thing to complete your total transformation. Rummaging through her purse, Madeline produced a pair of round granny glasses."Try these, the lenses are clear, but they will add to your disguise. Let's see how they look on you."

It was mid afternoon when her transformation was complete. Lilly returned to her apartment for a change of clothes. Before she left her bedroom she straightened the granny glasses on her nose, shook her auburn curls, and stared in amazement at the stranger in the mirror.

A few minutes later she was in the courtyard petting Topaz, as he sat on the rim of the fountain. With her head high, she took a deep breath, walked up the carriageway, through the gate and entered Panthea's Pantry. Jolene looked up and automatically inquired, "Can I help you find something?"

Lilly smiled and answered smartly, "I was told I had a job here today."

Jolene did a double take as her mouth fell open. "Oh, mon dieu, you look completely different. You will be safe."

The smile faded from Lilly's face, she shivered, fear churned in her stomach and exploded into anxiety. "Will I be safe? Can a disguise work? How long before he finds me? He will kill me if he finds me now."

"Nonsense," Jolene said firmly, "he is not going to do anything to you. I am going to teach you a quick way to protect yourself. The first step of self protection: Call on your spirit guides, guardians and allies. Speak these words out loud or in your mind, 'Spirit guides, guardians and allies, please be with me and protect me.'

"Second step: In your minds eye, create a mirrored, protective egg around your body. The mirrored-egg creates a bubble of protection and repels harmful energy. Positive energy will flow through to you. Make those specifications the first time you create your protective bubble."

"Third step: Thank your spirit guides, guardians and allies. You are safe to head out the door."

"I, as well as many of my students, have used the mirrored-egg protection. It works beautifully. Once you create it, with intention, it will become second nature for you to call on it before you step outside."

"Remember to create it before you leave the safety of Panthea's. Our wards are strong in the shop. Once you are out on the street, your mirrored-egg will provide the protection you need."

Biting her lower lip for a second, Lilly nodded slowly. "Thank you. I need to feel safe if Im going to make a new life for myself." After some discussion and a few giggles, Lilly and Jolene agreed she would go by the name of Lyla in the shop. The pseudonym was the final piece of her disguise.

After a week of working days and secluded nights in her apartment, Lilly grew weary of her self imposed confinement. On her first day off from her job at Panthea's she stood in her apartment, called forth the mirrored-egg of protection and ventured out the door and into the streets of the French Quarter.

Wearing large dark glasses and a big floppy hat, another gift from Madeline, Lilly set out to explore. She discovered a second hand store on Royal Street called The Far Out. Rummaging through used clothing, shoes, boots, jewelry, books, scarves and a hundred other unique items, Lilly created a new look for herself. She began to relax as she blended in with the artists, hippies and gypsies living in the Quarter. She walked among them dressed in long velvet skirts, colorful gypsy blouses, lacy, fringed shawls and knee-high suede boots. Striding confidently, she caught a glimpse of herself in a store window. Stopping to examine her reflection, she was surprised by the young woman looking out at her. The casual observer would never recognize the carefree, spirited, young hippie as the tortured, rail-thin, battered wife she had been a short time ago.

Even though her disguise was good and she trusted the mirrored-egg protection, wariness lingered. She continued to scan the sidewalks, determined no one from the Castiglio family lurked nearby.

Nurse Trudy had been right about the anonymity available in the French Quarter. Lilly was grateful she had taken her advice. The regular inhabitants of New Orleans: the affluent uptown families, the old money families in the Garden District and those who made the white flight to the suburbs, were not comfortable in the French Quarter of 1971.

Residents of the French Quarter lived along the narrow cobblestone streets, sat on balconies overlooking lush courtyards and called their home by its original name, Vieux Carre, or simply The Quarter.

Artists, musicians, and eccentrics frequented the sidewalk cafes near Jackson Square. Old men, with pointed goatees, smoked cigars as they sipped absinthe or drank rich coffee with chicory.

Young women sold beribboned head wreaths of dried flowers from kiosks in the square. Street musicians played on corners day and night. They dipped their heads in thanks, as bottom up hats caught the tossed coins of passersby. The scene thrilled Lilly. She entertained the idea of joining the ranks of the street musicians, but first she needed a flute.

Jackson Square was full of artists sitting under brightly colored umbrellas, smoking cigarettes and gossiping as they waited for their next customer to approach.

Bourbon Street bustled with tourists seeking forbidden thrills. Barkers opened doors allowing momentary glimpses of young women slithering seductively on silver poles. Captured by the darker side of the French Quarter, the young strippers tossed their long hair, revealing sequined pasties glittering the nipples of their ample breasts. Jazz musicians shook their heads as the dancers undulated to the hard beat of the psychedelic rock and roll blasting over the jazz that had once defined New Orleans.

The buildings, old and crumbling, the cheap rent, and the laissez-faire attitude of the inhabitants drew in the free love generation. The young freaks and hippies poured out of VW vans and old school buses painted in mind-blowing psychedelic colors. They came looking for the good vibes, sex, drugs and rock and roll that had played themselves out in San Francisco. The French Quarter opened its warm arms to their free spirits, long hair, and love beads.

Lilly blended and thrived in the colorful milieu of the Quarter. Although she had not yet awakened to the secret world of the French Quarter, the world of the supernatural, her gift of 'sight' once again kicked in occasionally. In those moments, she caught a glimpse of psychedelic fractals swirling around the newly arrived flower children.

Back at the shop, Lilly listened intently as Jolene discussed the practice of witchcraft and the mystic's path with regular customers in the shop. During her first month working at Panthea's Pantry, she absorbed bits and pieces of witchcraft lore, astrological phenomenon, ritual workings and visionary experiences.

55

As the Winter Solstice approached the tug of magic pulled Lilly towards the Craft. She did not speak of her interest, but began to read one of the magic books Jolene had written, *From Magick to Mysticism.* The ancient teachings, rituals and sacred paths described in the book resonated with Lilly's soul.

Sitting on the couch in her apartment, a cup of hot tea in one hand and Jolene's book in the other, Lilly was deeply immersed in the planetary aspects that effected life on Earth when voices in the courtyard drew her attention. Glancing at her wrist watch she remembered the Winter Solstice ritual in the courtyard tonight. Jolene had not invited her to participate, however she had suggested she observe. Lilly stood on the gallery overlooking the courtyard and watched in awe as the white clad group below created a sparkling energy within their circle and lifted their voices welcoming the reborn sun.

Chapter 8

TRUST YOUR VIBES

I t was January in New Orleans yet the cool autumn air lingered. Lilly danced around her apartment in her long, flowery diaphanous dress. Her heart stirred as she celebrated the freedom of her new life. *'It's a new year and I have a new life,'* she thought. *'I love my job, my apartment and my freedom.'*

Standing in the courtyard enjoying the cool morning breeze for a moment, Lilly's bright mood was dampened by worry. Sabine was scheduled to return any day and Lilly feared her services at Panthea's would no longer be needed. She knocked on Jolene's kitchen door, turned the doorknob and peaked her head into the kitchen. Jolene was taking cream from the refrigerator when she heard the door open. Turning with a smile, she greeted Lilly, "Come in, ma chérie, let's have a cup of coffee before we open the shop."

Sitting at the round oak table sipping coffee and nibbling on a croissant, Lilly voiced her job concerns to Jolene.

"Non, non, ma chérie, there is no need to worry. Mardi Gras is coming up and we will be over run with tourists seeking love potions, money-drawing oil, good fortunes and hangover cures. You will be needed, don't worry."

A sigh escaped Lilly as her body relaxed. "Thank you, Jolene."

"No need to thank me, Lyla. You are very enterprising and a great asset. We are happy to have you."

"You think I'm an asset?" Lilly asked, with a light tremble in her voice. "Sometimes my life here at Panthea's feels surreal. I have to pinch myself to make sure I am not dreaming. When I know I'm not dreaming, fear tries to overwhelm me. Maybe I don't deserve this life. Something could change and my new life might disappear."

Jolene put her coffee cup down, and looked into Lilly's eyes, "All of us experience fear, uncertainty and overwhelm during our lives. You are making big changes in your life. It is understandable you would feel discomfort, uncertainty and fear.

"You've been through hell and you're finding your way back to yourself. It may seem like you're doing a trapeze act without a net. Over time, taking each day, sometimes just one minute at a time, you learn balance. You learn to land on your feet and no longer worry about the net. From my point of view, you are doing fantastic!"

Lilly managed a weak smile. "I appreciate your faith in me. I'm glad to be free of Alex and making a life of my own. What's most frightening to me is groping in the dark. From the time I was a child I could see the swirling colors around people, animals, trees and plants. The colors were how I navigated the world. I could tell who was trustworthy, who was happy, who liked me. The colors faded slowly. Last summer they disappeared completely. Now I have no way to see who I can trust!"

Jolene spoke in a soothing tone, "You are talking about seeing auras. You were lucky to develop the ability when you were a child. No doubt, your father guided you in the process. Over time, your third eye closed as you had to handle the abuse from your family and Alex. Sabine and I will work with you to help you open it again. There are meditations, rituals and sacred sacraments to open the third eye. This is not a permanent blindness."

Lilly sighed partly in relief and partly in frustration. Jolene squeezed her hand, "Oh, Lilly, all is not lost. Everything is about energy. Learning to trust the way you feel around certain people and places will tell you if a connection with them is a good idea."

With a pinched, tension filled expression, Lilly shrugged her shoulders and looked at her hands. "I never had to try to see the colors, they were always there. Now, you're saying I have to learn a new way to navigate the world?"

58

Jolene smiled and reassured her, "Energy awareness is not difficult and it is often more informative than seeing the colors. Today you hear people talking about good vibes and bad vibes. They are talking about energy. You can tap into the energy of people and situations and get the same information you would get from seeing the colors."

A look of doubt passed over Lilly's face as a frown deepened between her brows.

"Oh ma chérie, how many times have you passed someone on the street and felt a chill go down your spine or goose bumps on your arms? Have you ever met someone who was saying one thing but you could tell their words were different from their true feeling? Oh, and think about people you spend a short time with who leave you drained of energy. What about people you love to be around because you feel joyful for no particular reason? You have experienced the energy field of others. Don't label yourself as blind! You don't have to perpetuate your victimhood. Tap into the vibes."

Lilly's hand flew to the center of her chest as the deep muscles surrounding her heart softened allowing fear to unwind. Absentmindedly she moved her hand from her chest to her forehead. She rubbed the space between her eyebrows, easing the tightness and tension causing a permanent crease between her eyes. She nodded at Jolene and agreed, "I suppose paying attention to energy would be beneficial on many levels."

"Yes," Jolene said, "Seeing the colors was easy. Listening, watching and opening to vibrations, brings you into a fuller engagement with people. I suggest you practice being present. Over time, you will develop a deeper awareness."

Lilly's felt the tingling beginning in her fingers. The tingling was stronger than every before. It engulfed her hands and wrists. She stood up, wringing her hands together. Jolene watched her for a few minutes before she asked, "What is going on Lilly? Is something happening to your hands?"

Lilly chewed her bottom lip, looked away and put her hands behind her back.

Jolene continued to stare at her. "Come on Lilly, what is going on with your hands?"

"They're tingling. It used to be only my fingers, but now the tingling moves up into my hands. I don't know what to do about it. Alex hated it and was always yelling at me about rubbing my fingers together. I know it is an annoying habit, but they tingle."

"Good Goddess, I missed this completely. You mentioned tingling fingers the first day we met. It went right past me."

"Have you ever heard of such a thing, Jolene? Do you know what I can do?"

Jolene nodded slowly, "I've never come across anyone who had them, I have only read about the phenomenon."

Lilly twisted her fingers then rubbed her hands down the front of her skirt, "Do you have any idea how I can get it to stop?"

Jolene closed her eyes and sat silently for a few minutes, Suddenly, she opened her eyes and began to speak. "It may be that your hands and fingers are filling with an energy for manifestation. Have you tried using them to direct energy?"

"Uh, no. I have never thought of that," Lilly said.

Jolene stood and took Lilly's hands, turned them over and looked at the palms. "Your fingertips and palms are thrumming with energy, Lyla. They may hold the power of focused intention within them, the same way a magic wand would be charged and used to focus energy. My wand is consecrated and imbued with personal energy. I use it as an extension of my hand, pointing to and defining my will. From what you are saying, and from feeling the energy emanating from your hands, you do not need an outside tool. Your hands are giving you a signal and sending you a message to focus."

"Okay, but how do I know what the signal means, or what do with it?"

Jolene answered, "I use a magic wand when I want to effect change or quickly manifest something. If I don't have my wand with me, my first inclination is to point my finger and use it as a wand. Anyone could use their finger in a pinch. It appears your fingers are exceptional. They have a sentience that gives you the signal to focus your intention. I suggest, when you feel the tingling, you put your awareness on the thought preceding the tingling or what you were looking at when the tingling began. The vision of what you can manifest, change or create will be held in your mind as you point your tingling finger."

A slow smile spread across Lilly's face, "This could be good news. Fingers that double as magic wands. What a convenient tool!"

Jolene agreed. "The power of intention is the core of magic. You have magical gifts and I would like to offer you training in the Craft. Would you be interested in learning and possibly joining us in our rituals?"

"Yes!" Lilly exclaimed.

Chapter 9

AN EARLY INITIATION

Jolene and James sat across from one another in a pool of candlelight. Eyes closed, minds stilled, hands in laps, they sat in silent meditation. They had been sitting for about an hour when James stirred, opened his eyes and stretched.

Jolene slowly opened her eyes and watched James. Her hands covered her heart as she sighed. James stilled and looked at her across the candle flame. Neither spoke until James lifted his eyebrows and tilted his head inquiringly.

"James, I've been having dreams for the last few nights. I have tried to ignore them but today, during our meditation, I received undeniable instructions."

James made a small inquiring sound in his throat and leaned toward her. Jolene's voice broke as she spoke, "I believe it is time to relinquish the crystal. The messages are coming from my guides and the energy of the crystal is leading me in this."

James slowly nodded, "We knew the day would come, Jolene."

Putting her hand out to James he moved next to her and put his arm around her, gently pulling her close to him. She rested her head on his chest for a moment, "I have prepared myself to relinquish it, however I'm surprised the chosen recipient is Lilly. It seems impossible. She's been here less than three whole months. She has not received her first initiation. The crystal is pulling towards her. Inanna's energy, my guides and hers are adamant she is the new guardian of the stone. We must initiate her into the priesthood immediately."

James held her tight for a moment, "Let's prepare to initiate her and gift her with the sacred stone. You will be able to guide her in its use and help her as she attunes to the power of the crystal. If the masters and guides and the crystal say this is what must be, we place the crystal in her keeping and allow the mystery of life to unfold."

Jolene put her hand on his cheek and kissed the lips she had known for over half a lifetime. "You are my wise Druid and I love you." James took her hand from his cheek and pulled her into an embrace, kissing her as they slowly lay back on the pillows.

The next afternoon, Jolene and Sabine had their heads together behind the counter as Lilly was stocking the book shelves. Jolene looked up and called to her, "When you are finished, please lock the front door and join me in my kitchen." Lilly assured her she would be there in a few minutes.

Several times during the week Lilly, Jolene and Sabine would meet for coffee and discussions. Some evenings they would meet in the Meditation temple. She was receiving instructions in the practice of 'the craft' and other esoteric teachings. Her mentors instructed her in the casting of magic circles, protective wards, properties of herbs and stones, the creation of crystal grids, meditation for self knowledge, transversing the pathways on the tree of life and their co-ordinates in the tarot.

It was an overwhelming body of knowledge. For the most part, Lilly had a strong attraction to the teachings and relished the time spent developing new abilities. She gave special attention to the practice of meditation for she was determined to focus and rebuild her life grounded and centered with strong, positive intentions.

Jolene placed a pot of tea and jar of honey on the table and spoke in a serious voice, "Before Candlemas, we want to offer you your first initiation into the mysteries. James, Sabine and I will be present."

Lilly took a deep breath, a big smile raced across her face followed by a puzzled look. "I haven't been studying a year and a day. How can I...?"

Jolene's gaze was serious as she leaned forward, took Lilly's hand in hers and spoke, "I have been getting messages from my guides and ancestors. They say you are ready. You have more training than you realize. Your abilities were highly developed in your previous lives. In this incarnation, you have been led to Panthea's to awaken your power and knowledge; to continue the training your father and your Aunt Pearl began when you were a child. In witchcraft, we call it coming in the back door. In other words, you were born into a magical family. Your family ties point to your many lives with highly developed magical abilities."

She paused, pursed her lips for a moment, and continued, "There is also the matter of your Fae bloodline."

Lilly tilted her head to one side and frowned slightly, "My what?"

"I noticed indications of a possible Faery connection the first time I looked at your palms. Sabine, who grew up in this area, says there are rumors of Faeries living in the Deep bayou near LaPoint.

Lilly blanched, set her tea cup down and stared blankly across the table. "No, this is crazy. There are no such things as faeries, are there?"

Jolene smiled her secret witchy smile, her black eyes sparkled for a moment and she nodded her head slowly. "Not in the way you may think about faeries. I'm not talking about Tinker Bell. I'm talking about ancient magical beings of great beauty. Ancient Sumerian and Babylonian tablets tell of the Anunaki, our star family ancestors, who visited our planet thousands of years ago. They came with great magic some interpret as highly evolved technology. The Faery were the first creatures the Anunaki created through DNA manipulation. The Anunaki loved them dearly. The Anunaki were giants. To them the faeries were tiny creatures, none more than four feet tall. When our star family departed from Earth, the Fae sought comfort with the humans created with Anunaki DNA. A new breed of Faery resulted as the two species mated. The offspring has the combined DNA of highly developed humans, which contains DNA from our star family ancestors and the beauty, sensitivity and magic of the Faery. This race of long-lived, musical, magical creatures is still alive on Earth. I believe you, Lilly, are one of them."

Lilly's head shook and she opened her eyes wide, "How? Who?"

Jolene tilted her head and said in a matter of fact voice, "Your dad, obviously."

"My dad was a Faery?"

Jolene laughed, leaned back and rocked the kitchen chair on its two rear legs. "Your dad was a descendent of a strong Fae bloodline. His ability to see auras, his fishing skills, and his amazing wood carvings are all indicators. Surely you have held his carvings in your hands and felt the magic."

A light passed before Lilly's eyes and she nodded her head. "I knew he was wonderful and special. Now, I find out he was truly a magical being. He was part Faery. It is crazy weird. Wait a minute, how do you know about his wood carving?"

Jolene looked surprised for a moment, but explained to Lilly, "When you told me about your dad, a light went on. I knew I had heard the name Avery La Couer before. I thought about it for a while and remembered the beautiful carvings he made. A friend of mine in Lafayette carried them in her art gallery. They demanded a high price. The magic in them is priceless."

Lilly shook her head, "This is a small world. I use to ride with him to Lafayette when he delivered his carvings to the gallery."

Jolene laughed and hugged Lilly, "Ma chérie, your magical path has finally brought you to us and we are thrilled. Your Aunt Pearl is your dad's sister. She is also part of the Faery clan."

"Wow, my Aunt Pearl was magical. When I think of her and the pink light around her as she worked in her garden, harvested herbs and made medicine, I am certain there is magic on my father's side of the family." Smiling, she lifted her arms over her head, threw her head back in amazement and exclaimed, "I have Faery ancestors!" Her exuberance faded and her face grew serious.

"What is it ma chérie?"

"My mother told me my dad's relatives weren't human. She said they were unscrupulous and mean."

Jolene shook her head back and forth quickly. "That is a misconception. Part of Faery magic is mirror power. Those who are ruled by the ego energy of the dark side see their darkness reflected back to them when they interact with the faeries. Don't worry about that aspect. It won't effect you. Your Faery ancestors are part of the group who have been communicating with me, encouraging your initiation. There is no need to fear and no need to wait a year and a day."

Lilly's eyes grew large, "Jolene, you're psychic, can you scry and locate my Aunt Pearl? She has the same Fae blood as my dad. It would be wonderful to have a real family again."

Jolene nodded in agreement, "I will be happy to scry for her. Do you have a picture or anything of hers?

Lilly's shoulders sagged, "No, I have nothing of hers. When I left Alex, I took a few of my necessities in a garbage bag. I am positive Alex will never allow me get the rest of my belongings.

Jolene put an arm around Lilly's shoulders, "Let us complete your initiation, Lilly. We can work on contacting your Aunt afterwards."

Regaining her composure, Lilly said, "You're right, Jolene, it is a discussion for another time."

"I'm so honored to be offered initiation. What do I have to do for the ritual? Is there something special I need to study?"

Jolene took a sip of her tea, "Ah, ma chérie, the road to mastery of spiritual magic, which is the heart of the craft, is a never ending journey. You will never stop learning. At Panthea's we believe the best way to approach the priestess process is in increments."

"For this first initiation, be yourself, trust your heart and all will be well. We will perform a consecration, ask you a series of questions, anoint you and welcome you into our coven."

"Let's do it tomorrow night, okay?"

Lilly's smiled and nodded her head vigorously.

Jolene continued, "On February 2 our coven will be meeting in the courtyard to celebrate Candlemas with a ritual honoring the Goddess Brigid. We would love for you to join us. It will be a perfect time for you to experience group ritual."

Sabine explained, "All of our members live at Panthea's and will be at the ritual. Oh, except one young man who is out of town."

Lilly sipped her tea and said, "I would love to be a part of the ritual if you think I am ready."

"You are ready," Sabine said. "It is time for your initiation and the beginning of your magical life.

Jolene agreed. "On Candlemas we sweep away ideas, attachments and judgements which no longer serve us. We focus our energy toward the increase of the new light growing within and without as spring approaches. We invoke the spark of creativity and the strength of Brigid, the Goddess of inspiration. Through the ritual we acknowledge our ability to shape our potential and consciously craft a new beginning with a will and purpose unique to each participant in the ritual."

Lilly could not stay in her seat. She stood up, leaned down and gave Jolene a hug and walked around the table to put her arms around Sabine's shoulders. Her heart was bursting with gratitude. She had found a loving, trusting relationship with these two women, similar to the one she had as a child with her Aunt Pearl. She trusted Jolene and Sabine and knew they held the keys to the wisdom she wanted and needed to live a life free of fear and insecurity. Lilly settled back in her seat at the round oak table and listened to the story of the Goddess Brigid and the part she would play in the Candlemas ceremony.

The sun was setting when a tall attractive, older gentleman entered the kitchen from the courtyard. He bent and kissed Jolene on the cheek, nodded to Sabine and introduced himself to Lilly, "Hi, I'm James, Jolene's husband. You must be Lyla."

Stammering a bit, Lilly replied with a quiet "Hello." After a moment she found her tongue and spoke up, "I didn't know you were married to Jolene. She kept mentioning James. I thought you were another member of the group." Lilly stood, put out her hand to James. He smiled charmingly, took her hand, lifted it to his lips and lightly kissed her knuckles.

Expecting a firm handshake, Lilly was surprised. James' blue eyes sparkled as he held Lilly's hand between both of his, "Ah, she didn't mentioned I was her crotchety, old husband, heh Lyla? I know I haven't been around much lately. I've got a shop on Royal Street and recently received a shipment of antiquities from Ireland. I've been busy overseeing the unpacking and the inventory."

Jolene took James' hand and gently pulled him into the chair next to her. Looking at Lilly she explained, "James will be joining us tomorrow for your initiation and for the ritual at Candlemas. The new shipment is taken care of. Now, you will see him more often and get to know his crotchety ways and his charm."

James smiled broadly, "Well said, Jolene!"

The next evening Lilly soaked in her candle lit ritual bath of scented oils. Sacred music flowed from her tape player and the sweet aroma of frankincense drifted in the air. Cleansed on multiple levels, she began to dress for her initiation. Her hands were shaking as she lifted her white robe from the bed. "I'm more nervous than I thought," she said to herself.

Putting her robe back on the bed, Lilly sat in front of her meditation altar. She lit the white pillar candle and opened to her place of meditation. It took a few minutes for her mind to clear and her nerves to calm. She sat, eyes closed, waiting for a sensation she had only recently become aware of.

The feeling was not completely physical, it began as a quiver permeating her aura. The tingling began in her hands and diffused through the essence of her being like the scent of a fine perfume or the remnants of a golden memory. As she embraced the feeling, she realized it was not new, but a familiar sensation. Scenes of childhood summers spent with Aunt Pearl returned. As memories flooded her inner eye, the quiver of magic increased, engulfing her in a golden light of bliss.

The memory of peace and joy, emotions she had once known well, reawakened in her heart, body and mind. This was the familiar, pleasant state she had known as a child. She put her hands over her heart, felt her body solid in the present moment, and returned from her mediation.

The rain had just begun to fall when James, Jolene and Sabine arrived at her door, greeted her warmly and walked with her to the temple. James and Jolene had created the sacred space years before in one of the two apartments enclosing the back of the courtyard. Interior walls had been removed to fashion a single large room. The back wall of the temple was made of the old brick used to build most of the French Quarter three hundred years before. The wide planked wood floor was covered with plush, oriental carpets and cushions for sitting. Tall cast iron candelabras stood in the four corners, each holding eight lit tapers, providing the only illumination.

James, as the high priest of the coven, cast the circle. Jolene called the Quarters. Sabine stepped forward with the censor allowing the sweet scent of frankincense to waft through Lilly's aura.

The elder magicians stood with Lilly inside the sacred circle of protection. In a strong voice, Jolene proclaimed, "Through this rite you cross the threshold into new territories of knowledge and abilities. We, the elders of this coven, have sensed the subtle shifts within you. We have watched you devoutly dedicate yourself to your personal and spiritual development. Today you put your foot intentionally on the path to your greatest good, you commit to the development of your full potential. Today you honor and accept your ability to be of service. Through this rite you embrace the journey to your authentic, magical self."

The elders questioned her, testing her knowledge and abilities. Lilly's voice quivered slightly as she spoke her truth, acknowledged her gifts and lack of understanding in some areas. Lilly thought the ritual was drawing to an end when James stepped forward and asked her to describe the path she was presently walking on the tree of life.

She licked her lips and began to recount the visions she was having during meditation and the slowly returning ability to see auras. "With these experiences in mind, I know I have been traveling on the path of the Universe. I travel the path on the tree of life from the earth to the moon, traversing the astral plane moving toward the higher realms."

Her mentors nodded and smiled. Jolene stepped forward and anointed her with sacred oils stating simply, "You are most welcome in our coven, Priestess."

Chapter 10

Matrix Magic

Lilly stood alone in her bedroom slipping her white satin ritual gown over a white leotard and tights. She tied a red silk ribbon with small gold bells on the end around her waist and slipped on a pair of white suede moccasins. Walking over to the mirror on the back of her bedroom door she chuckled and thought, *'I look like am about to go down to the river for a good old fashion baptism.'*

Sobering a bit, she placed the circlet of red roses on her head and recalled what she knew of the ritual. There was a light tap on the door and Jolene stuck her head in, "Are you ready, ma cherie?"

"I'm a little nervous, but I am ready. Can you think of anything else I need to know before we go down for the ritual? Do I look okay?"

"You look radiant, Lilly. Being part of Panthea's is good for you.

A few minutes later, the high priestess and the newly initiated priestess joined James, Sabine and the rest of the coven in the courtyard. They stood in a loose circle in front of the fountain, chatting among themselves. A large cauldron was raised on bricks, appearing to float in the fountain. The cauldron was filled with sand, a thick white candle stood in the center.

The group gathered as Jolene addressed them, "Tonight we affirm our connection to the rhythm of the Earth. We are reminded of the divine spark within each of us. This sacred ember has been tended through the dark days leading up to the winter Solstice. Tonight we celebrate Candlemas, the festival of the Goddess Brigid. We ritually honor the spark of divine light as it grows brighter. The flame is fanned as we continue to burn brighter with life, strength, passion and inspiration."

"On this Candlemas we welcome, Lyla, a new member into our midst. She has been studying and performing the personal rituals necessary to prepare for this night. She has passed the tests of her first initiation. Let us ask the Goddess Brigid for a special blessing on our new member." All of the members came up to her, said "Hello," and squeezed her hand as they moved into the sacred circle.

Sabine walked around the inside of the circle, anointing the members with consecrated oil. Lilly felt a light touch on her third eye. She lifted each hand as she had been instructed. Sabine rubbed a drop in the palm of each hand and spoke in a firm ritual voice, "May the sacred fire of Brigid purify, inspire and guide you as you walk the path to your greatest good."

"So mote it be," Lilly replied.

The group formed a larger circle. Swinging an incense burner on a long chain, a tall young woman walked behind them as they chanted in unison; "We are a circle, within a circle, with no beginning and never ending."

Jolene lifted her arms and called out in a powerful voice, "I do conjure that this shall be a circle of power, of inspiration where within the bonds of the supportive, protective love of brothers and sisters, we may raise, contain and release the energy of increased light. By the love of the Threefold Goddess and her mighty Consort, I do bless and consecrate this circle. As it is willed, so mote it be."

Lilly watched the corners of the courtyard burst into magical flame as the four directions were called. Her second sight awoke to reveal huge, glowing energies. Each corner was consumed in flame; silver in the East, gold in the South, turquoise in the West and deep green flames in the North corner.

Jolene and James approached the fountain and lit the tall, white pillar candle in the cauldron. Jolene stepped into the center of the circle and invoked the masculine energy, "Lord of Light, I call your spirit to this rite. The reborn sun of Yule, stands with us in our circle. We ask that you fill this priest with light, shine through him, kindle hope within us all. Through your touch the seeds of rebirth awaken. As it is willed, so mote it be."

James stepped into the center of the circle and invoked the feminine energy, "O bright Goddess of Fire and inspiration, mother of life who called us forth from darkness, I now call you to this celebration of increased light. Fill your priestess with the wisdom of your spirit, through your touch the Goddess is awakened within us all. As it is willed, so mote it be."

Two glorious beings of light overshadowed the high priest and priestess. The strength pouring through them was palpable. Lilly felt the air vibrating. Glancing at the others standing in the circle, she saw wonder and amazement on their faces.

Her attention turned to Sabine as she stepped into the circle, "The darkness passes, let it go. Foster the light as it grows stronger. Let us fill our selves with visions of new ideals and goals. As the light grows, may it crystallize into visible form, individual and unique for each of us. Tonight we call upon the Goddess Brigid, to ignite a bright new light within us with love and inspiration. May our light grow so we may share it with others."

Approaching the white candle, the members of the circle turned clockwise as each member stopped and lit a taper from the flame of the center candle in the cauldron. Standing in a circle of candlelight, the group chanted, honoring the Goddess Brigid in all her forms.

Lilly's fingers tingled and her body grew warm. The magic spread to the core of her being. Again, the circle turned as each member, continuing the chant, placed their burning tapers in the sand around the large white candle in the cauldron.

The circle reformed as Jolene instructed, "Keep the energy flowing. Focus your thoughts on sharing your creative healing light with others and with our Mother Earth. Feel the energy of this light flow from hand to hand and see it fill the circle and expand beyond. Your intention carries it."

73

Her instructions were not necessary, Lilly's attention was on her tingling hands, and vibrating body. A powerful wave moved through her as the energy passed from the young man beside her in the circle, into her left hand, through her body and out of her other hand into her neighbor, Madeline's, hand.

White light danced behind her closed eyes as the vibrations grew stronger. Energy was building and shifting within her. She opened her eyes, a rainbow of glowing color swirled in her vision. A cone of energy formed in the center of the circle. "Aaahhh!" she gasped, as she watched the cone spiral up into the star filled sky.

Closing her eyes, she floated in space through a matrix of energy. She felt herself connected to each person in the circle. Glowing hand in hand, they formed a circle of light beings. The bond was strong as each unique energy fed into the circle of light forming one powerful force. It was only a few minutes of earth time. To Lilly, it was an eternity of knowing oneness and unconditional love.

The vision slipped away as she opened her eyes and looked around the circle. For the first time in her adult life, Lilly experienced a deep sense of belonging. A huge sigh welled from deep within her. She exhaled and the weight of the world lifted. Her next inhale filled her with light. The members of the coven exchanged wide eyed looks of amazement at the powerful vision they had shared.

Jolene closed the ritual. "Mother of Life, of fire and inspiration. Thank you for your love and vision. We bid you hail and farewell. Blessed Be."

When the four quarters were released, the group joined hands and spoke as one;

"Merry meet and merry part and merry meet again."

Although the energy had been dispersed, Lilly was trembling. Each member of the coven pulled her into an embrace. As she put her arms around them, a matrix of vibrant spiritual energy began to build a bond of trust.

Lilly shivered slightly in the night air, ran up to her apartment and changed from her ritual gown into jeans and a sweater. Running back downstairs she joined the other members of the coven in Jolene's kitchen.

This was the first time Lilly saw all the members of the group together. She knew Madeline and was excited to meet the rest of the coven members in physical form, having already merged with them as beings of light.

The main topic of conversation was the shared visions the group had experienced during the ritual. They had never seen the flames appear in the four corners and the protective beings of light. Everyone was awed by the energy they experienced as one, floating in a glowing matrix of love and trust.

James sat next to Lilly on the couch, and put his great bear arms around. "Congratulations on your first ritual Lyla, you did beautifully. How did you like it?"

Lilly looked into the high priest's vivid blue eyes and spoke sincerely, "I loved it. I've never been a part of anything so beautiful. The energies, invoked in the ritual, vibrated through my body. Every cell was dancing with life, activated is the word that best describes it. I saw the guiding and protective spirits appear as they were invoked. Their energy was large, shining and benevolent as they surrounded our circle."

James was taken aback and took a moment to control his reaction, "Yes, you have a real gift. We all saw the beautiful energy you brought to the ritual. You are a welcome addition to this coven."

"Thank you. It is wonderful to be welcomed and appreciated." James patted her on the shoulder in a fatherly gesture and went on to speak to the other members gathered around the room.

Sitting next to Madeline on the couch, Lilly was introduced to the tall woman who had swung the censor during the ritual. Her name was Gemma. "Hi, Lyla, nice to meet you. I live on the

75

ground floor, across the courtyard in Apartment 11."

"I'm happy to meet you, Gemma," Lilly said, suddenly shy. A beautiful smile played across Gemma's full lips as she tossed her dark hair over her shoulders. Lilly noticed the heavy silver earrings set with glowing fire opals dangling from Gemma's ears.

"Your earrings are beautiful."

"Thanks, Lyla. These are from my collection of Gemma's Gems."

Realization dawned on Lilly's face, "Oh, you make the jewelry for the store!"

"Yes, most of it, I have my studio set up in my spare bedroom. Come over and visit anytime."

Sabine came into the room and announced the food was on the table and it was time to eat. The door to the shop was open and a long table filled the center of the store.

The group formed a circle, this time surrounding the feast laden table. They joined hands as James spoke the blessing, "Shining Sun, Holy Moon, Sacred Mother, Father, we thank you for this feast, for the blessing of good friends, companions and spiritual teachers. We thank the rooted ones, the winged ones and the four footed of this earth for their sacrifice which nourishes and strengthens our bodies and our spirits. Blessed be."

The circle responded with a resounding, "Blessed Be!"

Walking around the table, filling her plate, Lilly got a good look at the rest of the members of the coven. They all lived in Panthea's apartments. These were her neighbors and would be her friends. Smiling brightly, she took her plate and headed back to Jolene's apartment.

Jolene was sitting at the oak table in the kitchen and signaled Lilly to join her. They discussed the ritual for a few minutes, Jolene listened intently as Lilly told her about the experience of oneness she had during the ritual.

They finished their meal and Jolene leaned close to Lilly and spoke quietly, "I have tried to scry for Pearl. I am sorry to say, I get nothing. The mirror remains dark."

"Oh, no! She is dead," Lilly exclaimed.

"No, not necessarily, don't jump to conclusions, ma chérie. Remember, she has a strong Fae bloodline, strong enough to block me from finding her. The faeries are hard to find on the physical plane and much harder to locate on the astral. I'm not giving up."

Tears stood in Lilly's eyes, "Thank you, Jolene. I'm grateful to you for trying."

"I am happy to help," Jolene said as she shooed her out of the kitchen. "Go, go back into the parlor and have some fun. Get to know the other members of the coven. Enjoy yourself!"

Lilly blinked away tears of joy and joined the group as they began to sing a bawdy song. She took a seat between Gemma and Madeline and joined in on the chorus.

After hours of conversation, hugs, musical offerings and group songs, the members of Panthea's coven said their goodbyes for the evening. It was after midnight when Lilly returned to her apartment, softly humming a tune.

In the days following the ritual, Lilly was more determined than ever to learn all she could from Jolene, James and Sabine. She took advantage of quiet time in the store to read and listen closely to the teachings of her mentors.

"The power of intention is the core of magic," Jolene stated as they sat at the round table in her kitchen.

Sabine, sitting across from her, chimed in, "There are many ways to hone intention and develop a vibration in alignment with one's desire."

"This is the purpose of meditation and ritual. Through meditation you learn to know your true self. Through ritual you focus your intention," Jolene explained.

"As you progress in your studies of magic, as you increase your spiritual knowledge and strength, you will create a bridge of language between your conscious and subconscious mind. The language of the subconscious mind is symbology. Over time, you will learn to intentionally open and close your subconscious. Rituals will have deeper meaning and your world view will expand." Jolene explained.

Sabine's voice filled her mind for a moment, "It is imperative you remain grounded. You have a body to care for and an earthly life to enjoy. Don't get so enamored of the higher dimensions, you lose your footing in the third dimension. You have chosen to incarnate. Be present. Enjoy it."

Lilly's head turned from one to the other as the two priestesses seemed to bombard her with information. "Wait, wait a minute. You two are speaking too fast. Please give me time to take notes."

Sabine and Jolene nodded and repeated the lesson more slowly, giving Lilly time to take notes and absorb the information.

Chapter 11

THE JEWEL OF INNANA

Lilly was stocking the incense display when Jolene locked the front door and flipped the CLOSED sign over. "We are closing early, Lilly. I would like to have a meeting with you when you finish with the incense."

Lilly looked up from the display, "I'll be finished in a minute," she said.

Fifteen minutes later she was seated across from Jolene on a large cushion in the meditation temple. Jolene sat quietly, eyes closed, breathing deeply. Lilly followed her lead.

After a few minutes, Jolene opened her eyes, took Lilly's hand and spoke from her heart, "Lilly, I have been guided to present you with a sacred and powerful tool." She picked up the purple velvet bag resting in her lap and removed a large crystal suspended from a gold chain. An oval of lapis lazuli was set in the band of gold which encircled the top of crystal. The terminals were exposed and a subtle violet light moved within the six facets of the crystal.

Jolene's eyes looked steadily at Lilly. Her voice matched the intensity of her eyes as she spoke. "This crystal has been in my keeping for over fifty years. Its history is long, longer than the written history recognized by modern man."

Lilly's eyebrows rose as her mouth opened slightly. Jolene smiled reassuringly and continued, "Through the centuries the crystal has been called by many names, among them the Jewel of Inanna, the Witches stone, the Inanna Crystal, the Queens's stone and others. This crystal has a molecular structure almost identical to the quartz crystals found on Earth. However, there is a mutation in the crystalline structure which gives it advanced properties. Ancient Sumerian tablets contain information about this crystal and others like it. It was the Anunaki, the same off planet race that created the Faery people and added their DNA to the Earth's humans, who created the crystals. When they arrived on Earth they were integrating sciences and highly developed technology with spirituality. Some of their crystals were used to run their technology, others were used by the priests and priestesses to communicate with the invisible realms and speak to one another mind to mind.

"This crystal," she said holding it up to catch the candle light, "belonged to the Priestess Inanna. As you can see the crystal holds the violet flame. It has the ability to align electromagnetic fields with higher vibrations, activate psychic powers, and possibly serve as a teleportation device.

"There are those in the magical world, the military and political arenas who would kill to get their hands on this implement. You must be discreet about your guardianship of this ancient artifact and the powerful energy it holds."

Lilly's eyes grew large, "My guardianship?"

Jolene nodded. "Yes, I am passing the Jewel of Inanna into your hands."

"Listen closely as this is information you will need as you begin to align with the power of the crystal."

Lilly's shoulder's stiffened and her stomach churned as she squeezed her eyes closed and leaned away from Jolene and the ancient crystal.

Jolene smiled and took Lilly's hand. "There is no need to fear the stone. It is a tool for psychic development, awakening, and connection to universal wisdom. It will not harm you."

She saw the look of confusion in Lilly's eyes and tried to explain. "Everything vibrates at certain frequencies permeating time and space. This crystal vibrates at an extremely high frequency. It has the ability to shift and alter the frequencies of living organisms when they occupy the same space. Wearing it next to your skin will trigger a synchronization response."

"The physical law of resonance will lift your vibration to match the higher frequency of the stone. Your alignment with the crystal will happen slowly. In time, your nervous system will have the ability to develop and transmit information more rapidly. Aligning with the stone insures your consciousness will expand allowing you to see, hear and feel things others do not. It will also impact your health and longevity.

"Guardianship of the crystal is the reason I was guided to offer you an early initiation. The rituals of initiation open your system and assist you in adapting and processing a higher amount of energy. This enables you to handle the accelerated energy emanating from the crystal. As you progress in your studies and receive higher initiations, your ability to understand and incorporate the energy of the crystal will increase. Be patient, and allow it to influence you gently.

Lilly managed a whispered, "Oh." Jolene was silent waiting for her to say something more. "So, it came from aliens?"

Jolene drew a deep breath and looked into her eyes. "Ancient history, recorded on thousands of tablets in ancient Sumeria, clearly states that the crystals were brought to earth by a highly advanced race from the planet Niburu. They were called the Anunaki. Were they aliens? I prefer to call them non-terrestrials. The primitive humans they encountered on Earth considered them to be gods and goddesses.

"This crystal belonged to the Priestess Inanna, the most powerful Priestess of the Anunaki. Before she left Earth, Priestess Inanna entrusted her beloved servant/companion with her jewel encrusted scepter and the crystal filled with violet light. She charged her companion to safeguard the jewel and the scepter until she could return to Earth and claim them. Priestess Inanna, along with many of the Anunaki, departed Earth soon after.

"The history of Inanna's Jewel is long and filled with discrepancies and lies. One thing has been established as certain, the stone chooses the one who will most benefit from its properties. The stone and the energies surrounding it sense when it is time to move to a new guardian. The crystal sends out strong vibrations through the subtle realms and higher dimensions. The Guardian holding the stone, attuned over time to the vibration of the crystal, receives tones and messages indicating it is time for the crystal to be passed to a new guardian. I have been receiving strong messages and know it is time to relinquish the sacred stone into your keeping."

As Jolene continued, a frown creased Lilly's brow. "Mention of this crystal can be found in ancient texts from Malta to Italy to the Middle Eastern countries and throughout the continent of Africa. It was highly coveted. You can imagine, everyone wanted to be gifted with long life, knowledge, understanding of the subtle realms and unknown gifts unique to each guardian. However, no power play could force the sacred stone to belong to anyone. The crystal would attune to the one it chose and no one else.

"About 3500 years ago, during a cataclysmic volcanic eruption, the stone was buried with its guardian in a deep cave. Thus, the Jewel of Inanna disappeared. Generations passed and stories of the power of a magical stone became the stuff of myths and legends.

"Centuries later, a wandering Druid felt the pull of the stone and found it beneath bones and rubble in the ancient cave. The Druid treasured it. Using the strength and wisdom gained from his long life and the high frequencies imparted through the stone, he became a great teacher. He was known as the Merlin, Men-tor of Kings. From his example, future kings learned compassion. From the wisdom he shared, they learned the benefits of using power over force. These kings have passed from history and are the stuff of legend.

"From the line of Druids known as Merlins, the Jewel passed into the hands of the Priestesses on the Isle of Avalon. From there it has passed from one Priestess to another. Over the centuries,

Priestesses have found the power of the stone is most potent and benevolent when the one who holds it hears the signals and passes it quickly to the next chosen guardian. This way the power, focus and violet flame energy of the stone is maintained."

Lilly leaned forward to stare at the crystal, "What will it do to me, exactly?"

"I can't say exactly what it will do. We are all different. My experience, over time, has been an increase in psychic powers, knowledge of the subtle planes and those spirits who dwell there. Through the past fifty years, abilities and strengths I never dreamed I would develop have awakened within me. I am grateful for the gift of good health and long life."

Lilly gave Jolene a puzzled look. "Was it gifted to you as a child?"

Jolene shook her head slightly, "No, ma chérie, I received it when I was twenty-six years old. Close to the age you are now."

Lilly took in a sharp breath, "How old are you now?"

Jolene looked into Lilly's eyes, "I was seventy-five last Samhain. James, my close companion for the past fifty years, is eighty-two. His close connection to my energetic field has benefited him with good health and long life.

"The Jewel is now passing to you. Your awareness and power will increase. You will notice your aging …."

Lilly chest felt it would explode as she interrupted, "I don't know. How can I possibly be ready to guard something so powerful?"

Jolene put her arm around Lilly's shoulders, "Since you first came to Panthea's I have sensed a strong power within you, combined with a delicate sensitivity. While in the trance state of deep meditation, I received a clear message: 'It is time to initiate a new priestess as keeper of the crystal.' My guides insist it be given to you. I can't deny the strength of these messages. After your initiation, the messages became more insistent. The Jewel is gently pulling away from me. I know it is time for you to assume its guardianship."

Taking Lilly's hand, Jolene spoke in an authoritative voice, "The Jewel of Inanna is now in your keeping. Over time, you will recognize the matrix of energy it carries as it amplifies your own developing power. You will attune to the energy and become aware of the properties which will be unique in its relationship with you. Wear it *always* during ritual, meditation and your daily life. Sleep with it next to your bed."

Lilly opened her hand and received the crystal. It lay on her open palm, one terminal resting near her wrist, the other end touching the top of her hand beneath her middle finger. She spent long moments looking into the violet depths of its six facets, slipped the gold chain over her head and exhaled sharply. The crystal landed over her heart and pulsed a gentle energy through her body. Jolene smiled and gently, but decisively whispered, "Your life has begun anew."

"Lilly," Jolene began in a firm voice, "I don't want to harp on this, but I must stress discretion. This powerful magic must not fall into the hands of anyone who would use it unwisely. Legend says it will not respond to any but its chosen guardian. However, I would not like to deal with the person who would dare take it from you."

"Jolene, who has the jewel encrusted scepter? Does it hold properties similar to the crystal?"

"Some say the scepter is among the treasures stored beneath the Vatican. Others say it is lost. If someone is in possession of it, they are keeping silent. I don't know if the scepter is more powerful than the stone. I can only imagine the power the two would create together."

Lilly nodded in understanding as her body thrummed with new energy. "What did you mean, it can be used as a teleportation device?"

Jolene shrugged slightly, "I have never had the need or

desire for teleportation. I haven't a clue how one would use it to teleport. You can explore the abilities it offers you and focus on teleportation if you feel drawn to it. Over time, as you become attuned to the power of the stone, it will respond to your wishes."

"Do the members of Panthea's coven know about the stone?"

Jolene shook her head slightly, "All have seen it, however, none know of its true power. Only a few have asked questions. I find it better to be discreet and evasive."

The crystal pulsed between Lilly's breasts. Within days she noticed her awareness gently expanding as her studies became more clear and easily integrated. Wearing the crystal during meditation brought visions of multiple dimensions, communication with spirits, guardians and ancestors from her Faery lineage. Lilly had to set a timer to bring herself back to third dimension reality.

Part III

THE
GREEN MAN BAND

"I WANT TO BE MAGIC. I WANT TO TOUCH
THE HEART OF THE WORLD
AND MAKE IT SMILE.
I WANT TO BE A FRIEND OF ELVES AND
LIVE IN A TREE, OR UNDER A HILL.
I WANT TO MARRY A MOONBEAM AND
HEAR THE STARS SING.
I DON'T WANT TO PRETEND AT MAGIC ANYMORE. I
WANT TO BE MAGIC."

~ Charles de Lint

Chapter 12

KNIGHT OF CUPS

....

Roland jumped to the sidewalk from the door of the bus, and stood for a moment drinking in the sights and smells of Frenchman Street. He had been on the road with *The Green Man Band* for six weeks. The band had traveled from San Francisco through Arizona, New Mexico and Texas playing music at clubs and busking on city streets. This was their first trip to New Orleans and Roland was glad their stay was going to be longer than a couple of nights. Traveling with the band was great, but he was ready for softer company.

Trey hailed him from the door of Valentine's Restaurant. "Come in, have some breakfast and meet Jason."

Roland had been playing lead guitar in Trey's band for a couple of years in San Francisco. This year they were fulfilling their dream of traveling across America, playing music and having fun. Trey had made arrangements to park their bus in a number of great spots around the country. This one in New Orleans was spectacular. The band agreed to play music for the lunch crowd and happy hour twice a week at Jason's restaurant, Valentines. They played in exchange for parking their bus in Valentine's parking lot across from the restaurant.

Roland sauntered into the restaurant as Trey was introduc-ing the band to a tall man with a long blond braid. Each band member reached out to shake hands with Jason and thank him for his generosity.

Jason nodded welcome and invited them to have some coffee and croissants while he told them a bit about the neighborhood of the Fabourg Marigny where their bus would be parked for the duration of their visit. "The Marigny is almost as old as the French Quarter," Jason began. "It is the first area developed outside of

88

....

THE GREEN MAN BAND

the original city of New Orleans. Most tourists don't venture into the Marigny. They don't cross Esplanade Avenue which is the wide avenue at the end of the French Quarter. Hell, most tourist don't see more than the first few blocks of Bourbon Street and maybe Jackson Square.

"Music clubs and restaurants have been popping up in the Marigny in recent years and the word is getting out. The mule drawn buggies have expanded their tours of the French Quarter to include parts of the Marigny. Fortunately, their route includes Frenchman Street. It is fine with me, good for business, but hell on traffic. Tourists are starting to return to the area to try some of the authentic creole food at Valentine's. For the most part, you are among the locals in the Marigny and I hope you enjoy your stay."

The members of the band smiled and nodded, eager to cross Esplanade Avenue and explore the French Quarter. By midmorning, the members of The Green Man Band had grabbed their instruments and headed towards Jackson Square, the heart of the French Quarter. As they crossed Esplanade Avenue, leaving Frenchman Street and the Fabourg Marigny behind, the scenery changed. They stepped into a city 200 years older than the American cities they had visited on their musical tour.

The uneven brick sidewalks, called banquettes, led them past shops and restaurants with tall French doors and wrought iron gates leading to unseen lush courtyards. The band walked slowly, missing the sight of balconies overhead and historical buildings, as their eyes followed one beautiful Southern lady after another.

"I know I am going to love this city!" Trey exclaimed.

The rest of the band agreed with a resounding, "Yes!"

The ladies head's turned too, as the musicians, brightly garbed in medieval attire, long hair flowing and instruments strapped to their backs, walked slowly towards Jackson Square.

The scent of frying beignets, chicory coffee, briny river water, mule dung, stale alcohol and old oyster shells mingled and filled the air. Roland labeled the unsavory blend, French Quarter "Par-fume."

Turning the corner into Jackson Square, the miasma faded. A visual feast of green space filled with trees, and a splashing fountain, filled their senses. Three of the largest and most historic buildings in the French Quarter; Saint Louis Cathedral, the Cabildo and the Presbyter lined one end of the Square providing great acoustics.

The four musicians claimed a spot near the steps of the Cabildo. A crowd gathered as the music from The Green Man Band filled the square with ancient Celtic tunes tinted with mystical shades of magic.

Monday was Lilly's day off from her duties at Panthea's. She cleaned her apartment, did her laundry and walked to the A&P for groceries. After putting away her purchases, she paced around the apartment. She missed her flute. Before she married Alex, music had filled the empty spaces in her life. *'I will get a new instrument as soon as possible,'* she vowed to herself.

Sun poured through her bedroom window with a tantalizing invitation to bask in the warmth of the day. Often, she needed to pinch herself to believe she was free to go wherever she wanted. Donning a wide brimmed hat, sunglasses and her mirrored-egg of protection, Lilly walked out onto Rue Saint Ann. The general flow of foot traffic moved towards Jackson Square. Lilly moved along with the locals and tourists. As she sauntered around the Square, she nodded to several of the artists she had befriended on her afternoon walks. Lilly smiled, glad they were getting busy as tourists arrived for the Carnival season.

As she approached the Cabildo, she saw a crowd gathered around some sort of act. Unique, fun and often mind blowing acts were beginning to arrive in the Quarter. So far she had seen a bear ride a bicycle and a man fold himself into a small plexiglass box.

She stood on her tip toes to see what the new attraction might be. The music began and Lilly stopped struggling for a view of the musicians. She stood still listening to the music. It differed from anything she had heard before. Cajun music had filled her life on the bayou. Learning to play the flute, she became familiar with classical music, and of course, she loved the Beatles.

The music floating through the Square had elements of classical music blended with medieval tones. She stood tapping her foot in time with the music as a surprising lilt lifted her heart. Wiggling through the crowd until she had a clear view, Lilly stared at the four men creating the music. *'They have arrived from another realm,'* Lilly thought. *A place where faeries, unicorns and gnomes live.*

The guitarist, violinist, mandolin player and drummer, were all wearing white shirts with long billowing sleeves, silk vests, velvet britches and soft leather knee high boots. Each musician wore a jewel color; crimson, emerald green, gold and sapphire blue.

Backing slowly out of the crowd, Lilly sat on the steps of the Cabildo, closed her eyes and allowed the music to transport her through a portal where music filled the air and magic was afoot. She felt the music swirl around her and she drank it in like life's own sweet air.

The band took a break and most of the onlookers dropped coins or dollars in the instrument cases open to receive donations. Lilly sat studying the musicians. The mandolin player was truly beautiful. He was taller than Lilly by about six inches. His long dark hair fell in waves around his face and down his back. A short beard covered his cheeks and chin while a soft mustache framed his full lips.

Lilly, pulled a five dollar bill out of her pocket and dropped it in the mandolin case. "Thanks," the mandolin player said. As she was turning away she heard, "Wait, don't run off."

Lilly stopped and turned slowly, removing her shades to meet the gentle brown eyes of the mandolin player. A grin pasted itself on her flushed face as she blurted out, "Wow, ya'll are great! I love your music, I've never heard anything like it. Where are you from?"

The mandolin player smiled, "Uh, thanks. We're from San

THE GREEN MAN BAND

Francisco. Our band tour has brought us to New Orleans for the Mardi Gras. There are a couple of clubs we're going to be playing over the next few weeks. Let me introduce you to the rest of the band. This is our violin player, Bart, Trey on guitar and our percussionist, Leon. My name's Roland."

Lilly was tongue tied and her face glowed red for a moment before she found her voice, "Hello, I love your music."

The musicians smiled, nodded, glanced briefly at Roland and mumbled, "Thanks."

Turning back to the mandolin player, Lilly asked, "What kind of music are you playing?"

Roland turned the pegs on his mandolin, plucked a string and looked at Lilly, "It's Celtic music, from long ago in medieval Ireland."

Lilly chewed on her bottom lip and spoke shyly, "It is magical. I'd love to learn a few Celtic tunes."

"Are you a musician?"

"Yes. No, I mean I was."

Roland smiled and shook his head, "No, once a musician always a musician. There's no getting over the love of making music."

Lilly nodded in agreement, "I know, you're right, I haven't played for several years."

"What instrument do you prefer?"

"I played classical flute."

"The flute works beautifully in Celtic music, I'd love to share some of it with you."

Lilly shook her head sadly, "I haven't got an instrument right now. I'm looking for the right flute. I'll know it when I pick it up and play it. So far, I haven't found one that called to me."

"Ah, you're a true musician."

Conversation stopped and they both stood gazing at one another. Lilly stared at his full lips and caught herself running her tongue over her bottom lip. She felt her cheeks flush with warmth and hoped he didn't notice.

Roland spoke first, "I arrived last night in your fair city would you do me the honor of a tour around the French Quarter this evening? I will repay your kindness with a meal, however you will have to choose the restaurant as you would be the most qualified."

Lilly was at a loss for words. She stood very still for a moment, her green eyes wide drinking in the handsome musician. Gathering her wits, she responded, "Of course, I'd be happy to serve as your tour guide and have dinner with you. I have to warn you, I've only been living in the French Quarter for a short time. I am not exactly the perfect tour guide. My friends have been pointing out the best restaurants, bars and shops to me. Her fingers tingled and she put her hands behind her back. She shrugged off her nervousness and smiled, "I'll be happy to show you the places I know."

"Cool, we can explore together," Roland said as he beamed at her. She gave him instructions to meet her at Panthea's around the corner on Rue St. Anne.

Roland watched her as she walked away. Closing his eyes when she turned the corner, he took a deep breath inhaling the scent of magic filling the air. Bart gave him a friendly punch on the upper arm, "Hey man, in love already?"

Roland smiled for a moment then his face grew serious, "Bart, the scene in San Francisco is fun, but you and I both know the magic has dissipated. It is all fantasy now. The Big Easy is the real deal. Magic is still alive in this community. I want to know it, see it, feel it and be a part of it."

"Far out," Bart said with a slap on Roland's back, "I'm with you!"

Lilly laughed as Roland tried his first raw oyster with Louisiana hot sauce. She showed him how to put it on a cracker and put it all in his mouth at once. His eyes bulged and she thought she saw a gag reflex, but Roland quickly recovered, swallowed reached

93

for another one.

"You like them!" Lilly exclaimed, amazed after his facial contortions.

"I love them!" Roland said, stuffing another oyster topped cracker into his mouth.

She sipped her beer and leaned back enjoying the beautiful man across from her. They had only been together a few hours, but there was an easiness between them, the kind of relaxed banter shared by old friends. The scary ideas about the danger of falling in love again and fear of getting into another abusive relationship began to fade from Lilly's immediate attention. The sight of Roland's deep brown eyes crinkling when he smiled his impish grin and sent a shot of warmth right through her heart.

Roland took her hand as they walked down Rue Royal peaking into shops, bakeries and famous restaurants. Lilly lead him down Rue Dumaine to the last few blocks of Bourbon Street far away from the mayhem of the strip joints and night clubs. He squeezed her hand as they entered Lafitte's Blacksmith Shop."This place is the real deal," Roland said as they stood at the bar, threw caution to the wind and ordered Voodoo Cocktails.

They walked out to the patio soaking up the energy of the oldest bar on Bourbon Street and marveled at the sculpture of the man and woman lying entwined in the fountain.

"These are super potent," Lilly said as she drew a large gulp through a straw.

"In that case," Roland said as he gently removed the straw from her drink, "maybe we should drink them slowly." Lilly laughed and agreed.

The world tilted a bit when Roland stood. He noticed Lilly staggered slightly as they left Lafitte's and walked toward the river. They walked with their arms around each other's waists as they made their way a few blocks over to Harry's Corner Bar. Lilly's neighbor and hairdresser, Madeline, was moonlighting as the bartender. Lilly wanted to say hello and introduce her to Roland.

THE GREEN MAN BAND

Madeline's blue eyes took in the dark haired musician and a seductive smile played on her full lips. Looking around furtively, she pulled a bottle from beneath the bar and asked if they'd like to try some absinthe. Roland shot a look at Lilly and Madeline, "You have real absinthe?"

"Locally made, powerful and delicious," Madeline said. Lilly shook her head, no, but Madeline would have none of it. Looking Lilly in the eyes she said, "You must meet the Green Faery."

Lilly could tell Roland wanted to try it. Nodding her head in assent, she watched as Madeline poured the liquid through a strainer containing a sugar cube then presented a small glass to each of them.

The neighborhood inhabitants and a few tourists filtered in and sat at the bar. Madeline had no time to talk so Lilly and Roland waved quick goodbyes.

Mellow and more than a little woozy, they left the bar and turned the corner. Lilly saw the door open and the lights on in Mike Park's Mask and Costume Shop."I want you to meet Mike, she said as she took Roland's hand and tugged gently. "He is a wonderful mask maker, costume artist and a real French Quarter celebrity."

Mike often came into Panthea's and Lilly had grown to love this burly, bearded giant of a man with a contagious laugh and a gentle artist's soul. Standing up to greet them when they walked in, Mike smiled broadly through his bushy beard. Lilly made introductions and left the two men to chat as she wandered through the shop.

She took her time as the Green Faery, Madeline had promised, appeared and showed her the magic imbued in every mask and work of art.

Roland and Mike were getting along famously. They had their heads together speaking in low tones when Lilly approached the counter. Roland took her hand and squeezed gently, "Are you ready to continue our tour?"

95

"Yep, I'm ready," she said. The two men shook hands and hugged. Lilly gave Mike a hug and a goodbye kiss on the cheek.

The moon was high when they left the mask shop and walked slowly through Jackson Square. As they passed the Cafe du Monde the scent of hot coffee and beignets sent out tendrils of temptation. Ignoring the tantalizing aromas, they left the crowds of the French Quarter and let the Green Faery lead them over the levee. They stood together looking out over the river watching tugboats guiding huge freighters through the dark water. The wake of the ships sent soft waves onto the river bank at their feet.

Roland sighed, "I don't know if it's the Voodoo Cocktail the Green Faery, moon magic or your beautiful presence, but this night is amazing. Lilly smiled to herself as they stood together watching the moonlight dance on the rippling wake in the river. She stole a look at Roland, bathed in moonlight, a slight breeze lifting his long hair. The Green Faery whispered, "Enchanting" and faded away into the night. Roland drew Lilly closer to him. The fear imprisoning her heart began to melt.

Roland asked quietly, "Do you come here often?"

"Yea, it's my get away spot. I grew up on the bayou, fishing every day. Being near the water calms me and helps me think."

Roland turned toward her and took her hand, "What do you come down here to think about?"

"Oh, stuff, you know like what I am going to do with my life." "What do you want to do with your life, Lyla?" She smiled although tears filled her eyes, embarrassed she pulled away from Roland. "You can talk to me. It's okay," he said softly.

Retreating into herself, Lilly let everything fade away as she became one with the rhythm of the river. Roland squeezed her hand slightly and she remembered he had asked her a question.

"What?" she whispered into the wind.

Roland took her chin in his hand and turned her head towards him."Talk to me. You don't have to figure everything out right now. Take your time, flow like the river. Your life will unfold.

THE GREEN MAN BAND

Pushing the river won't bring you answers." Looking into her eyes, he said, "I am certain you will play music again. I want to be there to hear you when you do."

Lilly smiled and leaned into him as he gently put his arm around her waist.

"Thank you so much for this. I never dreamed I'd be in New Orleans only one day and meet the most beautiful, magical Faery on the planet."

Lilly blushed and laughed nervously, "I'm no tiny Faery, I am 5 foot 2."

Roland drew her into an embrace. "Yes, a delicate and beautiful 5 foot 2."

Alarms went off in her head. Her vision of Roland, as a benevolent friend, wavered as memories of Alex's easy embrace and initial gentleness warned her away from physical closeness.

"I'm sorry, Lyla. Did I frighten you? I am so drawn to you. I thought maybe..."

"No, Roland, it's not you, it's me. I am afraid. I've had a bad relationship, worse than a bad relationship, a scary marriage."

Roland's eyebrows flew up, his jaw dropped, "You're married?"

Lilly shook her head, "I'm getting divorced and I will never go back."

"Good news! I'm glad you've chosen freedom."

They walked in silence, watching the rippling waters of the river, enjoying the absinthe's emerald haze tinting the moon.

"I better get home Roland, it's getting late," Lilly said, breaking the spell of the walk. Roland nodded as they reluctantly retraced their steps along the riverbank, climbed the levee and walked slowly through the Square.

Lilly unlocked the gate and stepped into the carriageway. She smiled, but did not invite Roland further. The night had surprised her. She needed time alone to sort out her feelings and confusion.

Roland kissed her softly on the lips, expecting nothing more.

He squeezed her hand and backed away as she closed the gate.

She had every intention of getting to sleep and being fresh for work in the morning, but Roland's beautiful face swam before her every time she closed her eyes. The warmth he exuded, the safety she felt with him was wonderful. She was terrified. Letting her heart lead the way had gotten her into the dangerous mess with Alex. Fear and doubt begged her to be strong and resist the handsome musician. As soon as she resolved to resist him, she recalled his smiling brown eyes. She lay awake, questioning the fear and joy Roland stirred in her heart. The sky turned dove gray as she continued to twist and turn in the rumpled bed sheets.

Chapter 13

RESISTANCE IS FUTILE

Lilly stared in the bathroom mirror at the dark circles under her eyes. Her drooping eyelids and pallid face were the result of a sleepless night. She pulled herself together and went down to work in the shop. Jolene took one look at her and put a cup of coffee in front of her.

By mid-morning, she didn't know how she would make it through the day. At Jolene's suggestion, Lilly took a long lunch hour and went upstairs for a nap. She returned to work feeling a little better. Jolene took her off floor duty and assigned her busy tasks in the store rather than waiting on customers.

Lilly, sighing with relief, sat on a tall stool and began arranging the book shelves. Absorbed in her task, she yelped when she felt a hand on her shoulder. Startled, she spun around to find Roland smiling at her.

"I'm sorry, I didn't mean to scare you," he said, taking a step back.

"No, that's okay. I'm fine," Lilly said, smiling.

"I've come in to see if I can take you out to dinner tonight. Last night was wonderful. I would love to continue our tour."

Lilly almost blurted out, "Yes, of course," but remembering her resolve, she declined his invitation. Roland's face fell and he looked puzzled and more than a little hurt.

"I'm not in the mood to go out tonight," Lilly explained. Her stomach clenched as a wave of panic washed over her. Her mouth opened and she blurted out, "Maybe you could pick something up for dinner and come over to my apartment."

A smile stretched across Roland's face as he quickly took her up on her invitation. "I'll be over around 7:00," he said, kissing her on the cheek and sauntering out of the shop.

'Why did I do that?' Lilly plopped down on the stool wringing her hands and chewing her bottom lip. 'What's the difference if I go out with him or have him in my apartment?' She felt her heart flip flop in her chest, beat wildly and finally calm as she took a deep breath.

Roland arrived with a bag of takeout from Felix's Restaurant, a six pack of Dixie beer, a bouquet of flowers and his mandolin strapped across his back. Lilly put the flowers in water in an empty mayonnaise jar and lit a couple of candles on the coffee table.

They sat across from one another on the floor eating spaghetti and meatballs. Lilly was quiet, but Roland couldn't stop smiling. "What are you grinning about?"

"I'm happy. All this time on the road, traveling with the band, I was having a good time. Tonight, however, I am truly, deeply happy. There is nothing like a beautiful woman and good food to put a smile on my face."

A smile played on the edge of Lilly's lips, "I'm happy too. It is good to see you again."

Roland came around the coffee table and sat next to her. He took her hand in his and gently turned her face towards him. Looking into her eyes, he asked, "What is bothering you? Did I get my signals crossed? I thought we hit it off spectacularly last night. Am I wrong?"

"No, you are not wrong and that's the problem."

"How is that a problem?" Roland wanted to know.

"You don't know anything about me. I've escaped my husband. He was cruel and abusive. I didn't know this at first. I misjudged him. I thought we were in love and would be happy together. I don't know how I could have been so blind and stupid. Now, I am scared to...."

Roland pulled her gently to him, "I'm so sorry he turned out to be a jerk. What kind of man would do anything to drive you away? He obviously didn't know who or what you are."

Lilly's head lifted, "What do you mean, who or what I am?"

100

"Lyla, I know one of the Fae when I see them. You are the embodiment of enchantment with the charm and guilelessness inherent to all the Faery kin. A tender, magical, musical being, you must be treated with care and respect."

Lilly relaxed into his embrace, felt the tickle of his soft mustache as his lips found hers. Her arms went around his neck and her mouth parted slightly. He moved his head to the side and kissed her deeply. She pulled him closer as his tongue entered her mouth. Her body flamed with a surprising urgency.

In one swift motion, he stood up, lifted her into his arms and brought her into the bedroom. Placing her gently on the bed, he lay beside her. His mouth found her eyes, her lips, her chin, her neck. He kissed and tasted her until he found her breasts. Unbuttoning her blouse, he placed his mouth over one breast, as he gently rubbed the nipple of the other. Lilly's body lifted slightly as one of his hands moved up her skirt, and slipped beneath her panties.

In seconds, they lay naked together. Her hands moved over his back, pulling him closer. He gently moved his body on top of her. Their lips touched and his tongue explored her softening mouth. Instinct lifted her body, demanding more. She moaned as he entered her slowly.

Ripples of ecstasy flowed over them, a counterpoint to the fiery energy igniting their bodies. Lilly's spirit rose like a phoenix in the expert hands of the master musician. She opened her eyes for a moment surprised to see crimson red, deep purple and cerulean blue swirling around them as their auras joined. She clung to Roland, gasping, as her first orgasm in years rocked her entire being. Roland arched his back as he held himself on straightened arms and thrust deep inside of her, satisfying his need, delighting in her soft sweetness.

They lay together afterwards enjoying the gentle vibrations still coursing through their bodies. Lilly put her hand over her heart, fearful it might fly out of her chest. Roland took a deep breath and exhaled a great sigh of satisfaction.

THE GREEN MAN BAND

The alabaster glow of the moon poured through the window, bathing their bodies in its milky light. Roland's face was in shadow but Lilly could feel his energy thrumming beside her. It was unlike anything she had ever experienced. The word power came to her mind. It didn't feel like power over anything, more like an innate part of who he was.

"What is going on in your beautiful head?" Roland whispered.

Lilly gave an embarrassed laugh, "I'm thinking I've met a magic man. Not only met him, I've banished my resistance, taken him into my bed and rolled around in the moonlight with him."

Looking at her from the shadows, Roland smiled, "I was thinking something similar about you," he confessed. "Although, I believe it was a bit more than rolling around in the moonlight." Roland looked deep into her eyes, "Possibly, we are both enchanted tonight. Resistance to enchantment is futile. The only thing to do is surrender and enjoy."

Jolene and Sabine exchanged knowing glances and raised eyebrows throughout the morning. Lilly sang to herself, her bright pink aura filling the shop as she floated around the store charming every customer. No one could resist the jewelry she showed them, the incense and candles she suggested or the silver ritual chalices she removed from the case and placed in customer's hands. The ring of the cash register filled the air throughout the morning.

Finally, curiosity got the best of her and Jolene crooked her finger and signaled Lilly to join her. Lilly was oblivious to Jolene's signals until she finally registered her pseudonym, Lyla, being called. Looking around she noticed Jolene's puzzled face and followed her through the back door for lunch.

With the coffee pot on, Jolene turned to her, "Okay, tell me."

Lilly blushed, a mischievous grin lighting her face. "Tell you what?"

"Lilly, what is going on? You look like, you look like maybe... well, you look like you got laid." Lilly's laughter filled the room.

THE GREEN MAN BAND

Jolene had never heard this much merriment pour out of the young priestess. Lilly's laughter was contagious and Jolene joined in finally getting out a clear, "Will you tell me who?"

Setting two cups of strong coffee on the table, Jolene sat across from her curious as a cat. "It was a musician I met in the square Monday. We went out to dinner Monday night. He is from California, he plays mandolin with a group called *The Green Man Band.* They play Celtic music and rock and roll. His name's Roland. I wish I would have introduced you when he came into the shop yesterday afternoon."

"Wow, You obviously, trust this young man. You met him Monday and you slept with him Tuesday?"

Lilly's grin grew even broader, "Yes. I tried to convince myself to resist, it is too soon to get into a relationship, but resistance was futile. When he came into the shop yesterday afternoon, he invited me out again. I was hesitant, thinking I didn't want to encourage him. Ha! The truth, is I do want to encourage him. Instead of going out, we decided to have dinner in my apartment. He feels like an old friend, not like a stranger at all. It turns out it wasn't too soon. It wasn't sordid. It felt right. I'm almost certain he felt the same. He recognizes Faery energy."

Jolene's head tilted as her eyebrows shot up. "I want to meet this fellow," she said as she reached across the table and took Lilly's hand, "I'm so happy for you. It is time you had some fun!"

"Thank you Jolene. I'm curious, how did you know?"

"How could I not know? You have been filling the shop with pink love energy all morning. I knew something good had happened."

Lilly nodded, "Yes, it was wonderful. I can hardly believe it happened and I can't wait to see him again."

THE GREEN MAN BAND

Chapter 14

THE SECRET COURTYARD

When she returned from her talk with Jolene, Lilly began to watch the clock, waiting for her lunch break. When the clock struck one, she grabbed her hat from under the counter and flew out the door.

The music reached her before she spotted the crowd of people surrounding The Green Man Band. She found a warm spot on the steps of the cathedral, took off her big floppy hat and little round granny glasses. Leaning back on her elbows, she let the sun's warmth bathe her face as the Celtic music washed over her.

Lost in the music she yelped when someone grabbed her arm. Looking up with a ready smile, she stared into the cruel smile on Alex's face. "Time to come home, Lilly," he said as he tried to pull her up.

She jumped up, jerked her arm free, balled her right hand into a fist and swung into his face with all of her strength. Not expecting the punch, Alex swayed and fell backwards onto the bricks.

Lilly turned and sprinted to the corner. Running down the block and across the street, she rushed into the door of the Place de Arms hotel. She walked sedately through the lobby, out the back door, around the pool and made her way to the hidden courtyard in the rear of the hotel. Instinct guided her. She knew she did not want to lead Alex, or anyone with him to Panthea's. If he came into the hotel, she could scream and make a scene.

She squatted behind a stand of banana trees. Rivulets of sweat poured down her neck and between her breasts. Swarms of mosquitos found her soft flesh and set to work drinking her blood.

Time crawled. It seemed an eternity before she stopped trembling, cautiously stepped out from the banana trees, crept through the shadows of the courtyard and made her way into the lobby of the hotel. The young woman at the front desk looked up, smiled, and resumed her telephone conversation.

Lilly peaked out the front door, checked both ways, and gingerly stepped out onto the banquet. Panthea's front door was a mere ten yards from the hotel. She sprang into a run. Two meaty hands grabbed her shoulders. Jerking and twisting, she tried to shake off her assailant, lost her footing and fell heavily onto the brick sidewalk. Stars exploded before her eyes, as a black veil tried to drag her into unconsciousness. She lay motionless for a moment, her eyes flickering slightly. She fought off the temptation to surrender to the dark veil. She felt the bricks under her hands and remembered why she had fallen and why she needed to get up. Her head was spinning, as she tried to get to her feet. Strong arms pulled her up, grabbed her around the waist and lifted her from the sidewalk. A long, black Cadillac sped around the corner, its back door swinging open. The Cadillac slowed for a moment and Lilly was thrown into the backseat.

Another set of arms grabbed her around the waist. The smell of Alex's Old English aftershave assaulted her and she promptly vomited on his shoes. Grabbing a handkerchief, Alex cursed, pressed it into her hand and demanded she clean his shoes.

She spit in his face. Alex grabbed her breasts and squeezed until Lilly screamed, "Stop!"

Minutes later, his soft voice crooned into Lilly's ear, "Lilly, I'm so glad I finally found you. I've been so worried, I haven't been able to sleep. The whole family is distressed about the way you left. Your mother and Rex are worried and want to talk with you as soon as possible." Lilly moaned.

As they sped down North Peters Street, a voice from the front seat asked, "Where we going, boss?"

"Let's go to Guiseppe's warehouse over on Tchoupitoulas Street. This girl needs to be taught a lesson before she sees anyone." Alex squeezed the nipples of her breasts again, delighting in her screams. His eyes shown with malice as cruel laughter twisted his mouth. The moment he laughed, Lilly's fingers came alive, tingling with power. She took a calming breath and the tingling grew more insistent. The Cadillac slowed for the red light at Canal Street and came to a stop behind a mule drawn carriage filled with tourists.

Lilly saw her opportunity. The tingling power in her fingers moved into her hands. Grabbing Alex's arms, she focused on one thought, 'Release me!' Alex screamed, his arms flew open, as the bolt of power delivered a white hot shock to every nerve in his body. Lilly drove her elbow into his stomach, while she pointed a finger at the locked door. She pushed the heavy car door open and jumped into the street.

She ran toward the crowded sidewalk on Canal Street. As she passed the huge, gray government building on the corner, she glanced over her shoulder. The thugs were running around the corner of the building, with Alex trailing behind them.

Movement at the front door of the government building caught Lilly's eye. A group of business men were coming through the door, talking among themselves. Lilly followed her gut instinct, plunged up the steps between the men and entered the building.

She was in a huge room, 'Too exposed,' she thought. Her footsteps echoed as she ran over the marble floor. Ignoring the woman sitting at the front desk, she found the stairs and ran up flight after flight.

Out of breath, she stopped, bent over and put her hands on her knees. She took a moment to recover her breath, then stood and looked around. The wide hall was lined with glass doors leading into offices. 'Where can I get help, which door should I open?'

Her breath caught in her throat, as she heard footsteps running up the stairs. Lilly turned, opened the first office door and quickly closed it behind her.

THE GREEN MAN BAND

A young woman, in a navy uniform, looked up in surprise as Lilly burst through the door. Seeing the girl's head was bleeding, the receptionists quickly asked Lilly to sit down. She came out from behind her desk, as Lilly declined to sit.

"What has happened? Were you in an accident. Did you trip on the stairs?"

Lilly shook her head and wrapped her arms around herself. "Where can I hide? There are dangerous men chasing me."

"What?" The receptionist asked, "Who is chasing you?"

Lilly shook her head and spoke to the confused woman, "There are dangerous men following me, where can I hide? Is there a phone I can use?"

The young woman nodded and flipped the lock on the office door. Guiding Lilly by the elbow, she led her through a heavy door, down a long hallway, and into an office. "Admiral Schleinker is out of town, you can hide in here and use his phone. Dial nine for an outside line." As she stepped out of the office, she locked the door and went back to her desk, hoping she had not let a crazy girl into the Admiral's office. She picked up the phone and alerted the security team to be on the lookout for suspicious char-acters running around the building.

In the Admiral's office Lilly picked up the receiver, dialed nine and heard the dial tone. Holding the phone, she knew exactly who to call. The morning she ran into Tulane Hospital flashed in front of her eyes. It was the lowest point in her life. She had no one to call, not a friend or a relative she could ask for help. Nurse Trudy saw her crying and invited her to coffee. Lilly felt a pang of guilt. She hadn't gone back to see Nurse Trudy to thank her for her three steps to freedom.

Jolene picked up the phone, "Panthea's Pantry." Tears welled in Lilly's eyes. She couldn't find her voice.

"Hello, is anyone there?" Jolene repeated several times.

Lilly fell to her knees. Her hands shook and she was having trouble catching her breath. Cradling the phone, she found her voice, "Jolene, it's Lilly."

"Thank the Goddess you've called. We have been worried. Where are you, ma chérie? Are you okay?"

"I'm in Admiral Schlienker's office in the big gray building on the corner of Canal and North Peters Street."

"Stay there, I will get help! Do you know which floor you are on?"

"Uh, I don't know, maybe the fifth floor?"

"Okay, Lilly, stay where you are."

Hanging up the phone, Lilly released a sigh that turned into a huge yawn. She lay on the carpeted floor and closed her eyes. Her ordeal was over. The worst had happened and she had survived. The power in her tingling fingers had served her well. She had been doubtful when Jolene and Sabine told her to direct intention through her fingers. Today she had no choice, her fingers and hands had saved her. Emotionally drained and exhausted, she fell asleep on the floor of the Admiral's office. The next thing she knew, James was shaking her shoulder, gently. She opened her eyes to see him standing over her, Jolene next to him and three military police standing close by.

"Are you ready to go?" James asked softly.

"Are Alex and his thugs still outside?" Lilly asked.

Jolene shook her head, "No, the military police escorted them out of the building and made sure they left the area."

James helped her stand and put his arm around her as she began to shiver.

Sitting around the oak table in Jolene's apartment, they drank tea in silence for a few minutes. "We started to worry when you didn't return from your lunch break," Sabine said in her gentle voice.

Jolene nodded in agreement as she stood, dampened a paper towel and began to blot the dried blood from Lilly's face. You've had a bad scare, ma chérie. Take some time to get body and soul back together. We can hear about your dangerous encounter when you are rested and grounded."

Lilly nodded in agreement. She turned before she opened the kitchen door, "It was my tingling fingers that saved me. I am so grateful for your guidance. Using my own power to escape felt good. I don't have to be Alex's victim. Those days are in the past." Lilly walked slowly up the winding stairs to her apartment, closed the door and flipped the lock. Within five minutes, she was soaking in a warm lavender scented bath.

The scent of coffee and warm croissant drifted up through the floor boards in Lilly's bedroom. She stretched, inhaled the tempting scents of breakfast and readied herself to go downstairs.

She knocked on the door of Jolene's kitchen and opened the door.

"Come in, come in, have a cup of coffee." Jolene rose from her chair and put her arms around Lilly. James and Sabine smiled and invited her to join them at the table.

Lilly finished eating the last crumbs of her croissant. She sat staring at the empty saucer and sipping coffee. The elders waited until Lilly was ready to talk.

Sabine broke the silence, "How are you feeling this morning, Lilly?"

"Happy to be home. I had a close call yesterday." She sipped her coffee and began relating the events of the previous day. As she told them about the hidden courtyard, Sabine said, "You are a smart girl. Heading to the hotel next door and not leading him to your home was a good idea. How did you know about the hidden courtyard?"

"I went over and scoped out the hotel right after I moved into Panthea's. I thought it was a good idea to have an emergency place to hide if Alex showed up. It didn't do much good. The thugs hid themselves in a doorway and waited to see when and where I would step out."

Jolene's eyebrows rose as she asked, "Did you remember to

activate your protective shield before you left Panthea's?"

Lilly's face blanched, "No, I was in such a hurry to see Roland and hear the band, I went running out the door without a thought for my safety."

Sabine's mouth puckered, "I bet it will be the last time you forget your protection."

"You can bet on it," Lilly said. "The worst has happened and I survived. There is a positive lesson in this miserable event, I learned to trust my power."

Jolene nodded her approval and picked up her keys. "Time to open the doors to the shop," she said.

Looking at Lilly, she asked, "Do you feel like working, or would you like a few days to recover?"

"I want to get back to work, no need moping about," Lilly said.

Tourists, housewives, hustlers and hippies poured into Panthea's as Mardi Gras day grew closer. The list of clients waiting for appointments with Jolene and Sabine extended through the weekends and late evenings. Jolene's Friday night salon was suspended, along with all evening classes until after the Mardi Gras vacation.

Throughout the brisk morning business, Lilly rang up purchases and answered questions from curious customers. After lunch the rush of customers slowed. By late afternoon, Lilly had tidied all the displays in the shop and had time to think.

She suppressed a moan as Roland's eyes, full lips and gentle touch, filled her mind. She may have read too much into their lovemaking. Had she been foolish? Had she imagined their connection? Her head ached as she berated herself for falling for the first smooth talking musician she met.

An hour later, the bell on the shop door jingled and Roland sauntered in. Lilly's tight shoulders relaxed and the tense frown between her brows smoothed. She put her hand over her solar plexus and smiled. Roland returned her smile, and casually asked, "Hey sweet lady, how's it going?"

She couldn't answer or take her eyes off him. He was more beautiful than she remembered. His gentle dark eyes, long black hair cascading in waves down his back and his sensuous lips mesmerized her. Weak knees forced her to sit quickly on the stool in front of the bookcase. Roland stood close by "Are you okay?" She nodded and felt his fingers beneath her chin, as he leaned over and brushed her lips with his.

Jolene cleared her throat loudly, getting Lilly's attention. She raised one eyebrow with her "What's going on?" stare.

Jumping off the stool, Lilly walked over to the counter and quietly said, "It's Roland, he's here." Turning towards her handsome lover, she waved him over to the counter and introduced him to Jolene and Sabine. The elder priestesses were sufficiently impressed and encouraged Lilly to go on and enjoy the rest of the afternoon with Roland.

Pulling her floppy hat over her face and putting her oversized sunglasses on, Lilly went flying out Panthea's front door with Roland behind her. Walking up Rue Chartres, Lilly took a minute to silently invoke her mirrored-egg protection. Leading Roland around a corner onto Rue Ursuline she continued her roundabout journey to an Italian Deli on Decatur Street.

Roland gave her a puzzled look and she explained, "I'm changing the usual routes I take. Alex and his thugs grabbed me yesterday. It was terrifying and I don't want it to happen again."

Roland shocked, stopped and turned to look into her face, "Are you okay? What happened?"

Lilly told him briefly about the incident, trying to play it down. She didn't want him to think she was a drama queen with endless troubles and sad stories.

Roland put his arm around her and drew her close to him, "You are safe with me. No one will harm you while I'm around."

Lilly smiled up at him, "Thank you, that means a lot to me."

Shaking off the bad vibes from her encounter with Alex, Lilly grabbed Roland's hand and led him to an old fashioned Italian deli on Decatur Street. The moment they entered, the delicious aromas made their mouths water.

Turning to Roland, she said, "You are about to experience a magnificent delight, the joys of the Italian muffuletta." Picking up one of the huge sandwiches stuffed with ham, cheese, three different salamis and tons of olive salad, she grabbed a couple of root beers and headed for the river bank where she felt safe.

The wake of passing ships slapped the shoreline as they shared the big juicy sandwich. Olive oil dripped from the thick bread and ran down Lilly's chin. Roland kissed and licked it away, making his way to her mouth. Olive oil slipped through her fingers as she squeezed the sandwich tight with one hand. They separated and Lilly smiled looking up at Roland wondering if he could hear the wild beating of her heart.

They finished the last of the Muffuletta and sat sipping Barque's root beer, watching tiny tug boats move huge barges up the river. In tune with one another, they stood, joined hands and walked along the river's edge, leaving the crowds of the French Quarter behind. After a bit, Roland exclaimed, "Hey, let's go sit under that big old oak tree and have a smoke."

"A smoke of what?"

"Red bud" he replied as he lead her to the ancient oak.

They sat together on the lowest limb of the oak, their feet brushing the ground. Roland pulled a small, tightly rolled joint out of his shirt pocket, lit it and took a deep toke. He handed the joint to Lilly. She took it between two fingers, put it to her mouth and immediately coughed.

"Wait, wait, let me show you how to do this, Miss Lyla," Roland said in his best southern gentleman impersonation. "Take a tiny inhale, hold it in for a few seconds and blow it out." Lilly tried again and after a few more coughs and sputters was able to hold the potent smoke in her lungs for a few seconds. She relaxed as they passed the joint to one another.

They sat beneath the oak tree for hours. Roland told her about life in San Francisco, the music scene at the Filmore West and Haight Ashbury.

His face grew animated as he recounted the night The Green Man Band had opened for Jefferson Airplane at the Filmore, the time he met Janice Joplin at a party in Redwood City and the magical evening he jammed with Johnny Winter at a hole-in-the-wall club in the Haight. His stories made her want to run away to San Francisco right away.

He sighed deeply, the corners of his mouth turned down, "Unfortunately, things have taken a downward turn in San Francisco. The drug scene has gotten heavy and people are dying from overdoses of heroin and other nasty concoctions. There was this brief period when everything was perfect and magical and we were all part of something new and wonderful. Eventually, the whole scene became a caricature of itself. Busses arrived in the Haight carrying throngs of tourists pointing to the 'crazy' hippies and disparaging our way of life.

"The tourists, ridicule, noise and bus fumes slowly destroyed our tranquil haven. The magic dissipated and one day it was gone."

Lilly sighed deeply, "I'm glad you came to New Orleans. I think there is magic here in the French Quarter."

Roland threw his head back and laughed, "Miss Lyla. You are right. I am happy I came to New Orleans too." He put his arm around her and gently drew her to him. Her arms reflexively went around his neck. He kissed her gently on the lips, kissed both of her eyes and made his way back to her full lips, kissing her deeply.

Lilly could feel his kiss through her entire body. Her knees relaxed, her back arched slightly and she leaned closer to him.

Returning to Panthea's through Jackson Square, Roland was full of energy. He talked to tourists, artists and musicians along the way. Digging a handful of papers out of his back pocket, he began handing out the flyers advertising his band's premier gig at The Cave on Bourbon Street.

Soon after arriving in Lilly's apartment Roland dramatically stuck his nose in his arm pit and pulled an embarrassed face. Lilly could't help herself, she giggled uncontrollably.

"I haven't had a good shower in a couple of days, do you think I could take one here?"

"Of course, make yourself at home," she offered, trying to stop giggling.

As he closed the door to the bathroom, Lilly retreated to the living room with a cold Dixie 45. Sipping the beer, she sat listening to the shower run when Roland called out, "Lyla! Lyla!"

Running to the hallway she yelled through the bathroom door, "Are you okay in there?"

"No" Roland cried in a petulant voice, "I'm lonely."

Lilly laughed, cracked the door a couple of inches and said, "I'm lonely too, hurry up and come on out here."

Two minutes later Roland stepped out of the bathroom. Clouds of steam swirled around him, streams of water poured off his hair and beard. A drop of water dangled on the end of his nose. Lilly giggled as he took her face in his hands and drew her to him. He kissed her and she responded enthusiastically as he lifted her into his arms and carried her to the bedroom.

His warm, moist body engulfed her. Gentle hands found her breasts and his full lips tenderly kissed each nipple drawing one into his mouth as his hands explored the contours of her body. Lilly's hands moved over the muscles of his back as she pressed herself against his naked body. One of his hands made its way to the waistband of her jeans, quickly unbuttoned and unzipped. In mere seconds her clothes were on the floor.

Roland's tongue slid down her body to the bottom of her torso. Lying back, his tongue explored between her legs. She froze. Confused by his exploration, her body clenched. Roland looked up and said, "Relax, you're going to like this."

THE GREEN MAN BAND

Lying back, her body softened. Her breath quickened as his tongue worked magic and she arched her body. She teetered on the brink of orgasm. Roland stopped and made his way up her torso to her breast.

Lilly's legs opened and wrapped around Roland's waist as he entered her. Taking her legs in his hands, he placed them over his shoulders and penetrated her deeply. The feel of him inside of her was ecstasy. She lifted her body slightly, moving slowly at first. Abandoning all cares, her body demanded more. Roland brought her to the edge of orgasm, slowed, stopped, kissed her and began again. Their love making went on longer than Lilly thought possible.

She felt the vibration before she heard the sound coming from deep in his throat as his body moved faster and faster, penetrating her depths with each stroke. The momentum built quickly and they climaxed together releasing primal cries of ecstasy.

Roland awoke a few hours later and looked around for a clock. Lilly awoke as he sat up. "Hey, sweet lady, you want to do me a favor?"

Lilly ran her fingers through his tangled silky hair. "Ah, huh, what do you need?" she asked with an invitation in her voice.

"Will you braid my hair? Its too wild for me to deal with right now." Lilly grabbed a hair brush as Roland dug a piece of leather cord from his jean pocket.

She worked the tangles out and pulled his long thick hair up ready to braid. "What is this?"

Roland felt her finger tracing a familiar design on the back of his neck. "It's a birth mark,"

"No, I've never seen a blue birthmark and it looks like a knot. You know what it looks like? It looks like one of those things sailors get. Ya' know the heart with 'Mom' or 'Forever?' Oh, what do they call those things?"

Roland turned his head trying to see her sitting behind him, hair brush in her hand. "Do you mean a tattoo?"

115

"Yes, are you sure it is not a tattoo?"

"Yea, I'm sure it's a birthmark. I've had it all my life."
"I've got to get going Lilly, sound check is at 9PM and I've no idea what time it is." Lilly quickly braided his hair and tied the end with the piece of rawhide.

"It's 8 o'clock, you have time for some coffee and eggs before you head out," she said as she opened the refrigerator and lit the burner on the stove.

They ate quickly at the coffee table. Roland put his boots on and Lilly walked him to the gate. "Music starts at ten. Come on over when you are ready. I've put you on the guest list. Give them your name at the door."

"Thanks, Roland. I can't wait to hear the band."
Roland laughed, "We are in rock and roll mode tonight, it is going to be far out!" He kissed her like he meant it and walked off toward Bourbon Street.

Lilly returned to her apartment, lay back in her bed and replayed every moment of the most extraordinary love making she had ever experienced.

Chapter 15

WILD MAGIC

A rriving at The Cave a little after 10:00, Lilly could barely squeeze in the door. The city was working its way into Carnival mode and Bourbon Street was rocking. The Doorman gave her a thumbs up as she yelled her name over the music.

The afternoon's melodious music in the square had morphed into some serious rock and roll. The medieval costumes were replaced by bell bottoms and fringed leather vests. Roland was firing mind shattering leads on his electric guitar. Trey was playing rhythm guitar. Bart's long blond hair swung as his electric violin screamed. Leon, the gentle gnome, held it all together hidden behind a huge set of trap drums.

Lilly made her way as close to the stage as she could. The crowd pressed close dancing until the floor was overflowing. The tabletops became mini dance floors as young girls with short skirts and men with long hair undulated to the driving beat of the music.

Watching Roland play electric guitar was mesmerizing. Lilly swayed and danced until sweat was running between her breasts. She quenched her thirst with Dixie beers and finally climbed onto a chair, her arms pumping and her hips moving in time with the electric throb of the music.

The band announced a short break. Before Lilly could make her way to the stage, Roland was surrounded by a group of adoring girls. Lilly stood a few feet away and nervously rubbed her tingling fingers, wishing the girls would walk away. Instantly, the knot of women surrounding Roland dispersed as they turned as one and put their attention on a bearded, beaded hippy guy.

Roland looked around and spotted her in a heartbeat. He raised on eyebrow, pointed a finger at her and mouthed, "Did you do that?"

Lilly guiltily stared at her hands as Roland closed the space between them in two strides and put his arm around her. "I'm sorry," she said, laughing with a twinkle in her eye. "I am trying to learn to be aware of my thoughts when my fingers tingle. I'm afraid that wild magic escaped before I could stop it."

Roland smiled and urged her toward the back door. "Let's get out of here for a minute, okay?"

They sat on boxes in the closed courtyard and shared a beer. Roland sighed as he lifted her hand in his, gently pulling on each of her fingers. "These are your magic wands, Lyla. I don't mind you dispersing a few groupies, but I want you to be aware how and when you are focusing and channeling your energy. Remember you have a powerful tool at your fingertips."

Lilly was stunned. "How do you know about my tingling fingers?"

Roland responded in a matter of fact voice, "The power of observation. Those twitching fingers are dispersing bits of wild magic. Your ability is getting stronger. The run in with your ex-husband gave you more confidence in your magic, but it also threw you off balance. As long as you are centered, your magic stays in balance. Watch out that wild magic doesn't fly off those twitching fingers and create havoc."

Lilly didn't know if she wanted to laugh or cry. The idea she had power at the tip of her fingers had been exciting. Realizing it was something she had to control became a new responsibility.

Lost in revery, she was surprised when Roland lifted her chin with one finger, "No need for regrets, think about all the fun you can have."

Lilly's pensive frown transformed to a mischievous grin. She wiggled her fingers, nodded her head and said, "Yea, right on!"

Changing the subject she exclaimed "Y'all sound great! You know how to transition from Celtic music to rock and roll. I never dreamed it would be so electric!"

THE GREEN MAN BAND

Roland laughed, "Yea, we've discovered medieval music doesn't go over well in nightclubs. I like the electric music, it gets the crowd going. I like the way the energy builds and circulates. Its super cool. I could play all night."

Lilly smiled, "The music is great, but I don't think I can stay all night. I'll be heading home after I hear your next set."

"Oh, Lyla I was hoping you would stay and come back to the bus when we finished playing. You haven't checked out our bus."

Lilly locked her hands around his neck and drew him close to her, "I have to work in the morning at Panthea's. I've got to get to bed before dawn."

"You are too responsible," Roland said, looking slightly dejected. He took a long pull on his beer as she ran her hand down his back.

"I have an extra key to the front gate. You can come over to my apartment when you are finished here."

Roland leaned over and kissed her deeply. She slipped the key in his pocket and whispered, "We will have time later."

"I don't think I can wait until later," Roland said in a husky voice as he stood in front of her and pulled her close.

His passion engulfed her in a wave of deep longing, banishing any hesitancy and fear. Her legs went around his waist and she pressed herself close to him. The heat of her body radiated through his jeans. His hands slipped beneath her shirt and his thumbs rubbed her erect nipples. Lilly unbuckled his belt, opened his zipper and guided him to her. His fingers pushed her panties aside and found her wet and ready. Their bodies pumped together. Lilly watched as he moved rhythmically between her legs. The sight of him entering her faster and faster excited her. She matched his rhythm until they climaxed together.

Midnight found Lilly soaking in her claw footed bathtub, aromatic bubbles tickling her neck. She replayed the unexpected 'quicky' she and Roland had enjoyed in the courtyard of The

Cave. She blushed, smiled and anticipated the long slow sex they would have when he arrived later.

The bath water was growing cold when Lilly reluctantly climbed out, wrapped herself in her fuzzy, pink robe and placed the violet crystal over her head. She lit a scented candle on the night stand beside her bed, picked up a delicate crystal bottle and dabbed rose oil between her breasts. Her robe lay on the floor beside her bed as she slipped between cotton sheets. Turning on her side, she watched the moon floating through the clouds.

The morning sun found Lilly alone in bed. Roland had not arrived. Disappointment etched a frown between her eyes, as her hand reached out to the empty side of the bed. It was too late and he didn't want to disturb me, she assured herself, as she pulled on her robe and put on a pot of coffee.

Chapter 16

A RITUAL OF UNBINDING

illy had an apartment and a job. Meeting Roland brought home how much she wanted to be free of Alex. It was time for her to move into phase three, getting divorced. Jolene introduced her to a lawyer, Tyrone Williams. Tyrone was the son of the Vodou Mambo, Alustra Williams and her husband, Shemo. Both were long time friends of Jolene and James. Lilly was assured Tyrone could be trusted with her story and any secrets she may want to share.

She met with Mr. Williams in his office downtown on Baronne Street. "What are your grounds for divorce, Lilly?"

Lilly looked Mr. Williams in the eye, lifted her chin and spoke in a steady voice, "I thought Alex was a wonderful guy, but over the two years I was married to him he became cruel and abusive. He was hurting me, slapping me, choking me. When he took all the doors off the inside of the house I was upset. Not caring how upset I was, he proceeded to put new locks on the front and back door and would not give me a key. I couldn't get away from him. I was terrified."

Barely able to find her breath, Lilly continued. "Things kept getting worse. Last summer he was slapping me around daily. The abuse was escalating. I was afraid he would lose control and kill me." She stopped, clenched her hands together in front of her, and spoke in a strong voice, "I want a divorce and I want to get on with my life."

"I understand, Lilly. I'll put the papers together and meet with Alex's lawyer. Do you have any photographs of the bruises he inflicted?"

Lilly looked surprised, "No, I never thought about taking pictures of them. I was focused on hiding them."

Tyrone nodded, "I understand. Don't worry, I'll get this done quickly. Did Mrs. McCabe tell you about my fee?"

"Yes, Jolene told me about your fee. I have the money to pay you. I might as well tell you, I stole money from Alex. I used it to escape." Lilly spent the next few minutes explaining the red shoes and the socks full of money.

"This is why I want nothing from Alex but my silver flute. I took the money and my freedom. I don't want to ever see him again and I don't want him to know where I am."

A few days later, Tyrone called Lilly informing her he had met with Alex and his attorney. "Alex denies having your flute. He is also demanding you return the money you stole from him."

Lilly gasped! Tyrone gave a short chuckle advising her to deny having the money. "If the money was earned legally, it wouldn't have been hidden in shoes. It would have been invested. Alex is not going to squawk too loud or too long about the theft of, what may be, cash gained through illegal activity.

After much negotiation over nothing, Alex agreed to sign divorce papers. He stipulated there was to be a two year wait before the final decree. Alex was certain his wife would change her mind about a divorce when she realized how difficult the real world could be.

Lilly heard the terms for the divorce and surprised herself as she let a long loud exhale. "Ah, that felt good. I didn't realize I had been holding my breath for months. Her chest and shoulders felt light as she released the weight of Alex from her life. She lifted her head and spoke calmly, "Two years will not make a difference. I am never going to return to him."

With the legal divorce proceedings in motion, Lilly spoke with Jolene and Sabine about a ritual to dissolve her marriage on a higher level. "I'm sure vows resonate through the astral, and I want to be free from Alex in every dimension."

Jolene smiled, "I am so proud of you. You are thinking like a witch! You're right! Vows made in a binding ceremony do resonate through the dimensions of time and space, and possibly into parallel universes. I know a simple ritual to dissolve the bonds."

"Let's do it!" Lilly exclaimed.

Jolene, Sabine and Lilly met in the temple for a private ceremony.

Jolene cast the circle and called the guardians of the four directions.

Standing in the center of the protective magic circle, Sabine handed Lilly a sheaf of paper. "Write your name and Alex's in large letters." Lilly placed the paper with their names on it next to the brazier on the altar.

Sabine lifted a red silk cord from around her shoulders. Asking Lilly to hold her hands in front of her, she tied her wrists together.

"In this space, consecrated to Love, to the greater good and to the evolution of our hearts and minds, we are gathered to perform the rite assuring the welfare of our beloved Lilly. This rite insures the permanent separation and ritual unbinding of the body, mind and heart of Lilly LaCouer from Alex Castiglio through all dimensions of space and time. This unbinding permanently breaks the bonds formed by vows made, auras blended and body fluids shared between Lilly and Alex.

Jolene signaled Lilly to step forward, "Do you, Lilly LaCouer, wish to heal the rend in your heart by consciously releasing all past attachments of love and fear to Alex Castiglio?"

"I so desire."

Lilly heard Sabine's voice singing in the background, "Purify and heal us, heal us and free us,"

Jolene signaled Lilly to raise her arms. With one quick slash of her ritual knife she sundered the red silk cord in two.

"The ties which bound Lilly to Alex are severed. The vows made are undone, retracted and erased from the Akashic records. We ask the Gods and Goddesses to enforce this parting and soothe the heart and mind of Lilly."

"So mote it be," the three women said in unison.

THE GREEN MAN BAND

"Is it in your heart and mind to release all thought of Alex?"

"It is."

"Is it in your heart and mind to turn your attention to the present and the creation of a new life, free of attachment to fear and past hurts?"

"It is."

Jolene turned to the altar and lifted the paper Lilly had prepared for the ceremony. She handed the paper to Lilly saying, "Here in this consecrated circle before the eyes of the old ones, the ancestors, guides, guardians and angels, I bid you destroy this symbol of your togetherness." Lilly tore the paper in half, placed the edge to the candle and placed it in the brazier. She threw the two pieces of red silk on top of the paper and watched the fire grow in the brazier. She was surprised to feel tears on her face. Any residual attachment she had to Alex was released with those final tears. Her heart thudded sadly for what might have been and what her marriage had become.

As the paper and ribbons flamed and quickly turned to ash she heard Jolene chanting and joined in, "So mote it be, so mote it be, so mote it be." Sabine struck the gong as the three spoke in one strong voice, "And so it is!"

Over glasses of champagne Lilly laughed and joked and hugged her mentors. "I am completely free of Alex" she whooped.

Jolene smiled then cleared her throat, "Lilly, this ceremony has broken your bond to Alex. There is no doubt or regret in your heart or mind about your divorce. I cannot promise that Alex feels the same way. Attachments based on ego and entitlement tend to remain until a heart awakening occurs. The ritual was for you. We cannot do such a ritual for Alex unless he asks.

"I understand, Jolene. The ritual facilitated my unbinding. Disconnected from any thought form or regret about my marriage to Alex, I feel free. He can wallow in his darkness. There is nothing I can do about it."

Chapter 17

A CHAT BELOW THE PLEASURE PALACE

aturday evening the three adepts relaxed in the living room of Jolene's apartment. James held Jolene's feet in his lap, rubbing them gently while Topaz slept on her stomach. Sabine sat in the rocking chair, her feet up on the ottoman, eating chocolate mint cookies and French vanilla ice cream. "Only about two weeks and the madness is over," Sabine remarked, biting into another cookie. "It has been much easier having a third person in the shop. I am so grateful for Lyla."

Jolene nodded in agreement, "Even in her distracted state these last few weeks, it has been great having another pair of hands and she is good with the customers."

Speaking around a mouth full of cookies, Sabine stated the obvious, "She and her new fellow seem to be having a good time together."

"You don't have to tell us about it," Jolene remarked, "We live underneath their pleasure palace. I don't think they realize we're privy to the fireworks and ecstatic explosions."

The three of them laughed. James' face sobered as he mused aloud, "What do you suppose will happen when he leaves with the band?"

Sabine and Jolene sighed in unison. "She doesn't seem to realize or at least she is not admitting to herself the temporary nature of his attention," Jolene said.

Sabine put the cookies aside saying, "Lets not borrow trouble for Lyla. We don't know what is going to happen. Perhaps he will stay in New Orleans. Perhaps he will persuade her to go with him."

"Agh, no! "That is not going to happen," Jolene stated emphatically."She has recently escaped a terribly abusive relationship. It is wonderful she is enjoying herself and having great sex, but she is not ready for a long term relationship. She is exploring and discovering who she is. She needs time to attune to the crystal and anchor its violet flame within her. If she doesn't get distracted she can be empowered quickly and mature into a woman who trusts herself and knows her worth."

James nodded, "Convincing speech, Jolene, but there is a possibility she won't see it that way. You have to let her evolve and grow in her own way. The Priestess crystal will help her through whatever comes. You stay out of it."

"I intend to stay out of it. I don't interfere."

James laughed, "If you say so, my love."

"What upsets me," Jolene confessed, her voice ascending with every word. "She was doing so well in her training. Her comprehension of metaphysical concepts, symbology and ritual is impressive for one so young. I was thrilled when she told me of the visions she is having during meditation."

James spoke soothingly. "Jolene, she will come back around, it's Carnival time, she is in the middle of a new love affair, relax and let her enjoy her new freedom. She's young. Her Fae blood is strong. When it is time, she will come back to her studies."

"I hope you are right, mon biquet, she is the most promising student I have had in years, the only one with Faery blood. She has been chosen and entrusted with the Priestess Crystal. From her rapid understanding of the use of magic, deep meditation and focused intention, it appears she has lifetimes of experience in the magical arts. I have great expectations for the powerful priestess I know she will become."

Sabine changed the subject, "Where are you two going on your post Mardi Gras vacation?" Smiles appeared on James and Jolene's faces as they said in unison, "Florida Keys." James spoke up first, "We have decided to stay close to home this year. With Lyla adjusting to the violet fire crystal and Jolene adjusting to being without it, we have decided on a short vacation."

Sabine smiled as she took out her crochet needle and continued to work on a rainbow colored baby blanket. "I'm going to be with my daughter and my new grand baby. This year my vacation will be spent on the Mississippi coast with my new favorite person, baby Ivan Bourgeois.

James teased Sabine, "How many of those little blankets does young Ivan need?"

Jolene jabbed him with her foot as Sabine ignored James and mused aloud, "I wonder what Lyla is planning for her two weeks off."

"Aggghhhh!" Jolene exclaimed, "I haven't mentioned to her we're closing the store for two weeks after Mardi Gras. Oh, how could I have forgotten? Did either of you mention it to her?" Sabine and James shook their heads. Jolene nudged a slumbering Topaz off her stomach, jumped up, grabbed a pen and pad and wrote a note to put on Lilly's door.

Chapter 18

DIPPED WICKS AND FLYING BEER BOTTLES

lickering gas lights glowed through the fog as Lilly walked to The Cave on Bourbon St. She planned to arrive for the band's last set and bring Roland home with her. *'I can't get enough of him. Roland is my love drug,'* she thought to herself as her heart beat wildly. *'Having him in my bed for an entire night and day will be paradise.'*

A cool breeze swirled through the fog and swept up Rue St. Ann as Lilly turned the corner onto Bourbon Street. The band was taking a break when she arrived. Looking around she saw Leon tipping a beer back and Bart sitting on a table talking to a tall, thin young woman. Trey was adjusting equipment on the stage.

Lilly looked around for Roland and headed to the door to the alley. *'He may be back here smoking a joint,'* she thought. As she headed for the door, it swung open forcefully and Agnes, the barmaid, came staggering through. Lipstick smeared and mascara running, she quickly walked behind the bar, grabbed a handful of cocktail napkins and wiped her eyes.

Lilly turned back to the door and saw Roland come in with lipstick on his chin and a bright red spot on his cheek. She had never seen him angry, but there was no doubt about his mood. She took a tentative step toward him, he saw her standing by the door and pulled her into an embrace. Lilly pulled back a bit, "What happened? Agnes came in crying and you look like you have been slapped?"

Roland released her from his embrace, took her hand and lead her out the back door. He was silent, his mouth turned down and his eyes on the ground.

Lilly stared at him and finally said, "Well, what happened?"

"Lyla, this is so weird. Agnes seems to think part of our run

128

here at The Cave includes members of the band shagging her."

"Doing what?" Lilly said, not laughing.

"You know, she wants to have sex with all of us. I think a couple of the other members of the band have slept with her. Tonight, she decided it was my turn."

Taking a step back, Lilly stared at him, "What makes her think you want to have sex with her?"

Roland laughed, "Nothing, I came out here to have a couple of tokes and she came out behind me. She kissed me and expected me to kiss her back. I tried to tell her politely it wasn't going to happen. Her feelings were hurt, she slapped me, got all teary eyed and headed back inside."

Lilly looked at the back door hoping Agnes wouldn't come smashing through it. "How weird," was all she could say.

Roland put his arms around her and whispered, "You, on the other hand, are exactly who I want to kiss." Lilly's lips parted as he bent down towards her, his arms drawing her close. His hands moved down her back and into the waist of her jeans.

She stepped back a bit and said, "No Roland, lets not. I have tomorrow off and I want you to come over after your gig and stay the night. We can spend all day tomorrow in bed."

Before Roland could respond, the back door opened and Bart signaled for Roland to come in. "Let's finish up this last set, I've got a hot date,"

"So do I," Roland whispered in Lilly's ear.

Roland jumped up on the stage and Lilly sauntered over to the bar for her usual Dixie beer. Agnes stood at the opposite end of the bar and refused to look at her. Exasperated, Lilly walked to the end of the bar, stood directly in front of Agnes and ordered her beer.

Agnes glared at her, popped the top off of a Dixie Beer and slammed it down on the bar in front of her. "I've a good mind to throw you and your horny-ass boyfriend off this property."

Lilly sneered, "What?"

Agnes put her hands on her hips and sneered, "Your boyfriend is a creep. He thinks he can put his hands all over whom ever he wants, whenever he wants. Tonight, he tried to feel up the wrong broad. I don't let no idiot musicians touch me."

All the hairs on Lilly's body stood on end. "You have got to be kidding?" She said in a deep, guttural voice she didn't know she possessed.

"No, I don't have to be kidding, Miss Goody Two Shoes. You think he is all hung up on you. He's been dipping his wick in half the strippers on Bourbon Street. You, my dear, are nothing but a little piece of sweet meat. Don't be thinking you are something special."

Lilly's body flushed, as a wave of shocking red filled her eyes. She clutched the beer bottle in her tingling fingers. Electric shocks sped through her arms setting her elbows on fire. Her body trembled with pain and anger. Suddenly, the beer bottle flew out of her hand, grazed Agnes' shoulder dousing her with beer as it flipped around, arced through the air and smashed into the mirror behind the bar. Agnes screamed and Lilly ran out of the front door.

Running like a thief in the night, she headed for the river tearing through the tendrils of fog swirling in the damp night air. Her head was spinning, but an inner guidance brought her straight to the old oak tree near the river. Only a few days ago she had been sitting on its low branches with Roland, happy and carefree. Tonight, she clung to the tree, squeezing her arms around a low branch.

The moon rose and a cold wind blew over the river. Lilly remained hugging the wide low branch, her tears soaking the bark of the ancient oak. Cursing herself for being foolish, she berated herself for letting her guard down. If Agnes was telling the truth, Lilly had endangered herself and suddenly, for no reason, decided to trust some random guy she met in the French Quarter.

Beating her fist against the tree branch she cried, and muttered, "Stupid, Stupid, Stupid!" Finally, exhausted she lay her head on her arm and drifted into despair.

She felt a hand on her back and bolted upright. Roland lifted her from the branch and held her close. "I thought I'd find you here. I don't know what Agnes said to you, but know it is not true. She made some nastiness up because I blew her off. I paid for the mirror, so no worries, heh?"

Looking up into his face, Lilly almost smiled. The doubts and distrust plaguing her moments before were forgotten. "I want to go home," she whispered.

Roland took her by the hand and said, "Let's do something different tonight. I'm going to take you to my home."

Chapter 19

THE MAGIC FLUTE

....

The refurbished Greyhound bus glowed silver in the moon light. Lilly stepped up through the door and exclaimed, "Wow!" Gone were rows of seats and the narrow aisle. The bus had been transformed into an efficient traveling home for the band. Tonight Bart and Leon were off having their own fun and Trey was enjoying a real bed in Jason's apartment.

Roland turned on a small heater, lit a candle and looked back at Lilly. She was shivering and wringing her hands. He stepped close to her, took both of her hands, kissed her knuckles then turned her hands over and kissed her palms. Lilly took a long calming breath and managed a tentative smile.

Candlelight softened their surroundings and faux fur pillows cushioned their taught bodies. They sat in silence for a bit, Lilly chewing on her bottom lip as doubts returned. Had Agnes been lying? Looking Roland directly in his eyes, she asked "Ro-land, Agnes didn't only say you made a pass at her. She said you were having sex with strippers. Is it true?"

Shaking his head slowly, he replied in a hushed voice, "She is hurt and embarrassed. Agnes was striking out with the most hateful thing she could say. She is jealous of you and our relationship. Can we forget it? Tonight was our last night playing at The Cave. In a couple of days, we are going to be playing up the street from here at The Dream Palace."

Lilly looked surprised, "I didn't know it was your last night there. I'm glad you're finished with The Cave."

Roland nodded, "The whole band is glad. It was a good gig, lots of money, but dealing with Agnes was a drag. It will be more convenient playing up the street, easier to do our thing at Valentine's and closer to the bus.

Lilly looked out of the window at Valentine's Restaurant. The lights were dark and the Closed sign was on the door. "What thing at Valentine's?" she asked.

"A few days a week we play our Celtic tunes during lunch and a few numbers during happy hour to repay him for his hospitality."

Lilly nodded her head, "How did ya'll know about Valentine's in San Francisco?"

Roland shrugged and took a swallow of beer. "Trey is good at making connections. The bus is his, the band is his. He did most of the planning for this tour. He has arranged for parking the bus or has found us places to stay all along the way. Tonight, we have the magic bus to ourselves. The rest of the band has found the softer company we were all in need of."

Lilly frowned, her lips puckered and her back stiffened. "Is that what I am to you, Roland, softer company to play with while you are in New Orleans?"

Roland shook his head, closed his eyes and sighed. "I put my foot in my mouth there, didn't I?" He saw the doubt in Lilly's eyes grow into sadness. Leaning back on his arms, he sighed and closed his eyes. They sat in silence as time moved like a sluggish bayou between them.

Roland stretched out his arm and took a couple of beers from the mini-frig. He opened them and handed one to Lilly. She took the bottle and set it aside. Roland stood and took an ornate wooden box from a shelf. Sitting back beside Lilly, he began to roll a joint. He lit it and took a long toke. Lilly declined when he handed it to her.

Sighing, he put the joint aside and moved closer to her. He put his finger beneath her chin and gently turned her head towards him. His eyes were dark and serious, "You are much more than soft company. I thought you knew how enchanted I am, sweet Faery. You are the most amazing woman I have ever met."

Lilly shrugged and pulled away slightly. In the glow of the

133

candlelight, Roland saw the glint of tears on her face. "I've written something for you," he whispered. He picked up his mandolin, strummed and begin to sing softly.

Moon drops they fall on a red heart candle.

Gifts of love touch me again.

My Lilly bud blooms in our sacred union, her gentle hand telling me when.

Her secret life flowers in the late night hours. Robed in her indigo blue, gently she waits by the old iron gates, my inner life she does renew.

She stands in the moonlight, pale soft and lovely, shadowed in pastel delights.

She catches my eye and fills me with wonder, our loving lasts all through the night...

A smile played on Lilly's mouth, her sudden attack of fear and doubt diminishing as she lay back on the furry pillows. The heartfelt lyrics, written for her, touched her deeply. Her mind began inserting flute flourishes and trills, filling out the music.

Suddenly Roland stopped. "Wow, I have something for you. Well, you can see if you like it. If you do, it's yours," he rummaged around in the dimly lit bus, opened a chest under one of the beds along the wall and removed a long, dark case. He handed the case to Lilly, "Check it out, see what you think."

Lilly's breath caught as she opened the case. Candlelight gleamed on the silver keys of a classical flute. Lifting it from the case, she snapped it together and checked the finger pads. Bringing it to her lips she played. The tone was perfect. She ran through the scales and played a little piece she knew from Mozart's Magic

Flute. Roland grabbed his mandolin and led them into a Celtic tune. Lilly's eyes closed as she easily blended her flute into the ancient Celtic music.

Emerald green hills, standing stones, an ancient tor and a sacred well filled her vision. The smell of heather filled her senses. Transported, riding the wave of music and magic, their energy blended creating light and color. Ancient carvings of fanciful creatures and intricate knots danced in their shared visions as the two musicians balanced between the worlds.

The music played itself out and they opened their eyes to sunrise in New Orleans. "Now I remember how I know you," Lilly said. Roland put his mandolin aside and gently reached for her. Their lips joined, as they moved into the ancient dance of ecstatic love.

Lilly woke in the late afternoon to the clip clop of hooves. A mule drawn carriage, overflowing with tourists, rolled down Frenchman Street. Roland, lying nearby, smiled. Lilly smiled and leaned in to kiss him between his well defined brows. "I'm famished" they said almost in unison.

"Valentine's restaurant is right out the door, I'll be happy to buy you a meal, my lady. First, let me ask, 'Is this your flute?'"

It took Lilly a moment to answer as her heart fluttered wildly in her chest. "From the look on your face, I'd have to guess it is," Roland said, handing her the silver flute.

Lilly held it close and looked up at him, "Where did this come from? How can you give it to me?"

"It came from a musician friend of mine in San Francisco, Jake. He has a beautiful tenor voice and added lyrics to our music. Jake started the bus tour with us. By the time we reached Tucson it was obvious he was not into the tour. He found out his old lady back in California was pregnant, and all he wanted to do was go home. He left me his flute, which he said he couldn't play worth a damn, told me to use it, find a home for it or sell it. I can't imagine a better home for the flute than with you. If you feel it is your

135

flute, then it truly is. What do you say?"

Lilly's face lit up, "This instrument is amazing, I've found my magic flute. Thank you! Thank you! Thank you!"

They stood up, straightened their clothes and headed for the door of the bus. Lilly put her hand on Roland's arm, "Wait a second, I need to ask you something. In the song you played for me, you called me Lilly. Why did you use that name?

Roland's head tilted to one side. A quizzical look drew his brows together. Isn't that your name?

"How did you know that? I've told everyone my name is Lyla. It is part of my disguise."

Roland smiled and kissed her hand, "I've thought of you as Lilly since the day we met. The name fits you better than Lyla. It's beautiful and perfect for you." He stood silently for a few minutes.

Lilly shook her head in amazement. "You are full of surprises" she said, as she nudged him, "Are we going to get something to eat?"

Roland took her hand and looked into her eyes, "I have something to tell you, Lilly. You know the blue birth mark I have on the back of my neck?"

Lilly nodded, smirked and said, "It is a tattoo, right?"

Roland shook his head, "No it is not a tattoo. It is a remnant from my past life. My grandfather, my dad and my brother all have similar markings. I feel comfortable talking to you about this because I know you are a supernatural being yourself. Your Fae magic is strong. It is strange bayou Faery magic, but I recognize it. I know the idea of being with a Druid won't frighten you. Am I right?"

Lilly took a deep breath, "A Druid? I'm cool with it."

Roland smiled in relief and kissed her.

'What exactly is a Druid?' Lilly made a mental note to find out as soon as possible.

"Okay, let's eat," they said in unison and hopped off the bus.

They were absorbed in Valentines' menu when the waitress sauntered over to their table. Lilly looked up ready to order when she spotted Alex with his sister, Angelina, walking by his side. They were being seated at a nearby table. Lilly gasped, her chair fell over as she stood abruptly and headed for the front door.

"Hey, Lilly, where are you going?" Roland exclaimed standing quickly. Alex's head flew up as he saw the young woman running out the front door. He bolted from his seat, swept past Roland and pushed him down into his chair. Alex flew out the entrance of Valentine's and broke into a run as soon as he was out of the door.

Lilly was running down the block headed for Esplanade Ave. Alex caught up with her, grabbed her arm, and swung her around. Holding her in his iron grasp, he stood catching his breath, his eyes taking in every part of her. "You look like a whore," he spat.

"You look like a creep! Get your fucking hands off me!"

Her fingers tingled, the Fae magic stored in her DNA ignited. Without a moments hesitation, she channeled a powerful electric charge into Alex's iron hold on her arm. He flew across the sidewalk, hit a newspaper stand and fell into the gutter. "Don't ever come near me again," she said succinctly to his prone form as she turned and ran down the street.

Roland arrived seconds later to see Lilly running across Esplanade Avenue. The man who had been chasing her was lying in the gutter groaning. Roland ignored him and took off after Lilly.

Angelina found her brother climbing onto the sidewalk a few minutes later. "What happened? Did you catch her? Was it Lilly?"

Alex sat on the sidewalk, rubbing his head, "No, no it wasn't her," he lied. "I ran after her, only to be confronted by some asshole who shoved me. He tried to take my wallet but I fought him off." Shaking, he got to his feet allowing Angelina to help him back to the restaurant.

Roland caught up with Lilly in Jackson Square. She spun around as he called her name, her hands out, fingers spread ready for battle. Recognizing Roland, she dropped her hands and jumped into his arms. "It was Alex, my ex-husband," she cried.

Roland glanced down Decatur Street making sure he wasn't being followed. "Was he the guy who grabbed you in the Square?" Lilly nodded. "He looks like a soulless one," Roland said as he put his arm around her waist and led her back to her apartment.

A sigh escaped Lilly's lips as she collapsed onto the couch. Roland's stomach growled and his tone was brusk, "What's up with this guy? You left him. It's over. Why is he attacking you?"

Lilly looked up, "Roland, he is a member of a powerful Mafia family! I stole money from him to escape. I was his prisoner. Now, he wants retribution. He wants to bring me back to his home in the suburbs and make me his prisoner again." Roland sat back, surprised at the seriousness of her situation.

After a few minutes he took her hand, "He doesn't know where you live and...wait, did he catch up with you?

"Yes, he grabbed me, but I was able to fight him off. I told him to leave me alone."

"Wow, you did some damage. He looked messed up."

Lilly couldn't repress a smile, "Good!"

"Yea, he was lying in the gutter."

"I thought he got the message the first time he tried to drag me away from the French Quarter. I hope a roll in the gutter conveyed the meaning of, 'No, not ever,' to him."

Roland took her in his arms, "You're safe here in Panthea's. I guarantee the wards on this building are stronger than the Mafia. He won't get in here."

Walking to the front door, he examined the lock for a moment. "I'm going to set a protective ward on your front door as a reinforcement. No one with harmful intention will be able to come in, even with a key, unless of course, you invite them in."

Lilly looked baffled, "You can set a magical ward?"

"Yea, I can. I learned when I was a teenager. My dad remembers a smattering of Druidic teachings from his grandfather and he passed them on to me and my brothers. Warding, scrying and

THE GREEN MAN BAND

drawing energy from the earth and the oaks are a few things he taught us."

He walked to the front door and with a simple pass of his hand, a blue light appeared to penetrate the doorknob and the lock. The frigid air of warding filled the room for a moment. Turning back to look at her, Roland gave a sheepish grin.

"Thank you," Lilly said and tried to smile.

They sat silently eating peanut butter sandwiches at the coffee table. Suddenly Lilly exclaimed, "I forgot the flute. I left it in your bus. I was going to get it after we ate. When I saw Alex I freaked out and all I could think of was getting away from him."

"Don't worry Lilly, I'll bring your flute over tomorrow afternoon."

Breathing a sigh of relief, she relaxed and let Roland lead her to the bedroom. They cuddled in bed, falling asleep in each other's arms. Roland woke early and left for rehearsal with the band. As he walked out of the front gate and through the square he kept his eyes open for lurking thugs. The threat of Lilly's Mafia connected husband bothered him more than he had admitted to her.

Chapter 20

LOVE SPELL

Back at work on Thursday, Lilly was ready for a lunch break. When noon finally arrived, she bolted up the spiral stairs to her apartment and ran into Madeline carrying two bags of groceries up the stairs.

"Oh, my stars, I'm so sorry. I didn't see you. The lenses in these glasses are clear, but they do blur my vision a bit, Lilly explained, pushing the granny glasses up on her nose. She picked up one of the grocery bags and followed Madeline into her apartment.

"I'm glad I ran into you. Well, I don't mean it literally," Lilly laughed.

Madeline put the groceries on the coffee table, "Yea, why?"

"I need to make an appointment to get my hair cut and colored. Do you have any time this week?"

Madeline ran her hand through Lilly's unruly curls which were growing out quickly, "So you like it short and red, huh?"

"I do."

Madeline dug around in her desk, pulling out a calendar. "Hey, I'm not doing anything tonight. Do you want to do it this evening? We could have some dinner, drink some wine and do your hair. You know, a girl's night?"

Lilly nodded and gave Madeline a hug, "I'm so grateful you are my friend, thanks so much. If you had not cut and colored my hair and suggested the glasses, who knows what would have happened? My disguise has given me time to make a new life for myself and get strong enough to rebuff Alex's threats and abductions."

Later that evening, with her hair cut short and dyed even redder, Lilly leaned back on Madeline's couch with a glass of wine in her hand. The room was aglow with candlelight. Lilly studied Madeline's altar from her seat on the couch, "Will you tell me about your altar? It is different from mine."

"Grab a pillow and come sit here," Madeline said patting the floor next to her in front of the low altar. The two young women sat in silence for a few minutes staring into the candle flames on the altar. Madeline spoke, "You see the four quarters are represented here with candles and symbols of the elements."

"In the center I have a statue of the Goddess Venus. I keep a red candle burning before her when I am at home. I've created this altar for a love ritual I am working on my lover, Chas. This wax figure next to the red candle symbolizes Chas. The doll is dressed in clothes I made from a tie he left on my bed. I have a spell I speak and I circle a bright red thread around him and tie it to this wax figure next to him, symbolizing me. It is simple and effective so far."

Lilly took it all in. She sat quietly looking at the candles and the energy surrounding the altar. Finally she spoke, "This is powerful, I can see the energy flowing. There is something I don't understand. Jolene, James and Sabine have told me it is against the laws of magic to put manipulative spells on people. Love spells are particularly dangerous. Your man may be enchanted by the spell and when it is broken, you are left out in the cold as he realizes he has been manipulated!"

Madeline got up and stood shaking her head, "The high priest and priestesses can say what they like. I don't see the point of knowing how to use magic if you can't use it to get what you want. I need Chas to spend enough time with me to realize he is in love with me."

"I can understand wanting to use what you know, using the resources you have to get the results you want," Lilly said, diplomatically.

Madeline put her arms around Lilly and gave her a hug. "I knew you would understand."

141

Leaning back supported by her arms, Lilly breathed in the scent of candle wax and incense. "How did you learn about this kind of spell?"

Madeline laughed, "Lyla, there are many more books on magic than are stocked on the shelves of Panthea's. There is another magic shop in the Quarter."

Lilly's head jerked up. "There is another magic shop? Where? I haven't seen it."

"It opened a few weeks ago. You walked right past it only a few days ago. I was inside the shop and saw you walk by. You were with Roland and only had eyes for him. I swear Lyla, you are under his spell."

"I am? Is that a bad thing?"

Madeline shook her head, her long blond hair glowing in the candlelight, "I can't say what is good or bad. I can see you are so entranced by him you are not seeing the world around you. If you want to work powerful magic, you must be grounded."

Lilly sighed, "Ever since I met Roland, my heart has run away with my body and my mind has exploded. Knowing I am free, having incredible sex with a gorgeous loving man has changed everything for me. The river sparkles, the trees breath life into me. I'm in love with the world. Roland and I have melded together, a symbiosis of souls. It scares me and it thrills me."

Madeline nodded absentmindedly as she adjusted the clothes on the wax figurine. "Speaking of Roland," Lilly said, "I have a question for you. What exactly is a Druid?"

Madeline dropped the wax figure she was holding and stared at Lilly. "Roland is a Druid? How do you know?"

"He told me."

Madeline smirked as her eyes narrowed, "Hmm, a Druid as in he read a book about Druids and has a robe with a hood?"

Lilly shrugged her shoulders, "I don't know. I don't think that's what he meant. He has this weird blue birthmark shaped like a Celtic knot. He says his dad and his brother have them too.

They are remnants of a past life."

"Whoa, and holy shit, Lilly!"

"What? Is it a bad thing?"

Madeline's eyebrows flew up as she exclaimed, "It is not a bad thing. Druids have powerful magic. Some of them can shape-shift. I know they can bind and unbind anything and....oh, I don't know what else. We will have to investigate this further."

Lilly smiled nodding her head emphatically, "I am going to ask Jolene about it, maybe she has some books I can read."

"Ha!" Madeline exclaimed. "She is married to a Druid, you want to talk to James." Lilly sat open mouthed and speechless.

Gathering her wits, Lilly leaned back on her arms, "I'll talk to her about it. In the meantime, where is the new magic shop? What is it called?"

"It's called The Raven Moon. Its over on Decatur, right past The Abby Bar."

"Do they know Jolene?"

Madeline snickered, "They know of her. They do not know about James being a Druid, so don't mention it. Only a few people know."

Madeline looked intense as she continued, "They know about Panthea's, but are not interested."

"Claude and Regina are the owners of The Raven Moon. They are both extremely talented psychics. Claude follows the teachings of The Golden Dawn, a powerful secret magic society. Regina is into ancient occult teachings. She works from a centuries old Grimoire.

"I know Regina better than Claude and I guarantee she does not hesitate to use magic to get what she wants. Go check out the store when you have time. Tell them I sent you."

"I will. I'm curious and I'd like to meet more magic people."

Madeline stood, put her hand out and pulled Lilly to her feet, "I'm ready for dessert, how about you?"

"I'm always ready for dessert," Lilly said. Madeline walked

THE GREEN MAN BAND

into to her tiny kitchen and returned with a king cake.

"Come on let's see who gets the baby," she said as she cut into the sugar coated Mardi Gras confection baked with a small plastic baby inside.

They were sitting on the couch licking the sugary icing off their fingers when Lilly turned to Madeline. "I have the most wonderful news. I have a new flute. Roland gave it to me and it is magickal."

Madeline smiled and said, "That is great news, I can't wait to hear you play."

Lilly thought about Madeline's love altar throughout the next day. She knew she wanted another altar in her apartment, but vetoed the idea of an altar specifically for the love of one person. She decided to create an altar dedicated to the more universal themes of love and protection.

It was near closing time the next day when Lilly collected candles for the four directions and one for the center of her altar. She splurged on a brass pentacle with imbedded gemstones and a package of frankincense and myrrh.

Sabine eyed her selections as she tallied up the items and deducted Lilly's 25% discount. "It looks like you are preparing for a private ritual."

Lilly smiled, "Yes, I'm building an altar focused on love and protection. I feel safe in my apartment, however it never hurts to boost protection. I want to fill my life with more love and less fear."

Sabine smiled, her eyes filled with admiration as she looked at the young witch, "You are a wise young witch, Priestess Lilly."

"Thanks, Sabine. I have a long way to go before I am wise as you are. I truly appreciate your kindness. I think I am on the right track."

Taking her bag of magical implements upstairs she dragged the end table from the living room into the corner of her bedroom. She wanted to put the altar together immediately, but disciplined herself to take a ritual bath, dress in her ceremonial robe and place Inanna's crystal around her neck.

A silk scarf decorated with moons, stars and planets made an excellent altar cloth. She spent time dressing each candle with oil, visualizing the elements each represented, finishing with the white pillar candle for the center. Collecting the small cut crystal bottle of water from the windowsill, where it had spent the night absorbing the light of the moon and the day absorbing sunlight, she cleaned and consecrated each magical tool with the charged water. A small bouquet of flowers was the last element she added, bringing earth energy to her ritual altar.

She sat quietly for a moment, picked up matches and lit the incense and each candle invoking the Elements of air, fire, water and earth. In the center she lit the white candle dedicated to the Goddess. Sitting crossed leg before her altar, she breathed slowly, staring into the candle flames.

"This altar is consecrated to the Goddess of ten thousand names. I ask for her blessing of love and protection." Slowly she chanted:

"Maiden, Mother, ancient Crone,
Bless my altar and my home.
Free from all fear and woes
Now my home with joy be sown.
Maiden, Mother, ancient Crone,
Bless my life with loves true tone
Released from all doubts and cares
Now my heart I'll truly share."

She chanted for a long time, inviting the triple goddess, her guardians and guides to be present. Her eyes were closed as she drifted through pastel colored mists and floated through the astral plane into the fourth dimension.

THE GREEN MAN BAND

A shining pink light appeared from the mist, followed by a beautiful face. The Goddess smiled kindly, a silver circlet shown within her golden curls. Lilly recognized the youthful face of the Maiden goddess.

The vision faded and another appeared. Ancestors, guardians and guides appeared in the misty periphery of the vision. A new aspect of the Goddess appeared. Tall with brown skin and a swollen belly, the Mother goddess rubbed her pregnant belly, smiled at Lilly and slowly faded.

Milky white mist swirled through the higher dimensions as a grandmother Goddess approached leaning on her staff. Her long gray braid hung over her shoulder. Lilly could feel the arms of the Crone surround her and draw her close. The feeling faded slowly. Lilly smiled, grateful for the love and protection of the triple goddess.

She continued to sit absorbing the higher frequency of love permeating her home. She was about to stand and close her ritual, when another vision appeared. The room vibrated with power as a tall woman with flowing black hair stood before her suspended in a galaxy of swirling stars. The Goddess's deep set eyes stared into Lilly's as violet light shot off the crystal hanging between the goddesses breasts.

"Greetings, young priestess. I see you guard the crystal of the violet fire in this lifetime. The stone's greater power is unknown to you at this time. Through the centuries on Earth there has been no Priest or Priestess, king or queen who sought to activate the true power of the stone. My hope is with you, young priestess. You are gifted with the desire and ability to delve deep into the soul. I have great hope that you will, in time, know the true power of the violet flame. The human race still carries the wounds of a great cataclysm in their ancient history. I wait patiently for total activation of the crystal for the wisdom it carries is the only way your world can begin to heal."

When the vision faded completely, Lilly put one hand on the

pentacle and one hand on the floor to ground herself into third dimension reality. She stood, swaying on her feet, overwhelmed by the intense energy of Inanna.

After a few minutes or maybe it was hours, she remembered to thank the Triple Goddess, her guides, guards, angels and ancestors for their presence and gifts of love and protection.

Chapter 21

OF PAN, DIANA AND THE LADIES OF THE NIGHT

L ife in the French Quarter sped up to overdrive as Carnival approached. The crowds quadrupled, as did the customers in Panthea's Pantry. Because she had ful employees hilly was able to take off work a little early Wednesday afternoon to join her friends for her first Carnival Parade.

She knocked on Gemma's door and found Madeline, Gemma, Forest, and Owen sitting on the floor of the living room. She joined them as they passed a joint around their small circle. They were all in high spirits as they grabbed jackets and shawls and headed for Canal Street to wait for the parade.

The colors, lights, textures and mythical themes of each float in the parade lit up Lilly's entire being. The god Pan adorned one float, magic flute to his lips, head gently swaying as the float made its slow progress through the crowded street.

The masked riders on the floats twirled strands of colorful beads and teased the roaring crowds. In the streets below the floats arms waved trying to catch the beads flying overhead. Voices called out, "Throw me something, mister!"

Dark men danced behind the floats. Oily flames dropped from the flambeaux they carried. The burning torches flickered wildly above their heads as they swayed to the music of the marching bands. Owen cupped his hands around Lilly's ear and asked, "Do you want to get up on my shoulders, you can catch more beads?" Lilly nodded. Owen bent his six foot frame over so Lily could mount his shoulders. She let out a whoop as she took in the crowds and the line of floats parading up Canal Street.

The Goddess, Diana, her bow drawn, the crescent moon at her back, hunting dogs at her heels, stood larger than life on the next float. Her glossy paper-mache eyes reflected the light of the flambeaux. Lilly's heart thumped in time with the music of the marching bands.

The last float rolled past them at 11PM. The group of friends, weighed down with multi-colored strands of beads, left Canal Street in high spirits. They walked through the Quarter all the way to Frenchman Street to catch The Green Man Band's debut at The Dream Palace. Arriving foot sore and thirsty, they grabbed a table, ordered a pitcher of beer and sat back to enjoy the music.

Roland had not seen them come in. He was absorbed in the music as his guitar rang out in crystal clarity. The opening chords to *Dancing in the Street* brought almost everyone to the dance floor. The band members floated in a sea of flashing purple as a fog machine filled the stage with billowing clouds of purple, green and gold. The Mardi Gras colored mist tumbled from the stage and swirled around the dancers. The music built as the strobe lights came on and Roland's guitar notes reverberated through the fog. The music penetrated into Lilly's core, but she was happy to sit back and let the music wash through her.

Around 1:00 AM the band wrapped up the set with one of their original tunes. As the lights came up in the club, Lilly left her table of friends and walked towards the stage. She was half way through the crowded club when she saw a short blond girl jump up onto the stage and wrap her arms around Roland's neck. She kissed him on the lips and from where Lilly was standing, he kissed her back. Lilly froze in place as Roland removed the girl's arms from around his neck and gave her a pat on the butt. He turned away from her, unplugged his instrument and helped to clear the stage.

Lilly kept her eyes on the blond girl standing by the side of the stage. After a few minutes the petite blond walked over to the heavy set guy seated on a stool by the front door. Putting her arms around the big guy's neck, she wiggled up onto his lap. Within minutes the unlikely couple headed to the back of the Dream Palace and through a door marked employees only.

THE GREEN MAN BAND

Lilly walked up to the side of the stage and called to Roland. Hearing her, he put the thick black cords he was winding around his arm on top of a speaker and jumped down from the stage. He took her in his arms and kissed her, pulling back he looked at her and said, "How was the parade? Did you like it?"

Lilly couldn't respond. As much as she didn't want to say it, the words flew out of her mouth, "Who was the blond who jumped up and kissed you?"

Roland looked confused, "When?"

"A few minutes ago. I was in the middle of the room and saw her jump up and kiss you."

Roland laughed and shook his head, "She was a working girl Lilly, she wanted to sell me some loving tonight."

"What? A working girl?"

"Yes, you know a prostitute."

"No. I've never seen a prostitute, I thought they would be easily recognizable."

"Well, Lilly, she must have forgotten her name tag tonight. I assure you, she was selling it. I wasn't interested."

Feeling foolish Lilly blushed. The memory of Agnes' jeering comment about Roland dipping his wick in the working girls on Bourbon Street echoed in Lilly'a mind. A red haze filled her vision for a moment. The voices of her friends calling her name brought her back to herself. She looked at Roland, waiting for a sign he wanted her to stay. He was looking at Madeline, Gemma, Forest, and Owen smiling and waving.

Forest gave a thumbs up and said, "Good show!"
Lilly lingered by the stage for a minute, waiting for Roland to invite her to the bus, or ask to come to her apartment. "My friends are leaving, I better go."

Roland looked at the stage and said, "Yea, okay. Oh, by the way, tomorrow night I want you to come to a party with me. It's a party and a drumming ritual. We are playing the early set here and heading to the party afterwards. Can you meet me here, around

150

10PM?"

"I'd rather you come to Panthea's and we go together from there, Lilly said."

"That would be a good idea, but the party is close to The Dream Palace. If you feel uncomfortable walking through the Quarter at night, I will come by and we can go from Panthea's."

Lilly blushed, bit her bottom lip and shook her head. "No, that's not necessary. If the party is close by it makes sense for me to meet you here."

Roland nodded in agreement as Lilly ran to catch up with Madeline, Gemma and the guys as they headed out the door. "Hey," Lilly called as she caught up with her friends. "Did ya'll notice any prostitutes in The Dream Palace tonight?"

Madeline's guffaw was followed by Owen's deep laugh. Forest walked beside Lilly and looked serious. "I don't know if they are prostitutes on the side, but I did see a couple of strippers from Big Daddy's in there. Maybe they make extra money turning tricks on their night off."

Gemma's head swiveled around as she glared at Forest for a minute, "How do you know strippers from Big Daddy's?" Forest looked sheepish, caught up with her, and put his arm around her waist.

Madeline put her arm through Lilly's, seeing her shiver. "Lilly, my sweet innocent friend, you are going to have to toughen up. When you are seeing a musician, you can expect the groupies are going to surround him, flirt with him and try to get into bed with him. This is the French Quarter, so you have to know the prostitutes are going to be offering their wares also."

Lilly gave half a laugh, "Is that what you call it, their wares?"

Both girls giggled for a moment. Madeline put on her serious face and looked at Lilly, "If you are going to be his old lady, you have to learn to trust, or you will drive yourself crazy. Remember, nothing repels a musician like a jealous old lady."

Lilly shrugged, "I'm not his old lady. I have no real claim on him, or he on me. I have no reason to be jealous."

Madeline laughed, "You may keep telling yourself that sister, but I have seen the magic between you. The love vibes are alive and well." Lilly smiled as they made their way home to Panthea's.

Chapter 22

The Order of Interplanetary Adepts

The Green Man Band finished their set around 10 the next evening. Roland stood on the sidewalk in front of the Dream Palace and looked around for Lilly. She hadn't arrived, so he waited as the rest of the band headed to the party. It was unlike her to be late. She was always so eager to please and ready for new experiences. She had been upset after her run in with her ex-husband at Valentines. Maybe she decided it was too risky to walk down to Frenchman Street. He didn't want her to get caught up in some godawful drama or get hurt. He paced a bit, berating himself for not going to Panthea's and walking with her to the party. *'You are a fool! You don't make your lady walk alone to meet you, you go get her!'* There was nothing he could do, but hope things were cool.

He had been pacing for a few minutes when he heard footsteps running toward him. He opened his arms to embrace Lilly as he saw her running up the sidewalk. "I'm sorry Roland. I was with Gemma, we were talking and I didn't realize it was so late."

Roland held her close and kissed the top of her head. He reluctantly released her from his embrace, "It's okay, I should have come to get you. I'm sorry for making you walk through The Quarter alone."

Lilly looked puzzled and out of breath. "How far is it to the party?"

"I have the address. He took a wadded piece of paper out of the pocket of his jeans and showed it to Lilly. Bodhi Sala Temple, 627 Rue Ursaline, she read as he put his arm around her waist, pulled her close and began to walk.

Within minutes they stood in front of an open set of ornate iron gates. The sound of music drew them into a huge courtyard.

153

Tiny white lights draped the upstairs balcony overlooking the courtyard. Tiki Torches flamed in the courtyard and groups of candles flickered on tables grouped to one side. A large vat of punch and a tray of cookies stood in the center of a table.

Lilly and Roland made their way through the festively attired guests to the refreshments. They drank deeply of the punch and grabbed a few cookies. Roland took Lilly's hand and drew her up the stairs to the balcony overlooking the courtyard.

They stood arm in arm watching the stream of people pour through the gates bedecked with Mardi Gras beads and multi-colored capes, their arms filled with drums and rattles. The drummers gathered together and a loose circle formed. Women, wearing white dresses with Mardi Gras beads draped around their necks, moved gracefully to the steady beat of the drums.

Swirls of color caught Lilly's eye as she watched the dancers move. An older woman with bright red hair hanging to her waist entered and stood at the center of the circle. Roland whispered in Lilly's ear and pointed at the woman in the center of the circle, "Her name is Kumira and she is the guru or priestess of this group.

Lilly nodded her head as Kumira lifted her arm, pointed her finger and drew a circle with a triangle in the center. Lilly recognized the cardinal cross from her studies. The circle of dancers added their voices to Kumira as they toned in one powerful voice, "OOOOO, EEEEE, AAAAHHH." The sacred tones activated the cardinal cross and it burst into flames which hung in the air.

Four cardinal crosses were drawn, each activated and flaming in the four directions. Kumira spoke in a powerful voice, "We are the interplanetary adepts, priests and priestesses of Atlantis. We are the old ones, we are the new ones, come to reawaken the people from a dream, come to open the portal of energy waiting to flood the earth with love." She pointed at the drummers and the mesmerizing beat of the drums worked its magic on those moving in the circle.

The dancers undulated, whirling faster and faster. Roland grabbed Lilly's hand and pulled her towards the stairs, "Lets go dance."

Joining the circle, Lilly looked towards the center. The woman with red hair had disappeared. In her place stood an ancient one, a man wearing the ornate robes of a high priest. Power emanated from the crystal atop the staff he leaned on. The old man was speaking, but Lilly was dancing near the drums and couldn't hear what he was saying.

As she danced, colors swirled and spun with her. She danced ecstatically, celebrating the return of her inner vision. The world looked as it always had. Colorful energy spiraled, swirled and eddied around them. The circle was a vortex of color. Powerful cries of "OOOOO, EEEEE, AAAHHH," rang out calling forth a gigantic winged serpent spiraling over the circle of dancers and drummers.

The serpent was weaving its way through the circle, moving between the dancers, forming an intricate knot with its glowing light body. She heard someone exclaim, "Quetzalcoatl our protector, is with us. Feel his fiery energy!"

The drums continued to beat out rhythms faster and faster, the crowd dancing and exclaiming "OOOOO, EEEEE AAAH-HH." Quetzalcoatl circled over head, spinning faster and faster, following the ecstatic beat of the drums. Lilly watched the snake transform into an explosion of brilliant colors sending streams of three dimensional patterns spiraling into the night.

As the geometric figures split apart and coalesced, disappearing into infinity, Lilly looked for the old man in the center of the circle. The ancient high priest had disappeared. Kumira stood in the center, her mouth moving in some ecstatic chant as her arms swung, moving the energy above her.

She pointed to the drummers and they stopped. Putting her hands on the earth, all the participants followed as she intoned, "The energy of the drums, the energy of love, of fiery creation

155

is within us, let us share it with the earth so we may continue to draw from her strength." "OOOOO,EEEEEE,AAAHHH," they all intoned.

"Through all dimensions of time and space, we are here tonight to celebrate the truth of love. Love without fear, love un-ashamed, the creative energy of the universe as it manifests here tonight, as it has manifested for eons. We, the original Atlantean's, The Order of Interplanetary Adepts have returned to Earth to open the portal for a new paradigm to emerge. We are fearless, we are one, we are love, "OOOOO, EEEEE, AAAHHH!" The beat of the drums propelled the dancers into a coiling and uncoiling serpent sinuously moving through the courtyard.

The drumming and dancing continued for hours. The horizon was tinged with the first gray light of dawn when, exhausted and hungry, Lilly and Roland joined a group headed for an all night Chinese Restaurant on Decatur Street. Thirty minutes later, Trey, Leon, Bart several of the drummers from the ritual and assorted girlfriends and boyfriends were sitting under paper lanterns pass-ing crawfish fried rice, shrimp with lobster sauce and Kung Po chicken around the table. Lilly picked at her food. The ecstasy she had experienced earlier was slipping away. The swirling colors were disappearing.

Roland spoke quietly in her ear, "Don't like Chinese food?"

She shook her head, "I'm not as hungry as I thought I was."

"It's the acid," he said in a matter of fact voice.

"What acid?"

"You know the punch? You drank two whole cups of it. It was electric punch."

"Why didn't you tell me?"

"I didn't know until everything turned into psychedelic pais-leys," he explained.

Lilly sat back in her chair and sighed deeply. "I have to be in the shop by noon tomorrow. I've got to go home."

Roland kissed her on the cheek squeezed her hand and said,

"Okay baby, lets head back to Panthea's." They made a quick goodbye to their dinner companions and headed for the door.

Expecting the sky to be pink and gold with the rising sun, Lilly was surprised to find a thick shroud of fog blocking the dawn light. She and Roland stepped onto the damp banquette slowly making their way towards Jackson Square..

Ghostly figures appeared suddenly out of the fog, footsteps muffled as they passed in the dampness. Lilly saw floating forms and colors drift through the fog, transforming as they floated into her. Laughing nervously, she followed the tug of Roland's hand. They turned a corner and continued through the pea soup fog. Roland held tight to her hand, and stopped abruptly, "Was I supposed to turn the corner back there?"

"You turned a corner? What street is this?"

A dark form approached through the fog. Roland stepped up to the form in the mist, "Oh, sir can you tell us which way to Jackson Square? We've gotten turned around in the fog."

A hand reached out of the swirling fog, grabbed Lilly's arm. "I don't know where your going fella,' but this sweet thing is coming with me." The man elbowed Roland in the face as his meaty hand pulled Lilly close and dragged her away through the fog.

Bright red flashed behind Lilly's eyes at the same moment she became aware of the tingling in her fingers. She concentrated on the feeling and invited it up her arm. As soon as she felt her entire arm tingle she sent a shocking spark of pain to her abductor. His body jerked and she took advantage of the moment to direct a powerful punch to his ample gut. Doubling over, he lost his grasp on her arm. She stumbled and fell onto the damp bricks of the banquette. She lay there for a moment before climbing to her feet as she saw the glowing form of Quetzalcoatll chasing the dark form into the opaque wall of fog. Laughter bubbled from her lips as she stood watching the glowing feathered snake fade into the mist. "Thank you!" She called.

Following the sound of low moaning, she walked back

THE GREEN MAN BAND

through the fog to find Roland lying on his back. She knelt over and help him sit up. "I'm okay, he pushed me and I lost it for a minute when my head hit the bricks. "I may have a hell of a headache tomorrow, but I'm okay. Where did he go?"

"My tingling hands, a well placed punch and a little help from Quetzalcoatl scared him off."

With their arms around each other, they back tracked and found their way to the Square. A breeze blew in from the river tearing the fog into ribbons which floated away on the breeze. The glorious dawn light bathed their faces as Lilly placed the heavy key in the gate to Panthea's apartments.

Roland fell into a deep sleep when his head hit the pillow. Lilly lay in bed and closed her eyes. Her outer vision had cleared, but her inner vision tripped on, revealing psychedelic realms. Swirling colors filled her vision morphing into weird animals, faces and geometric shapes. The vision danced before her closed eyes and sleep would not come. She opened her eyes and saw her small apartment. She closed her eyes and let the psychedelic vision take her. The visions faded by 7AM and Lilly's mind finally relaxed into the oblivion of deep sleep.

A loud knocking woke her at 12:30 as Sabine came to remind her she was due in the shop half an hour ago. Lilly dragged herself through the afternoon as Roland slept through the day. She was sitting on the stool behind the counter, sipping her third cup of coffee staring into space. Jolene sat on the stool beside her, "Late night?"

"Yea, we went to a drumming ritual. Afterwards we went to the Chinese restaurant for dinner."

"So you've met Kumira?"

"I didn't meet her. I saw her in the center of the circle, but I never spoke with her."

"You know," Jolene said in a whisper, "Her rituals are fueled by LSD. She has even formed a church with LSD as its sacrament."

Lilly nodded slowly, "Yes, I had some of the acid punch. I

didn't know I was drinking LSD, but it was wonderful. My aura vision fully returned after I drank it. I could see the colors. I could see the energy building. I even saw a huge flying serpent. I saw him twice. He rescued us from a drunk on the way home. The flying serpent seemed real! I'm sad to think it was an hallucination."

"Your visions are not less real because you took LSD," Jolene said in a matter of fact voice. "Our brains block over 90% of the energy surrounding us. LSD's magic works on the brain and lifts the veils of illusion. When the veils are lifted the energy, always there, is visible to us. Your ability to see more energy than most is strong, so don't think what you saw wasn't valid. If you were at the ritual, you were supposed to be there. You are part of the energy invoked within the circle. The Bhodi Sala are reincarnated Atlanteans and I would not be surprised to find you have a connection to them through a past life or many past lives. The visions you enjoyed were gifts to you, windows into your deeper knowing. Be grateful."

Lilly smiled sadly, "Since I've been wearing the Inanna Crystal my abilities have been returning. I see a bit from the corner of my eye. I wish my vision was as vivid as it was on the LSD. Everything was beautiful."

Jolene put her arm around Lilly's shoulders, "It will return, give it time. The process of healing the trauma you have suffered will take time, ma chérie. You can work on forgiveness. It is forgiveness which will accelerate your healing."

Lilly shrugged out of Jolene's arm, "Forgive? You think I'm going to forgive Alex for what he did to me? I will never forgive or forget. I'm not opening the door to abuse again!"

"No, Lilly, I'm talking about forgiving yourself. Have you considered you may be harboring blame for what happened, believing you invited it, deserved it and allowed it? These deep seated, unknown, unacknowledged and false beliefs churn in the subconscious mind. Over time they create fear, doubt, self loathing and havoc in your life. It is the unexamined and unhealed parts of you that will allow the abuse to return in myriad ways. I am not asking you to deny the abuse you suffered or pretend it didn't happen. I am saying examine your feelings, allow them, embrace yourself in love and forgiveness, those are the thoughts, feelings and attitudes that will speed your healing and raise your energy to the point where you will reactivate your gift of auric vision. You are on the path don't let attachments to the past get in your way. Reclaim your personal power. Knowing and appreciating your true self will be the greatest deterrent to allowing abuse again."

Lilly stared at Jolene for a minute, a frown burrowing between her brows. Too tired to argue or even assimilate Jolene's advice, she shrugged her shoulders and sipped her coffee.

"You and Roland have experienced the removal of the veils of illusion together. Your bond will be stronger. He is a good man with powerful magic," Jolene continued.

Lilly's eyebrows raised as her head flew up, "You think he has powerful magic?"

Jolene tilted her head, "Don't you?"

"Yes, yes, I do. I need to talk to you about something."

Jolene opened her hands and lifted an eyebrow, "Okay, ask me anything."

"Jolene, Roland is a Druid. Well, he was a Druid in a past life. He has a blue birthmark and he told me it was a remnant from his past life as a Druid. He is a powerfully good musician. He may have powers he hasn't tapped, I don't know."

Jolene took a deep breath, sighing softly, "I knew there was something familiar about his energy. Lilly, we will have to talk with James. He may be willing to help Roland develop the talents of his birthright. In the meantime, ma chérie, concentrate on you. The better you know yourself, the more you will be able to see and appreciate the truth of others.

Chapter 23

LUNDI GRAS

At 3PM Monday afternoon, Jolene locked the door to Panthea's Pantry and put the key away. "I've had enough of the tourists and the Mardi Gras madness! I'm going to serve up some red beans and rice and enjoy my sweet friends tonight. It is Lundi Gras. This is the day when the fun and excesses of Mardi Gras rev up. We have been so busy with the influx of customers for weeks, it is time to take the day off. I am ready to relax and enjoy myself," she said as she playfully danced out of the door and into her apartment.

All of Panthea's tenants gathered in the courtyard for a Lundi Gras celebration. James and Forest were getting a fire going in a firepit when Lilly joined them.

She had taken a nap and spent over an hour looking for Roland. She had borrowed Gemma's bicycle and ridden to Frenchman Street. He was nowhere to be found.

Disappointed she couldn't find him, Lilly returned to her apartment and put the crystal she had bought for him on her dresser. She had chosen the crystal from Gemma's new collection. It was double faceted, clear as glass with three strands of white curling through it. A fleck of red Carnelian glowed in the center. The crystal held and radiated magic and Lilly wanted Roland to have it.

'It looks like I'll have to celebrate Lundi Gras without Roland,' Lilly mused sadly. Shrugging off her disappointment, she took a long bath, dressed casually. Before she left her apartment, she placed the Jewel of Inanna beneath her shirt and grabbed her flute. Walking out onto the gallery she saw her friends gathering in a circle in the courtyard.

Sabine stepped into the circle, "Tonight we come together to celebrate our connection, the love, joy and trust which binds the members of this coven. We will separate soon for a few weeks but our sacred connection to one another remains in our hearts.

"Let's close our eyes as we stand in this circle. Our connection is strong. No need to hold hands, this night, instead feel your energy radiating out and around the circle. Feel the energy as it moves and allow it to enter your heart. Continue to circulate this powerful energy around the circle from your heart. Feel the power of our connection, the strength of our magic together, the bond of love and trust we share."

Sabine was silent as the members of the coven let the energy build and circle from and through them. A bell sounded and Sabine's voice softly said, "Release and return."

Lilly opened her eyes and looked around the circle, radiant colors shown in swirling patterns. Each member of the coven contributed a different shade and pattern of light and color to the matrix. She drank in the vision and made eye contact with the new friends she was getting to know and love.

The circle morphed as friends gathered. A musical chord was strummed loudly on a guitar and the beat of a drum joined it. The strum of the guitar evolved into intricate chords blending passion and devotion. Gemma moved her willowy body in smooth arcs. Soon the entire group was dancing.

Lilly closed her eyes and let her body move. She was transported from the courtyard to another time and place. She put the flute to her lips and magic flowed. A bright fire danced behind her eyes, throwing shadows on a magnificent tent. She danced in the sand beneath her feet, as camels, legs folded beneath their lumpy bodies, watched the desert scene unfold. All the while she played her flute, moving and swaying as swarthy men sat near by, hands clapping, dark eyes flashing in the firelight.

The music continued to drive her vision, filmy clothes adorned her body which moved sensuously. Rows of tiny bells, jingled on bracelets around her ankles. The music was inside of her as she moved sinuously over the desert floor, wildly rotating her hips to the beat of the drums. The music of her flute followed her steps as she danced.

The music stopped, Lilly opened her eyes and found herself in the courtyard. She looked up and her eyes locked with the guitar player sitting on a stool nearby. He stood and came over to her.

She spoke softly to him, "I was in the desert, dancing. I was wearing bells. There were camels. I swear I could smell them."

The guitar player laughed and said, "It was Shaharazad."

"Did you see the desert vision too?"

"Of course," he replied as he put out his hand to her and said, "Lucky."

She shook his hand and replied, "Not so much."

He threw his head back and laughed as he squeezed her hand, "We will have to do something about that!"

Forest, Gemma's live in boyfriend and a member of the coven, picked up Lucky's abandoned guitar, strummed it a few times and played a melody.

Lucky took Lilly's hand, pulled her into his arms and danced her around the courtyard. His eyes locked with hers. She looked away and looked back. Butterflies filled her stomach and she had trouble catching her breath. She had the feeling they had met before, or maybe he reminded her of someone. Dimples creased his cheeks as he smiled at her. His deep set gray eyes exuded intensity, interest and mischief. Lilly smiled back trying not to stare as his eyes continued to hold her in a steady gaze. She had to admit he was beautiful. His strong jawline, black curly hair, slightly hooked nose combined to form a strong handsome face with a touch of vulnerability. He pulled Lilly slightly closer, his fingers slipping between hers as he danced her over the cobblestoned courtyard.

When the music stopped, Jolene was ringing her dinner bell announcing the red beans and rice were ready. Lilly stepped out of Lucky's embrace, smiled and headed for Jolene's kitchen.

Sitting next to Madeline on the floor of Jolene's spacious liv-

163

THE GREEN MAN BAND

ing room, Lilly whispered, "For heavens sake, why didn't you tell me a Marlon Brando look alike lived here?"

Madeline looked puzzled, "Who are you talking about?"

Lilly let her eyes wander to the couch where Lucky was talking to James. She gently nodded her head in his direction and looked at Madeline.

"Oh, Lucky, yea he is something. He is a bit too intense for me but, now that you mention it, he does look like young Marlon Brando in *On the Water Front*."

"Yea," Lilly sighed.

"He comes and goes, travels for his work," Madeline said, cutting her eyes in his direction. "I haven't gotten to know him."

When the dishes had been collected and the last beer was gone, the group wandered back out into the courtyard. Forest placed more wood on the fire and Lucky picked up his guitar. Lilly stayed for a few minutes listening to the music, drinking in the magic of the night. The fire burned to ash and the moon silvered the faces of her friends. Lilly smiled, waved goodnight and headed upstairs to her bed.

THE GREEN MAN BAND

Chapter 24

THE BLISS OF KOSMIC DEBRIS

MARDI GRAS

"Keep still, don't move your face," Madeline instructed as she applied the face paint.

"It tickles," Lilly said while trying not to move her mouth.

Madeline stood back and examined her art work. "Check it out," she said handing Lilly a mirror.

"Oh, wow, I can't believe it. You did a great job Madeline. I look like some otherworldly magical Faery being."

"Exactly my intention," Madeline said smugly.

"Thank you, I could have never done anything like this myself," Lilly hugged her, careful to keep her newly painted face clear of Madeline's blond hair. "Can you help me get into this costume? I'm going to need some assistance with the wings."

At 11AM a beautiful, sparkling and unique creature opened the gate from Panthea's Apartments and walked out into the Mardi Gras milieu. Her bright red hair glittered with golden bits and tiny flowers. Her face was a swirling mask of mystery, eyes up tilted with fine lines of golden paint, tiny dots and swirls declaring her affinity with the Faery tribes. Two breasts peaked out from a lacy golden bodice atop a shimmering Faery skirt floating around her thighs. Soft leather boots embraced her feet and calves to her knees. Faery wings of finest filament stirred slightly as she walked. A small velvet pouch was wound about her waist with a golden cord.

The Inanna Jewel was stored safely in its velvet bag on top of the altar in her bedroom. The crystal she was gifting Roland dangled between her breasts.

Lilly made her way through the crowd in Jackson Square to Decatur Street. She was stopped several times along the way for photos. She smiled and curtsied for the cameras and continued her journey to Frenchman Street.

She hadn't worn a costume since she was a kid at Halloween and didn't remember it being so exciting. Today every fiber of her being thrummed with new life. Lilly LaCouer was reborn as she embraced and displayed her magical self.

The walk towards Frenchman Street was slow as the Carnival revelry was building. Some of the masked faces delighted and some frightened her. Pushing gently through the crowd, she thought she saw Alex's face. Fear paralyzed her for a moment. She quickly lost herself in a group of pink pigs with glittering wings. She walked with them for a little while laughing at their nonsensical conversation as they ate beignets and drank beer.

Leaving the flying pigs behind, her heart grew heavy as she thought of Alex and the mask he had worn before they were married. She had believed his mask of sincerity, love and caring. Overtime, she came to see he was an impostor, an unkind, wicked and cruel man hiding behind a handsome smile. She shook her head slightly, opened her eyes to the sunny morning and banished thoughts of Alex.

Making her way through the colorful crowd, her thoughts turned to her new relationships, her friends at Panthea's, Roland, *The Green Man Band* and the dozens of artists and vendors in the Square. She admitted to herself she, as well as everyone else, wore masks. They put on a personality mask hiding their deepest selves. Not everyone had a monster hiding behind the mask of their personality. Lilly saw the brave, wild, colorful beings full of love, hiding behind the masks her friends wore. The marvelous and beautiful powers hidden in many of her friends at Panthea's were unmasked during the rituals they performed together and the sharing of their lives as friends. As their shadow selves and greatest powers were unmasked, they stood in awe of one another,

THE GREEN MAN BAND

filled with compassion, acceptance and love.

'Possibly,' Lilly mused, 'the true purpose of life is to unmask oneself and become an authentic being. Those who shed their mask, also shed self deception and live their lives fearlessly with open hearts. They become beacons of light for those who yearn for freedom from fear, doubt and judgement.'

Lilly wondered how she had masked her own power. When did she lock it away at the bottom of her heart? She stopped and looked around at the costumed crowd realizing, 'Everyone locks some part of themselves away along the road to adulthood. Rejection, family problems, heartbreak and a thousand cuts and bruises to the psyche create a web of fear, a ball of darkness to hide from the light. Everyone is apprehensive about how the world might perceive their unmasked self. Would they be stared at, punished, laughed at, abused and judged as frivolous, ridiculous or unworthy?'

Lilly laughed thinking of all the brave, wild and cunning, marvelous and beautiful parts most people hid away in fear. Carnival day everyone had permission to unmask. This was the day to courageously paint and costume yourself, revealing an essential expression of your true self. The parts hidden in fear were given a free pass, unbound and celebrated on Mardi Gras day. She remembered something Sabine had told her the day before, "Laughing at the shadow, dispels its power. Embracing your true self, liberates creativity."

Basking in the freedom of her new life, Lilly spun around in a little dance as she made her way through the French Market. 'There is nothing freer than a Faery.' Smiling to herself, she crossed Esplanade Avenue hurrying to meet Roland at the Dream Palace.

Frenchman Street was filled with throngs of costumed revelers. Lilly peered through feathers, satin, sequins and half nude bodies filling the street. She and Roland had planned to meet in front of the Dream Palace, so she made her way to the sidewalk, scanning the crowd in search of him.

She stood for a moment directly in front of The Dream Palace. The crowd parted nearby revealing a group of women standing in a circle around a handsome musketeer. Bowing at the waist over soft leather boots, sweeping a wide brimmed, plumed hat to one side, the crimson velvet and lace clad character appeared to have stepped out of a Faery tale.

The musketeer straightened and looked around. His mouth, framed by a Van Dyke beard and mustache, broke into a grin. Excusing himself from his admirers he made his way to the sidewalk. Sweeping his wide brimmed hat off, he made a courtly bow, his dark wavy hair falling over his lacy collar. "I wish you a good morning, your highness, queen of the Faeries." With a serious face and a respectful tone he spoke only to her, "Today I see you as the true magical, mystical, multifaceted being you are. When I look at you I look into a window of light."

Flustered for only a moment, Lilly responded respectfully, "You may rise, musketeer, and let me look at you in all your glory."

The crowd surged around them. A thousand strands of color and energy intermingled with their own drawing them through a portal of sparkling carnival spirit.

The wave of unfamiliar energy subsided, Lilly's vision cleared and her awareness focused on the beautiful man smiling broadly in front of her. *'He is a beautiful musketeer with more than a touch of sorcery in his eyes. What does this tell me about him? He is brave, loyal, magical and something of a dandy,'* she mused silently, smiling to herself.

Taking the crystal from around her neck, she stood on her toes and slipped it over Roland's neck. "This completes your costume today and I hope you will wear it everyday."

Roland held the crystal on his palm, closed his fingers around it and smiled. "I feel the magic of it. Thank you."

They stood staring at one another witnessing the powerful beings hidden in their daily lives. Today they were expressed for all the world to see and know. Roland laughed exuberantly as he took

THE GREEN MAN BAND

the Faery queen into his arms and kissed her thoroughly.

When they separated Lilly asked, "Where did you get this beautiful costume.

Roland turned around allowing her to view him for all angles, "You are looking at one of Mike Parks creations."

Lilly laughed, "I knew you two were planning something the night you had your heads together in his shop."

A gong sounded and the lovers watched as the Pope, holding onto the golden miter atop his head, walked regally up the sidewalk A tall nun with a bushy beard and mustache accompanied him.

The nun helped the Pope climb into the back of a pick up truck. Climbing in beside him, the nun struck the gong several times.

The crowd in the street and lining the sidewalks quieted as the Pope raised a frosty mug of beer and addressed his subjects, "Hail to all the Kosmic Debris gathered before me today. I hereby issue an edict to be enforced through midnight tonight. All shall revel, dance, sing, drink and make merry. We do this in honor of the gods of merriment and Kosmic Debris everywhere. It is our sacred charge. Go forth and make merry!"

The crowd responded with a roar. The Krewe of Nutria, dressed in ragged animal skins and furs, pounded a primal beat on their goat skin drums. The revelers followed in loose lines and small clumps, all swaying to the beat of the drums, smiling and waving as they made their way into the French Quarter.

Lilly and Roland danced in the streets, lingered with the Kosmic Debris at bars along their route and toasted gods of merriment with beer, wine and an occasional glass of champagne.

The radiant couple caught the eye of wealthy party hosts standing on balconies above the crowds. A few of the party hosts managed to get Lilly and Roland's attention and invited them up winding stairways to private parties. Lilly and Roland happily agreed. Relaxing in sumptuous apartments, they met famous artists and musicians, philosophers and gurus. They filled fine china plates at tables laden with rich, spicy food, drank exotic cocktails and, most importantly, made use of the bathrooms.

Leaving one of the balcony parties, a wave of delight washed over Lilly as she stepped into the street. The sun was shining on throngs of joyful people. Roland was at her side. Laughter, music and magic filled the air.

The bright colors of a long silk banner unfurled from a third floor balcony. The silky material, light as a kiss, floated over the crowd. Lilly could feel waves of ecstatic love magic floating through the exotic Indian silk, falling softly on the lighthearted crowd below.

The world slowly stopped. For a moment she embodied all the joy and magic of the day. Abandoning all care, she floated like a Faery above a sea of color. Soaking in the benevolent energy, she stored the scene in her minds eye and held the moment of perfection close. As the afternoon wore on, the magical couple decided to head to Panthea's for rest and recuperation before the closing festivities on Frenchman Street. Sitting on the couch rubbing one another's feet, they enjoyed some quiet time.

"Where did you disappear to yesterday? I wanted you to come to our Lundi Gras celebration." Roland looked puzzled for a moment, "Yesterday? Oh, I was at the park."

Lilly shook her head, "What park?"

"City Park. James told me it was filled with ancient oaks. He was right. I spent most of the day, lying on the ground beneath a five hundred year old oak tree. The energy of the earth and the oaks renews my strength and my spirit like nothing else. I feel great today."

Lilly sat up for a moment and gave him a quick kiss. "You look wonderful,"

Roland's hands massaged her calves and thighs, moving up slowly. Suddenly he stopped. Lilly opened her eyes to see him blushing slightly.

She lifted one eyebrow in inquiry. He laughed nervously and explained, "I've never made love to a Faery queen. I'm afraid I may fall short."

Lilly laughed, "You? My cavalier, my musketeer, my invigorated Druid, I find it impossible to believe one little Faery could unman you." Laughing, he scooped her into his arms and carried her into the bedroom.

They awoke at twilight to voices in the courtyard. Roland made a pot of coffee and Lilly walked out onto the gallery to greet her friends below. Robin Hood, Friar Tuck and Gemma, dressed as Maid Marion, waved. Madeline, a convincing Marilyn Monroe, beaconed her to join them.

Lilly threw a kiss to her friends, leaned over the wrought iron railing and asked, "Where are the rest of the merry men?"

"Sodding drunk on Bourbon Street," Owen replied in mock horror.

Lucky came strutting out of his apartment in full Pirate attire, announcing a pot of gumbo was available for the hungry group.

Before joining their friends, Lilly touched up her face paint and Roland straightened his lacy shirt, collar and cuffs. As they were going out the door, Lilly turned and put her hands on either side of Roland's smoothly shaved face. I almost didn't recognize you this morning without your side whiskers. You are even more handsome than I imagined under all your hair. Rubbing her hands on his face she kissed both of his smooth cheeks.

The moon was rising over the Crescent City as Frenchman Street filled with disheveled, drunk and stoned revelers. Many of the bright smiles of the morning had transformed into the faces of unrepentant sinners.

They gathered in the darkness for the final celebration of the sensual pleasures. A band set up in front of *The Green Man* bus across from The Dream Palace. Stilt walkers and fire jugglers arrived. A man, bare except for a pair of leather chaps, put the torch to a bonfire in the center of the street.

The Krewe of Nutria added primitive drum beats to the electric rock. Primal impulses possessed the crowd, the waking world abandoned or forgotten. Consumed by a wave of atavistic resurgence they danced wildly around the fire. Costumes came off, inhibitions disappeared and discernment dissipated in Bacchanalian frenzy.

Like Cinderella's ball, the party ended at midnight. Police riding abreast on tall horses made their way slowly through the French Quarter, crossed Esplanade Avenue and onto Frenchman Street. An authoritative policeman's voice announced through a bull horn "Mardi Gras is over. Clear the streets."

The department of sanitation truck followed the line of horses.

The sanitation truck halted at the glowing embers of the bonfire. Disgruntled firemen arrived from the corner fire house. They were not amused and shouted threats about jail time for whomever had built a bonfire in the middle of a city street.

Lilly and *The Green Man Band,* minus Bart, headed for the shelter of their bus. The rest of the Kosmic Debris scattered into the cosmos until next time.

Chapter 25

SEX SLAVES = FREEDOM

t was after noon when Lilly slowly opened her eyes. She had to pee, but didn't want to disturb anyone. Lying quietly, she noticed something was missing. She lay still for a moment listening. It was quiet. There were no mule drawn buggies rolling by, no sidewalk conversations or delivery trucks squeezing through the narrow street. She sighed and closed her eyes. Her mind sought the sweet rest and oblivion of sleep but her bladder broadcasted a persistent message. She slowly crawled over Roland and tiptoed to the tiny bathroom at the back of the bus. The light went on automatically when she shut the door and she let out a scream as a strange creature stared at her. She burst out laughing as she realized it was her reflection in the mirror. The face paint, so beautiful yesterday, had become a mess of streaks extending into her hair which stuck out stiffly in all direction.

One breast had popped out of her gold bodice, and where was her skirt? After a failed attempt at getting the paint off her face and out of her hair with the trickle of cold water the bus provided, she slowly opened the bathroom door and peaked around to see several people stirring.

Roland was sitting up rubbing his eyes as she climbed back into the narrow bed. He looked at her face, smiled and shook his head.

"I've got to go home immediately and clean up," she explained.

Roland shook his head, "You don't want to walk through the Quarter. I'll take you up to Jason's apartment. You can wash your face and brush your hair."

"Roland, where are my clothes? Where are my wings?"

Looking around, Roland pointed to a big mirror inside the

173

bus. Hanging over the mirror, draped across the dash board were a pair of glimmering Faery wings and a luminescent skirt, dirty and a bit torn, but still recognizable. Lilly sighed. "No worries, baby, I'll get some clothes from Leon, he will have something that fits you."

By 1PM the group, minus Bart, was sitting at the round table in Valentines. The place was closed for Ash Wednesday except for the members of The Green Man Band who were Jason's guests. He put a pot of coffee on the table and joined them. "Is Bart here?"

Everyone shook their heads. "Last seen yesterday with Joan of Arc," Trey explained.

The timer on the oven binged and Jason brought out scrambled eggs and piping hot biscuits with butter and jam. As the group dug in hungrily, he went out to get a newspaper from the stand in front of the restaurant.

Jason opened the paper and sat, sipping his coffee. Lilly looked up, yelped and almost dropped hot coffee in her lap. Everyone stared at her. She couldn't speak for a moment but kept pointing to the newspaper. Jason turned it over to see what she was so upset about.

Pointing frantically, Lilly spoke in a strained voice, "Let me have it, please."

Staring at her from the front page of the New Orleans Times Picayune was Alex's face beside an older man. The headline read, International Business Man and Local War Hero Arrested for Sex Trafficking. Lilly was shaking so hard she couldn't hold the paper, her eyes were bugging out of her head so shocked she couldn't focus on the words.

Jason took the paper from her and read. "Lawrence Brankston, an international manufacturing executive and local Vietnam War hero, Alex Castiglio, were arrested Mardi Gras day in New Orleans. The charges: Sex trafficking. Allegedly the two men have been trafficking young women from Southeast Asia to various countries, including the United States. The arrests come after an extensive investigation by the FBI into the sex slave trade growing in the U.S.

"Lawrence Brankston." Lilly interrupted him, "Read the part about Alex, please."

"Alex Castiglio, youngest son of the New Orleans Castiglio family, a veteran of the Vietnam war and highly decorated Air Force officer returned to New Orleans after his discharge from the USAF. He became the private pilot for New Orleans native and international businessman, Lawrence Brankston. The Castiglio family has been attempting to shed their Mafia profile since the murder of Carlos Castiglio Sr in 1960. There has been no comment from the family since Alex Castiglio was taken into custody yesterday.

"The arrest took place at Lakeside Airport in New Orleans early Mardi Gras day. Fifteen young women, ranging in age from fourteen to seventeen were on the plane. Castiglio was arrested disembarking from the plane. Brankston was arrested at his home on Audubon Place. At this time, neither Brankston nor Castiglio have made a statement."

Lilly's mouth hung open as she shook her head slowly back and forth. Finally, she took a breath and banged the flat of her hand on the table. "This explains a lot! The mother fucker was involved in this horror while he was married to me. I don't doubt he would have sold me into sex slavery if I hadn't escaped when I did."

Tears burned her eyes. She couldn't catch her breath. Jason jumped up and grabbed a glass of water from the kitchen. Roland held her hand as she sipped the water slowly, taking great gulps of air between swallows.

Her body shook and she laughed hysterically. The band members stole glances at Lilly and each other, not knowing what they should do or say in this awkward situation. Lilly calmed herself and looked from face to face. "Thank ya'll for being here, for being kind to me. This is huge! You have no idea! This is great news. I am free and I'm sure the girls he was kidnapping and selling into sex slavery think this is great news too. This explains his aura looking like a dirty rag. Wow! I am so grateful to be here safe with you sweet, gentle men. I am blessed to be alive.

Roland put his arm around her chair, "This is big news for you and for those who love you. It's been hard knowing that there is someone out there who wished you harm." Tears filled Lilly's eyes and she laid her head on Roland's shoulder. Roland put his arm around her and kissed the top of her head.

Lilly gathered herself together, looked up and said,"I want to go home and soak in a bubble bath and really relax. I'm ecstatic, excited and exhausted."

"Do you want me to walk you back to Panthea's?"

Trey cleared his throat and gave Roland a hard look. Lilly saw Trey's pointed stare. Not wanting to come between Roland and his band mates, she kissed Roland on the cheek, "Thank you, baby. I'll go by myself, no one is threatening me any longer. You enjoy some time with your bandmates. I'll be fine. I'm sure the Castiglio family has more important things on their minds than me. I'm going home to take a long hot bath, change my clothes and revel in this new development. I was married to a monster and now, thanks to his own wicked nature, I am free of him and his family."

Chapter 26

VENUS AND THE MOON SPELL HEART ACHE

*L*illy walked home on a cloud of euphoria. Arriving at her apartment, she lit scented candles, put on soft music and sank into a warm bubble bath. She began to breathe deeply, filling her lungs completely. Yesterday she had hoped to embody the freedom of a Faery and today she succeeded. Her diaphragm relaxed, her worry lifted and her mind floated free. All things were possible as the world without the threat of Alex was gone. She no longer had to be called Lyla. She was Lilly LaCouer and she was 100% free.

Slipping into her fluffy pink bath robe, she lay on her bed and closed her eyes. Several hours later she woke, made coffee and sat cross legged on her bed. She placed the Priestess crystal on a tiny hook on the window and watched it catch a ray of sunshine and splash a violet tinted rainbow on the wall.

Her flute lay on top of the near by dresser. She picked it up and lifted it to her lips. The music flowed effortlessly as she closed her eyes and let the music flow.

In her mind's eye, the room filled with iridescent butterflies floating through the air. Marveling at the musical vision, she silently thanked Roland. Playing music with him had opened a portal of magical visions and music. Sheet music was a thing of the past. It seemed she only had to close her eyes and let the music pour forth.

The sun was beginning its descent into twilight when Lilly put the flute away and thought about getting some food. She was getting dressed when there was a knock on the door. Looking through the peep hole, she recognized Mr. Marlon Brando look alike, Lucky. She threw open the door and smiled broadly. Lucky returned her smile and stood looking into her eyes. *'What is with this guy and the eye contact?'* she wondered. "Hi Lucky, what can I do for you?"

She stepped back and Lucky stepped into the living room. "A few of us are going out on my sailboat. We are going to have dinner on the boat, watch the moon rise and look for shooing stars. You know, it will be far out."

"Far out, huh? I'm ready for something far out. When do we leave?"

Lilly climbed into Lucky's VW van along with Forest, Owen and Gemma. "Hey, Lucky can we drive down Frenchman Street? If Roland is around, I'd love for him to join us."

The VW bus drove slowly past The Dream Palace and stopped in front of Valentines. Lilly hopped out of the van and knocked on the door to the bus. There was no answer.

She got back in the VW van and shrugged, "He's not here. He is going to miss a good time."

Lilly sat quietly as Lucky drove and her friends chatted, exchanging stories about their Mardi Gras adventures.

When the van turned onto Pontchartrain Blvd Lilly called out, "Hey everyone! From now on I want ya'll to call me Lilly. I've been going by Lyla as my crazy ex-husband and his family were looking for me. They are a dangerous bunch so I've been keeping a low profile. Now, it is over. I am free to be myself. Please, call me, Lilly."

Her friends called out, "Hi Lilly!" and the riders in the VW bus dissolved into laughter. A few minutes later they were carrying baskets of food, bottles of wine and packs of beer as they climbed aboard Lucky's 36 foot sailboat, Cat Eye.

They set sail as the sun dipped into Lake Pontchartrain. The water was smooth as glass forcing the Cat Eye to rely on her engines to propel them into the lake. Leaning back on a cushioned bench on the deck, Lilly watched the stars as they appeared one by one on a canopy of indigo blue. She lifted her glass of wine and sniffed the sweet aroma. Lucky lit a fat, oily joint and passed it around. Lilly took deep breaths of the briny sea air, closed her eyes and smiled to herself. *'My life is practically perfect. I've got a good man, a job, an apartment, a beautiful flute and friends. It's smooth sailing from now on.'*

The wind picked up as they ate dinner on the aft deck. Lilly shivered and Lucky grabbed a blanket. His arm went around her shoulders with the blanket and stayed there. His arm tightened slightly around her shoulders as he spoke quietly in her ear, "Did you bring your flute?"

Lilly shook her head. "No, I wish I had."

Lucky shrugged, "Okay. I've got an instrument and I thought it would be nice if you had the flute. That's cool, You can sit back and enjoy the trip." He disappeared below deck and reappeared with a violin. He sat near her, put the beautiful instrument under his chin, ran the bow over the strings and tightened one of the keys. The next thing Lilly knew, the night was filled with pure enchantment.

Lilly watched Lucky play his violin, mesmerized. *'Who is this guy?'* she thought to herself, *'and how does he own a huge sailboat?'*

After the shocking news about Alex in the morning, the red wine, powerful pot, good food, violin music, hours on the water and the celestial beauty of the crescent moon, Lilly leaned back and drifted, falling deeper and deeper into a state of total relaxation. Her head nodded to one side as her breath slowed and she fell into peace.

Opening her eyes, the first thing she was aware of was her world rocking crazily. Climbing out of a narrow bed, she instantly fell to the floor. She was on her hands and knees when Lucky pulled aside a curtain and helped her up. "You don't have your sea legs yet," he explained.

"What happened? The water was so calm?"

"It was calm last night," Lucky explained. "The wind picked up this morning and it is getting rough. We are heading back and will be in the marina by 4:30 or so."

179

Lilly looked at him incredulously. "We slept on the boat?"

"Yep. Everyone was tired and wasted, including the pilot, he said pointing to himself.

"What time is it now?"

Lucky looked at his wrist watch, almost 3 o'clock."

"Wait, I've been sleeping all day?"

"It appears so. I think you were more tired than you knew. You fell asleep out on the deck."

"Oh, yea, you were playing your violin. You play beautifully, by the way. I can't believe I slept until 3 in the afternoon" she said rubbing her head. "Wow, I feel so out of it."

Lucky put his arm around her and gently lead her through the curtains, "Let's get some coffee."

It was after five o'clock PM when Lilly opened the door to her apartment. *'It feels so good to be home,'* she thought switching on the table lamp. She went straight to the bathroom and turned on the tap in the bath tub. She turned and walked into the bedroom to grab her robe.

There on the bed lay a dozen red roses and an envelope addressed to her. Opening the envelope she took out the card and read:

My beautiful Lilly,

I don't know where you have gone, but I am sad and distressed, I cannot find you. I wanted to say goodbye in person and I thought I would have time. We finally rounded up Bart and packed all of our equipment. Trey has decided we are heading out of town today. I can't tell you how much these past few weeks have meant to me. You are a special lady, one deserving of all the good things life has to offer. Right now, I am a vagabond musician, traveling where they will have me. You are so talented and carry a bright light no amount of abuse has been able to or would ever be able to extinguish. I am grateful our paths have crossed and I have gotten to know you. I will be trav-

eling with the band to Florida, up the East coast and back across the country to California. We will be in San Francisco by early summer. Trey wants to make the whole trip again next year. Hopefully, the tour will happen again and I will return to the magical city where a part of my heart lives with a beautiful Cajun faerie.

Love, Roland

"NO! No, no, no no, no." Her throat closed, her heart constricted. Her body tensed and, finally, the tears came. Sobbing hysterically she fell onto the bed, holding the roses in her arms. Her world fell away and she plummeted into despair.

Later, water crept into the room as the bathtub overflowed. Lilly screamed in frustration. Anger bubbled up as she mopped the floor with towels. *'How could I have been so stupid? I never allowed myself to think of him leaving. He was magical, he was every- thing I ever dreamed of. He couldn't just leave on a bus.'*

Pounding on her head with her hand she berated herself. *'I let my guard down and spazzed out over a traveling musician. I thought we were falling in love, but no, he, he was having a frolic. He knew he would be leaving, but he never mentioned it, never said a word. Agnes may have been telling the truth, when he was nowhere to be found, he was dipping his wick in strippers on Bourbon St. I have been a fool. I have ignored my studies and my meditations for a romp with a musi- cian.'* Putting her head in her hands she sobbed, *'I knew he would be leaving. I chose not to see it, or think about it or mention it. Putting blinders on, I pretended we could go on forever.'*

Three days of seesawing from self reproach and fury to mind numbing grief left Lilly depleted physically and emotionally. On the afternoon of the third day she was exhausted and out of food and coffee. She took a deep breath and decided to suck it up and walk to the A&P for groceries. Despite her half hearted efforts, a splash of cold water did little to shrink her swollen eyes and red face. She pulled a brush through her tangled curls, pulled on a sweat shirt and a pair of jeans and headed out the door.

Pulling open the gate to the street, she turned left instead of heading to the A&P grocery, her feet carried her towards the Square. She had traveled only half a block when a mongrel dog jumped out of nowhere, hackles raised menacingly, emitting a low, threatening growl. Backing away from the dog, she ran across Chartres St. into the Square. Looking over her shoulder to make sure the mongrel wasn't chasing her, she ran into a smelly drunk who grabbed her breast and breathed an obscene invitation in her face. Slapping his hands away, she ran to Decatur Street and kept her eyes on the ground, watching her footing on the uneven banquette.

Part IV

THE RAVEN MOON

"SAY 'NEVERMORE,'" SAID SHADOW.
"FUCK YOU," SAID THE RAVEN."

Neil Gaiman
American Gods

Chapter 27

CRYSTAL VISIONS

Lilly sprinted down Decatur Street until her breath gave out. She stopped in front of the Abby Bar, put her hands on her knees and took a moment to calm her ragged breath. She stood, took a deep breath and inhaled the odor of stale beer oozing out of the Abby Bar. When her breath quieted she noticed the music rolling out onto the sidewalk from the jukebox, "You don't have to say you love me, just be close at hand," Dusty Springfield sang. Lilly threw her head back as an anguished howl moved up from the depths of her being.

It was then she saw the sign hanging on the building next door. It squeaked gently on its hinges in the afternoon breeze. The black metal raven perched on the crescent moon, urged her to enter.

The OPEN sign hung in the door. Directly over the door a sign declared, Magick & Alchemy. On either side of the door hung long black signs displaying The Raven Moon's services in archaic white letters

The left sign listed: Psychic Readings, Occult Books, Incense Candles, Charms, Talismans, Occult Jewelry, Statues, Herbs, roots, Tarot Cards, Anointing oils.

The right sign read: Classes in Ritual Magick, Alchemy, Gnostics, Metaphysics, Astrology, Ancient Wisdom, Tarot Reading, Scrying.

Lilly stood for a moment reading the offerings. *'Many of these same services are available at Panthea's,'* she thought, *'but Panthea's is closed.'*

She opened the door and stepped into The Raven Moon. Tall shelves lacquered midnight black, lined the blood red walls. A scattering of crystal balls reflected the afternoon sun. Human skulls, carved in crystal, glowed on beds of black velvet. Fractured light, from red and purple crystals hanging in the window, threw patterns of light around the store. Lilly stood, taking in the visual feast.

Despite the crystal skulls, crystal balls and a variety of brass dragons reflecting the sun light, Lilly sensed a cloud of darkness hovering around the edges and settling in the corners of the shop. Sweet clouds of incense were unable to mask the century old miasma of decaying brick walls, old wine, strong tobacco and French perfume. Beyond the mingled scents lay the energy of men who long ago married ivory skinned ladies, bid on human lives, and bought dark women for secret pleasures.

A tall, broad shouldered young man stood behind a glass counter. His blonde hair was pulled back in a long pony tail. Blue eyes lit his face as he smiled and came from behind the counter and greeted her. "Hi, I'm Claude, welcome to The Raven Moon. How can I help you?"

Lilly blinked away her vision and managed a weak smile, "I'm Lilly. My friend, Madeline, told me about your shop and I happened to land on your doorstep today."

Claude looked puzzled for a moment, "Madeline? Is she a blond?"

"Yes, she is a blond and she is my neighbor at Panthea's. She told me about your shop."

"Oh, yea, I remember Madeline. How is she doing? Did she leave on her trip?"

"I'm not sure what is going on with her. She was supposed to leave the day after Mardi Gras on a cruise with her lover. I saw her going to the laundry room yesterday. I didn't say anything, but I think the cruise fell through."

"Oh, I'm sorry," Claude said.

"Madeline has good things to say about you and your partner. With Mardi Gras madness over, I finally have an opportunity to meet you."

"I'm glad you came by. I remember Madeline telling me about you. She says you are new to the coven at Panthea's."

"Yea, I lucked out when I rented an apartment from Jolene a couple of days after Thanksgiving. I didn't know I was finding my true family and what a big change it would make in my life."

Claude smiled, "That is amazingly good karma. I'm hoping The Raven Moon will also be beneficial for you."

Lilly was silent for a few minutes as she looked around the store. "What I would like today is a reading, if you have time." Claude assured her he had plenty of time.

He walked over locked the front door, flipped the open sign over, and explained, "My partner is out at the moment. I will lock up so we won't be disturbed."

He lead Lilly through an arched opening into a crimson velvet tent. The top of the tent was drawn up into a point and attached to the ceiling. Thick gold fringe decorated the edges. He pulled aside the front flap and invited Lilly to enter. A little light filtered in but Claude quickly lit a candle and gestured for Lilly to sit at the round table in the center of the tent.

"Have you had a crystal ball reading?"

Lilly shook her head.

"I am going to do a general reading for you. I use the crystal ball as a focus point. Colors and shapes trigger insights. Sometimes visions come, sometimes not. Whatever I see, I will relay to you. If you have any specific questions we can address them later in the reading."

Lilly's fingers tingled and her palms grew damp. "I invite you to relax, Lilly. The only information I would like is your birth date."

"My birthday is November 10." She stared into the crystal ball for a moment, the candle appeared burning upside down within it.

Claude encouraged her to take deep breaths. After a few minutes, he thought she might hyperventilate so he suggested she take slow even breaths.

"I'm going to do a little something to help you relax and enjoy your reading, Lilly. Allow your eyes to close. As I count from ten to zero you can relax a little more with each number I say." Claude began counting, 10, 9, 8. He repeated his suggestion to Lilly, "With each number, you will relax more and more, 7, 6, 5, 4...."

Lilly's head fell slightly forward and Claude spoke as he stared into the crystal ball. "Lilly, you posses an innate power and the gift of magical vision. Your talents are not merely gifts, they are part of an ancient Fae bloodline. In your past lives you followed the path of the priestess. You are not new to the ways of magic."

"During your present life power has eluded you. Abuse, betrayal and abandonment have caused you to loose touch with your abilities. Now you are blind to the powerful visionary talent which is your birthright. As you struggle to define a new reality for yourself, it is important you have the right teachers. Learning to focus and harness your power is crucial in order to manifest the life you want. It appears there is an urgency to achieve contact with your power as dark energies seek you."

Claude paused a moment and looked at the slip of a girl sitting across from him. He studied her for a moment, sighed and let the trance take him again.

"Recently, you have become enchanted by the craft. You are renewing your ancient wisdom and building a stronger, more complete magical practice. The goddess has lead you to teachers in the French Quarter and to The Raven Moon. Lifetimes of strength and dedication have recently been rewarded with the gift of a powerful, ancient tool."

"A great love can be yours if you are able to develop your gifts and use them to create the life you desire. I am here to help you. Do you have any questions at this time?"

Lilly's head moved slowly signaling she had no questions.

Feeling the energy fading, Claude closed the session. "In a

187

few moments you will return to ordinary waking awareness. You will know I am a trusted friend."

On Claude's command Lilly opened her eyes and looked around. In the candle lit room, an aura of golden light surrounded Claude. His blue eyes stared into hers. "You have great potential. I hope you will allow me to be a part of your journey and assist you in remembering the wisdom you embodied in previous lives."

Lilly blinked and looked around. The air was thick and warm in the velvet tent. She put her hand out to open the flap. Claude's hand covered hers, "Let me get that for you."

They walked back into the main shop and sat on the two wooden stools behind the counter. "How did you like your reading?"

Lilly thought for a moment and spoke quietly, "It wasn't what I expected. I don't know how you know those things about my past life. The information is surprising and, shocking. I hope, one day, I will be able to awaken the knowledge and power I once owned."

"On a more immediate note, I thought I would hear a message from my friend, Roland. I wanted to know if he is coming back or how I can be with him. You asked if I had a specific question at the end of the session, but my mind went blank."

Claude's face grew serious, "At this point, as much is concealed as is revealed. It appears the most immediate and important focus is developing your power and controlling the magic you hold."

Lilly's attempt at a smile resulted in a grimace. She sighed, venting her frustration, "I keep being told I have this ancient knowledge and magical energy. Some days I feel it. Other days, I have a hard time believing it is real. The Cajun girl within me has a hard time wrapping her head around Faery blood and ancient magic.

Claude smiled and tilted his head to one side, looking at her intently with bright blue eyes, "It was obvious in the reading. You are more than a Cajun girl from the Bayou. You have an inborn power. It may be untapped, but I can help you awaken your magic."

Lilly leaned forward, "How?"

Chapter 28

REGINA VALRAVEN

illy's question was left hanging in the air as the doorknob rattled and a key quickly opened the lock. The bell over the door chimed as a willowy brunette entered like a queen surveying her kingdom. Long dark hair and straight bangs across her forehead gave the illusion of a modern day Cleopatra, if Cleopatra had worn a leather mini skirt, knee high boots and a tight red cashmere sweater. Big brown eyes, painted with a touch of dark witchery, focused on Lilly as full red lips curved into a smile.

Claude introduced Lilly to Regina and she came around the counter to give Lilly a hug. "Hi Lilly, I'm so happy to meet you. Madeline says you are the star initiate in Panthea's Coven."

Lilly rocked back on the tall stool, surprised at this description of her. "I don't know about being the star initiate. I love learning about the craft and sometimes, I'm told, I become a bit obsessive about learning more."

"Perfect," Regina purred. "Now you are here, you must stay. Our business is slow as New Orleans gets over its Mardi Gras hangover. Please say you will stay and have dinner with us. This way we can get to know one another better. I know we are going to be great friends."

Lilly agreed to stay for dinner. She was ready to branch out from her family at Panthea's and meet more magical friends. With her soon to be ex-husband in jail and his mafia family no longer looking for her, she was free to go and be and do anything she wanted.

Seated on a red velvet sofa, Lilly admired the mahogany coffee table and blanched as she realized it was a small coffin. She diverted her attention to the painting over the fireplace and allowed her eyes to wander to the group of fancy glass jars lining the mantle. She got up to inspect the jars and flinched when she saw the contents. Each jar held the body of, what appeared to be, a small black bird suspended in viscous fluid. Claude came in, put a few logs in the fireplace and noticed Lilly chewing her fingernails as she stared at the jars on the mantel.

"Hey Lilly," he said, as he stood next to her and looked at the glass jars lining the mantel piece. "Regina decorated the apartment. Her vision prevailed as she had the money to furnish it. I had no say in it."

"I understand," she said smiling as she returned to her seat on the sofa. She sat back and continued to chew her nails.

Claude studied her for a moment and said, "I know exactly what you need." He whisked off to the kitchen and returned with two glasses of wine.

Lilly rubbed her hands together and wiped them down the front of her jeans. She took a deep breath, lifted her wine glass from the coffin coffee table and took a deep swallow. Turning to face Claude she leaned slightly toward him and asked, "I hear you are from New York."

"Yep, I have escaped the madness of the Big Apple and landed in the Big Easy. I'm loving it.

"Where are you from, Lilly?"

"I'm from a small town on the bayou. I've only been in The French Quarter a few months."

"You haven't been a part of Panthea's Coven for long?"

"I was initiated right before Candlemas, but it feels like I have always been part of the coven. Living at Panthea's feels like coming to my true home. Jolene says I am a pagan priestess reborn. You spoke of it in my reading. I was amazed you picked up on it. I hope I can remember everything you said."

"You will. I had the tape recorder on. I'll give you the cassette before you leave so you can listen to it again."

"Super," Lilly said, taking another sip of wine.

THE RAVEN MOON

Claude leaned towards her as he spoke, "I haven't had a chance to meet Jolene, the famous Witch Queen of New Orleans. Do you get along well with her?"

Lilly laughed, "I haven't heard her called the Witch Queen, but the title fits. Jolene is knowledgable, powerful, kind, ethical and a great teacher. I feel blessed to be a part of her coven."

Claude nodded. "I hope you will have time to take part in some of my rituals. I know my process would be good for you."

Lilly took a deep breath. "I don't know what to say. Until recently I knew nothing of rituals or magic. I am part of Panthea's coven. Is it okay to do ritual with someone outside of my coven? I've never thought of it."

Claude smiled and took her hand, "Lilly, it is okay for you to do whatever makes you happy. I believe in the philosophy of Alistair Crowley, 'Do what thou wilt, shall be the whole of the law.' I like to say: Do what you want, do what you will, what gets you off will fill the bill."

Lilly laughed, "I feel like I've been trying to obey the rules all my life. In retrospect, it seems it has gotten me nowhere. Possibly you are right, I should do what feels good."

Claude laughed and squeezed her hand, "I knew I was going to like you."

After Regina served a three course gourmet dinner which they ate from platinum rimmed plates on the coffin table, she opened a bottle of champagne. "Okay, its time to partake of my favorite beverage. This is a night for celebration. I have a new friend and we all survived our first Mardi Gras." She poured champagne for each of them and lifted her glass in a toast, "To Lilly, may our friendship grow stronger with every passing day."

Lilly lifted her glass and took a sip. "Wow, this is delicious. I've never had champagne. Until a few days ago I had never had a glass of good wine. I've been a beer drinker. However, this champagne makes me want to change my mind."

Claude spoke in a mock serious voice, "Well, Miss Lilly, hopefully you have the pocketbook to afford a champagne lifestyle. Regina has the good fortune to be born in the lap of luxury. She is able to indulge her expensive tastes."

Regina poured herself another glass of Pierre Jouet, "Pay no attention to him, Lilly. He is jealous because I have a small income from my family and he has none. The money is my parents way of saying, 'Don't bother us.' I'm happy to oblige."

Claude laughed, "How astute of you to observe my minor fit of jealousy, Regina. I have had to scrimp and save and work since I was thirteen. I am delighted to have the good fortune of going into business with someone with bread to spare."

Regina looked stricken by Claude's words. "I may have an income, but you know I didn't have and still don't have, a family. My parents were traveling the world, living in grand hotels, wheeling and dealing the Valraven fortune. I have no idea why they had a child. I imagine it was a mistake."

Claude put his arm around Regina's shoulder and pulled her into a hug. "You have a family now and the longer you live in The Big Easy the larger your family of friends will grow."

Regina, lingered in Claude's embrace. Lilly thought she saw her flick a tear from her cheek with the back of her hand. She stood and joined Claude in a group hug around Regina, "I want to be a part of your family. We can be sisters," she said genuinely.

A weak smile flitted across Regina's face as she pulled away from the supporting arms of Claude and Lilly. She poured everyone another glass of champagne and sat on the red velvet couch.

Her sadness was soon replaced by a bright smile as she turned to Lilly, "This was your first carnival, right?" Lilly nodded. "Did you costume for Mardi Gras day?"

Lilly smiled remembering her Faery costume and Roland as the attentive musketeer. "Yes, I was a Faery. Madeline did a great job of painting my face. It was the first time I've costumed since I was a kid. Did you go out into the madness?"

"Of course," Regina replied. "I've never seen anything like

193

it. Some of the costumes were more elaborate than anything I've ever dreamed of. Walking through the streets I felt I was a part of a moving, breathing work of art."

"Did you costume?" Lilly asked.

"Yes, I was a witch and Claude was a sorcerer. It was the most fun I've had in ages. The costumed people in the streets played a part in the great comedy, drama of the day. I saw the soul of New Orleans, crazy, colorful and unselfconscious."

Lilly laughed, "You have summed it up perfectly! Were you on Frenchman Street at the end of the day?"

Regina looked puzzled. "No, I was in the Quarter where everything was happening? Why do you ask?"

Lilly proceeded to tell Regina about the Krewe of Kosmic Debris and the Bacchanalian behavior on Frenchman St. "You and Claude have to check it out next year."

THE RAVEN MOON

Chapter 29

An Unexpected Oath

....

Lilly noticed gray light filtering through the lace curtains of the living room. Fuzzy from the champagne, she stood on unsteady feet, "I better get home."

Claude stood up with her. "Okay, if you must go, let me walk you back to your apartment. I would not feel good about you walking through the Quarter alone."

"Thanks Claude."

Regina hugged her and gave her a kiss on the cheek. "You must come back soon and often."

"I will, I promise," Lilly said as Claude opened the door and lead her downstairs.

The chilly evening air had Lilly turning up her collar as she and Claude walked up Decatur St. towards the Square. "It feels like winter is finally arriving," Claude mused.

Lilly agreed, "The weather has been beautiful. It is only fitting the cold comes now."

Claude took her hand in his as they walked, "It has been a magical time and it will be again. Winter is the time to go within and reflect, to fortify ourselves for new growth coming in the spring."

Lilly blinked away tears, "Yes, however I wasn't planning on reflecting through the winter by myself. My Aunt Pearl told me, 'In times of hardship and disappointment, the universe is always unfolding the way it is supposed to. It is our resistance to what is happening and laying blame outside of ourselves that makes our lives difficult.' "It's hard to embrace that belief when I feel so sad and abandoned."

"Your Aunt Pearl sounds like a wise woman," Claude said as they approached the gate to Panthea's Apartments.

195

"Yes, she was. I wish she was here to help me now. Her words are meaningful, yet don't seem help me much without her strength behind them. I am grateful for the time I had with her. I wish I knew what happened to her. One day she was simply gone."

Claude looked pensive, "Maybe we can find out what happened. I'm sure the two of us together could scry the astral plane and the physical plane. I want to help. I swear I know we can find her."

Lilly gave him a hug, "I am glad I landed on your doorstep today. I've been lost the last few days. I needed a friend. You and your wife have come into my life at the perfect time."

Claude stepped back, "Whoa, Regina is not my wife. Regina is my business partner. She came into Spell Caster's Emporium in New York. Later, over drinks in the Village, she convinced me to open an occult shop with her. She had the funds, lots of magical knowledge and the will. I had the psychic ability and muscle to get it all happening.

At one time, I thought there might be more between us. In the long run, I knew I couldn't pursue it. I'm not attracted to her in a romantic way. She has some serious baggage around her family. It seems they have a lot of money and the power they once wielded through the magical realms is gone. Regina is determined to discover and reclaim the power her family once took for granted. From what she says, no one else in her family is interested.

Lilly gave him a puzzled look. "I didn't want to get intimately involved with someone so focused on the past," Claude explained. "She was disappointed when I told her I didn't want a romantic relationship. She is cool with our situation now. We are roommates and business partners, nothing more."

Lilly nodded her head, "I didn't sense a romantic vibe between the two of you, I assumed you were an old married couple."

"Well, we are not. I am hoping you and I can be close friends," Claude said as he put his arm around her. "I meant what I said, Lilly, I swear I will help you discover what has become of

THE RAVEN MOON

your Aunt."

Lilly smiled grateful for his offer of assistance. "Goodnight, Claude" she whispered as she slipped from his embrace and stepped through the gate.

Regina sat in her bed, the cushioned red leather head board supporting her back. She heard Claude's footsteps on the stairway and sighed in relief. He was back quickly, which meant Lilly had not invited him into her apartment.

Claude passed Regina's open door and she called out to him, "Claude, wait a minute. I want to talk to you."

"Yea, about what?" He asked, stepping into the door frame of her room.

"Our new friend. Do you like her?"

"Yea, what's not to like? She has an appealing innocence and vulnerability in contrast to the depth and magic in her eyes. I'd say, she is very interesting and definitely worth getting to know."

Regina's mouth puckered, "Did you sense power in her?"

Claude shrugged his shoulders. "Powerful lifetimes showed up in her reading. That is all I'm going to say about it" he said and walked down the hall to his bedroom.

The next morning business at The Raven Moon picked up as the Mardi Gras daze lifted from the inhabitants of New Orleans. Claude was managing the store while Regina guided a young guy with a fuzzy beard to the red velvet tent for a Tarot reading.

"Would you like me to record your tarot session," she asked smiling at the nervous young man. "You can listen to it again and gain more insight."

The young man responded with a vigorous "Yeah!" Regina slid her hand to the shelf underneath the table and grabbed a blank tape.

Her blood red fingernail clicked on the button when she opened the recorder sitting next to her on the table. "Oh," escaped her lips when the machine popped open. There was a tape in the machine, wound to the end. A small smile lifted the corners of her mouth as she slipped the tape into her pocket.

After an interminable hour, Regina handed the young man his recorded tarot reading and directed him to Claude at the check out counter. She pulled the velvet flap closed, grabbed the braided cord, and tied it into a tight knot. Her hand wrapped around the tape in her pocket. In one swift move, she had the tape rewinding. When the rewind motion stopped, Regina hit the *play* button, turned the volume low and leaned close to hear the voices on the tape.

"Your talents spring from an ancient Fae bloodline strengthened by lifetimes of esoteric study and ritual. You have followed the path of the priesthood many times. The ways of magic are not new to you."

Regina tapped her fingernails on the table as her mind absorbed the information, *'So Lilly LaCouer, her new best friend, held Faery magic in the present and past life powerful magic lay dormant within her.'* Regina's finger nails continued to tap on the table as her eyes stared into the future.

Chapter 30

AN INTERLUDE WITH LUCKY STAR DIAMOND

illy closed the gate and heard the sound of Claude's boots walking away on the brick banquette. She sighed and walked through the carriage way, pausing in the courtyard. The Fountain, silvered by starlight, made gentle music as the water danced from tier to tier. On any other night, the music of the fountain would have soothed her. Tonight it brought tears. The visit with Claude and Regina, the excitement of making new friends had temporarily distracted her from her grief.

She walked into her apartment, the scent of roses permeating the air unleashed an avalanche of emotions. Her heart clenched and her stomach bloomed with nausea. The taste of bile filled her mouth and mingled with her salty tears. The velvety rose petals so soft earlier, lay dying, staining the sheets like drops of blood. Scooping up the stained sheets and the rose petals, Lilly wadded them into a ball and held them close to her body. She swayed as she stood beside her bed, resisting the urge to vomit. Blinking away tears, she took a deep breath, ran down the spiral stairs to the courtyard, through the carriage way, out the gate and onto the street. The metal dumpster cast a shadow onto the banquette as Lilly walked into the street, opened the heavy top and threw the wadded sheets into the dumpster's dark maw.

Her hands clung to the railing of the winding staircase, the last vestiges of Regina's champagne spinning through her head. She reached the gallery to find a narrow line of light spilling from her front door. In her haste she had left her front door slightly ajar. She pushed the door open, slipped inside and turned the key in the bolt lock. Leaning back against the door, her breath lay stagnant in her lungs. Her eyes surveyed the apartment and her ears listened for any noise that did not belong. The air burst from her lungs, she pushed herself off the door and strode into the bathroom. An hour long soak in a hot bath relaxed her muscles. She wrapped herself in a crimson towel and crawled into bed.

The next morning she awoke to an empty cupboard and no coffee. She made a quick trip to the store returning with food, coffee and new resolve. Recalling her talk with Trudy, the nurse at Tulane Hospital, she decided it was time to implement step three. She was going to make an appointment to audition for work as a musician. Her musical plans had taken a detour, but now she resolved to get her life on track. She couldn't work at Panthea's forever. Determined to avoid spending any more time grieving for Roland, she sat in the center of her bed and placed the flute to her lips. The music, awkward at first, spiraled upward as she relaxed and opened to the magic. The easy flow of music she had enjoyed with Roland came back to her, but cosmic visions failed to appear.

The day crept by. Lilly thought about taking a walk around the square or down to the river but her legs felt heavy and her head hurt. She made a pot of coffee, toasted a croissant and sat in her rocking chair dipping the croissant into her coffee. She sat rocking slowly until her coffee was cold and the croissant was soggy. The clock ticked and Lilly remained in the old rocking chair staring at the front door. A chill ran down her arms, her throat unlocked and a bellow of grief filled the room. She slipped from the chair, lay in a ball on the floor and sobbed.

Eventually, she uncurled from the fetal position, stood and found her flute. She played for a while, her music formed nothing, but flat notes which hung limply in the air. Frustrated, she lay the flute on the coffee table, stretched and walked out onto the gallery for a breath of fresh air.

Topaz, Jolene's cat, was sitting at Lucky's front door. Lilly watched as the cat stood on his hind legs, lifted his front legs and scratched on the door. The door opened just enough to let Topaz scoot inside. Before she allowed herself to think about it and lose her nerve, Lilly grabbed her flute and rushed down the stairs and

THE RAVEN MOON

across the courtyard. She knocked on Lucky's door. He opened it and enveloped her in his intense gaze. A smile spread across his face as he invited her into his apartment.

Lilly's jaw dropped. She stood in shock for a moment. Lucky's apartment was stunning. It looked more like a New York penthouse, she had seen on TV, than an apartment at Panthea's. The living room was large with white shag carpets, a baby grand piano and sumptuous, soft leather furniture. Track lights illuminated rows of paintings hung along the walls.

She looked around and looked at Lucky. As usual, he was staring at her. "Hi," she said nervously.

"Hi, come in and sit down. I see you have your flute. You want to play some music?"

"Yes, I do. I want to learn the *Shaharazad* piece. I think it might be perfect for an audition."

Lucky grabbed his guitar and sat on an ottoman covered with tooled Moroccan leather. Lilly made herself comfortable on the piano stool.

As Lucky tuned his guitar he explained, "You won't find sheet music for this piece. I listened to the original music many times. I played with it until the piece took on a life of its own. It is my version of *Shaharazad*."

"Would you mind if I used it as an audition piece?"

"Not at all, I would be honored."

He strummed the first cord. Lilly listened as the music built. She sensed the moment to join in. Together they played a beautiful piece of music. However, Lilly failed to visit the desert dwellers who had been so vivid a few days ago. She tried to visualize the desert scene, the camels, but the look and feel of it eluded her. The guitar stopped and Lucky looked up at her. "What is it, Lilly? Is something bothering you?"

She put the flute aside and stood up stretching her back and legs. "I've been having a full blown pity party. Roland left unexpectedly while I was out on the boat with you. I've been grieving like a school girl."

Lucky's eyes filled with compassion as he gave her a rueful smile. "Let me cook you something delicious. I bet you haven't had a decent bite of food in days. My mama always said, '*A good meal can cure much heartache.*'"

Lilly nodded, "I don't know if it will heal me, but since you mentioned it, I am hungry."

She sat on the butter soft leather sofa and listened to Lucky in the kitchen. He was cooking and singing along with the radio, Neil Young's, *Heart of Gold.*

Delicious smells drifted through the apartment. Lilly's stomach gave a low rumble as she stood and walked around the living room examining the painting hanging on the wall. She stood in front of each painting for a few minutes amazed at the emotions a painting could evoke. They were mostly seascapes. One had rugged faces etched in rocky cliffs, watching tall ships list in a heaving sea.

She moved from one painting to the next and stopped. Ah, this was her favorite. A small wooden boat, its sails billowed slightly, moved through turquoise water headed for shore. Above the shoreline the sun shone on yellow stucco houses with bright red tiled roofs. They decorated the mountain side like strands of exquisite golden beads. Lilly sighed as she looked at the painting.

Lucky came up beside her and spoke softly, "You like this one?"

She nodded. "What do you see in it that pleases you?"

"It's filled with hope and the promise of pleasure."

He reached over and took the painting from the wall, "It's yours."

"No, no I couldn't possibly take something from you. It must be valuable. It wouldn't be right."

"Lilly, I painted it, I can give it to whomever I please. I would love you to have it. Perhaps you can bring it to life with your magic flute."

THE RAVEN MOON

"You painted this?"

"Yes, you see my initials on the bottom of each one." Lilly looked closely and her mouth fell open, "LSD?"

"Yea," Lucky laughed as he responded, "Lucky Star Diamond. These are all my paintings. Well, this is not all of them, but these are the most recent."

"I thought you worked on boats. You're a painter?"

"Where better to paint the sea than on a boat?"

"Ah, right. But still I couldn't possibly take your painting." She went back to the piano stool and sat, picking out a tune with one hand. Lucky came over and sat next to her.

Keeping eye contact he spoke sincerely, "You can come by anytime. If you want to talk or play music or visit, I'm here. I will be here for a few more weeks."

"Your leaving?"

"Only for a short trip. I'll be gone a few weeks. This is my home. I always return."

Topaz came sauntering into the room and jumped on top of the piano. Lucky laughed and began to run his hand down Topaz's back, "I would miss my feline friend dropping in for a visit. All the people at Panthea's are my family. I've been here a long time and this is where I want to stay. I belong here."

Lilly stood beside him scratching Topaz behind the ears, "I am beginning to feel like my friends at Panthea's are my family too. I am grateful to be here."

"Gratitude is the best attitude," Lucky said as he put his arm around Lilly's shoulders and led her to the small alcove off the kitchen. They fell into a pattern of easy banter enjoying a simple meal of gulf shrimp sautéed in butter and garlic served over brown rice and vegetables.

After dinner, Lucky made her a cup of herbal tea. He swore the hot brew would restore her good vibes. His potion worked. Her body relaxed and she laughed and basked in Lucky's encouraging attention.

203

When she stood to leave, they lingered in the doorway as Lilly said, "Goodnight."

Lucky didn't respond. He stood near her, keeping the intense eye contact she had come to expect. She held his gaze and, for once, his eyes closed.

Lilly leaned slightly toward him, felt his arms surround her gently pulling her close to his body. She tensed and moved back. Lucky smiled sadly, took her hand and drew her back into his apartment.

He sat beside her on the sofa. "Lilly, you must know how attracted I am to you. I see the vulnerable situation you are in and I don't want take advantage of your grief. I do want you to know I am here for you. I will help you in any way I can. When you are feeling stronger and able to see your way more clearly..." his voice trailed off and ended in a sigh.

"Oh, Lucky, what have I done to deserve your friendship and support? What have I done to deserve my new family? I am thrilled to be here and terrified it will all go away. I don't know how it all came to be and I am scared I don't know how to make it stay."

Lucky looked into her eyes, "There is nothing you did or did not do. You are here because you were drawn here. You belong here. We are an ancient coven coming together again to pave the way to the new millennium. You are a vital part of our family. Have no fear of losing what is so intimately and eternally yours." A huge sigh escaped from the depths of her being. She lay her head back on the sofa, all thoughts of running back to her lonely apartment slipped away. Hours later, Lucky stood in the doorway and watched Lilly dash across the moon frosted flagstones of the courtyard, his painting tucked under her arm.

Chapter 31

CRYSTAL SKULL PORTALS

illy climbed between the cool clean sheets of her bed and drifted to sleep. Dove gray light began to tease the horizon as Lilly entered a dreamscape.

She was in Jackson Square, under an indigo sky. A new moon was rising over the Cathedral on the edge of Jackson Square and Venus shown in all her glory.

A loud dissonant cawing, within her dream, broke the celestial spell. The source of the racket, a huge black bird, was perched atop the gate to Jackson Square. As soon as she saw it, the dark form took flight down Decatur Street. Lilly ran through the square following the huge black bird. She stumbled for a moment as music surrounded her. The lilting strumming of a mandolin rang in her ears as a Celtic tune filled the air.

Shutting her ears to the music, she turned to follow the bird. She stopped, the sidewalk was deserted. She had lost sight of the bird. She walked down Decatur Street and caught sight of it perched atop the metal sign of The Raven Moon. With no conscious thought or movement, she was standing beneath the creaking metal sign. Frozen in place, she stared into the darkened window of the magic shop.

Her eyes picked out a glimmer. A glowing crystal skull rested on a bed of red velvet. She stared at the pulsing light within the skull. As she watched, empty crystal eye sockets morphed, expanded and swirled. A spiraling portal opened and drew her into a smooth crystal cave.

Purple light illuminated the walls leading into the crystal cavern. The light slowly faded and Lilly found herself standing still in the darkness. She placed a hand on the smooth wall of the crystal cave, and waited for her eyes to adjust. A dim green light began to glow, painting her face as she watched a tableau unfold before her. A thin, young woman, her face hidden by a bonnet, collected herbs in an ancient wood. A group of horsemen approached, jumped from their mounts and lassoed the young woman. They pulled her by the rope and threw her over a horses back, touching her as little as possible. Tying her hands and feet, they secured her to the horse, mounted their steeds and galloped into the dark woods, pulling her horse behind them.

The cruelty of the abduction sent shivers through Lilly's astral body. She turned, wanting to return to the sidewalk and back to the Square. A dim orange light bloomed in the corner of her eye, and drew her deeper into the crystal cave. Slowly, she approached the fiery glow and recoiled at the scene illuminated before her. The same young woman, abducted in the woods, was bound to a post atop a pile of sap filled logs and kindling. A filthy hand tossed a burning torch into the wood at her feet. The flames grew bold, moving through the wood pile scorching the hem of the young woman's dress.

A crowd chanted, "Burn witch, burn." The young woman tied to the post, paid no attention to the chant or the men surrounding her pier. Lilly watched as the woman's eyes rolled in her head and focused on the sky. Surely she was entreating the sovereign Lord of all to remove her quickly from her reddening body. As the flames rose, a cry escaped her lips and her search of the sky grew more desperate. Lilly's eyes searched with her and caught sight of what the woman was seeking. A dark shadow became a pitch black raven plunging from the sky. He flew around the head of the woman. Lilly yelled, "Quickly, quickly!" Valiantly the bird attempted to cut the bindings with his razor sharp beak. The smell of burning flesh and singed feathers filled the air. The fire roared as flames crackled rising high, almost obliterating the site of the woman tied cruelly in its center. Lilly stepped back in horror expecting fire and smoke to engulf the scene.

A loud caw of triumph split the air. Sooty hands grabbed the

THE RAVEN MOON

raven's back. The huge bird lifted the young woman from the fire, flew through the billowing smoke and disappeared into the night sky.

Lilly turned to run, but a solid glass wall restricted her escape. She could only go forward. Visibly shaken, she continued through the dark corridor lined with grottos, each offering a haunting tableau.

A pulsing purple light drew her to the next scene, a sacred temple, three marble steps leading to a center altar covered in royal purple cloth. On the altar an ornate silver bowl glowed with an otherworldly light. Eight tapers in tall candelabras created light and shadows around the altar.

A door clicked quietly and Lilly watched a priestess walk across the marble floor. Lilly's heart lurched. She gasped and fell to her knees in shock. The priestess embodied an energy she knew well. It was Lilly's own divine spark, the light of spirit burning within her, the energy she had come to know through her meditations and rituals. "Oh Great Goddess, can it be? Do I look upon myself in a different life?"

The priestess leaned over the silver bowl and spoke a slow incantation. She lifted her hands and moved them gently, as a column of smoke curled from the silver vessel. A sickening green light exploded from the bowl accompanied by a putrid odor. The priestess fell back, the shadow of a raven shot from the bowl and began to circle inside the temple. The priestess watched in horror as the unnatural creature found a high window and flew out into the night.

The priestess fell to her knees in front of the altar. A sigh, a sob and a cry of anguish escaped her throat. *'She must be awakened. The evil in her heart must be transformed. Somehow she must turn to the light. No one is safe as she sleep walks through the world, using her ensorceled raven to do her blind and evil bidding.'*

Turning her head slowly from side to side, she placed her hands on the edge of the altar and pulled herself up. Standing at

THE RAVEN MOON

the altar, she lifted her hands, forming them into a triangle, she voiced a long incantation which ended with the proclamation, "May her body be captured, her soul cleansed. May the darkness within her be transmuted, may her quest for power and disregard for all living things come to an end, may she be shorn of her magic, cleansed of her misdeeds, may she choose peace over power." As the priestess finished her incantation, disembodied laughter echoed in the high vaulted ceiling of the sacred temple.

The tableau faded as Lilly fell and jolted awake in her bed. The dawn light filtered through the window of her bedroom as she reached for the fluffy pink robe at the end of her bed.

The day crawled past while Lilly moved numbly through meaningless tasks. She tried to block the disturbing scenes from her dream, but they would not be ignored. Her nocturnal journey and all it had revealed churned through her being. Visions of the young woman lassoed and placed on the stake to burn clawed at her heart. The cawing of the huge raven who rescued her echoed through her mind.

She sighed heavily, wishing Jolene was home! Placing the priestess crystal around her neck, she sat before her altar and took centering breaths. The dream, or was it a nightmare, had effected her more than she wanted to admit. She called upon her guides, guardians, ancestors and allies to protect and guide her. She felt nothing. No smiling goddess appeared. No ancestors whispered, no angels comforted her. She received no solace. After an hour, she stood and walked away from the place of solace she thought she could always depend on.

Chapter 32

THE FOOL

Roland sat alone on the beach in Coconut Grove. He rubbed his hand over his weary eyes. He had come to the beach desperately seeking some time to himself. He needed the energy of the earth to renew him. He needed the earth mother's powerful healing, to soothe his emotional turmoil.

Traveling on the bus with the band members was fraying his nerves. His lifelong dream of being in a band, traveling across the states in a bus was wearing thin. He was no longer the carefree musician who had left San Francisco a few months ago, nor was he the self assured young Druid exploring his magical path. Living in a big tin box, rolling along on asphalt roads left him drained of energy and inspiration.

He missed Lilly and New Orleans. He thought he might be in love with both of them. The realization confused him. *'I've never gotten this hung up on a lady before,'* he said to himself.

Lying back on the sand, he put his hand over the crystal on his chest, closed his eyes to the bright sun and found a vision waiting for him. Jewel toned butterflies fluttered, dancing to faint flute music. Lilly appeared in a mist, but faded too soon. Roland's hands clenched, as he opened his eyes. He sat up slowly, blaming the blazing sun for the tears filling his eyes.

Thoughts of Lilly overwhelmed him. He remembered her delicate features, her laughing green eyes and the look of ecstasy on her face as she lifted the flute to her lips. Flopping back onto the sand, he berated himself for being a fool.

He fell asleep on the beach and woke to the soft cadence of Lilly's voice. "I miss you, I love you, return...." Feeling a visceral connection to the young woman he had known so briefly, remembering his vision of the butterflies and her music, Roland tried to convince himself he had been dreaming. *'Am I going mad? I swear I saw her face and heard her speak to me.'* Brushing the sand off his clothes, he walked to a nearby convenience store and dialed Panthea's Pantry. The phone rang and finally the answering machine picked up, "You have reached Panthea's Pantry, we are closed for the two weeks following Carnival. Please leave a message and we will return your call when we reopen. Blessed Be." Putting the phone down, Roland shook his head. *'I don't know what to say. I have never been this hung up on a chic before. Leave it to me to fall for a Faery witch with no home phone.'*

Chapter 33

DESPERATE MEASURES

ays passed and Lilly was unable to calm her nerves or meditate. She paced through her apartment, the weight of the Priestess Crystal heavy on her heart. Her need for Roland's touch was physically painful.

Deciding on a course of action she pulled a knit cap over her curls, threw on her jean jacket and a pair of sneakers and headed out the door. She walked fast, trying to contain her nerves. She was going to ask Jason if he knew the bands schedule. "Oh, jeez, this is so lame! I can't stand it," she muttered to herself as she crossed Esplanade Avenue, entered the Marigny and walked down Frenchman Street.

She stood in front of Valentine's, hands stuck in her jeans pockets, head bowed, kicking at the sidewalk with the toe of her shoe. Jason came out to grab his morning paper and Lilly stepped up to say hello. "Well, hi there Lilly. Its good to see you. Hey, why don't you come in and join me for a cup of coffee?

"Add an almond croissant and I'm in," Lilly said sounding much more casual and relaxed than she was.

"Of course, come on in," Jason said as he held the door open.

Seated in a booth in the back of the restaurant, Lilly and Jason exchanged pleasantries for a few minutes. The conversation began to dwindle. Lilly was determined to get the information she had come to gain.

"Oh, by the way, Jason, have you heard from the band. Do you know where they are?"

"I don't have any idea, Lilly. I knew when they were arriving here and approximately how long they would stay. Once they left, it wasn't my concern. Trey mentioned Gainsville Florida and a trip to Coconut Grove. At some point, they are going up the East coast to New York."

Lilly finished her coffee and licked the sugary croissant crumbs from her fingers, "Thanks Jason. I am not going to be chasing after the band, don't concern yourself. If any members of the band contact you for any reason, please tell them it is of utmost importance Roland contact me immediately."

Jason leaned back and put his hands behind his head. "Lilly, are you in trouble?"

A furrow appeared between Lilly's eyes, "Trouble? What do you mean?"

"You know, pregnant?"

Lilly let out a whoosh of air, "No, I don't have that problem, thank the Goddess."

Jason looked relieved as he stood up and grabbed his newspaper. "I've got to get into my office, Lilly. I will pass on your message if I hear from them."

"Thanks, I appreciate it," Lilly stood crimson cheeked as she watched Jason walk down the hall to his office.

She walked up the block slowly, said hello to a group of handsome young firemen in front of the fire station and crossed Esplanade Avenue into the French Quarter. Walking up Decatur Street toward the Square, she passed The Raven Moon. As she approached a hand flipped the open sign over on the front door. Lilly walked in and found Claude and Regina standing amid unpacked boxes of incense and candles.

They looked up and smiled. Regina came over and hugged her. "How are you doing?" Lilly assured her she was feeling better.

Claude, however, gave her a hard look and voiced his concern, "Are you sure? I sense there is something bothering you?"

Lilly looked at him in surprise. "I guess having a psychic for a friend means I will never be able to keep a secret."

Claude smiled, "I would never pry into your personal business. I was merely picking up a sense of unrest."

Lilly released a frustrated sigh, "I miss Roland. I mean, I more than miss him. I am in physical pain like a vital part of myself is missing. I'm having weird nightmares. I don't know what to do about it. I need to speak with Roland. I have no idea where he is or how I can get in touch with him. Maybe you or Regina have an idea."

Lilly sat on a stool and explained the note she had found from Roland and how she had missed telling him goodbye.

"So you think Roland left believing you were not truly interested in him. He thought you were enjoying a Mardi Gras fling?" Regina asked.

Lilly shook her head slowly as tears filled her eyes, "I don't know. While he was with me, I never thought our relationship was a Mardi Gras fling. I may have put too much meaning into it."

She opened her mouth to tell them about her dream of the crystal skull in the shop window, but a frisson up her spine warned her to keep the dream to herself.

Lilly's tingling fingers fidgeted with the Inanna crystal through the fabric of her shirt. Regina watched her for a moment, "Do you have a love talisman under your shirt?"

Lilly shook her head, "No it's a crystal."

"Oh, can I see it? I love crystals." Lilly slowly pulled the golden chain from under her shirt and let the crystal dangle before Regina's eyes.

Regina's eyes grew wide. "Amazing! May I touch it?"

Lilly nodded seriously, "Yes, but be aware it is powerful and you could be incinerated immediately." Regina stepped back as Lilly laughed. "I'm kidding. You may have a look at it, but I am not taking it off."

Regina cupped the multi-faceted crystal in her hand, turning it gently as the violet light moved within. "It is beautiful and ancient," Regina said in a low voice filled with awe. Where did you get it?"

"It was an initiation gift from Jolene," Lilly said only partially lying.

"Some gift!" Regina said. "I've heard something about a crystal with violet light," Regina said slowly, staring at the crystal in her hand.

Lilly gently lifted the crystal from Regina's hand and placed it out of sight beneath her shirt.

Smiling brightly Regina changed the subject, "Oh, Lilly, I'm glad you showed up. Would you like to make some extra money today. Claude has several readings scheduled and I would appreciate your help in the shop." Lilly smiled and agreed to help.

They passed the day chatting as they waited on a few customers, packaged orders to be mailed to distant customers and unpacked several boxes filled with statues of deities from Baal to Quan Yin.

Claude bid his last client, 'Goodbye,' and locked the door to the store. Turing around he smiled at Lilly, "How was your day?"

"Busy, and I know yours was too, but I'm, uh, maybe you could..."

Claude tilted his head slightly and gave her a puzzled look, "What do you need, Lilly? I'm happy to help."

Lilly smiled shyly, "Do you think you could scry for Roland? Can you find out where he is?

Claude rubbed his hand across his face, "I think so but I think it will take more preparation than merely looking in the crystal ball. Do you have anything of his I could use as a contact?"

Lilly shook her head. "No, only the card he wrote me. Wait, yes I do! He left a necklace he wore, a silver spiral on a leather cord. It is on my dresser."

Claude smiled, "Okay, sounds perfect. Bring his silver spiral and I'll see what I can do."

Lilly ran to her apartment and put Roland's spiral around her neck and ran back to The Raven Moon. As she entered, Lilly sensed tension in the air. She looked back and forth between Claude and Regina "What is it?"

Regina sounded exasperated as she explained, "Nothing, I have an after hours client coming in for a reading. She made the appointment before Mardi Gras. I can't cancel. I'm upset I won't be able to participate in the scrying. I wish you could wait for me and do it later, but Claude says it is too important to put off for another minute."

There was a knock on the door and Regina admitted a nervous middle aged woman wearing a pants suit. Regina was leading her tarot client to the reading tent when Claude grabbed Lilly's hand and lead her out of the shop. They made their way up a flight of stairs, but didn't stop at the apartment. Instead, they entered another narrow stairway which lead to the magic temple in the attic of the old building.

It took a moment for Lilly's eyes to adjust to the shadowy attic. One end was lost in darkness, while the dim winter sun poured through the dormer window overlooking the street. The attic was long and the roof over head was high enough for Claude, at six feet, to easily stand and walk. Looking around, it was obvious he had already been upstairs and turned on a space heater. Two large pillows were placed beside a low altar, a crystal ball glowing in the center.

Claude took her hand and guided her to a pillow. He stood and cast a magic circle, called in his protectors and assisting energies as well as Lilly's. Returning to the center of the circle, he sat beside her and lit the candle. As he put his open palm on the table, Lilly laid the silver spiral necklace in his hand. She watched as Claude took three deep breaths. She breathed along with him and felt the tingle of magic awaken in her fingers as Claude slid into trance. His voice was deep and low as he began:

"Scrying orb before me rest, a vessel strong
to manifest he that I would conjure here,
by Baphomet come through clear.
Roland now, arise, draw near."

215

Swirling smoke filled the crystal ball. Colors appeared, vague at first, but growing brighter. There! Lilly could see him dimly. It was Roland. His beard had grown back since Mardi Gras and his dark hair hung over his shoulders. He was staring out of the crystal ball. Claude drew her near and said, "Speak to him."

"Roland, it's Lilly. I miss you, I love you. Is there any way you can return to New Orleans?"

Roland nodded his head. Before he could speak, the image faded. Lilly grabbed Claude's arm, "Bring him back, I want to talk with him."

Claude lay back on his pillow. Sweat poured from his pale face, "Maybe later, Lilly. I can't do it right now."

Lilly looked at him, her eyes wide. "Does this exhaust you?"

Claude nodded. "Yes, it has been a long day for me and this was no parlor trick. True magic takes its toll."

"Thank you, thank you so much for doing this for me. Please let me compensate you," she said as she reached for her purse.

Claude put his hand on her arm. "Ah, Lilly, it is not your money I yearn for."

"Well, how can I thank you for helping me. This is so important."

Claude shook his head slowly. "I would like to think we are friends. Possibly we could be more than friends."

Putting her purse aside, Lilly nodded. "Claude, I am happy to call you friend. You are, without a doubt, a kind and powerful ally. But, surely you can see, my heart belongs to Roland."

Sitting up slowly, Claude took her hand and put it to his lips. He gently pulled her forward and kissed her lightly on the lips. Lilly pulled back as the door opened and Regina came in full of questions.

Lilly stood and filled Regina in on the scrying. "I think we made contact. I saw him and I think he saw me and hopefully heard me. I guess I will have to wait and see if he calls or shows up."

Claude nodded wearily, "If not, we will have to try again."

216

Regina entered the circle without a thought and put her hand on Claude's shoulder, "You have exhausted yourself. We could all use a glass of wine. Come on, lets go back to the living room where it's warmer."

Chapter 34

CONTACT AND CONFUSION

Four days later, a postcard of a bright white beach and turquoise water arrived for Lilly. Turning over the card she read, "My dear Lilly, I sit on a beach in Florida missing you. I know my leaving was a mistake. Your music and beautiful face have filled my vision. I have my obligations to fulfill with the band. I'm looking for replacement so I will be free to return to New Orleans. Love, Roland"

Lilly laughed and cried simultaneously. Her loneliness disappeared momentarily along with her doubts. The lock on her heart fell open and she was flooded with memories of his touch, his scent, his soul.

'*I want to tell Claude the scrying was a success,*' she thought as she grabbed her jacket and headed for The Raven Moon.

The bell jangled and Lilly heard Regina's voice coming from the back room. "I'll be with you in a second."

"Hey, Regina, its me, Lilly, take your time." Lilly busied herself reading the titles of books on the shelf near the check out counter.

Regina appeared taking off an apron. "Hi, Lilly, I'm trying to get the backroom cleaned out. We have more books coming in soon. I want to make sure we can move things around, store what we must and display the new books." Lilly nodded only half listening.

"I've got some news," she announced. "Where is Claude? I want him to hear this too."

"Oh, I'm sorry Lil, he is in New York. A collection of rare magic books is going up on auction and he left this morning. It would be wonderful if we could buy a few for the store at a decent price. Antique magic books are something we want to specialize in. But, I digress, what is the big news?"

Lilly reached inside her pocket, removed the post card and handed it to Regina.

Regina read the card quickly, "It sounds like he is going to be returning," she said smiling.

"Yes, I know he is going to come back. I don't know when," Lilly said.

"Oh, Lilly, I'm glad for you. I'm glad you showed up with good news."

Lilly stood grinning and nodding her head as Regina continued, "Could you help me out again today. With Claude gone, I need some help if I am going to get the back room organized and keep the shop opened." Lilly agreed, glad to have something to do with the nervous energy coursing through her body.

The two young witches passed the morning chatting as they worked. Regina had a hundred questions for Lilly about her life, her magical training and abilities. Lilly answered innocently, giving Regina an inside view of her life. She told her about her father's death, her Aunt Pearl, her abusive husband and the power awakening within her as she studied and participated in rituals at Panthea's. She avoided mentioning her slow adjustment to the violet Jewel of Inanna. Regina had seen it, but she didn't know the extent of its power.

Regina locked the front door a few minutes after noon and the two young witches went upstairs for lunch. They made pineapple and cottage cheese salads, poured themselves glasses of tea and settled on the couch. Lilly had taken a few bites of her salad when Regina placed a pipe and a couple of buds of Acapulco gold on the coffee table. They leaned back, put their feet up and shared a bowl.

"I don't know much about you Regina. Are you from New York?"

Regina sat back in her chair and sipped her ice tea, "No, I'm from California, the Santa Cruz area. I was in New York shopping when I walked into The Spell Casters Emporium and met Claude. We talked for a bit, I invited him to join me for a drink when he got off work. A few hours later we were sitting in a bar in the East Village. A few weeks later we were moving to New Orleans to open The Raven Moon."

Lilly sighed, "Such a magical story."

Regina nodded her head, "Indeed, it seemed magical at the time. Now it seems like a lot of work. I'm loving it, don't get me wrong. Adjusting to New Orleans, the climate, the people, the food, is a lot to get used to."

"Has your life always been so magical. What was it like growing up in California?"

Regina leaned forward, tapped the ashes from the pipe's bowl and refilled it with the second bud. She lit the pipe, took a long toke, leaned back, closed her eyes and began to speak.

"My childhood was not as happy as your early years with your dad and your aunt. My parents traveled constantly. I was left at home with a series of nannies; some kind, some bitter, some cruel. My parents came home for my 13th birthday and decided I no longer needed a nanny. I needed to go to boarding school. I was packed up, put on a plane, and enrolled in Saint Mary's Catholic boarding school in Ireland.

"The only male allowed to enter the school was Monsignor Scotty. The nuns, especially Mother Superior, cowered in his presence. He was the high hot-in-tot and demanded we agree and submit to his constant demands and attend his long winded Catholic rituals. It was months before I discovered the uniformed girls, meekly approaching the altar for communion at daily mass, secretly chafed under his domination.

"On the night of the full moon girls from every level at St. Mary's climbed through windows, shimmied down drain pipes and clung to tree branches before dropping silently onto leaf covered ground. I saw them leave but had no idea where they were going. My first impulse was to follow, but something inside told me to wait for an invitation.

"At the beginning of the second semester, I received an invitation to join the mysterious full moon exodus. Following the group, I arrived in a grove of ancient oaks next to the graveyard filled with the moldering bones of long dead nuns. I stripped off my night clothes, along with the others, linked hands in a circle and began to dance.

"Circe, a senior from South Africa, led us through the full moon rituals and, occasionally, placed the sacrament of sacred mushrooms on our tongues. The light of the full moon shone through the boughs of the ancient oaks, as we touched our hidden and forbidden power.

"It was towards the end of my first year at St. Mary's that Circe approached me and asked if I was a member of the ancient Valraven family. Although my name is Valraven, I had no idea if my family was ancient. I have no grandparents, aunts, uncles or cousins. The family I am aware of consists of my mysterious and mostly absent parents. For all I know, they could be aliens traveling the galaxies.

"With that, Circe nodded, leaned towards me and whispered, 'Let's get together tonight after lights out. I have some interesting information for you.' Hecate ruled the moon that night. I lay in pitch black darkness waiting for Circe. She came silently through the door, put her hand on my shoulder and pointed to the window with easy access to the extended roof of the floor below us. We settled down on the tiled roof and leaned our backs against the brick wall of the dormitory building. We sat quietly admiring the cascading starlight in the dark velvet sky.

"Circe lit a cigarette and began, 'Before I get caught up in studying for finals, I want to see how much you know about your bloodline. From what you said today, I'm guessing it is nothing. I'm not surprised. I will tell you what I know and you can follow up on the information if you want to.'

"I sat dumbfounded thinking, how could this South African

girl know anything about my family?

She calmly continued, 'Your ancestors on your father's side of the family, the Valravens, carried powerful magic in their blood. Through many generations the family used their magic and power to amass a great fortune. The secret of their bloodline was held close. The Valraven's were recognized in the wider community not for magic, but for philanthropy. They donated money to schools, libraries, hospitals and charities. By the late nineteen thirties, the family began to fray along the edges as the older generations passed away. The family fortune, tucked away in secure investments and stabilized by the family's vast gold collection, was safe and continued to grow. The Valraven reputation for philanthropy, kindness and generosity faded. The younger generation, undisciplined in the greater mysteries and workings of magic, replaced the family honor with self-entitlement, disregard for community and, sometimes, cruelty.

'A distant, but powerful branch of the Valraven family had settled near Lake Tahoe. Three Valraven brothers, their grandfather and two great uncles carried the power and wisdom of the true Valraven bloodline. They began to hear tales of the debauchery and destruction wrought by the young egotistical Valravens of Santa Cruz. The three brothers argued among themselves, the uncles could not agree to a plan and the Grandfather was dead set against any plan but annihilation of the self-entitled Valraven youth. After weeks of heated debate, the brothers, uncles and grandfather agreed to wage war on the Valraven estate, not through violence, but through an exorcism by the Catholic church. When the young Valraven's crossed the pond and began gambling their way through Europe, the exorcism began.

'The walls, rafters, mantels and curved stairways of the main house were filled with intricately carved symbols and grounded the magic of the Valraven blood on to the physical plain. The Catholic bishop, hired by the Lake Tahoe Valraven's, was denied permission to burn the house to the ground. Instead, the bishop, carrying a crucifix mounted atop an ornate silver staff, walked with intention through the house. A half dozen priests followed behind him, twisting, defying and creating an invisible barrier to the magic in the Valraven estate. Chanting their own incantations in Latin, the posse of destruction set about burning the large library filled with the history of the Valraven family. They carefully packed the ancient grimoires they found, the powerful artifacts and magical implements. The boxes containing an inestimable value and power were sent to the Vatican to be stored in the below ground vaults. My blood boils when I think of the power and knowledge they stole and locked away for their own use.

'Lacking the vision to see the house as a potent cauldron of magic and the patience to reverse the spells of corrupted religious control, the infuriated young Valraven's gathered their belongings and abandoned the last vestige of their inherited power. Returning to Europe, the youths began to feed off the blood of old Europe's most magical families. Having exhausted their welcome in Italy and France, they traveled down the Mediterranean coast to befriend a family in Malta. This was a mistake as the magical families of Malta recognized the youths as the blood sucking, energy hungry miscreants they were. Warnings went out through the eastern countries and Europe. The young Valraven's, labeled as energy vampires were, turned away from the powerful families the Valraven's had been friends with for generations.'

"I turned to look Circe in the eyes. "Is this true? Is this why my parents travel the planet? Are they looking for a way to restore their magic? Have you heard they are vampires? Tell me!" I pleaded.

"Circe flipped the butt of her cigarette over the edge of the roof and shifted her position. 'Your parents lived on the Estate, at least that is where you were lodged. Possibly they travel as they have a hard time being in the house. I have heard nothing of them being vampires, at least not blood drinking vampires. They may be energy vampires, preying on the powerful and ritually syphoning off their magic.' Shrugging her shoulders Circe continued, 'I don't know why they travel or what they are seeking. I swear I don't.'

"I asked Circe how she knew this story of my family and she calmly turned and looked at me saying, 'The story of the loss of the Valraven magic is a story known to all of the prominent magical families of Europe, Africa and the Middle East. I wanted to tell you what I know before you heard the crueler version from someone else. You deserve to know.'

"Circe's revelations turned my world upside down. My parents had sent me to Ireland, a particularly Catholic country, and enrolled me in a Catholic school. Did this indicate they were comfortable with Catholicism? Another twist entered my mind, or were they were using the Catholic Church as a smoke screen.

"After two semesters in the midst of the Papal loving nuns at Saint Mary's, I hated my parents. My blood ran cold when I thought of them. I had so many boiling questions. Were they comfortable with the loss of the Valraven magic, or were they seeking to restore it? Regardless of what they were doing, I vowed to reclaim and restore the Valraven magic in my blood." Regina blinked her eyes, shook her head, and roused herself from her stoned monologue. Realizing she had been talking, revealing who knows what, her eyes flew to Lilly who smiled with compassion and understanding.

"I'm sorry to bore you with tales of the distant pass. Let's get back to work," Regina said, not sure how much of her past she had revealed.

Lilly took Regina's hand and squeezed it gently, "You can count on me if you need any help." Regina slipped her hand from Lilly's, stood, pocketed her pipe and again suggested they return to work.

By late afternoon the storeroom was full and a shelf in the shop was ready for the magic books Claude was sure to bring home.

It was after five when they washed their hands and headed out for a drink and supper. Sipping beer and eating a shrimp po' boy, Lilly noticed soft colors filtering into her vision. The auric fields of the customers in the bar appeared. Her breath caught in her throat for a moment as she gauged the moods of those around her. Most were harmless, some were disturbed or sad, others were drunk.

Glancing at Regina, Lilly's auric vision faded. Regina appeared to be motionless. Her red fingernails reflected the glow of the flickering neon light on the wall. Lilly caught no trace of swirling color or floating symbols.

She's shielded! Lilly realized. Since Alex had been arrested, Lilly had stopped using her mirrored-egg spell to shield herself. 'What is Regina hiding from? What or who is frightening her?' She wondered. Curious, and ready to try her skills at reading energy, Lilly decided to explore Regina's shield. A line from one of her magic books popped into her head, "Stay with a situation, a vision or a feeling until you gather insight or understanding."

She looked at the beautiful young woman with dark witchy eyes and bright red lips. Closing her eyes, she opened to her feelings. She sat back in her chair as Regina's need, frustration and thwarted desire, showed themselves to Lilly's inner eye.

Regina suddenly shifted in her seat when she noticed how quiet Lilly had become, "What is it, Lil? Are you feeling okay? You are so quiet."

Lilly managed a smile. "I'm fine. I think you wore me out today."

Regina picked up her purse, "That reminds me, let me pay you for your work." Digging through her wallet, Regina pulled out three twenty dollar bills and handed them to Lilly. "Thanks so much. I would never have been able to do it without you."

Lilly took the money gratefully. Putting her napkin aside, Lilly decided to tease out Regina's hidden emotions. "How about you, how are you feeling? Tired from all the work or excited to see the

225

vision you have for your business manifesting?"

Regina thought for a moment, "Both. When Claude and I consulted the oracles, they pointed to the South. The only place in the South we both agreed on was New Orleans. I contacted my bankers in California and my parents. It was only a matter of weeks before Claude and I secured the building and decided on a name for the business."

"What reaction did you get from your parents when you told the you were opening a magic shop? Were they supportive?"

Regina smirked and waved her hand in front of her face, banishing the idea of their support, "My family has no idea exactly what kind of business I have and they don't care. The knowledge and practice of deep magic was lost to my family generations ago." A wave of sadness rolled off Regina, catching Lilly by surprise. The story of her boarding school days was entertaining, recognizing the pain and loneliness she still suffered filled Lilly's heart with compassion.

"I'm sure you and Claude will make a great success of the business. You are both lovely people. I'm happy to have you for my friends." The corners of Regina's mouth twitched into a brief smile. Lilly pushed her chair away from the table, walked over and gave her new friend a hug. Regina sat stiffly, raised her arm and patted Lilly briefly on the back.

Chapter 35

POPPY SEED TEA

....

The Inanna crystal hung in the window, catching the sunshine. Shades of violet dominated the fractured light, glowing from deep purple to softest lavender. Lilly watched the play of the violet tinted rainbows on the walls as she played her flute. An insistent buzzing interrupted her musical trance. Putting her flute down on the bed, she ran to the speaker button by the front door. "Who is it?"

"It's Regina, can I come up?"

Hitting the buzzer to unlock the gate, Lilly opened the front door and stepped out onto the gallery to greet Regina. "Come on up, I'll make a pot of coffee?"

As she came up the stairs, Lilly noticed how haggard Regina looked. Her usual perfect make up was missing replaced by dark circles under her eyes. She put her arm around Regina's shoulders and lead her gently into her apartment.

"Coffee sounds great, I need it. I didn't sleep at all last night. I realized as I lay in bed, listening to the old building creak, I have never spent a night alone. I grew up in a large house with a nannie, a maid and a cook. There was a security gate at the front entrance to the house. Our Dobermans were released onto the grounds at night. I have always travelled with someone. Since I've been in New Orleans, Claude has been in the apartment. I realized I am a complete scaredy cat. I have never slept in a house alone and it is freaky."

Lilly nodded in sympathy as Regina continued, "Would you be a doll and stay with me while Claude is gone? It won't be every night. I'm thinking of getting a dog."

"Of course! I'll be delighted to come stay with you," Lilly said.

Regina finished her coffee and stood with a look of relief

on her face. "I better get back to the shop and open the doors for business. Come over anytime your ready. I'll cook something special for us tonight." The two young women hugged and Regina walked towards the front door.

She stopped abruptly and stood in front of the sofa staring at the painting Lucky had gifted Lilly. The morning sun pouring through the transom window brought life to the painting. Leaning closer to the painting, Regina exclaimed, "Wow, this is lovely!"

Lilly beamed and leaned over to straighten a corner of the painting. "My friend Lucky painted it."

"Cool," Regina said pensively. "Who is Lucky?"

"He is a guy who lives here at Panthea's. He works on ships, travels, paints and plays music."

"It appears he is an excellent painter. I'd like to meet him sometime," Regina said. She turned back towards the door, looked at her watch and she hurried out the door with a wave.

The door closed and Lilly immediately took the crystal from the bedroom window and placed it around her neck. A shock went through her as the crystal fell over her heart. The raven from her dreams flashed quickly before her eyes. It was only a moment and she shook her head, took a deep breath, picked up her flute and played, setting her mind on practice and working as a musician again. *'I must discipline myself to practice if I'm going to make a living as a professional musician.'*

It was late afternoon when dark roiling clouds began to obscure the winter sun. Lilly pulled her jacket close and her knit cap over her ears. Dampness seeped into her bones as she walked down Decatur Street to spend the night with Regina.

Candle flames flickered as Lilly closed the door to The Raven Moon. Wax dripped from long tapers in black candelabras. Trails of incense floated in thick clouds above the displays. Regina slumped in an intricately carved antique chair she called her throne. With shallow breath and glazed eyes she stared unblinking at the crystal skull nearby. Lilly pried Regina's fingers from the tea cup she grasped in her hand. Taking the flaccid hand in hers she patted softly and called, "Regina, Regina, Regina." Long minutes passed before Regina blinked and squeezed Lilly's hand. She slowly straightened on her throne and spoke slowly, "Lilly, you've come to keep me company."

"Yes, yes I have. Can you make it upstairs?" Regina stood, swaying slightly as Lilly helped her through the shop and up to the apartment. She settled her on the couch and ran downstairs to put out the candle flames and make sure the front door was locked.

Regina remained motionless on the couch, her eyes closed and her breath shallow. Lilly made grilled cheese sandwiches and tomato soup in the kitchen. Returning to Regina's prone form, she rubbed her hands and called her name until she stirred. "Wake up Regina, it is time to eat."

Sitting side by side the young witches ate slowly in the darkening apartment. Placing her barely touched plate on the floor, Regina stood and shuffled off to her bedroom. Lilly took a pillow and blanket from Claude's room and settled on the couch. She turned on the television and watched the news, a comedy and an episode of *The Six Million Dollar Man* before drifting off to sleep.

The smell of pancakes, bacon and coffee drew Lilly from her restless sleep. Regina served breakfast on the coffin table in the living room. She was wide awake and feeling chatty while Lilly rubbed a kink in her neck and sipped the hot coffee.

"I'm so sorry about last night. I made some special tea for myself to help me relax. I'm afraid it was more potent than I expected. I'm lucky you came into the store and not some stranger. Anyone could have emptied the cash box. I was so out of it!"

Lilly nodded as she enjoyed the hot blueberry pancakes. Not sure what to say, she let Regina continue to chat on about her plans for The Raven Moon. After breakfast Lilly said goodbye and walked to the river's edge leaving Regina to open the shop.

THE RAVEN MOON

She took in a deep breath of the morning air, and recognized the aroma of Roland's French Quarter Par-fume. Smiling to herself, she touched the crystal around her neck and called out to Roland in her mind, I wish you were here, I miss you. The crystal warmed a bit as she sent her longing out through time and space.

Thick pieces of colorful river glass worn smooth by the water decorated the sandy shore along the river's edge. Lilly collected a few pieces, watched the slowly moving river for a few minutes, buttoned her jacket and left the windy shore line. Fatigue pulled at her as she climbed the spiral stairs to her apartment. Kicking her shoes off, she flopped onto her bed, closed her eyes and fell asleep, dreaming.

Swirls of darkness surrounded her. With her arms extended in front of her, she groped through the swirling murk. Something bumped against her shoulder and she screamed silently. Her first instinct was to run. She tried to move her legs, but found they were numb and unresponsive. She couldn't run, yet her dream body lifted and floated through a dense fog. Bare tree branches scraped her body, huge black birds swooped out of the darkness, their beaks tinged with blood.

A light glimmered in the distance. Her body propelled itself forward. As she grew closer to the light, it flickered orange against the stark tree branches. She grabbed a branch and clung to it as she looked down at a small fire in the center of the clearing. Her body jolted as screams filled the air and a blaze of light flashed through the night. Sparks flew as the fire grew into a bonfire. The smell of burning flesh filled her nostrils. Lilly leaned over the branch and vomited.

A continuous buzzing dragged her back through the fog and she awoke to the sound of the gate buzzer. Rushing to the inter-com by the door she pushed the button, "Telephone company, we are here to install your phone."

Lilly sighed in relief as she released the lock on the gate and stepped out of her front door into the sunny afternoon. She had

THE RAVEN MOON

forgotten about the telephone. A surge of happiness washed through her as she realized Roland could call her, if she could get her phone number to him.

It was sunset when Lilly walked over to The Raven Moon to check on Regina. She nearly fell over when she walked into the shop and was greeted by the biggest dog she had ever seen.

Stepping back she looked around for Regina. "Hey, come on in, he won't hurt you." Regina shouted from the storage room.

Lilly shut the door and approached the dog slowly, "What kind of dog is it?

"Silly Lilly, he's a Great Dane."

"He's big. How old is he?"

"He is three years old, his name is Dodger and he has a mate," Regina said as a second huge dog walked up to her and stood by her side. "This is Priscilla, called Prissy for short. She and Dodger came as a package."

Lilly was speechless. The dogs were intimidatingly huge. "Where on earth did you get them? Were they at the dog pound?"

"No. I ran into the woman who owns the little junk shop on the corner. She was walking these two beautiful babies. No, it was more like they were walking her. I fell in love with them and she offered them to me for free. It seems her boyfriend split, went back to his wife in Minnesota. He left his two dogs. She can't afford to feed them and doesn't want to take care of them. I was glad to take them.

"Wow, what a...a...a...great deal!" Lilly stuttered.

Regina frowned at her, "What is with you, have you never been around a dog?"

"Sure I have, just never one, uh two this big."

"Don't worry, Lil, you'll get used to them. I grew up with Dobermans. I love big dogs. I feel safe with these babies in the shop and sleeping on either side of my bed."

Lilly nodded and agreed they would be great protection.

Once The Raven Moon was locked up for the night, Lilly and

Regina, Dodger and Prissy went up to the apartment. The two dogs filled the living room, waging tales knocked over lamps and thrashed against Lilly's thighs. Regina got the two dogs settled on blankets in the corner of the room and went into the kitchen to open a bottle of wine.

"How was your day, Lil?"

"Good, I now have a telephone in my apartment."

"Let me get a pen and write your number in my address book," Regina said as she disappeared into the bedroom and came back with a pen and leather bound address book. She sat down, then immediately jumped up and slipped into the kitchen. She returned with two wine glasses brimming with red wine.

Regina opened her address book, "Ok, I'm ready, give me your new phone number."

Lilly had to think for a few minutes before she replied, "Twinbrook 7-2219. She sighed, took a sip of wine and leaned back on the sofa. "Call me often, I am having trouble being alone."

Regina frowned, "Are you bored? We can spend as much time as you like together."

Lilly gave a weak smile, "As long as I'm staying busy I'm okay. As soon as I have time to myself, I feel the loss of Roland like a knife in my heart. I can't believe he's gone. The only thing keeping me going is knowing he is trying to get back here. I am grateful I met you and Claude. Spending time with you is wonderful and I can't wait for you to meet Roland."

They emptied their wine glasses and Regina headed to the kitchen for refills. Returning to the red velvet couch, she suggested a toast, "To the return of Roland," she said. Lilly smiled as she lifted her glass and drank the sweet red wine.

Within minutes Lilly's vision blurred and her chin fell forward onto her chest. She tried to sit upright but her head was spinning. She looked at her glass, 'How much did I drink?' Wine was swirling in the bottom of the glass as it slipped from her hand onto the floor.

Regina finished her glass of wine before dragging Lilly's legs onto the sofa. She ran into her bedroom and returned with a pillow and a blanket. "Poor dear," she said softly in Lilly's ear, "you've had too much. Yes, you've had too much."

Moonlight was pouring through the living room windows when Lilly woke. She looked around the room and made out the shadowed figure in the wing backed chair across from her. One side of Regina's face was silvered with moonlight, the other was hidden in shadow.

"How long have I been here?"

"You've been here since sunset. You passed out and I let you sleep on the couch. I thought you drank too much wine. You were vomiting. I don't know, maybe you are coming down with something."

"I didn't drink too much wine," Lilly said weakly, "I can't remember ever being sick so suddenly."

Regina made a soothing sound as she stood and headed for the kitchen. She returned with crackers and a cup of herbal tea. "Try to nibble on these Lilly, and sip the tea slowly."

Lilly ate one half of a cracker and drank half of the tea before falling back on her pillow and passing out again.

Gray water lapped the shore of a lake. Huge black birds darted overhead, their piercing eyes glowing yellow in the twilight sky. Wet sand squished between the toes of her bare feet as she walked along the shoreline. She wrapped her arms around her trembling body as a dank cold sank into her bones. The search for shelter drove her onward.

She saw torch light glowing in the distance and stopped, wary of the tone of the voices traveling down the beach. She ran to an outcropping of rock with scraggly bushes at its base. Peering through the sparsely leafed branches she watched as several men gathered around a small boat with something tied to the mast.

233

The men pushed the craft out onto the lake. The boat drifted on the receding tide as flaming arrows arced across the sky thudding into the small wooden boat. A woman's scream filled the night, as the craft burst into flames. The scream stopped abruptly.

A growling voice rose to a bellowing threat, "I told you not to shoot her. She was to experience the full horror of the fire. Now you have given her a short cut out of her punishment. I have a strong urge to put you in her place."

A whimper answered the growling voice. Lilly remained motionless, watching the fire on the water as it drifted and sank into the cold gray water.

She struggled through a dark fog and fought her way to consciousness. The sight of the burning woman tied to the boat, lingered in her head and bile rose in her throat. Her head spun when she moved quickly. Swallowing bile, she inched her way up to a sitting position.

"Where the hell am I? Oh gods!," Putting her head in her hands she cried. "What has happened to me?"

There was a movement near the door. She looked up and saw a dark silhouette standing motionless. *'I'm hallucinating,'* she thought as the black silhouette approached her.

"It's me Lilly," Regina said, taking her hand. "Are you still feeling ill?"

Lilly nodded her head, but the spinning reminded her to be still. A low moan escaped from deep in her throat.

"You've come down with something awful. Don't worry, you can stay here. I will take care of you."

No longer able to sit up, Lilly slid onto the couch and passed out again.

She awoke in the late afternoon, her head fuzzy and her stomach growling. Regina served her tea and toast. She ate slowly and felt a little better.

"I need to get to the bathroom," she moaned. Her rubbery

legs collapsed as she plopped back onto the couch. Regina took her arm and helped her to the bathroom. Lilly splashed cold water on her face and rinsed her mouth.

Regina, Prissy and Dodger were waiting for her when she opened the bathroom door.

"Lilly, can you make it up the stairs? We have a bed up there and I am sure you would be more comfortable in bed than lying on the lumpy couch."

Lilly nodded, her thoughts fuzzy and her tongue too thick to speak.

Her head was spinning again as Regina lead her up the stairs. The click clack of the dogs nails on the old wooden stairs, followed behind them. A dim light filtered through the dormer window of the attic and Regina led her to the futon near the magic circle where Claude had contacted Roland through the crystal ball.

She stretched out on the futon on the floor. Regina suggested she take off her clothes. "You know you have been in those jeans and sweater for a couple of days. You have been throwing up. I think it is time to throw your clothes in the wash."

Lilly nodded, slowly sat up and slipped her sweater over her head. Regina unsnapped her jeans and slipped them off along with her socks. Lying naked, Lilly's skin chilled and erupted in goose bumps.

Suddenly the soft lighting disappeared and she lay in semidarkness. Regina's velvet voice grew spikes, "How gratifying to find you vulnerable and innocent! You are exactly who I've have been waiting for. I will relish harvesting your power before your beloved Roland shows up, if he shows up. Your centuries of power as a priestess and your Faery magic, will be mine. Surprise! The powerful Jewel of Inanna will also be mine. What do they call it down here in N'Orleans? Lagniappe, yes, that's it. You are a package with an extra bonus. Thanks to you, I will regain the power my Valraven blood craves."

Chapter 36
CARRION OF THE SOUL

illy heard the door open and close. She called out when she heard the click of the key in the lock. "Regina, what did you say? Bring me a blanket."

Her head ached ferociously as she tried to sit up. Lying down again, she grabbed for the sacred Jewel around her neck as it thrummed gently beneath her fingers. Miserable, cold and disoriented, tears wet her face and rolled slowly down her neck. Soaked with tears of frustration, she called out to the empty room, "What is going on? We are friends. Why are you doing this?"

Her drugged mind drifted into an uneasy sleep. In her delirium, she was looking into a black mirror. Her pale face and sunken eyes stared back at her for a moment. She blinked, and mist drifted over the surface of the mirror. Out of the mist, Roland's face appeared. He was sitting staring into the still water of a pond. His eyes widened as he saw Lilly's face in the dark water. Shocked, he leaned forward and spoke to the vision, "Lilly, Lilly, what's going on?"

Lilly lifted her hand to the mirror. She touched the surface just as Roland hand lifted. For a moment she swore she could feel his warmth. Suddenly his hand disappeared into blackness. Her heart ripped as she cried out in her sleep, "I miss you, I love you." She tossed restlessly and awoke to the sound of sleet beating on the slate roof. Shivering in the darkness of the attic, she groped around the room looking for something to cover herself. She found the door, twisted the doorknob and fell to her knees. Crawling through the room, she found nothing to warm herself. Standing on shaky legs, she found the futon, lay down and sought the refuge of oblivion.

"Hiss, scratch, creek, flutter," Lilly lay barely breathing, listening to the small sounds. It didn't sound like a rat. The fluttering and scratching with an occasional hiss continued intermittently. She curled into a tight ball, closed her eyes and ears and cast her mind into the past. Her memories sustained her for a time. Slowly the memories faded, replaced by thick, cold fog.

Regina's Chanting cut through the fog in Lilly's mind. The sickly smells of storax and sulfur filled the air. Lilly opened her eyes. Flickering candles surrounded the futon and arced out into a wide circle. Regina stood over her, "You are mine now, Priestess. I have tracked you through centuries of incarnations as priestess, princess, sea captain, high lord of the manor and now pitiful little bitch from the bayou. You cannot believe how easy this has been. You are finally in my grasp and it was worth the wait!

"I am so close, so close to having what I want!" She exclaimed as she moved within the circle and lifted her arms in front of a tall triangular mirror. Now she would get revenge for all the lifetimes she had been thwarted by the soul known by many names over the centuries; Marga, Elsbeth, Loren, Elric and now, Lilly.

Finally she would reap the reward for her years spent summoning the Raven to her service and honing her ability to use its magic to manipulate human hearts. Ah, and a bonus, this time her nemesis through many lifetimes, held the sacred stone. Stupid girl did not know how to use the power.

"I will make the crystal mine and learn to wield the violet power." Heart thudding with the thrill of success and the taste of retribution on her tongue, Regina stood before the triangular mirror in the circle. Her voice rose to a crescendo over the approaching storm:

"Raven come as black as night,
Magic take her inner sight.
Mystic carrion of the soul,
breath in her power, be so bold,
Enter through the rift now torn,
That my full power shall be born."

237

Lilly squinted. Her eyes burned in the putrid smoke. She kept her half closed eyes focused on the standing mirror. Her breath caught in her throat, her eyes blinked away smoke and her body trembled. A creature, larger than a man, appeared in the mirror. Her eyes widened when she saw a vulture, quickly morph into a huge spider, then a scorpion. A scream clawed at her throat, as the huge form of a raven stepped out of the silvered triangle.

Thunder shook the old building. Lighting flared at the gable window. In a moment of total darkness Lilly saw the glowing yellow eyes of the raven. Closing her eyes, she prayed she was hallucinating. Scrambling to her knees she stood searching wildly for a place to hide. She thought briefly of jumping out the window.

The man sized raven approached and knocked her onto her back. It loomed over her for a moment, moved quickly and engulfed her trembling form. Discordant chimes grew louder, thunder boomed as Regina struck a gong, chanting louder and louder.

Lilly's body grew rigid as the huge figure moved on top of her. The raven's burning eyes stared into her soul. His razor sharp beak opened inches from her face. She twisted her body, tried to turn but the creature's weight held her pinned to the floor. Pain seared across her cheek as the black beak slashed at her. A powerful voice invaded her mind. "BE STILL! This won't hurt a bit."

Her hands tingled, and for a moment, her mind cleared. She willed the tingling in her hands to move through her entire body. Gathering her Faery magic, she drew strength from her connection to her soul group, the members of Panthea's coven, her bonding with the Druid, Roland, and the ancient crystal between her breasts. Power stirred as the crystal grew warm. The persistent thrumming heat of the Jewel energized her. She continued to struggle until she got her hand up under the beast.

In one quick motion, she jerked the crystal from around her neck and stabbed it into the raven's eye. With a screech, the creature dissolved in a rancid plume of smoke. Dark, oily feathers drifted through the room as Regina's scream filled the night.

The room swirled in slow motion. Lilly tried to get up from her splayed position on the floor but her legs wouldn't work. She lay still, hoping Regina would disappear. The odor of decay filled the air. Lilly turned her head and vomited. Regina stepped forward and slapped her. Her voice, sharp as a whip lashed through the air, "Enough of you're spewing." She turned and fled through the door leaving the candles burning.

Lilly heard the key turn in the lock. Sitting up slowly, she took control of herself. In spite of being brutally violated, or possibly because the horror had passed, a calm came over her.

The diabolical machinations of Regina's twisted mind were no longer hidden. Lilly was aware of what she was up against. *'Goddess take me, how did I get myself wrapped up in this mess?'*

Regina's actions were unexpected, still Lilly berated herself for trusting her and failing to examine the negative vibrations the young witch masked with her friendly overtures. Lilly's hands balled into fists, *'I've been stupid, a part of me knew something wasn't right yet I denied it. I sensed the emptiness around Regina and I knew she was shielded. If I had explored a little deeper and trusted my feelings, I may have avoided this debacle.'*

The dark cupboard opened in her mind once again, as blood from the gash across her cheek, ran into her ear and hair. She tossed her body around in misery and the warm sticky blood ran down her neck and between her breasts. She was trapped in a nightmare panting in fear and exhaustion. Her hands began to tingle and Lilly paid attention. She focused on gaining control of her breathing. As she calmed herself, the dark dreams she had been plagued with recently came into focus in her mind. They had been trying to shake her memory, to warn her of danger!

Lying back, she closed her eyes. Lifetimes of study and practice rushed before her eyes. She recognized Regina in a variety of guises, as centuries passed in a heartbeat. The tableaus from her dream journey through the eye of the crystal skull came to life.

For many lifetimes Lilly had encountered the dark sorceress

THE RAVEN MOON

now known as Regina. Through centuries the sorceress insatiable hunger for power and control grew. Lilly became her nemesis using the white light to absorb the dark manipulations, lies and thievery Regina used indiscriminately. It was Lilly who had brought charges against the power hungry sorceress. It was the information and accusations the Priestess of the Light brought forth that lead to Regina's disgrace and banishment in more than one lifetime. It was Lilly's testimony that sealed the ruthless woman's fate. It was for this, Regina was determined to destroy her.

Recoiling in horror, she told herself it was not so. Immediately, a powerful voice filled her mind, "Her craving for power is bottomless, you have been the agent of her doom in the past, you can do it again."

"I don't want to be an agent of doom," Lilly declared. "I want her to wake up and develop her own power and leave me, and everyone else, alone."

Her stomach clenched with dread. Regina had been scrying her for years, searching for the signature of her power. She had tapped into Lilly's awakening energy from her home in California. Securing the cover of a partner and a shop, Regina had come to New Orleans to find her and drain her power for herself. Finding her nemesis was the guardian of the Jewel of Inanna had been an unexpected bonus. She stepped up her plans to annihilate Lilly, drain her power and claim ownership of the ancient crystal.

Aware of the danger she was in and the possibility of losing the violet crystal, Lilly mustered her energy, stood up and dragged the futon out of Regina's dark magic circle. Crawling around the circle she blew out all of the candles, but one. She piled the remaining candles next to the futon. Her mind and emotions were blunted allowing the instincts developed over many lifetimes as a priestess to guide her. Weakly, she felt around for the crystal. She ran her hands along the floor nearby. Staring into the darkness, she saw a dim glow of violet light. The crystal, her sacred responsibility, lay tossed on the floor amid a whirl of dark feathers. The

THE RAVEN MOON

gold chain was broken. She took the crystal into her hand and stared into the violet light. She lay back on the futon placing the crystal over her heart. Her breathing slowed, her fear subsided and she slept.

Chapter 37

ASTRAL SCRYING

She woke in total darkness, sat up, pulled her shivering legs up to her chest and wrapped her arms around them. Long moments passed as she rocked back and forth in the darkness. *'There has been enough blame and retribution,'* she thought. *'Reconciliation is needed in this lifetime, but now is not the time to initiate a reconciliation. I am in danger and I must get out of this attic.'*

Lilly knew she needed help. The person she had the strongest psychic connection with was Roland. He had connected with her on the dream plane earlier. Possibly, with the help of the crystal, her emotional connection with him was strong enough to call him forth in waking time. She chewed on her lower lip, took a deep breath and exhaled loudly, *'It may be a long shot, but it's the best option I have for rescue.'*

The hissing and fluttering continued in the darkness. Lilly closed her eyes and ignored it. She focused on her in-breath and out-breath, held the sacred crystal in one hand, opened her eyes and stared into the tiny candle burning beside the futon.

"Great Goddess hear me and look with favor upon me. I am your servant in this physical world. I seek your immediate assistance in the dimensions free of time and space. I travel the astral planes in search of assistance and rescue. Guide and guard me with your love and ancient power, bright glow and glimmer, sparkle and shimmer. The magic of my inner sight, spring to life on this night."

Pulling the rhythmic chant from the air, she chanted until the violet light of the crystal flamed brightly. It was then she felt the magic stir. Releasing all attachments, she lay on the filthy futon and allowed her physical form to release her astral body. She drifted through the astral plane surrounded by the light of the violet fire.

She sensed the cool marble floor beneath her feet when she stepped into an astral temple. Soft light infused the space and columns of lapis lazuli soared into the shadows of the high vaulted dome. Lilly drank in the sacred beauty of the astral temple and gathered energy. She approached the raised altar in the center of the temple and mounted the three wide marble steps. Leaning over the delicate jade bowl in the center of the altar, she saw her reflection in the still water. A bloody gash glowed red on one cheek. Despite her bruised and swollen face, her eyes were clear, opened and aware.

A series of ripples disturbed the smooth surface of the water. When the ripples calmed, Lilly was looking into the eyes of a Goddess. Her presence was magnificent. An ethereal halo of golden hair surrounded her face. A woven silver band adorned with a sapphire encircled her head. The Goddess held Lilly in her gaze as she touched the sapphire on her third eye, smiled and faded slowly.

Once again, ripples crossed the surface of the water. Holding her hand on her heart, Lilly leaned over the jade bowl. Roland appeared, sleeping soundly. Lilly spoke quickly, "Wake up Roland, I need you. Wake up Roland, I need you. Wake up Roland, I need you!" She spoke firmly and he stirred slightly. She focused her mental energy on her need and sent the message to Roland through the scrying bowl. His human figure remained still but his astral body sat up. "Roland, it's Lilly. I need you. I am in danger."

His astral figure rose and Lilly saw the powerful Druidic energy he carried within his shining form. The crystal she had given him radiated white light in the center of his chest. His hands closed around the crystal and he held it before him. Looking within the clear facets, he spoke "What is it? Lilly? Where are you?"

"Roland, I have been poisoned and kidnapped. I am in the attic of The Raven Moon on Decatur Street. Regina Valraven is

THE RAVEN MOON

trying to destroy me. Please help me. I am in danger."

Roland repeated her message, making sure he heard her correctly. She thought she saw his head nodding as the water rippled and his image faded. Satisfied Roland understood her message and would come to help her, Lilly curled into a ball and fell into a deep sleep.

The light of a monochrome dawn crept through the dormer window as Lilly awoke shivering. She could see her breath clouding in the frigid air of the attic. Sitting up, she almost knocked over a glass of water beside the futon. *'Regina has been in here.'* Despite fear of more poison, she took a sip of the water to soothe her dry and swollen tongue. The cold water splashed down her throat freezing her internally. *'I must find something to cover myself or I'm going to freeze to death.'* Crawling onto her hands and knees she stood slowly. Her legs felt wobbly as she stared into the gloom and the dark corners of the attic.

The hissing, fluttering, clicking sounds grew louder as she began to walk. Stopping, she stifled a scream. A pair of yellow eyes glowed in the back corner of the attic.

Straightening she called out, "What are you?"

A black mass separated from the darkness and flew toward her, its talons catching strands of her hair as it flew to the ledge of the dormer window. She stared at the raven, her heart pounding and bile rising in her throat. Perched on the windowsill, the bird cocked its head to the side, getting a close up view of her. It turned and beat its wings against the window pain, tapping the glass with its huge beak.

"Don't worry, I am not going to climb out of the window, or is it you who wants to escape?"

In answer, the bird beat on the window pain, paced about on the sill and lifted its wings again and again. Lilly screamed as the bird shot into the air. It flew back and forth through the attic, screeching and cawing in anger. Lilly curled into a ball and put her arms over her head. The horrid bird finally flew down the center of the attic and back to its perch in the darkness.

Trembling and numb from cold, Lilly peered into the darkness at the back of the attic. Slowly she got on her hands and knees and crawled back to the futon.

Weak sunlight barely pierced the darkness of the attack. Lilly was determined to use whatever light she could to search for a warm cover. She kept one eye on the glowing eyes of the raven and felt along the walls and floor for something to warm herself. She found a coat rack with one long ritual robe. "No!" she said firmly, "I won't wear Regina's ritual robe." Beside the coat rack, her hands found a large sweatshirts. "This is Claude's," she spoke, as she held it close and felt no malevolent energy. "As far as Claude, I don't know what he has to do with this or where he has gone."

She quickly slipped the large sweatshirt over her head. The sleeves encased her arms and hands and dangled down to her knees. The shirt fell to her ankles. Returning to the futon, she pulled her legs up into the warmth of the sweatshirt and curled into a ball.

The key turned in the lock and Regina arrived carrying a bucket, a bag of warm beignets, a cup of coffee and a roll of toilet paper."Good-morning Priestess. I know you are ready for some breakfast." She walked to the futon and held the bucket out to Lilly."I bet you are needing this badly. Take it into a corner and relieve yourself."

There was no point resisting, she removed the warm food and gratefully took the bucket to the back corner opposite the raven. Peering into the shadows, she could make out the form of the bird, but his eyes were closed, his head down.

Regina unwrapped the beignets and removed the plastic top from the styrofoam coffee cup. Tempting as it was, Lilly resisted. It could easily be laced with poison. Ignoring Regina's manic chatter, Lilly lay on the futon and closed her eyes. When she heard

THE RAVEN MOON

the lock click open and the door slam, she opened her eyes and glanced to the rear of the attic. The ravens yellow eyes were glowing.

Sitting up she looked for her crystal. She always kept it next to her body. Panic built in her chest as she searched. She picked up the futon, retraced her steps to the coat rack, and the corner of the attic where she had relieved herself in the bucket.

The sun was setting before Lilly gave up her search for the crystal. Great sobs shook her body as she admitted to herself Regina had taken the Jewel of Inanna.

Chapter 38

THE KNIGHT ARRIVES

Roland woke with the sunrise in Richmond, VA. He quickly dressed and left a note for Trey explaining there was an emergency. He didn't want to explain his dream message. Trey had trouble understanding Roland's Druidic gifts. He put the note where Trey would be sure to see it, threw some clothes and his mandolin in a duffle bag and called for a cab to the airport.

It was a little after noon when he arrived in Jackson Square. He wasn't sure exactly where The Raven Moon was, but he knew it was on Decatur. *'I must have passed it on the way from Jason's up to the Square,'* Roland thought as he ran down Decatur Street.

He slowed when he reached the Abbey Bar which was unusually quiet. Squeaking metal drew his eyes upward to the huge metal raven perched on the crescent moon. He stopped and slowly approached the magic shop. He sauntered past the large front windows, but the shop was dark. On the opposite side of the building, he found a narrow alley. The old brick wall that housed the shop was windowless. Higher up, there were the windows of an upstairs apartment.

Walking across the street he examined the roof line of The Raven Moon and gave a silent cheer. There was an old chimney towards the back of the building. Perfect! He looked up at the gable window and saw a shadowy figure standing there. He couldn't see if it was Lilly so he made no sign. He ran to the sporting goods store on Canal Street. Thirty minutes later, he was standing in the narrow alley on the side of The Raven Moon holding a grappling hook and a sturdy climbing rope. He hoped no one would notice him climbing up the side of the building and call the cops.

It took him a couple of throws, and then the hook finally caught on the chimney. His booted foot found small niches in the

247

THE RAVEN MOON

old bricks as he made his way up the vertical wall. A brief flash of summers spent in Yosemite, climbing the sheer face of El Capitan, gave him a surge of confidence.

He made it to the second floor windows which were locked. In minutes he was grappling across the slate covered roof. Tapping on the glass of the dormer window, he made sure Lilly saw him. The old window frame had been painted shut at least a half a dozen times. Signaling Lilly to stand back, Roland turned his face aside and smashed the window panes with his elbow. Removing large shards of glass from the edges, he kicked in the frame. Lilly ran to him. In one swift move, she was in his arms. He carried her out of the window and onto the roof as Dodger and Prissy sounded the alarm.

The slate shingles were damp and Roland slipped for a moment. He put Lilly down, keeping a strong arm around her waist as they carefully crept across the slippery roof, down the pitched roof to the ledge.

The barking grew closer and Lilly heard Regina screaming. She turned and looked over her shoulder. Prissy had two front legs out of the attic window, barking and growling. Regina leaned out of the window with the raven on her shoulder. She screeched a curse and extended her arm, one finger pointing at Lilly. The raven sprung from Regina's shoulder and slammed into Lilly's back. Roland grabbed her, steadied her and held her for a moment. The raven circled over them and with a loud screech flew at Lilly's face. She ducked and the raven circled again. Roland took the rope in hand, let him self over the edge and signaled for Lilly to do the same. She wavered for a moment and peered over the edge of the roof. "No, don't look down," Roland said calmly, "come on, I won't let you fall."

Lilly took hold of the rope and lowered herself over the edge. The raven harried them with its wings for a moment, lost interest and flew down to examine the contents of the metal dumpster in the alley.

Roland sighed in relief when their feet hit the ground. His eyes met Lilly's for a moment, she nodded and they ran to the end of the block. Turning the corner they ran toward Chartres Street. Lilly's legs buckled, Roland scooped her up and ran along the banquet towards Jackson Square.

Jolene and James were getting out of a cab in front of Panthea's, arriving home from their vacation, when Roland came around the corner. Jolene dropped her luggage as she saw Lilly wearing nothing but a sweatshirt, blood running from a gash across her cheek.

"Can you open the gate?" Roland gasped. James ran to the heavy wooden door, passed his hand over the lock, dissolving locks and wards in seconds. He pushed the gate open and followed Roland into the courtyard and up the stairs.

Roland placed Lilly on her bed. His eyes roamed quickly over her body looking for blood or injuries. She stared at him, hardly believing he was there. She caught her breath as he sat next to her on the bed. "I knew you would come," she said weakly.

Roland kissed her lightly on the lips, nodded and smiled.

"Regina won't come after me here," Lilly whispered, "the wards are too strong."

She sat up slowly, "I want to have a bath, immediately." Roland drew a bath and helped her get out of the oversized sweatshirt. She sank into the warm water holding a cool, damp cloth to her bloody cheek. Roland grabbed a bath sponge and a bar of soap and gently washed her body and her hair.

He helped her out of the tub and was wrapping her in her pink fuzzy bathrobe when Jolene came in. "What has happened? Was there an accident?"

Lilly gave her a short and garbled version of what had transpired over the last three or four days. She wasn't sure how long she had been at Regina's.

"We must get your cut looked at right away," Jolene said as she disappeared out the door.

THE RAVEN MOON

Lilly returned to her bed, holding a clean cloth to her cheek. Within minutes Jolene returned with Lucky who took one look at her face and said, "I'm going to call my doctor. That gash will need stitches."

"Wait a minute," James said steadily. "Let's slow down and look at this wound." Sitting on the edge of the bed, he took Lilly's face between his hands. He passed his hand over the bloody wound and it seemed to fade in and out of existence. "This was created magically and can only be healed magically. I seriously doubt a regular doctor could see it much less stitch it up. Let's get into the temple."

Without a word, Lucky stepped forward and lifted Lilly into his arms. He carried Lilly down the winding stairs, a slightly puzzled Roland close behind. James walked ahead and opened the door to the temple. Jolene knocked on doors, summoning Sabine, Gemma, Forest, Madeline and Owen, explaining Lilly had received a magical wound and needed healing.

Jolene was unsure of what had happened. Lilly's explanation was garbled and Roland said something about a kidnapping. Jolene held her hand over her heart, fearful the Inanna crystal was the motivation behind the abduction. She was desperate to hear the details, but first they must tend to Lilly's wound.

The coven gathered around the young priestess as she lay still on a large cushion. Jolene cast the circle quickly, invoking the healing guardians and guides who moved through time with Lilly. Together the members of the coven placed their hands over Lilly calling on universal healing energy to pour through their crown chakras and healing earth energy to rise up from the ground into their heart centers The energy of celestial light and the healing energy of mother earth circulated, forming a taurus of energy which exited through the palms of their hands into Lilly's prone body.

As the members of the coven poured healing love over Lilly, James called upon the Druid power of binding to seal her wound. He began to move his hands slowly across the side of her face, around her head and down to her heart. Time passed and the group slowly lowered their hands placing them on Lilly's body allowing the last of the healing energies to fill her physical, emotional and spiritual bodies.

Lilly lay with her eyes closed for several minutes. Her eyes fluttered as she sat up and rubbed the side of her face. The bloody gash was gone. With the tips of her fingers she could feel a small seam that had not been there before. She smiled and opened her arms to her friends. She looked into their faces and thanked them for their care. Her eyes found Roland, "You saved my life. I am so grateful. Thank you for your courage."

Roland smiled and scooped her into his arms. Back in her apartment, he set her feet on the floor of the living room, and drew her close. With his hands tangled in her red curls he brought his mouth to her cheek and kissed the narrow white scar. He kissed her eyes and lingered on her lips. Lilly's arms went around his neck, she leaned into him and pressed her mouth to his.

Despair, longing, fear and grief melted; her world blurred for a moment. Everything she had longed for was here. She was home and safe, Roland was here and she wanted nothing more than to lie with him and melt into his warmth.

The rest of the coven gathered in Jolene's kitchen to discuss the attack and injury. "Are we equipped to deal with this," Sabine asked with an angry sob in her voice.

The members of the coven raised their voices in response, "We will deal with this!"

Chapter 39

TAINTED BLOOD

Lilly's bare feet stood on the damp bricks of the banquette. Her hands found a metal post to cling to as she tried to get her bearings in the thick fog. A dank scent wafted through the mist as a dark figure approached silently. She turned to run but the dark figure flapped it's wings, landed in front of her and blocked her path. The Ravens' eyes glowed red as it opened its beak blasting her with the fetid smell of death.

A hand reached out and grabbed her as she took a step back on the slippery bricks. Regina held her arm in a vice grip as she spoke, her voice razor sharp, "You will not escape this time. You will suffer! Your blood will spill! Your life will be ruined!" Lilly struggled to get away but the fog grew thicker and the oily wings of the Raven engulfed her, pulling her close.

The Raven's beak brushed the top of her head and she froze. "Ah, you don't want another scar to match the one I gave you earlier? You are mine, marked by the raven. I have tasted your blood, I can find you anywhere. There is no place to hide."

Roland heard Lilly struggling and ran to her bedside. He shook her shoulder gently, "Wake up, Lilly, wake up."

She slowly opened her eyes and propelled herself into his arms. "It is Regina, she is never going to leave me alone. She says the Raven has tasted my blood, she can find me anywhere and take my power."

"Not while I am on this planet!" Roland exclaimed.

Jolene, had insisted on keeping watch over Lilly with Roland. Sitting patiently in the living room rocking chair, she overheard their conversation. She moved quickly to the bedside. Taking Lilly in her arms, she rocked gently and made soothing sounds.

Lilly's body shook with sobs as she pulled Jolene close. "I am so glad you are here and I lived to see you again. I thought I was going to die in Regina's attic."

Jolene tightened her hug and spoke quietly, "I need to know what happened, exactly. Lilly, can you tell me?" Dizziness overtook Lilly as her mind began to spin. Jolene placed her hand on Lilly's and repeated the question.

Looking into Jolene's loving eyes, Lilly nodded slowly. Putting her hand up she ran her fingers over the seam across her cheek. Her eyes filled with tears. "Oh great Goddess, it is true. The raven has marked me and I will be in its power forever!"

"Poppycock!" Jolene exclaimed. "Tell me what happened."

Propped up on pillows, Lilly related the details of her visits to The Raven Moon and her new friendship with Regina and Claude. She described the disturbing dream visions which had started to plague her immediately after meeting Regina. Tears ran down her face as she berated herself, appalled she had not seen through Regina's offer of friendship.

"It was in the wine. Whatever she gave me, it was in the wine," she repeated, "it knocked me out, made me ill," Lilly's voice faded.

"I think she needs some rest," Roland stated. Jolene agreed, kissed her and assured her they would be nearby.

Over the next few day, the bits and pieces of her ordeal in the attic of The Raven Moon began to come together in her mind. Lilly was able to relate her story with more clarity. Looking at the faces of her friends, she was still bewildered by the sudden twisted behavior of Regina. "Initially, I liked Regina, I was happy to have a new friend. She gave me no reason not to trust her. It was after I drank the wine she gave me that I became disoriented and nauseous.

"There was a thick fog, I was in the attic alone in the dark. Regina came in and cast a circle. She was chanting. She is always chanting! I saw the raven step out of a mirror and stand over me. It tried to draw something from me. It hurt me and I stabbed him in the eye with the crystal. Oh, I don't know how it all happened! When he was gone, I remember Regina slapped me and locked the door to the attic.

"I scavenged the candle stubs from the circle Regina had cast. Keeping one candle lit I called upon the Goddess, invoked my inner sight, lay down and left my body. I contacted Roland and he came and helped me get out of the attic and back to Panthea's."

Lilly closed her eyes. "That is all I can remember. Maybe I will have more clarity later," she said putting her head in her hands. Roland sat close and put his arms around her. Jolene looked at James and lifted an eyebrow. Sabine broke the silence and gave voice to what they all knew, "Thank the Goddess your strong Fae blood and your guardians and ancestors assisted you."

Lilly shrugged one shoulder, "How does Fae blood have anything to do with this? It was Roland who helped me."

James answered, "The Fae have a strong talent for communicating clearly through the astral plane. You were in great distress, injured and afraid. Your Fae instincts, combined with your training as a Priestess, saved your life, Lilly."

With the help of Roland and her friends at Panthea's, Lilly began to recover from the emotional trauma she had suffered at Regina's hands. Jolene insisted she drink gallons of cleansing tea to wash any remaining poison out of her body. Her spirits lifted and she was feeling stronger every day. There was one constant reminder, the narrow white seam adorning the side of her face. She knew only those with magical vision could see it, but it tightened and tingled at weird moments.

She and Roland renewed their relationship making love slowly, getting to know one another again. Roland had recovered his duffle bag from the locker at the airport and spent hours playing his mandolin. He made up silly songs to make her laugh and love songs that made her blush. "I wrote this on the beach, remembering you, missing you. As I wrote it I realized what a fool I was.

> *When the meeting of our eyes becomes obsession, emotion*
> *and longing start to play*
> *When getting what I want becomes, I love you, the attraction draws us closer every day.*

*Then bring me to your Venus violet lady, wrap me in
your subtle strands of silk.
Touch me with your tender hands, have mercy, let me
touch your skin as white as milk.*

*I hear your radiating laughter, like a holy mother god-
dess of the Earth.
Drive me to the center of your passion, show me the
measure of your worth.*

*Then bring me to your Venus, Violet lady. Wrap me in
your subtle strands of silk.
Touch me with your tender hands, have mercy. Let me
touch your skin as white as milk.*

*Dream me in your nights. I'll be your lover. Let me ride
the cresting of your wave.
Thrill me with the pleasures of your body, roll me in the
caverns of your cave.*

*Then bring me to your Venus, Violet lady. Wrap me in
your subtle strands of silk.
Touch me with your tender hands, have mercy. Let me
touch your skin as white as milk.*

Lilly blushed to the roots of her hair, but quickly gained her
composure. "Sounds like you were mighty horny. So...was it love
or lust which lured you back?"

Roland's eyebrows rose as he bit his lower lip. "Ah, I must
confess it was both," he said as he put his mandolin aside and
took her in his arms.

Chapter 40

THE THREAT OF THE RAVEN'S CLAW

illy resumed her classes with Jolene and Sabine, Roland spent time with James delving into Druidic teachings. He wanted to continue to study and unlock whatever powers he might have. After the attack on Lilly, he was determined to explore all possibilities in order to protect her.

On a sunny day, a week after the rescue, Roland took a walk to Frenchman Street to say hello to Jason. He sauntered down Decatur Street past The Raven Moon. The energy was dense, dark and malevolent. The 'Open' sign was not on the door.

Feeling stronger, Lilly took her flute into the courtyard. Sitting on one of the wrought iron benches near the fountain, she closed her eyes and allowed the music to move through her.

Fields of swaying wild flowers filled her vision as she recovered her inner joy. The flute Roland had given her was not only an instrument of expression rather, as Lilly was discovering, it was also an instrument of invocation. With no warning, she felt a pressure in her head as her joyful vision began to twist and change. The sunny sky filled with ominous black clouds. The swaying field of flowers withered.

Taking the flute away from her mouth, she opened her eyes and screamed. A huge raven twice the size of the normal bird, sat on the edge of the nearby fountain staring at her. Its mouth opened and closed as it made a terrible screeching sound.

Grabbing her flute, Lilly ran towards Jolene's kitchen door. The raven swooped after her, trying to entangle its claws in her hair. Bursting through the door, she slammed it closed turned and almost tripped over Topaz as she made her way into the shop.

Jolene and Sabine, sitting behind the counter chatting, saw the look of distress on Lilly's face. They jumped up as she pointed to the courtyard gasping, "Raven."

Jolene ran past her, grabbing a broom as she rushed through her kitchen. Sabine was on her heels with Lilly following cautiously behind them. The raven had returned to the rim of the fountain. Spying the witchy trio, it tilted its head and made its loud, unnatural screeching sound.

Jolene raised her broom and swung with all her strength at the evil creature. Screeching even louder, the raven flew up a few feet to avoid the broom. With glistening talons extended it attacked Jolene.

Lilly opened the palms of her tingling hands repelling the creature as Jolene brought the broom up again, swatting the creature on the side of its head. It plunged to the ground for a moment. Jolene quickly hit it again. Screeching wildly, the raven extended it's wings and flew from the courtyard.

Landing on the edge of the rooftop, it stopped to give one last piercing screech as it tilted its head to stare at them with one eye. Lilly lifted her hands sending repellent energy as the avian creature swiftly flapped its huge wings and fled.

The three witches sat on the edge of the fountain. Jolene sat with broom in hand, ready to take another swipe at the hideous creature if it returned. "This won't do," Sabine said seriously.

Jolene nodded her head in agreement. "The question is, what are we going to do about it?

Sabine shrugged and said, "Well, you are adept with the broom. Possibly you could train us in the use of your implement."

Jolene looked at the broom in her hand and laughed. "I grabbed the closest thing at hand. It worked pretty well. Lilly's energy helped to keep the raven at bay so I could get a swing at it."

She and Sabine sat on the edge of the fountain their momentary mirth overshadowed by the grim look on their young friends face. Lilly chewed her lower lip and tried not to cry. Her voice cracked as she shared her outrage, "Regina grows more brazen everyday. She is sending her creature after me in my own territory,

257

in broad daylight. She has the Jewel of Inanna! What more does she want?"

The two older witches looked at her, eyebrows raised, "Indeed, what does she want?"

"I know," Lilly gasped, "She wants to draw magic from me. I remember her stating I had power over her in the past. In this lifetime she would take my power and destroy my life. How could she take my inner power? The idea seems ludicrous."

Sabine said in a hard voice. "It is ludicrous and vicious. Do you know where Roland has disappeared to?"

"He went to talk to Jason about playing music at Valentines."

Sabine pursed her lips, "Uh huh, and I bet he went down Decatur Street, right past The Raven Moon. Possibly Regina saw him go by and decided to attack while he wasn't here."

Lilly shrugged her shoulders, "I don't know, Sabine. I don't think Regina has seen Roland. If he walked by there, he was betting on his belief she has never seen him."

"You forget, Lilly, she saw him the day she rescued you from the attic. She also has the crystal and may be able to scry."

"I don't doubt her psychic abilities," Jolene injected, "but I think the crystal is dormant in her hands. It did not choose her. There has not been even a shadow of its energy in my awareness. I would recognize it. I think it has gone dormant. I could still feel the energy when Lilly was wearing it. The glowing violet stone, filled with potential, is nothing more than a dull rock in Regina's hands."

Lilly nodded in agreement. "I have felt nothing from the stone. It must be dormant. As long as it remains in Regina's hands, let's hope it remains a dull rock."

Jolene nodded at Lilly, "Ma chérie, you are right about her motives. She wants something more of you. She wants your magical essence. The raven is her tool, but it will only comply with her wishes for a time. The raven spirit is strong, it does not bow to control easily or for long.

"She is getting desperate, stepping up her game. We don't know how she plans to obtain your energy, however we are going to put a stop to this. We are going to free the raven and get the Priestess Crystal out of her hands and back to you, my dear."

Lilly nodded automatically, her mouth dry and her heart pounding. As Sabine and Jolene left to close the shop, Gemma and Forest came in the front gate and found Lilly standing in the courtyard scanning the roof. She filled them in on the incident. Gemma hugged her, "You have had enough. I am here to help in any way I can."

Forest echoed, "Me too." They hugged and Lilly knew a moment of peace, grateful she had friends who would protect and support her.

As the shadows lengthened, Lilly decided to take a walk through the Square. Reinforcing her mirrored-egg protection, she grabbed her hat and left. The crowd of people would be safe and she needed to focus on something else and let go of the knot in her stomach.

She walked around Jackson Square aimlessly for a while, stopping to listen to a tall black man wail on his saxophone. The blues filled the square, purging sorrow from the soul, pouring healing balm over the pedestrians walking nearby. She felt Roland's energy coming toward her.

Seconds later, Roland touched her arm as she swayed, eyes closed, absorbing the magic of the music. He smiled at the site of her, and pulled her gently into an embrace. "How is everything? I was feeling strange vibes and rushed back."

Lilly took his hands and walked towards Panthea's, filling him in on the raven attack and Jolene's retaliation with her broom.

"Wait, Jolene attacked the huge raven with a broom?"

Lilly nodded smiling, "Yep, it was the closest thing at hand and she used it with great precision."

Roland devoured one of Felix's extra large oyster po' boys as

259

Lilly sat picking the shrimp out of the french bread on her plate. "You need to eat, Lil, you have to build up your strength."

"I'm not hungry right now."

"Do you want to wrap it up and bring it with us?" Lilly nodded assent and had a sip of ice tea.

As the waxing moon rose they made their way through the streets of the French Quarter hand in hand. Entering the courtyard at Panthea's, they saw Lucky sitting on the old iron bench with Topaz. They stopped to tell him of the day's events.

"Something has to be done," Lucky said looking worried. "I'm postponing my trip. I want to be here for you."

Lilly thanked him, rubbed Topaz behind his ears for a moment, took Roland's hand and led him up the winding stairs.

Curling up in bed together, they watched a rain of starlight silvering the rooftops of the French Quarter. Soon they were asleep. In the darkest hour of the night, an insistent rapping woke the sleeping couple. Roland put on his pants and head for the door.

Lilly looked up and screamed, "No it's not the door. Look!" Pointing to the window, they watched as the raven balanced on the narrow ledge beating his sharp beak against the window pane.

"Holy Hell," Roland exclaimed, as he and Lilly ran from the bedroom. He slammed the door and traced a ward of protection across it. Lilly saw the ward's blue glow and gave a sigh of relief. The tapping continued as they paced around the tiny living room.

"I'll make some coffee," Lilly said. "Maybe it will wake us from this nightmare."

Roland touched her shoulder and said, "No, you stay here. I'll make coffee."

The insistent rapping continued. Lilly was about to burst. "What if he breaks the window? What if he gets into the bedroom?"

"He will have to get through the door and that is not going to happen," Roland said grabbing the broom from its hook on the

260

wall near the stove. He brandished it around and managed a smile from Lilly.

Feeling her hands tingle, Lilly gathered the surge of energy. She centered herself and called to Roland. "Come! Join your energy with mine."

As they stood in the center of the living room, Lilly drew a large pentagram in the air before them. She could see it glowing through her second sight. As the star within spun clockwise, a portal was created. The magical couple drew a pentagram in violet light over one another's third eye. Joining hands, they turned slowly clockwise, feeling for the direction from which the attack originated. No surprise, the attack had come from the West, the direction of The Raven Moon. Bringing their hands up in a triangle shape over their foreheads, they called in protection from all five points of the violet pentagram. Stepping forward together they projected their triangular hands forward, sending the pentagram's violet fire through the portal, to the source of the attack. Feeling the link sever, they relaxed and embraced.

As suddenly as it had begun, the rapping stopped. They stood still. The only sound was coffee percolating on the stove. Roland put his ear to the bedroom door. Unable to stand the suspense, he cracked the door open, broom ready for an attack. He flipped on the overhead light, ran to the window and stepped back, "It's gone."

The coffee boiled over, and Lilly turned the stove off, taking two cups out of the cupboard, she poured the dark liquid. They sat on the sofa, silently sipping scalded coffee.

"Do you think it is gone? Maybe it is in the courtyard waiting for us to come out. What if it attacks another member of the coven?"

"I'll go look around," Roland said.

Lilly grabbed his arm, "Don't go, I'll call Lucky. He has a good view of the courtyard. I'll ask him to see if its out there."

Lucky was glad to help. He looked out of his window, but

could see little in the dark courtyard. Grabbing a baseball bat, he walked out of his front door, through the courtyard and around the fountain. He examined dark shadows and peered through the darkness searching the roof top.

A few minutes later, he knocked on Lilly's front door. It's clear in the courtyard, he reported. Lilly took his hand and gently tugged him through the front door. She gave him a cup of coffee and the three of them went over the events of the late night intrusion. When a soft gray light filtered through the transom over the front door, Lilly called Jolene's apartment. James answered groggily. She apologized for the early hour and told him briefly of the raven's latest visit.

By 6AM, Lilly, Roland, Lucky, Sabine, James and Jolene sat around the oak table eating warm almond croissants and drinking hot coffee. "We have to have a plan to deal with this creature," Jolene said. "Chasing it with a broom is not going to stop these attacks. I'm proud of you" she said nodding towards Lilly and Roland. "In the midst of an attack you were able to act like warrior priest and priestess and protect yourselves. I'm concerned next time you won't be in the comfort and safety of your home."

Roland licked his lips and looked around the table, "Regina has already sent the vile creature to invade Lilly's dreams. Now, she is sending it to threaten her home. I'd say the attacks on both fronts are sure to escalate. We have to take action."

Sabine suggested they call in other members of the coven, "Gemma and Forest know a bit about what is going on already."

James, who had been silent, spoke up, "Let's make sure all of our members are informed. I don't think there is a need to get everyone involved at this time, however they need to be appraised of the situation. We may need some members of the group to watch the shop, or help out in other ways. Let's work on a plan and call on the other members when we need their help."

Jolene spoke with authority, "We will gather in our meditation temple tonight when the moon rises. Be prepared for invocation, deep meditation and multi-dimensional journeying. We will seek the council and protection of our ancestors, guides and guardians. We will call on the wisdom of the goddess and the strength of Mother Gaia before deciding what course of action to take." Everyone nodded in agreement.

When the meeting dispersed Roland and Lilly took a walk by the river bundled up against the chill morning air. "So what did Jason say about the music?"

"Ah, good news! He wants us to play for happy hour on Friday night and on Saturday and Sunday for brunch. It's not much money, but we can get use to playing together in public and refine our music."

Lilly smiled, "It is nice to hear a bit of good news." They walked in comfortable silence, arms around each other's waists, as the morning sun turned the river to molten gold.

Part V

SUPERNATURAL INTERVENTION

THOSE WHO DON'T BELIEVE IN MAGIC WILL NEVER FIND IT

Chapter 41

The Forces Unite

P anthea's apartments were quiet throughout the day. The members of the coven rested, preparing to offer support, magical or mundane.

As the moon rose, those directly involved gathered in the meditation temple. Tall candelabras stood in the four corners, providing the only illumination. A small brass gong hung on a stand and a Tibetan singing bowl rested on a cushion next to the gong.

The group stood in the center of the temple holding hands. Sabine cast the circle, James called on the powerful protection of the four watchtowers. Jolene lit the candle on the low table in the center of the circle. Together the group called upon ancestors, guards and guides of all present asking for protection and assistance. The circle quickly filled with benevolent energy.

Sitting on cushions the small group formed a close circle filled with intention. Sabine tapped on the Tibetan bowl with the wooden mallet. She slowly rubbed the mallet around the edge of the bowl, the tone and vibration cleared their minds of all thought and distraction. As the clearing tone faded, the group's attention focused on the inhale and exhale of breath. They breathed together, becoming empty vessels.

Lucky was the first to see the vision and the others quickly followed. As the higher dimensions opened, intricate designs filled the minds eye of each participant. The mandalas swirled and morphed into flames.

The flying serpent, Quetzalcoatl appeared forming a circle of glowing green light. The ancient Atlantean priest from the Order of Interplanetary Adepts stood within the glowing circle.

The serpent faded as an expressive and beautiful face appeared in Jolene's vision. It was her long time friend and Vodou

Mambo, Alustra. The mambo was dancing through a ritual Vévé, invoking the Loa. Alustra's consort, Shemo was dancing by her side. In a circle of fire, an unfamiliar energy emanated power. The spirit took form as a large man, brandishing a flaming sword.

James sat motionless in deep meditation. A swirling black hole filled his vision. The akashic egg formed before his inner eye, "Ah," he voiced, "The zero point." The group breathed together in the dark void.

The visions slowly faded and Sabine tapped the gong softly, calling everyone back to waking reality. It was clear, the three strongest magical powers in the French Quarter; The Mystical Witches of Panthea's, the Atlantian Order of Interplanetary Adepts from the Ursuline Temple and the Vodouns lead by the Mambo Alustra and the Hougan Shemo, must work together.

It would take their combined power to break the magical hold the sorceress, Regina, held on the raven and return the ancient Jewel of Inanna to its rightful protector.

By noon the next day, Lilly, Roland, Lucky, Jolene and Sabine, the Druid high priest James, the leader of the Atlantian Temple, Kumira, the Queen of the Vodouns, Alustra and the Hougan, Shemo, were gathered in Jolene's living room.

Alustra spoke up, "From what ya'll are describing it sounds like we're gonna' need the help of Ogue La Flambo." Her heavy lidded eyes looked from face to face at the table. She licked her thick lips before continuing, "I'm willin' to help out as much as I can. No way can I promise the Loa will respond. They are temperamental and may not feel this is their problem."

"We understand, Alustra. But think of this, the Valraven sorceress, most likely, has little or no experience with Vodou. Your help may be the key to our success. She is here in the French Quarter. If she is not vanquished it won't be long before her eyes fall on another. She will covet your power sooner or later and go after it." Jolene sat back, tilted her head and raised an eyebrow at Alustra.

SUPERNATURAL INTERVENTION

"Yep, that's fa' shore," Alustra responded, nodding thoughtfully.

Kumira, looking matronly, her long red hair in a bun at the back of her head, spoke up, "I'm in! I think she is a real threat. Together we can create a ritual unlike any she has ever encountered and defeat her quickly. You say Quetzequatel appeared in your meditation? I believe the winged serpent will lend powerful energies to the ritual. Let's do this as soon as possible. No need dragging it out."

Jolene poured coffee all around as the Circle of Adepts created the ritual the way they hoped it would play out.

James spoke solemnly, "I recognized the energy of Pluto in my vision. A swirling black hole appeared. As I watched, the dark void fell in on itself, forming a huge black egg. The black egg will absorb and dissolve matter. This energy appearing in my meditation, strongly implies it will be needed."

Roland, looking more serious than Lilly had ever seen him, spoke softly, "If the raven appears, possibly we can disrupt its DNA sequence with the help of Ogue Flambo. When the black egg appears, it will pull the ravens scattered molecules through the hole into another dimension. The distorted Raven energy Regina controls would be gone forever."

"Possibly, the essence of the poor creature she has been using, will survive the ritual," Jolene added.

Lilly looked puzzled, "How do we invoke this black egg?"

"This type of energy is usually evoked by aligning your energy to Pluto or the center of the galaxy. You, Jolene, Sabine and Kumira will be scrying through the cauldron, watching as our mission unfolds. You will know when it is time to allow its manifestation, for all thought will stop. Your eyes will see only the dark waters of the caldron. From this space of the great nothing, which contains everything, the entities we summoned at the beginning of the ritual, will allow the dark egg to appear where it is needed."

"I'm seeing two magic circles overlapping." James continued.

On the left is the circle filled with the Vévé to call in the Loa. The second circle overlaps the first, forming the Vesica Piscis, honoring the feminine and doubling the power of both circles. Sabine, Jolene, Kumira and Lilly will be within the safety of the right hand circle scrying through the cauldron, and sending help as it is needed. Roland and I, hopefully with the assistance of Ogue La Flambo, will travel the astral, find and confront Regina Valraven."

Lucky spoke up, "I will enter The Raven Moon, find the crystal or remove it from Regina as she is busy dealing with your astral attack. I may need one more person to go with me. Back up is always a good idea."

Someone, pounding loudly on the front door of the shop, interrupted their conversation. "What in blazes?" Sabine exclaimed.

Jolene and James got up simultaneously. "You stay here Jo, I'll go see what's happening." Before James stepped out of the kitchen door, the assault on the front door stopped, replaced by the insistent buzzing of the gate button.

Distraught, was the first impression James got when he opened the gate. A tall blond man, extreme distress stood before him. "What is it?" James inquired calmly.

The young man, blond hair tumbling to his waist, shirt tails hanging out and two days of grizzle on his chin blurted out, "Is Lilly here?"

James spoke to the young man with an authoritarian tone "Who are you?" What do you want with Lilly?".

"I'm Claude Mckenzie. My partner and I own The Raven Moon. I've been in New York recently. I returned last night and uh, where is Lilly?"

James signaled for Claude to come in, lead him through the carriage way and offered him a seat on the bench near the fountain. "How do you know Lilly and what do you want?"

Claude's fists curled as he heaved a frustrated sigh, "First tell me if she is okay?"

James nodded, "Yes, she is fine."

Claude sighed in relief. "I got in from New York last night. This morning when I saw my partner, Regina, she was wearing, what appears to be, Lilly's crystal. I demanded she tell me how she got it. Regina swears Lilly gave it to her. I know Lilly wouldn't give up her talisman willingly. Regina was evasive and refused to tell me how she came to be wearing it.

"I had a bad feeling in my gut and I ran upstairs to the ritual temple in the attic. Something dark has been going on up there. Pages of the Goetia grimoire are scattered all over the floor, the window has been smashed and the whole place reeks. I'm afraid my partner is not who she presented herself to be. She is into dark magic and I am worried about Lilly."

The door to the kitchen opened. Jolene and Lucky came out followed by Kumira, Alustra and Shemo. James introduced them to Claude and had him repeat his story. As he finished recounting his morning findings, Lilly and Roland stepped out of Jolene's kitchen. Peering through the group, Lilly spotted someone sitting on the cast iron bench. The group parted as she exclaimed, "Claude!"

Claude jumped up and pulled her into an embrace. Kissing the top of her head he said, "I'm so glad your okay. I don't know what Regina has been up to. I'm afraid my worst fears about her may be true."

Lilly stepped out of his embrace and confirmed his fears were valid. Introducing him to Roland, she sat next to Claude on the bench and gave him a quick rundown of the happenings since his trip to New York.

Placing his hand gently over her scarred cheek, Claude apologized and adamantly stated he was not involved with Regina's dark witchery nor her obsession with the raven. "I am here to help. I'll do anything I can."

Jolene and Sabine looked at one another, gave a quick nod, turned and invited everyone, including Claude, back into the apartment.

SUPERNATURAL INTERVENTION

The expanded group flowed into the living room and made themselves comfortable as they questioned Claude in great depth. Convinced he was an ally, James designated him to accompany Lucky into The Raven Moon during the ritual and assist in anyway possible to reclaim the crystal.

Shemo and Alustra ended their whispered conversation. Alustra stood on her sturdy legs and looked at each member of the group. "I know some of ya'll have knowledge of what Vodou is about, but some have only false ideas.

"Vodou is the living experience of the Divine. The Divine presence is encountered through our practice. It is a powerful practice with powerful results. That's why so many folks have a negative idea about Vodou. Where there is great power there is a great capacity for good. Where there is great power, the shadow side also abides and there is great capacity for evil. This here girl, Regina, is a perfect example of an unhealthy craving for power in the realm of the sacred Craft."

"Our spirits in Vodou are called the Loa. They were once livin' people, charismatic souls who are remembered and honored. It is these charismatic, powerful energies we call on to help us.

"In the ritual we'll perform together, we are gonna' call on Legba to open the pathway between the astral world and the physical world. After Legba opens the door to the spirit world, we'll call on Ogou La Flambo, a powerful warrior, to assist in the confrontation with Regina.

"The purpose of the ritual is to become the divine horseman, to be ridden or possessed by the spirit in physical form. In this ceremony we are gonna' be askin' Ogou La Flambo to take the spirit of two of you and carry you into the spirit world. The two will be with Ogou La Flambo and he will lend his powers to you. Like I say, this is most unusual. It may or may not work. I can't guarantee any of it."

Shemo spoke up, "If Ogou La Flambeau can be enticed to assist you, he will call upon the sacrificial knife of his relentless raw

SUPERNATURAL INTERVENTION

power to protect you and overcome the dark force. Ogou's great strength and endurance will be of a mighty benefit to you."

Alustra added, "Understand, those who open to this journey will be under the power of Ogou La Flambeau. You will be imbued with his astral power and you will act as he acts. Hopefully, you will be able to reason with Regina and get her to relinquish the sacred stone."

"Her resentment towards Lilly has spanned lifetimes. She may not go gently into the night. The raven is her servant and she has twisted the creature to her will, beware! Lilly, I agree with James, it is best you stay within the magic circle with Jolene and Sabine. Your presence on the astral would inflame Regina's rage."

Roland and James spoke simultaneously, "We will go." Lucky and Claude will enter the building physically, subdue Regina if necessary and retrieve the crystal."

Kumira spoke, "I will stand within the witches circle with the drummers from our Temple. I will lead the call of the Interplanetary Adepts and summon our protector, Quatzquatel. Lilly has bonded with his energy and the strength of the winged serpent will be a strong defense against the raven. Together we can take care of this little witch."

Everyone joined hands. Sitting thus, hand in hand, eyes locked upon one another, the group made a solemn vow to work together to dismantle the web of revenge and malevolence Regina had created. "We will replace the darkness with the light," they said with one voice.

Chapter 42

In the mid-sixties the Vodou Priestess, Alustra, purchased an old building near the river in the area behind the Faborg Marigny called the Bywater. The area was less than a mile behind the French Quarter and a world unto its self. The old brick building, once a cannery, stood three stories tall with huge windows. Alustra had one end of the building renovated, creating a section of spacious apartments for her extended family.

The rest of the building had been gutted. The huge open area, on the ground floor, was consecrated as Le Peristyle de Vodou Orleans. The poto mitan (center post) stood firmly in the middle of the sanctuary connecting the astral worlds with the physical world. It was through the poto mitan the Loa (Vodou spirits) entered into the peristyle during ritual. A large circular area was cleared around the center pole. Altars overflowing with statues, candles, flowers, beaded bottles and Vodou flags, stood on the edge of the sacred space, honoring the various Loa. Beyond the center ritual space, was jungle. The room was filled with tropical plants thriving in the humidity and bright sunlight pouring through the many windows of the old cannery. On the day of the intricate ritual, the group gathered around the poto mitan. Alustra went on, to explain in great detail, what might happen during the ritual invocation ending with a sigh, "We can only plan so much. The energy will play itself out as it sees fit."

The witches cast their circle of protection with salt as Alustra created a circle using a thick line of cornmeal. Following James's suggestion, the two circles overlapped, doubling the strength of both. The Mambo sang and called out to Legba imploring him to open the gate to the spirit world. As the choir added their voices, Alustra slowly drew a Vèvè within the Vodou circle. Lilly remembered the design Alustra created was Ogou La Flambo's sigil. The drummers added the intricate beat which would entice Ogou La Flambo to appear.

The Vèvè was created slowly, as hand full's of cornmeal sifted through Alustra's fingers. Radiating lines, intricate swirls, dots, curves and, what appeared to be flaming arrows, appeared. The process was slow and filled with respect for the spirit they were calling forth. Surely, Lilly thought, the intercession of Legba, the Power of the Vèvè , the ritual dancing, the voices of the choir and the dedicated beat of the drums would open the gate to the spirit world and call forth the mighty Ogou La Flambo. Once he arrived, it was up to Alustra and Shemo to entice him into assisting.

Lilly swayed slightly, entranced by the beauty of the voices, and the intricacy of the design. She was surprised as the Vodou priestess took a mouth full of rum, pursed her lips and blew a fine spray of rum around the circle. After blowing rum around the circle, Alustra nodded to her consort, Shemo. He lit a big black cigar and blew smoke across the circle.

The air was filled with the scent of the sweet liquor and pungent tobacco when Mambo Alustra lifted her voice, "Oh Legba, ancient one, gatekeeper, expression of primordial energy, master of the crossroads be pleased by our offerings. Open the gateway to the Flambo. Call upon Ogou La Flambo. Open the gateway, thank you."

Alustra and Shemo stood still, the choir was silent the drums resting. The calm was banished when Shemo lifted the ritual machete over his head and danced, swinging the machete, tossing it from hand to hand, twirling it over his head, his body shaking. Alustra ran to his side and slapped rum on the back of his neck signaling Ogou La Flambo that Shemo was not the one he was to ride this day.

Shemo's shivers ceased, his eyes opened. He nodded slightly and Alustra signaled James and Roland to step into the Vèvè . The two Druids moved slowly. The drums resumed their persistent

SUPERNATURAL INTERVENTION

beat energizing the circle for Ogou La Flambo. Alustra called out in a sing song voice, enticing the Loa to assist them.

James and Roland's feet tapped, keeping time to the drums as the energy of the Vèvè moved through their bodies. The design beneath their feet swirled as the drum beats filled their consciousness. Soon they were dancing wildly, spinning and waving their arms above their bodies.

Ogue La Flambo appeared in his astral form. Alustra called out in the language of Haiti, a Creole French dialect, asking Ogue La Flambo to reverse his usual ride and take James and Roland into the astral. James and Roland fell to the ground simultaneously. Alustra placed cushions beneath their heads. Ogou La Flambo lifted the spirits of the two men, drawing them to him on the astral plane. As one fiery astral entity, they headed for The Raven Moon.

The large metal sign of the raven perched upon the crescent moon, creaked on its hinges. When the disembodied trio arrived at the front door, the sign fell to the sidewalk with a loud clatter. Regina jumped to her feet, heading for the front of the store. The double doors slammed open admitting a rush of wind smelling of cigar smoke. Regina ducked behind the counter as the powerful energy swirled past her. The two Great Danes barked wildly and ran out the opened doors, tails between their legs.

Within seconds Regina heard the stairway door slam open. Shaking, she ran up the stairs. Her head spinning with panic, adrenaline pouring through her veins, she ran wildly into the attic into the center of her circle of protection.

The astral trio grinned in anticipation as it watched her trying to get her bearings. She managed to calm herself and called the raven through the mirror. The creature responded quickly and poured out of the triangular mirror into the circle. Its oily black form overshadowed Regina. Standing a bit taller, Regina shrugged the raven on like a coat. Enfolded in the power and protection of her ensorcelled creature, she turned and saw the astral form of her

SUPERNATURAL INTERVENTION

attackers. "Who the hell are you and what do you want here?"

They answered as one powerful voice, "We have come for the Jewel of Inanna and to free the raven."

Regina, laughed and shook her head. "You will never get the crystal. It is mine as is the power of the raven. You have no way to force any of this. I banish you from my ritual space. Be gone."

The trio ignored her banishment with a sneer. James and Roland knew the first order of business was to breach her circle of protection if the mission was to be successful. They focused their energy towards her.

Regina's laugh echoed through the astral plane as she spun inside the body of the raven. The circle filled with an oily darkness. Her laughter died in her throat as the power of the Vodou spirit filled the air.

Three hands held the flaming sword of Ogue La Flambo. The trio carved a huge X filled with reverse DNA spirals. The flaming coils permeated the astral and expanded to surround the circle.

Back at Alustra's, the witches were bending over their scrying mirror, seizing the moment to evoke and allow the ancient power of Pluto to rise. There are no words to the invocation. The powerful trio of witches focused into the void waiting to see the atomic egg.

The water of the cauldron continued to reflect the battle raging in the attic of The Raven Moon. The witches could see the Plutonian egg shimmer and disappear. Regina grasped wildly, trying to reassemble the DNA spirals fragmenting her circle of protection, weakening the solidity and power of the raven.

Staring into the cauldron, the witches groaned in dismay as the egg disappeared. Wild eyed, they looked at one another in horror.

Kumira stood apart from them, eyes closed hands opened in supplication. An ancient Atlantean Priest appeared where she had stood. His eyes were dark pools of infinity. As the witches stared, a tone resonated from deep within his being. Jolene, Sabine and

Lilly added their voices, matching the tone and directing it into the cauldron. They gasped as the black egg appeared.

Kumira, blinking her eyes and shaking her body, joined them as they watched the black egg appear over the spiraling circle of fiery coils in the attic of The Raven Moon.

Kumira took Lilly's hand, and called upon the winged serpent, Quetzalcoatl to speed the black egg into the path of the raven.

Dark feathers exploded filling the circle with a black cloud. The creature screamed with ear splitting shrieks as the atomic egg, wrapped in the glowing green light of Quetzalcoatl, absorbed the dark energy. The ensorcelled raven was free.

Regina's concentration faltered. Panicked, she followed her first instinct to use the raven wings to fly. She catapulted toward the window, abandoning her circle of protection.

Ogue la Flambou laughed as Regina fell through the window, rolled down the slate covered rooftop and landed on the broken sign of The Raven Moon.

Lucky, standing guard outside the doors of the shop, leaned over Regina's body and lifted the ancient crystal from her neck. Claude headed for the telephone to call an ambulance.

Lilly, scrying the scene in the cauldron at the Peristyle, cried for the young woman she had believed was her friend. Kumira, smiling broadly, lifted her head and exclaimed triumphantly, "OOOOOOEEEEEEAAHHH!"

Chapter 43

THE DIVINE HORSEMAN WIELDS A RUSTY SCIMITAR

The still figures of James and Roland stirred within the Vodou circle at the peristyle. Shemo and Alustra approached them, ready to assist as the two Druids oriented back into their bodies.

James sat up slowly, but Roland jumped to his feet. A wild grin distorted his handsome face. Dancing through the Vèvè, he grabbed a woman from the Vodou choir and rubbed himself on her in a blatantly sexual fashion. She screamed and was thrown to the floor. Roland bellowed a sound close to a roar, as he looked around the room. In a split second, he ran out the door. For a moment everyone stood motionless, a frozen tableau. Shouts, car doors slamming, the smell of fire and the screams of the innocent shook the magical group into action.

Shemo, followed by James, ran into the street spotting a car in flames and people huddled on the sidewalk. They watched the form of Roland, possessed by Ogou La Flambo, running towards the French Quarter at an inhuman pace.

Shemo ran for the parking lot on the opposite side of the building and started his van. Barreling down the street, he stopped only long enough for James to jump in. "Where did he go?" James yelled as he hung out of the window.

Shemo shook his head, "He is on the loose. I don't know how we gonna' find him." They continued through the Bywater area looking up and down every cross street. Suddenly, Shemo slammed on the breaks as they neared the railroad tracks past Piety Street. The bodies of half a dozen men lay scattered across the tracks.

James jumped out of the van to investigate. "They are not dead, thankfully. They look like they took a beating, though."

Shemo shook his head in disbelief, "All six of 'em?"

"Yea, unless there was a group brawl going on, this may be Ogou's work."

"I gotta tell ya' this has never happened before," Shemo explained sadly. "He must be taking his reward for agreeing to help on the astral. Oguo La Flambo loves to ride a body and have some fun. His fun usually includes creating chaos."

James looked worried, "I'm concerned about Roland. This spirit could run him to death, get him in bad trouble, get him arrested."

The men lying on the tracks, stirred, some sat up. One man stood and walked around checking on his friends. "Let's keep going," Shemo said, climbing into the van.

After a couple of hours of searching the streets of the Bywater and the Marigny, they parked the van and walked into the French Quarter.

"You want to split up?" James asked.

Shemo shook his head, "No, cause when we find him we gonna' need to restrain him. It will take both of us."

James scowled, "What do mean restrain him?"

"The Loa don't like to be confined. If the horseman is restrained the Loa will depart."

"So you are saying Roland is being ridden, he is a vehicle and once the vehicle can no longer act out the will of Ogou La Flambo, he will be released?"

"Tha's right. At least, tha's what I'm hopin' is right."

James heard the tinge of fear in Shemo's voice which worried him more than he wanted to admit.

Walking slowly through the main aisle of the huge open market on the edge of the French Quarter, James and Shemo scanned the crowd.

"This is going to take forever, there are hundreds of booths and look at the number of people," James said, discouraged.

Shemo rubbed his chin and frowned, "We're lookin for a

278

disturbance in the pattern. We can't possibly examine every face. Look for an area that is hyper energized or disturbed."

James's face lit up, "Ah, yes, that makes sense and makes it easier."

The two men turned the corner and entered the aisle on the far left of the market. "There!" James exclaimed, pointing to one of the stalls. The display table was pushed out into the aisle and there was a police officer talking to the agitated vender.

"What happened here?" James asked the guy selling tie dye shirts in the next stall.

"Craziness, man. This dude came up to Omar's display and picked up this old scimitar he has had for sale for years. This long haired guy looked mellow until he waved the big, old, curved knife over he head. The look on his face was scary. Omar yelled at him, but the guy was, like, deaf. Finally, Omar tried to grab him but the dude swung the scimitar at him. He was going to take Omar's head off with it. Omar went running back behind the display table. He told the guy he could have the scimitar. He wanted him to get outta' here, man."

James nodded, "How long did it take the police to get here?"

The tie dye salesman glanced at his watch, "About half an hour."

Shemo cursed under his breath, "Did you see where he headed?"

"He cut across the area with the displays on the ground and disappeared around the corner."

James and Shemo exchanged glances as they set off at a run. Ogou La Flambo running through the French Quarter brandishing a scimitar was not good.

'Where would he go?' The two priests thought simultaneously.

Shemo stood still, closed his eyes and shook his head in frustration, 'Anywhere he wants to go.' They searched for another fruitless hour and decided to return to the Peristyle.

The magical group was performing a ritual scrying for Roland.

They looked up as James and Shemo entered. The two men could tell, from their distraught expressions, they had been equally unsuccessful in their endeavors.

The sun was making its slow descent into the river, when Jolene announced she was ready to close the circle at the Peristyle and return to Panthea's. "We are exhausted. We have been scrying for hours with no results. Let's have something to eat, get some rest and resume our search."

After a light dinner, the group gathered again. James had slept for a bit, but still looked exhausted. They divided the areas of the French Quarter, Rampart Street and the Desire Housing Project between them. James nodded to each member as he explained, "We will search these areas and regroup here by 10PM. If anyone finds him, restrain him quickly."

Sabine handed keys to the team, "Try to return here immediately. This is the key to the gate. Get Roland back into the courtyard. If he is calm, get him into the meditation temple. If not, tie him to one of the gallery poles. I will be placing rope on the iron bench closest to the fountain."

"This can't be happening," Lilly cried.

Alustra and Shemo spoke up simultaneously, "It won't be necessary to restrain him for more than a few minutes, Lilly. Once the vehicle is stopped, Ogou La Flambeau's fun will be over. He will exit Roland's body quickly."

Lilly nodded numbly, as Jolene put her arms around her and held her for a moment. She turned Lilly towards her and moved her hands up to Lilly's shoulders, "You have got to be strong. Roland is going to need you. We will find him. All will be well."

Lilly nodded as the group spoke as one voice, "So mote it be."

Lucky and Claude headed towards Rampart Street. Shemo and Alustra decided to drive the van into the housing project adjacent to the French Quarter. Jolene, James and Lilly headed for Bourbon Street. The search was underway and everyone squared their shoulders and put on a determined face. Each member secretly nursed a heavy heart and the fear Roland would not survive his possession by an unrestrained Loa.

It was a moonless night with dark clouds scuttling across the sky. A cold drizzle began which made sure they were all miserable. Alustra and Shemo parked their van and went door to door through the housing project asking about a wild white man, wielding a curved knife. Some of the tenants laughed, some looked terrified, some simply slammed the door in their faces.

Lilly had a photo of she and Roland taken on Mardi Gras day. She was going to show it around to people, but the Roland in the picture with his Van Dyke beard, smooth cheeks, lacy collar and plumed hat looked nothing like the possessed man running through the area with a rusty scimitar.

After walking up a few blocks on Bourbon Street, James led Jolene and Lilly towards a side street. "I'm feeling we need to head over this way and get off of Bourbon Street." Picking their way gingerly over the bricks of the banquette, slick with spilled beer, they cut over to the seedier end of Chartres Street.

"There is an old apothecary shop on one of these blocks. The owner deals in herbs, St. John's root and magical supplies. He conducts rituals of some sort in the back of the apothecary. Let's go take a look."

Lilly gave a quizzical look at James, "Later," he whispered. Although it began to rain, Jolene had brought along a couple of umbrellas and they pressed close together, avoiding puddles and derelicts huddling in doorways.

They stopped in front of a dimly lit shop. Apothecary of the Magical Light was lettered in gold across a large plate glass window. Lilly put her hand on the window and peered in. Two huge Doberman pincers jumped in front of her face, barking madly, slobbering and wild eyed on the other side of the glass. Lilly jumped back, startled by the ferocity of the animals.

James made for the front door. "Wait," Lilly yelled, "The

dogs."

The dogs turned to give chase as James strode into the store. The Druid stopped, extended one hand out, palm up and made a small gesture towards the two canines. The dogs stood, whimpering, bound to the wooden floor. Jolene and Lilly gingerly entered, continuing to stand close to the door.

"Is anyone here?" James called out.

A hand pulled aside a curtain covering a doorway in the back of the shop. A thin, bearded man responded rudely, "I'm here, what do you want?"

"We are looking for a white man with dark hair and beard. He may be carrying a large curved knife. Have you seen anyone fitting this description?"

"Yea, the crazy bastard was in here. He came in and went right for the herbs," he said as he pointed to hundreds of glass jars on shelves behind a long counter.

"I couldn't tell what he was looking for. He seemed to have a lot to say, but I couldn't understand him. He wasn't speaking English. For a minute, I looked into his eyes and, I swear, he had a haunted look. It was like he was begging for help; I couldn't understand. I've got a magic circle set up in the back room, I thought I could do a banishment and whatever had gotten into this fellow might exit. I signaled for him to follow me into the back. We got back there and everything was cool. I lit some storax and signaled for him to step into the circle.

"He wouldn't move. I made a mistake when I grabbed him by the arm and tried to lead him into the circle. He pulled the knife from his belt, waved it in front of my face, ran to my altar and grabbed the chunk of John the Conqueror root. He ran back into the store and the dogs attacked him. I was afraid they would kill him or he would injure them with the blade. The dogs let him go at my command; the guy was wild eyed. I opened that door," he said pointing at a metal side door. "He ran into the alley."

"Did you call the police?"

"No, no I didn't. No need to get the cops over here; the guy was gone."

"Thank you," James said as he released the spell binding the dogs to the floor and lead Lilly and Jolene out the front door.

Jolene took a long look at James, put her arm through his and walked toward Rue Saint Anne and the comfort of Panthea's. "James, you are exhausted. We cannot do more. You need to be home resting."

"But!" James said, trying to challenge her decision.

Lilly had noticed James's stooped shoulders and haggard face as he learned of Roland's visit to the store. "I agree," she said.

James grabbed Lilly's arm, "What about the crystal? Have you felt anything from the crystal yet?"

Lilly shook her head and let out a heavy sigh, "I have it on, James. It feels cold. Before it was always warm and, sort of, thrumming. Since Regina had it, the violet light is gone, there is no warmth."

She looked inquiringly at Jolene and noticed the puzzled look in her teacher's eyes. Lilly's shoulders sagged and she ground her teeth in frustration.

"Possibly a ritual cleansing at your altar will wake it. Continue wearing it. It may realign with your energy," Jolene suggested wearily.

Lilly squared her shoulders, "I'm ready to try anything. Gently taking James' other arm in her hand she spoke to him in a firm voice, I agree with Jolene. We have done all we can. Walking aimlessly around in the rain is not going to produce any results."

James shook his head, ready to disagree, but Jolene gave an insistent tug on his arm and he knew it was futile to argue. The trio made their way back to the warmth of the kitchen and steaming cups of restorative tea.

The day weighed heavily on Lilly and her two mentors as they sipped their tea in silence. Regardless of their fatigue she decided to speak up, "I thought I had been introduced to all of the magical practitioners in the Quarter. I was surprised you never mentioned the guy at the Apothecary."

James wiped his mouth with a napkin and sat back in his chair, "He is a 3-D practitioner. He has no real power. His magic exists on only one dimension, this one."

Lilly frowned slightly, "What dimension does your magic exist on?"

"I work with energies in multiple dimensions. Those who are playing at magic have no idea how to access multiple dimensions and parallel worlds. The guy at Magical Light is a dabbler. He is merely a dream twister."

Lilly's mouth hung open until James smiled wearily and said, "I don't want you to feel overwhelmed by this information. You will develop your talents over the years. I have had a long life to study and practice multi-dimensional magic."

On Rampart Street, Lucky pulled the hood of his sweatshirt up and Claude pulled his hat over his ears as the rain fell harder. They crossed Esplanade in silence, their eyes peering into the darkness.

Alustra and Shemo pulled to the curb as Lucky and Claude were crossing Elysian Fields Avenue. "Get in," Alustra ordered, "we are feeling some disturbance a few blocks down the street."

They sped through the next few blocks until they heard music. Shemo made a loud grunting noise as the sound of people yelling and crying came through the Motown beat.

Within minutes they drove up in front of a squat looking yellow brick building with big black letters across the entrance, CLUB GEMINI. People were pouring out onto the sidewalk. Many of them held bloody handkerchiefs up to their faces. Scantily clad women were hollering and weeping.

"This must be the place," Lucky said with some relief. Claude pointed to the alley and they went around to the back of the club and entered through the service door. In the smoky gloom of the club, they saw Roland's back as he stood on the bar, a bottle of rum in his left hand and scimitar in his right hand. He was fending off the bar owner with the rusty old knife.

Shemo, Lucky and Claude moved quietly forward and grabbed Roland by the legs. He toppled over backwards. As they caught him and dragged him to the floor, Lucky held Roland still while Shemo pried his fingers from the hilt of the knife and tied his hands with an old bandana he had in his pocket. As Shemo predicted, Roland's body went limp when he was restrained. Alustra grabbed the bottle of rum, poured some into her hand and slapped Roland on the back of the neck signaling Ogou La Flambo his time was up. When the Loa released his hold on him, Roland collapsed into unconsciousness.

The bar owner was picking up the phone to call the police when Shemo intercepted him. "Let's have a talk, okay? My name's Shemo I'm the Mambo Alustra's husband. You see the Mambo over there?"

The owner nodded slowly. "This here is a bit of work gone bad, if you know what I mean. Alustra is gonna be happy we found this young man here in your establishment. She will be in the mood to do some favors for Club Gemini over the next few months."

The owner nodded his head and put the phone back on the receiver. "Glad to be of help," he said cordially as he picked up beer bottles and overturned chairs.

Claude and Lucky dragged Roland out of the club and laid him in the back of the van giving apologetic looks to the irate clubbers standing with bleeding faces in the rain.

Roland slowly lifted one eyelid. Lilly sitting beside the bed moved forward slightly and he opened both eyes. Squinting in pain, he put his hand on his forehead. His voice was hoarse as he croaked, "What happened? Was I in an accident, or am I horribly hung over?" His blurred vision cleared slightly and he could see

Lilly smiling.

Lifting his head she put a glass of water to his lips. Placing a cold damp cloth over his eyes, she made shushing noises and encouraged him to rest. "Time enough for explanations later. You need to rest and get your strength back." Nodding, Roland drifted back to sleep.

Chapter 44

Normal Life?

....

A week had passed since the ritual at the Peristyle. Claude's visits to Hotel Dieu, the hospital where Regina was taken, yielded no information until her parents arrived. They were happy to share details of her condition with her business partner. Regina had a concussion, two broken ankles, a shattered right wrist, and a deep cut along one side of her face. She was scraped and bruised but the doctors expected a complete recovery.

Claude pleaded with Regina's parents for permission to see her. He had to speak with her. After consulting with her doctors, they consented to a short visit.

Standing beside her bed, Claude took Regina's hand and squeezed gently. She opened her eyes and stared at him. He struggled for a moment, not knowing how to approach the vast ocean of questions he had.

Finally he asked the question at the top of the list. "Why did you do it, Regina? What did you hope to gain?"

Regina licked her dry lips and spoke hoarsely, "I want the crystal. I thought I could use it as a time travel device. I need to go back and undo the mistakes my ancestors made, prevent them from squandering the power of the Valraven bloodline.

"Once I had the crystal, it didn't work. It would do nothing. I needed time to research, to find a ritual to make it mine. I need to fix the past." Her voice grew weaker as she spoke, her hand slipped from his and her eyes slowly closed.

The nurse came in and signaled for him to leave. "She needs a great deal of rest, her injuries are severe." Claude nodded and walked into the hallway, closing the door behind him.

He thanked Regina's parents and said goodbye. Mr. Valraven

....

stopped him and insisted Claude take a check and sign legal papers relinquishing his partnership with Regina and their ownership of The Raven Moon.

Claude readily agreed. He wanted nothing more to do with The Raven Moon. Returning to Panthea's he walked with a lighter step.

He reported his conversation with Regina to James, Jolene and Lilly. They were relieved she had survived the fall and would recover.

"The strange thing about my visit," Claude said, "Regina remembered the crystal and why she wanted it. Yet, according to her parents, Regina told them she remembered nothing about her fall or anything about the previous week."

"The doctors assured the Valraven's amnesia could be expected with a concussion. Regina's memory of the events may or may not return. Her parents were concerned and intend to have her air lifted to a hospital near their home in California where she will receive extended care."

James shook his head, "I'd venture to say the extended care will not be very extended. Regina is not one to lay idle. Weaving a web of lies about what she can and cannot remember will be taxing."

"Why did she want the crystal?" Jolene asked.

Claude shook his head, "That is the crazy part. She said she had to go back in time and change something with her ancestors. She thought the crystal was a time travel device."

Jolene and Lilly exchanged glances. Jolene's lips tightened and Lilly nodded slightly.

Roland's memory returned, at least the memory of the astral confrontation with Regina in the attic. His friends were grateful he had no recall of his possession by Ogou La Flambo. There was a silent agreement between everyone concerned that he need not be reminded.

Life at Panthea's returned to some semblance of normal. The shop opened and Jolene, Sabine and Lilly went back to work. James spent hours with Roland teaching him the ways of the Druids. Lucky headed for New York to attend his art opening.

Claude couldn't return to his apartment over The Raven Moon. Jolene was happy to have him as a tenant at Panthea's. He moved into the apartment next to Madeline. Her relationship with Chas had fizzled and he had returned to his family. Madeline, already acquainted with Claude, was delighted to have him for a neighbor.

Roland was staying with Lilly, but they both knew it wasn't a permanent arrangement. The apartment was too small for the two of them and Roland still had an obligation to The Green Man Band. He wanted to spend a few more weeks training with James before he flew to Boston to reconnect with the Band. Once their gigs in Boston and New York City were done, he would return to New Orleans permanently.

Lilly, immersed in her life with Roland and her efforts to revive the Priestess Crystal, paid little attention to her mentors for several weeks. Her first day back at work, she was shocked to see a change in James when he sauntered through the shop on his way to an appointment. His shoulders seemed stooped and the snow white hair at his temples had expanded. The change in his appearance prompted Lilly to take a closer look at Jolene. Has her hair always had so many silver strands? Did her cheeks always sag a bit? She stole glances at Jolene throughout the day. The changes were subtle, but she was certain they were there.

It is the loss of the Priestess crystal, Lilly thought with a sinking heart. Jolene who appeared to be a spry fifty something had already told her she was seventy-five years old. James was older by five years. Fear and grief clutched at Lilly's heart, I cannot loose these two beautiful, people, she vowed to herself.

After work, Lilly followed Jolene back into her kitchen pretending she wanted a cup of tea. Jolene invited Lilly to sit while she prepared tea for both of them. Lilly sat across from Jolene and looked in her beloved friend's eyes. She spoke with resolve, "Jolene, I must speak with you about something of great importance." Jolene nodded as she sipped tea. "I want to return the Priestess crystal to you. Obviously, I am not ready to have it. I made a mess of things! I was easily duped and fell in with the first sorceress who flattered me with her friendship. The crystal should be returned to you. I will happily accept it in a few years."

Jolene grimaced slightly, "I've been anticipating this, Lilly. First let me tell you I will not accept the crystal from you. I was expecting you would feel guilt and remorse and try to return it. I also know you are noticing I am looking my true age."

Lilly's voice sounded strained when she responded, "Yes. It makes perfect sense. I am not ready to be responsible for the crystal and I need you here for many more years healthy and vibrant. You are my teacher and I am not done learning."

Jolene pressed her lips together and blinked away tears before she looked up at Lilly. "You were chosen by the crystal. Encountering Regina and falling into her trap was part of your learning. Everyone is your teacher. All life experiences are for your edification. No need to judge yourself harshly, life's lessons are learned as they occur. You benefit from the lessons through integrating your experience into your being. Those experiences and your responses to them, are the foundation of wisdom."

"Secondly, I have had a long and happy life. It is unnatural to prolong it beyond what seems reasonable. You don't have to worry. I am not on death's doorstep. I have many more years here on earth."

"It would be selfish of you to deny me the natural order of my life and to burden me with the ownership of the crystal. It is your burden and your joy, there is no way you can surrender it. We made an agreement beyond the veil of illusion, before we accepted incarnation into this life. We agreed to assist, yet not coddle one another.

SUPERNATURAL INTERVENTION

"I have taken on the role of teacher in this lifetime, but we have had been many life times when you were the teacher. All knowledge is available. Teachings, books, rituals merely shake the memories loose so you may bring them into present time. You have a great deal of time and energy. There is no hurry. Everything is unfolding perfectly. We cannot retrace our steps, we can only go forward into the ever present now."

Tears battled with an incredulous smile as Lilly took Jolene's hands into hers. "I have been your teacher? How can it be? I feel so small compared to your enormous wisdom and power. If you say it is so, I believe you. I will try to be worthy of the teachings you share with me. I think losing my Aunt Pearl so suddenly when I was a child has scarred my heart. I worry about those I love disappearing. First my dad was gone, then Aunt Pearl disappeared. When Roland left I almost lost my mind. The thought of losing you is more than I can bear."

Jolene squeezed her hand, "Take heart sweet Lilly, you are not about to lose me. Changing the subject she said, "In fact, I think its time you actively search for information about your Aunt Pearl. I also want to know what became of her. Did she pass away or was she threatened into leaving her home and breaking her connection with you?"

Lilly looked shocked, "Who would do such a thing? Why would my Aunt Pearl agree to such an arrangement? She may be dead, but I would like to know how and when and I'd also like to know where she is buried."

Jolene nodded as she stood up, "Possibly James can lead you into a hypnotic trance to help you recall details of your time with her. There may be small things, clues you've forgotten. "

"I'm open to it," Lilly said.

"Okay, it is settled, I will speak with James."

Lilly smiled, nodded and stood to leave. She opened the kitchen door and Topaz scooted through her legs, announcing he was ready for his dinner. Lilly turned and said, "Thank you, dear

SUPERNATURAL INTERVENTION

Jolene," as she headed to her apartment.

Lilly and Roland strolled by the river in the purple haze of twilight. They walked silently for a while and stood together looking over the dark waters. The moon rose and, still, neither of them had broached the subject of their future together. They watched the Cotton Blossom paddle boat leave its dock along the shore. With hundreds of lights bobbing and swaying the boat made its way out to the center of the river. From where they stood on the shore, they could hear the music from the calliope gradually fading as the paddle boat disappeared down the river. Lilly glanced at Roland, surprised to see tears on his face. "What is it, baby? Are you feeling sad tonight?"

Roland rubbed his hand over his face and quickly flashed her an embarrassed smile, "I'm feeling nostalgic for the city I haven't left yet and I'm thinking about you and how much I will miss you."

Lilly took his hand, "It will only be for a short while, a week, two the at most. The city will be here when you get back. I will be here too, if I don't get myself abducted by another evil sorceress," she said with a grim laugh.

"I'm glad you can laugh at your misadventure," Roland said. "I'm not able to think of it as amusing. Frankly, I'm more concerned about the way Claude looks at you and the unwavering and unashamed way Lucky stares at you. Who knows? You may be involved in a ménage à trois by the time I get back."

Lilly stepped back and looked up into his face. For a moment he looked deadly serious then suddenly burst into the contagious laugh she loved.

"A threesome is not going to happen, you can rest easy," she assured him. "However, the fellow who comes in for tarot readings five days a week, he may be a contender."

It was Roland's turn to be surprised, "What guy?"

Lilly laughed and said, "Gottcha." Their light hearted banter continued as they headed out to meet Gemma, Forest, Owen, Madeline, and Claude for Roland's bon voyage dinner.

Chapter 45

MANUAL NEEDED

James put his coffee mug carefully on the arm of the couch and looked at Lilly with his gentle eyes, "How are you doing, Lilly?"

"I'm okay. Planning the Spring Equinox ritual is fun. It's giving me something to think about and look forward to. I miss Roland terribly, even though I know he will be back soon."

James nodded, as he wrapped his hands around the warmth of his coffee cup. He turned to look at Lilly again, "And the crystal?"

Lilly shook her head as her mouth turned down slightly, "The fog within it seems to be clearing, although the violet light has not returned."

Jolene leaned forward from her seat in the rocking chair, "Don't worry Lilly, I know you can fix this. I believe the crystalline structure of the stone will respond to a certain set of energies and reset itself."

"You mean there may be some sort of ritual I can do?"

Jolene shrugged her shoulders, "I don't know of any rituals. It may need time to recalibrate and reactivate."

A frustrated sigh escaped from deep in Lilly's chest. "There was no manual or grimoire with the crystal when you received it? Information about how to awaken the violet light must be somewhere!"

Jolene shook her head. Suddenly, there was a light in her eyes, "There is not a grimoire, however, we know a savvy Atlantean Priestess who might have some ideas about what, where and when an ancient crystal may be restored."

Lilly sat up, "Kumira!"

The next afternoon Lilly sat on the sofa in Kumira's elegant living room overlooking Royal Street. The pair sipped guava juice, nibbled on banana chips and discussed the reactivation of the Priestess crystal.

Kumira brushed crumbs off her hand and took the stone Lilly held out to her. "There are a number of things used to activate a crystal. This one is ancient and contains great potential. I believe there may be a combination of things which may awaken it."

Lilly leaned forward, "A combination of what things?"

Kumira sighed deeply, "Possibly a combination of heat, light, sound, gamma rays and the energy of consciousness. When specific vibratory frequencies and energy transmissions come together, I believe the crystal will reactivate."

Lilly shook her head in frustration, "I have no idea where I can find those elements together and what about the specific amounts? How can I find out what, how much and where they might occur?"

Kumira stared at her for a moment. With the Inanna crystal clutched in her hand, she closed her eyes and sat back in her plush purple velvet chair.

Lilly followed her lead, closed her eyes and took long cleansing breaths, relaxing into meditation.

Shadows were creeping across the ornate Persian carpet when Lilly heard mumbling. Her eyes flew open. The ancient Atlantian priest, his crystal topped staff in hand, stood beside the now empty purple chair.

The ancient priest, while wiry limbed, stood straight and strong and spoke directly to Lilly. "The power lies in the pyramid where two great waters meet. Beneath the stones, within the temple, the portal leads to healing light to set the gem aflame once more."

Lilly nodded and opened her mouth to ask, "Where do the waters meet? What pyramid?" Without knowing how or when, Lilly saw Kumira sitting in her velvet chair, the priest was no where in sight.

"Did you get that child?" Kumira asked, reaching for her glass of juice.

Lilly nodded, "There is a pyramid where two great waters meet. Inside there is a portal leading to healing light that will ignite the violet flame."

Kumira quirked her mouth to one side and made a loud hmmmmm! "I've been hearing about this pyramid for years. It appears circumstances have come together and now is the time to find it."

Lilly looked worried, "Have you any idea where it is?"

"Uh huh, I have an idea. I would like to speak to someone who could help verify what I think I know. It would be great to find a guide to lead us." Kumira cleared her throat and spoke tentatively, "Lilly, if I remember correctly, you have relatives in South Louisiana. Do you think one or more of them might be willing to act as guides through the Deep Bayou?"

Lilly gave a sarcastic snort, "My Mama and Rex may live near the bayou, but I can promise you they do not venture deep into it or know anything about a pyramid. They would ridicule us mercilessly if we asked for their help. The only things they believe in are money, power and the Catholic church."

"I'm not thinking about your mother and stepfather. Didn't your father have interesting family in the bayou?"

Lilly heart sped, "Yes, my dad took me to visit them a few times when I was young. Frankly, I don't know how to find them. I tried several times after my dad disappeared. I could never reach them. I would catch a glimpse of the village and row towards it, but the more I rowed, the further away it moved. It must be shielded in some way."

"It sounds like a telescoping spell. The right person would know how to counter it," Kumira said. "You are of their bloodline. If you could not get past the shield, we will need someone who knows how to dispel it and get us to the bayou faeries. They are the ones who hold ancient knowledge and know the lay of the

295

land in South Louisiana."

Lilly's heart continued to pound, "It is dangerous in the bayou. There are alligators and supernatural entities. People make fun of the stories of Lougarou, but my dad assured me the stories were not all myths."

Kumira frowned, "Ah, Lougarou, one more thing to worry about! Legends say he is only a problem for humans when the moon is full. Let's make sure we venture out early in the day and not the full moon."

Lilly heaved a sigh, "There are more dangers than Lougarou. My dad told me there were weirder things lurking in the dark waters, hidden behind the cypress knees and hanging moss. I'm willing to venture out and find the Faery village. It may be the only hope we have."

Kumira pursed her lips, her face grew calm before she spoke. "A challenging adventure, to be sure. Your father was instilling respect for the energies of the Dark Bayou in you. He didn't want you venturing out on your own when you were a child. Together, I'm sure we will be safe. We have work to do. Let me think on it, talk to some of my people. I know it will all come together at the perfect time," she said calmly ending their visit with a gentle, "OOOOO, EEEEE, AAAHHH."

The late afternoon sunlight stained the clouds crimson as the sky slowly faded to indigo. Madeline, Claude, Lucky, Gemma and Sabine were sitting together in the courtyard when Lilly arrived home. Her heart leaped as she saw her friends waiting for her. She filled them in on her visit to Kumira. The group sat silently for a few minutes contemplating the situation.

Claude spoke up, "Lilly, I promised you I would help you find your aunt. You said she was your dad's sister and she was a magical being. It seems to me, she may be the person who could lead us to the rest of your family in the bayou."

Lilly's face lit up for a moment but her smile quickly faded.

"She might be dead by now. I haven't heard from her in years. If she is not, I have no idea where to find her."

Sabine spoke with a gentle voice, "Jolene spoke to you about having James hypnotize you. Accessing your deep subconscious mind could reveal a hidden clue, something you have forgotten or missed."

"Yes, I'm going to take James up on the offer for a hypnosis session. I hope it reveals a clue to where she has gone. I don't want to get my hopes up and be disappointed."

"Hypnotic recall or not," Claude said, taking her hand, "I promised I would help you find her and I meant it. Hiring a private investigator, would be the quickest way.

Lucky nodded his head, "I'm in, I can help with the payment for a private eye."

Sabine spoke up, "I'm in too. I'll be glad to help with the finances and anything else you need."

Lilly looked at their serious faces and had to smile, "I can't believe we're sitting around talking about hiring a private investigator, it's so *film noir.*"

Madeline giggled, Claude ignored her and said decisively, "*Film noir* or not, we are going to search for Pearl." The friends all nodded in agreement.

The moon had risen above the rooftops when the phone rang in Lilly's apartment. "Hello, Lilly, it's James. Are you up to exploring some things through hypnotic trance this evening?" She agreed, threw a sweater over her shoulders, and made her way down the stairs and across the courtyard.

The temple was dimly lit with one candle burning on a low table. James instructed her to lie comfortably on the velvet cushions. He put a light blanket over her and casually suggested she relax.

He sat on a cushion beside her and his gentle, melodic voice guided her attention to the top of her head, "Lilly, you become aware of a wave of relaxation at the top of your head. As the wave

297

of relaxation moves over your head, you feel the muscles in your scalp release and relax. The relaxing wave moves over your forehead and all the muscles relax, all furrows and lines of concern melt away in the wave of relaxation. As the wave moves over your eyes, allow all the tiny muscles in your eyes to relax, feel your eyes sinking into the eye sockets as you relax. Your eyelids are feeling so heavy you cannot keep your eyes open...you may try to open your eyes, you will find they are so relaxed, so heavy you cannot manage to open them.

Allowing the wave of relaxation to do its work, Lilly's body lay limp and relaxed within minutes. Her mind was focused on James's voice as he lead her awareness back through the years.

"Lilly, you are with your Aunt Pearl. It is the last time you see her. Tell me how old you are and where you are."

"It is summer, I'm fourteen. I'm with my Aunt Pearl for my summer visit at her house in Abita Springs."

"Is your Aunt Pearl in good health?"

"Yes."

"At any time during your summer visit does Aunt Pearl mention leaving her home permanently?"

James waited patiently as Lilly lay still and quiet for several minutes.

"No, we are making plans for my visit during Christmas vacation."

"When did you leave Aunt Pearl's house for the last time?

There was another long pause and James saw tears running from the corner of Lilly's eyes.

"My Mama and Rex come to pick me up in the middle of August. I don't want to leave."

"Why Lilly, why don't you want to leave?"

"Being with Aunt Pearl is my true home."

"What happens when your Mama and Rex arrive?"

"I am begging Rex and Mama to let me stay, live with Aunt Pearl and go to school in Abita Springs. They are angry. Mama

298

gives me her mean look. Rex grabs my arm and drags me to the car."

"What happens when you left Aunt Pearl's house? Are you on the trip back to your parent's house?"

"Yes, I am sitting in the back seat of the car crying. I am angry with Mama and Rex. I hate them. I...I...am afraid. I have felt the sting of Rex's leather strap and I don't want any more of it. I am sad. I lay back and watched the stars through the back window of the car."

"Do Rex or your mother say anything to you or each other?"

"Yes, they think I'm asleep. I'm not and I hear them talking."

"What are they saying?"

"Rex is angry and he says, 'This has got to end, I don't want her around Pearl again.' Mama shushes him and whispers, 'She loves Pearl. She would never agree to not seeing her again. We will have one hell of a rebellious teenager on our hands if you try such tactics.' Rex makes a nasty snorting sound. His voice is cruel, 'Not if Pearl were dead.' Mama gasps. I can hear the fear in her voice as she tells Rex, "That is not going to happen!" Rex nods his head, 'No, but Lilly will think it did.'"

"When you get to your home in LaPoint, do your mother or Rex mention Aunt Pearl again?"

Lilly was quiet for several minutes as her mind traveled through time.

"Where are you now, Lilly?"

"I'm in my bedroom. Mama comes in and tells me Aunt Pearl has died suddenly of a heart attack. I start to cry. Mama says, 'She didn't suffer and she died in her garden.' 'I don't believe you!' I scream. I couldn't stop screaming. Rex came into my room, removing his belt. He was hitting me and bellowing about respecting my mama." Lilly was shaking and crying. James gently lead her away from the memories of abuse into a relaxed and peaceful place.

"In the following years, did you hear your mother or Rex

SUPERNATURAL INTERVENTION

mention Aunt Pearl?"

"No."

"Have you ever returned to her home in Abita Springs, and if so, when?"

"Yes, the spring after I got my drivers license I took mama's car and drove to Aunt Pearl's house. It was empty and looked as if it had been empty for a long time. The garden was overgrown with weeds. The kumquat tree was heavy with fruit and leaning over the tall fence near the garden." Her body tensed as she struggled with emotion. James spoke calmly, bringing her gently back.

"In a few minutes you will come back into your normal waking awareness. You will remember all conversations, insights and scenes you accessed during this session. You will feel calm and grateful. You now have useful information concerning your Aunt Pearl."

Lilly opened her eyes, took a deep breath and sat up. She looked at James with tears in her eyes, "I always thought they lied to me. Now I know, with certainty, they did. She didn't die."

James agreed "Yes, it was a ruse to keep you away from her. Your Aunt's power and her loving heart threatened their need to control."

"You're right, James. I still don't know why she agreed to disappear but I am going to find her."

Chapter 46

Psychic P.I.

The next evening Claude knocked on Lilly's door. He had the thick New Orleans Yellow Pages in his hand. "Let's find a private eye, ok?" Lilly brought the phone with its long cord from her bedroom and sat next to Claude on the couch. Claude ran his finger down the lists of Private Investigators. He stopped suddenly and exclaimed, "Here he is!"

"Which one,"

"This guy here, Vic Benton, Psychic P.I."

Lilly sat back on the couch and laughed, "A Psychic P.I.? I didn't know such a person existed."

"One way to find out," Claude said as he picked up the receiver and dialed Vick Benton's phone number.

Vic Benton Psychic P.I.'s office was located on the wrong end of Magazine Street above a junk shop next to a dive bar. Lilly knocked timidly on the frosted glass door. Claude and Lucky stood on either side of her. A strong voice, invited them in. They introduced themselves and sat on wooden chairs in front of Vic's battered desk. Immediately Vic's attention focused on Lilly. "You are the one searching for a relative, correct?"

Lilly nodded and decided to say nothing more. 'Let's see how much he can read without my giving him a verbal clue, she said to herself.'

"It is a female relative, someone who has been missing for many years," Vic said with a note of inquiry at the end of his statement. Lilly nodded. Vic leaned back in his chair, smiled and said, "So, tell me everything you know and I will see how I can help you."

Lilly spent the next few minutes telling him the story of her

301

SUPERNATURAL INTERVENTION

Aunt Pearl. She finished with her visit to the empty house in Abita Springs.

Vic took notes as she spoke. After she had shared her story, he had a barrage of questions. "Do you know her birthdate? Was she married, was McAllen her married name? Does she have children?"

Lilly answered the questions easily. "Aunt Pearl was my father's sister so her birth name was LaCouer, the same as mine. Her married name had been McAllen. Her birth date was June 9. She and Uncle Liam had a son, Evan, who is grown, in his thirties by now. He didn't live closeby. We saw him on Christmas and other holidays. I have no idea where he lives."

"What type of person was Pearl? Did she have a lot of friends? What were her interests?"

"My Aunt Pearl was a healer, gardener and herbalist. Everyone loved her. She had lots of friends. I have spoken with her neighbors and friends and no one knows where she went."

Vic rocked back in his office chair and nodded. He closed his eyes and Lilly saw him sigh deeply. She thought he had drifted off to sleep when he sat up and spoke, "I'm seeing mountains when you speak of her and her son. Her husband has passed away?" Lilly nodded. "Do you know if your Aunt Pearl or her son had any relatives or friends in the mountains?"

"Oh," Lilly said sitting up straight, "she did have a friend in the mountains. They spoke on the phone sometimes. Aunt Pearl often said she would like to go visit her. I don't remember her name."

Vic took out an empty folder and wrote Pearl McAllen on the tab. He looked at Lilly and quoted his fee. Lucky reached in his pocket, pulled out his checkbook and made a generous deposit to Mr. Benton. Taking the check he responded, "Thank you, I'll be in touch, I have your number."

Lucky, Lilly and Claude were smiling broadly as they came out into the late winter sunshine on Magazine Street. "Let's celebrate," Lucky said. Soon they were in the van headed to the West End for dinner at Fitzgerald's.

A week passed and Lilly had to restrain from calling Vic Benton again to inquire about the investigation. Sabine, Jolene and James urged her to be patient and visualize a positive outcome. 'Easier said than done,' was her inner response.

Several weeks passed. Lilly was working in the shop, silently worrying that Lucky had paid Vic Benton for nothing. She was waiting on a customer when the door between the shop and Jolene's kitchen opened. She heard Lucky talking in excited tones. Her hands shook as she hurriedly wrapped her customer's newly purchased crystal ball, placed in a box and collected payment. '*Of all the times to have a chatty customer,*' Lilly thought, as the young woman lingered, obviously wanting to talk. Lilly walked to the front door of the shop, opened it and had to refrain from tossing the girl out. "Thanks for coming in," she said politely signaling the young woman it was time to go. She locked the door as soon as her customer walked through it. Turning back into the shop, Lilly could here more voices coming from Jolene's kitchen. She ran through the store into the kitchen to see what the excitement was all about.

"Ah, Lilly, I have good news! Our P.I. appears have a lead on your Aunt Pearl. He has located a woman living in North Carolina who may be your Aunt. I don't want you to get your hopes up too much, but this sounds like a good lead."

Lilly returned Lucky's penetrating gaze, "How did he find her? What did he learn? When will we know if it is her?"

"The first thing Benton did was check with utility companies in every state with mountains. He used Pearl's name and her son's name. The name P.V. McAllen pops up in Western North Carolina for electricity and gas. He checked with the public libraries. In Asheville NC there is a library card issued from the Haw Creek library to P.V. McAllen. According to Vic this confirms his findings. The utility bills give us the exact address."

"Vic gave me the phone number he got from the telephone people in Asheville. He can call her, or you can call her, or we can pay him to go to North Carolina and see if it is her."

Lilly grabbed the piece of paper Lucky was holding and ran to the phone next to the cash register in the shop. She quickly dialed the number and held her breath as she heard it ringing. It rang ten times and she was about to hang up when a breathless voice answered, "Oh, hello."

Lilly's hand shook and dropped the receiver. Lucky, standing next to her, caught it and put it to his ear. The breathless voice repeated, "Hello, hello?"

Lucky took a breath and began, "Mam, I'm sorry to disturb your afternoon, but I have a friend with me who has been looking for her aunt for sometime. Her aunt's name is Pearl. Do you know her or possibly are you Pearl from Abita Springs, Louisiana?

Dead air from the other end of the line. Lucky heard the phone hit the floor in North Carolina. After a few moments, the breathless voice spoke. "Yes, it is me. What is the young ladies name?"

Lucky smiled, "I'll let you talk to her and she can tell you herself."

Lilly spoke through tears, "Aunt Pearl, its me, Lilly."

The phone at Panthea's Pantry was tied up for a solid hour as Lilly and Pearl caught up on each others lives. Exhausting the basic information Lilly exclaimed, "Aunt Pearl, I need you here."

Without hesitation, Pearl declared, "I'm coming. I will catch the first flight I can. Give me your number so I can let you know my arrival time."

Lilly hung up the phone shaking her head. "I can't believe it! After all these years, she is on the phone. She will be here soon, maybe tomorrow or the next day."

Throwing her arms around Lucky, she thanked him, took his hand and ran up to Claude's apartment to give him the good news.

SUPERNATURAL INTERVENTION

Once they had toasted their success with cold bottles of Dixie 45, Lilly called Vic Benton to tell him the good news and thank him. "If it weren't for your psychic abilities, we would never have found her. The simple fact you saw mountains made all the difference. I am going to spread the word about your talent Mr. Benton. You deserve a much nicer office and I hope to see you get it."

Lilly joined Lucky, Claude and Madeline for dinner in Lucky's apartment. After dinner Lucky brought out a bottle of champagne, filled glasses for everyone and raised his glass, "A toast to Vic Benton, Psychic P.I."

When the champagne glasses were filled for the second time, Lilly raised her glass, "A toast to my friends, I am grateful for your assistance."

The group clinked their glasses together. Claude spoke up, "We love you Lilly and we were happy to help." Everyone clinked glasses again.

When the second bottle of champagne was opened, Lilly thanked Lucky for the dinner, hugged her friends and returned to her apartment. She wanted some quiet time to process the wonderful turn her life had taken.

She sat before the altar beside her bed. Lighting a new white candle, she thanked her guardians, guides and ancestors. She knew their assistance had played a part in leading her to Vic Benton and locating Aunt Pearl quickly.

The only heaviness in her heart, as she sat in gratitude, was the missing piece traveling with Roland. She wished he was here to celebrate with her and meet Aunt Pearl when she got off the plane.

Extinguishing the candles on her altar, Lilly climbed into bed, turned off the bedside lamp, curled around her pillow and closed her eyes. The sound of Roland's mandolin and his loving voice

SUPERNATURAL INTERVENTION

filled her mind as she remembered his song to her, "Moonlight falls on a red heart candle…" She drifted to sleep with his song in her heart.

Chapter 47

A Pearl Beyond Price

The sun was rising, when Lilly awoke to a persistent tapping on her front door. "What the dickens?" she thought, as she tied her pink fuzzy robe around her. Peaking through the fish eye on the front door, she squealed, threw open the door and flew into Roland's arms. "Now, everything is perfect!" she said.

The phone next to Lilly's bed rang at 8:30AM. Roland was closest to the phone and grabbed blindly for it. "Hello," he said sleepily.

"Uh, hello. A reticent voice spoke from the other end of the line, I am calling for my niece, Lilly. Is this her number?"

Roland sat up perfectly straight, shaking Lilly gently, he responded, "Yes, yes it is. Here she is."

Lilly shook her curls out of her eyes and took the phone. "Hi, this is Lilly," she said in the most alert voice she could muster.

"Lilly, this is Aunt Pearl. My flight is arriving at 3:17 this afternoon. Shall I take a cab to your apartment?"

"No, no! No way you are going to take a cab. I'm going to be there to pick you up." Lilly hung up the phone and bounded out of bed. "She will be here this afternoon! I have to talk with Lucky. I want to borrow his van to go pick her up at the airport."

Roland sat up, "Why borrow it? Why not get him to drive us out there?"

Lilly shook her head, "I don't want to arrive with a posse. It has been more than ten years since I have seen her. I want her to myself for a while."

"So, are you going to drive the van or do you want me to come along?"

Tilting her head and grinning she jumped back onto the bed

and into his arms, "Hell yea! You are coming. I'm not letting you or Aunt Pearl out of my sight!"

Roland laughed, tumbled Lilly over onto the other side of the bed and rolled with her, landing on top. "She's not getting here until this afternoon. For now, you are mine alone." He kissed her and Lilly threw her arms around him. A few moments later her legs circled his body.

Their love making was swift and passionate. They fell asleep curled together and awoke again for lingering kisses and more slow, deliberate love making. It was noon when they climbed into the shower together.

Lilly called Lucky on the phone and arranged to use his van, while Roland made coffee and heated up two croissant.

The drive to the airport took forever. Lilly found herself biting her nails and twisting her hair. "You nervous about something, baby?"

Lilly took a deep breath, "I don't know why I am feeling so jittery. I haven't seen her in so long and I don't know what to say."

Roland laughed, "Knowing you, my love, I'm sure you will think of something. Plus, you will do it rapidly and appropriately. It's the way you roll. I've seen you rise to the occasion more than once."

"I'm glad to hear you have confidence in my social skills."

"Yep, you are more together than you know. Stop worrying and enjoy the anticipation of being reunited with her. It is going to be super groovy."

"I love when you talk hippie to me," Lilly said, laughing.

She saw the rosy glow of her Aunt before she spotted her white blond hair and serene face in the line of passengers spilling out of the airplane. In only a moment, Aunt Pearl was there before her smiling brightly, a divine blush infusing her entire being.

Lilly stood still for a moment, taking in the presence of the woman she had loved so dearly and missed for so long. Aunt Pearl opened her arms and pulled Lilly gently into an embrace. "It has

308

been too long," she said in her musical voice.

Lilly put her arms gently around her, afraid she was an apparition and would disappear into air. "I can't believe this is happening. It is really you!" she said at last, stepping back to get a good look at Aunt Pearl's face.

Pearl's green eyes shown as she smiled, "Is it you Lilly, all grown up and beautiful with red hair?"

Lilly's hand flew to the curly mop on top of her head, "I'll explain it later on," she said as Roland stepped up to her side. She introduced him to her Aunt and the three of them headed to baggage claim.

Tiny tears glimmered on Lilly's eyelashes as they stepped into the sunny parking lot. "What is it Lilly? I'm hoping those are tears of joy," Aunt Pearl said.

"Oh, they are tears of joy. It has been an amazing twenty-four hours for me. Roland has been away and he surprised me around dawn this morning with his return. Now, I am here with you and it is a dream come true."

Pearl smiled, "For me too, my love" she said as tears sparkled in her eyes.

Once Pearl was settled in the open apartment next to Sabine's, Lilly told her to put on her walking shoes. "I'm taking you to eat at one of the best restaurants in the city." Pearl nodded enthusiastically.

Soon the two women were strolling arm in arm down the quiet blocks of Chartres street towards the Marigny and Valentine's Restaurant. Gumbo and crawfish pie were placed before them and for a while there was no talking. The waitress came over to check on them and Pearl ordered bread pudding with rum sauce for desert. Looking across the table at Lilly she licked her lips and said, "It is so great to be back where food is rich and spicy."

Lilly agreed, "So where have you been? Why did you leave and why didn't you...?"

Pearl put her hand up and shook her head gently, "One thing

309

at a time. I know you have a million questions, first let me say it was never my intention to hurt you. I did not want to leave my home and I didn't want to leave you. I was threatened, you see. Threatened with my life and yours, if I did not comply with the *request*."

Lilly's green eyes narrowed as her mouth pulled into an angry grimace. "Who?"

Pearl took a breath, "It was your stepfather, Rex."

Lilly's hand slammed on the table and she exploded, "I knew it! He is a low life bastard."

Aunt Pearl nodded in agreement and took Lilly's hand in hers. "He is a dangerous man. I have seen things in his aura which lead me to believe he may have committed murder in the past. From the look in his eyes and the swirling darkness around him, I believed him when he promised to make you disappear by accident. He scared me thoroughly. I agreed to leave my home."

"I am so sorry Aunt Pearl. I feel terrible. Your home was such a refuge and your gardens, your beautiful gardens…."

"It is not your fault, Lilly. Rex is filled with fear and anger. He sensed you and I are different. To a man like Rex, different is dangerous."

Lilly's face darkened as she stared at her Aunt for a moment, "Who do you think Rex murdered?"

"I'm not certain. It is a feeling I hesitate to look deeply into. For a long time I ignored my intuition regarding Rex's activities. I adopted a better not to know attitude. You are no longer a child living under his roof. You and I are free to do what we please. I tried to contact you several times. I called all the universities in Louisiana, but none would confirm you were a student there. I get the Times Picayune delivered to my home in North Carolina and I saw your wedding announcement. I had no problem getting Alex Castiglio's phone number. I called several times hoping you would answer. He picked up every time and was very rude. He finally told me to never call again. I was concerned for you. First you had

Rex, an abusive stepfather and then a rude and callous husband. I had to relax and trust you would find me when the time was right."

They sat in silence as the waitress removed their plates and brought the bread pudding and coffee. Lilly tasted the sweet concoction, grinned and wiggled her eyebrows at Aunt Pearl. Pearl closed her eyes as the bread pudding melted in her mouth, "Mmm, I haven't had this in years."

After a few bites of the bread pudding, Lilly couldn't contain her curiosity, "How is life in North Carolina?"

"It's been fine, other than missing you, I've been happy. As I told you on the phone, Evan lives in Asheville and I was happy to be near him. He has a wife now and they always make me feel welcome. North Carolina is lovely. It is a bit colder than I'm use to yet the snow in the mountains is beautiful and peaceful. The people are kind and..."

Lilly frowned and interrupted her Aunt, "Are you planning on returning to North Carolina? I was hoping you were here to stay."

Pearl took a moment to reply, "I don't know yet. Let's see how things go. I would like to visit the North Shore and see what condition my house is in." Lilly nodded slightly and blinked away tears, she couldn't bare to lose her Aunt again. "Now, tell me all about you, sweet Lilly," Aunt Pearl said as she poured cream into her coffee.

Lilly looked into her Aunt's up tilted green eyes, so much like her own and shook her head slightly, "I'd prefer to continue this conversation in my apartment, if you don't mind."

Aunt Pearl nodded, "I understand, some things are best said in private."

Lilly led them up Decatur Street to the building that had housed The Raven Moon. The windows were dark, the building empty. A *"For Sale"* sign hung on the front door. Aunt Pearl shivered when she placed her hand on the door. "The vibrations are askew. There needs to be some psychic clearing, a lot of psychic

311

clearing. This place is broadcasting negative energy."

"Yes," Lilly agreed, "But there is something else we need to take care of first."

Pearl raised an eyebrow, "The important thing we need to discuss in private?" Lilly nodded.

Roland was waiting for them when they arrived at Lilly's apartment. He sat on the sofa with his arm around Lilly as she told Aunt Pearl about her abusive marriage, her escape, finding Panthea's, her early initiation, the gifting of the Inanna crystal, her kidnapping by Regina, the theft and recovery of the stone and the reason they needed her help.

Aunt Pearl sat in the rocking chair, hands resting in her lap and listened to the tale of Lilly's recent past. The strength of the young woman astonished her. "I am so proud of you Lilly," she said when the tale was done.

Lilly looked astonished, "Proud of me?"

"Yes, you have come through so many challenges. You have had an exceptional life, and I have no doubt it will continue to grow and expand in intensity as you continue to grow in wisdom. There are many adventures ahead of you."

Lilly sat silently staring at her Aunt.

Roland patted her gently on the shoulder, "See, I told you. You are one special lady."

Lilly shrugged, "Okay, I'm glad y'all think so. When you say challenges, it does put things in a new perspective. I tend to think I've made a royal mess of things since the day I met Alex. I have to stop berating myself and congratulate myself for rising to the challenges. Although, I don't know how many adventures I can stand," she said with a touch of sarcasm.

"Speaking of adventures," Lilly said, "have you heard of a pyramid in the swamplands?"

Pearl was silent for a few minutes then spoke in a halting voice, "My mother told me bedtime stories about a magical pyramid when I was a child. I don't remember where it is. She sighed and released a small "Hummm" as she sat back and closed her eyes. After a few minutes, she looked at Lilly and Roland, "I vaguely remember hearing the pyramid was built near the mouth of the river by Toltecs or maybe the Mayans, I forget. There are stories about the pyramid and portals, however, it has been a long time since I heard anyone mention it. The stories may be based in fact or merely Faery tales."

"No, it is real!" Lilly exclaimed. "During my visit to Kumira, the powerful Atlantian priest she channels appeared and confirmed there is a pyramid nearby where two great bodies of water meet. Kumira says the Fae may have knowledge of the pyramid where the violet light in the stone could be awakened and its magic returned."

"If that is the case," Aunt Pearl said, "we will have to visit our family in the Dark Bayou to get that information."

A frown creased Lilly's brow, "Do you have any idea how we can approach the Faery village in the swamp. How can we get close enough to make contact? Will they know it is you and I coming and let us in? I haven't been able to get close to the place."

"Yes, I think I can help," Pearl said as she pulled a heavy silver chain from around her neck. A highly polished and exquisitely carved wooden egret dangled from the end of the chain.

Lilly gasped, "One of daddy's carvings!"

Pearl nodded, "Yes, it is. Do you have any of his carvings?"

Lilly's mouth dropped open, "Yes! She said as she dashed into the bedroom, opened the drawer beneath her altar and returned holding a carved wooden alligator the size of her thumb and a long leather cord. The alligator had a small ring in its nose and she quickly threaded it onto the cord. "This will do until I get a chain to put it on," she said as Roland tied the cord around her neck.

"Excellent, I knew you would have at least one of his carvings. Hopefully, these two talismans will be enough to get us through the telescoping portal and onto the front porch of my mama's house."

Roland looked at the intricate carving around Pearl's neck, "How are the carvings going to help?"

Folding her hand over the small wooden bird, Pearl held it to her heart, "All of my brother's carvings were imbued with magic. Each member of our family has a carved talisman which connects them to the village in Dark Bayou."

"Lilly, Do you still wear your talisman?" Pearl asked,

Lilly gasped, "No, no I haven't worn it since I married Alex. He told me I looked like bayou trash when he saw it. I tried wearing it under my shirt, but he knew it was there and made such a fuss about it, I put it away."

Scooting up to the edge of her seat on the couch, Lilly leaned forward and spoke seriously to her Aunt, "There is a small group who have agreed to go to the Faery village with me: a powerful Atlantean Priestess, Kumira, Roland, you and I. Everyone wants to come, but I think a small group may have a better chance of getting close and being welcomed. Kumira has some idea about where the pyramid might be. She is hoping the faeries will have more information and one of them will come with us as a guide."

"I want in on this trip," Pearl said. "I would love to see my family and learn what is known of the lost pyramid."

The next moment Pearl was overcome with a huge yawn. "Excuse me, I didn't realize that was going to happen," she said blushing slightly.

Lilly stood and grabbed a set of sheets and towels from the bathroom closet, "Come on Auntie, I'm going to walk you over to your apartment and make sure you have everything you need. It has been a long day and I know you are tired."

Roland stood, gave Aunt Pearl a gentle hug and said goodnight.

Chapter 48

JOURNEY INTO THE DARK BAYOU

T he next morning Pearl sat in Jolene's kitchen sipping her second cup of coffee. "I know all of you want to meet Lilly's Faery kin, but I think Lilly's idea of a small group is a good one. Only essential persons need to come on this trip." Jolene looked around the table. James and Sabine had disappointed faces, knowing their presence would not be essential.

"The plan Lilly has discussed with me has our journey scheduled for the morning of the new moon," Pearl continued, "I don't think leaving in the morning is a good idea. The bayou faeries are night owls. They feel most comfortable under indigo skies and moonlit waters. Their magic is strongest in the swampy landscape of hanging moss and night blooming flowers. Their own inner light and glowing lanterns illuminate the darkness. Daylight finds them sleeping or having breakfast at 3PM. There are a few who must rise early and get the children to school, they rotate this chore. We would not be a welcome sight early in the day."

James sat silently listing as Pearl described the life of the bayou faeries, "How is it you and Lilly's dad left the village?"

"A good question," Aunt Pearl replied. "Those who choose to live in the secret world of the swamp know the world of man encroaches on their lives and will continue to do so. They want their children to be aware of the world outside and prepared to deal with the people and technology they will encounter. Some of the children are sent to the local school to learn the ways of men. A few of them mate with land-dwellers, birth their babies in the village and raise them in the Faery culture. Others, marry land- dwellers which is what Avery and I did. It doesn't happen often, but it is necessary some of the children integrate into the outside world. Choosing to bring our magic to the world of men was a difficult decision. It became apparent if those with Faery blood did not enhance the world of men and share healing energy, the people of the Earth would devolve. The animals and plants of the Earth would perish at a rate more rapid than they are at this time. Faery blood is strong. Our family in the Dark Bayou are descendants of humans and faeries who mated hundreds of years ago. It takes eons of mating with humans before the Fay power is diminished. We don't want to become isolated from outside influence or risk our village becoming too inbred."

Everyone was digesting the information when the gate buzzer sounded and Kumira's voice came through. James buzzed the gate opened. Within seconds, Kumeria joined them at the table. Lilly looked around at her friends and broke the thoughtful silence. "Aunt Pearl and I need to speak with Kumira and make plans."

The three powerful women sat together in silence. Kumira began to speak and the plan unfolded. "Tomorrow is the full moon. After learning about the nocturnal habits of the bayou faeries we are going to postpone our trip for at least a week."

Pearl nodded, "While the light of the full moon would be a blessing, I agree with you. The sickle moon would be a safer time to make our way through the bayou."

"Good, I don't like the idea of us floundering around in the black waters of the Dark Bayou with a half baked plan," Kumira stated in a matter of fact voice.

"We can easily rent a boat, a motor boat would be best." Pearl stated. "I would like to set off in the late afternoon."

Lilly nodded in agreement, "We may arrive at the Faery village before the sun has fully set. If our relatives are still in their pajamas, I don't care. I would prefer to arrive for afternoon breakfast than be detained by slimy swamp things." The three women looked at one another and laughed nervously.

"All will be well," Pearl said in a matter of fact voice. "We are not helpless. I lived in the village for many years and managed to avoid being eaten by an alligator."

Kumira nodded her head and looked from Lilly to Pearl, We have talismans, Lilly's tingling hands, the protection of Quetzalcoatl and the power of love accompanying us on our journey. The sacred chant, Ooooeeeeaaaahhh," vibrated through the room.

The week passed quickly and everyone was ready to go. The day of their scheduled departure arrived bringing torrential rain, followed by another day of steady rain. The group struggled to stay calm and centered.

They had packed, discussed, meditated and cooked together. Everyone was ready to go. The missing light of the Inanna crystal worried Jolene more than she dared say. Lilly held the dull crystal in her hand as she paced around her apartment chewing her nails. Heavy morning rain cleared by lunch of the third day and the group began their journey.

The sun shone through low hanging clouds in LaPoint, trapping the humid air at 70 degrees. Quickly loading overnight bags into the boat, along with fruits, candies, soaps, lotions and a variety of other gifts for the Fae, they gingerly climbed into the boat.

Roland had a compass on a cord around his neck, sun glasses, a straw hat and a serious look on his face. The ladies, similarly attired, were quiet. Steering the boat across the basin into a nearby channel, they traveled at a steady 15mph. It was a good ten or twelve miles before the purple irises and pink azaleas lining the channel gave way to the red swamp maple, cypress trees, thick vines and hanging moss of the Deep Bayou.

Roland looked at Pearl, "Which way?" She nodded her head to the left. He steered the boat around a clump of land where a flock of Ibis gathered beneath a willow tree. He slowed the boat to a crawl as he navigated through cypress knees.

Lilly took out a bottle of Bug Off from her bag and slathered it on her exposed skin. She passed it around and everyone applied the oily herbal concoction, hoping it would be strong enough to repel the enthusiastic mosquitos inhabiting the bayou.

317

Kumira jumped suddenly and the boat rocked precariously as she pointed silently to two eyes floating eight feet from their boat. Lilly had seen many gators on her trips to the bayou. Obviously, Kumira was shaken by the site of the huge reptile. Roland sped the boat up a bit and left the scaly creature behind.

"Okay everyone, relax," Pearl instructed. "Let's all take a deep breath. We are enjoying a peaceful boat ride in one of the most beautiful natural environments on the planet. Let's enjoy the sites and one another." Kumira gave a nervous laugh, Roland took his sunglasses off and wiped the sweat off his forehead with the back of his arm. Lilly opened her canteen, took a sip of cold water and passed it around to her friends. The tension eased a bit as Pearl and Lilly exchanged a smile and a wink.

Pearl spoke softly to Roland and pointed, "Steer towards the big oak tree."

Roland's eyes widened, "The one with the snake hanging off the low branch?"

Pearl made a simple grunting tone, cleared her throat and with patience instructed, "Yes, but go around the left side of it, no need inviting a snake into the boat."

Roland maneuvered the boat around the small island hosting the ancient oak.

Pearl nodded her head again and continued, "Let's find a way around the wall of hanging moss and go straight for a bit."

The Deep Bayou brought back bittersweet memories for Lilly. She and her dad had shared many lazy summer afternoons fishing on the bayou. Avery LaCouer had spent those precious hours teaching his daughter how to bait a line, the best places to fish and how to charm the fish onto the line. Lilly had vague memories of other secrets he had shared with her, but nothing she could grab onto and pull into her present reality. She remembered how it felt to be with her father more than what he had said. His sparkling eyes, easy smile and gentle voice appeared in her mind. Tears pricked her eyes and she sighed.

Aunt Pearl put an arm around her and drew her close. Putting her head on Pearl's shoulder, Lilly let the tears come as Aunt Pearl reminisced about growing up with her dad. "Avery was a sweet child, mischievous but never mean spirited. His Faery blood was strong and manifested in his ability to create beauty. He embodied the soul of an artist and a philosopher. He loved you so much, Lilly. It is a great mystery to me what he saw in your mother. She was his opposite. Over time their relationship fell apart. Once your mother took Rex as her lover, the situation became unbearable. Avery was planning to bring you out to the bayou village and raise you with your Fae family when he disappeared."

"Aunt Pearl, you mentioned murderous tendencies apparent in Rex's aura. It was my father he murdered, isn't it?"

Pearl nodded her head and sighed, "I have no proof, no hard evidence. Avery's disappearance in the bayou didn't make sense. Your father grew up in the Deep Bayou. He knew how to survive, how to deal with animal threats and he had magic of his own to defend himself. I don't know how Rex managed to overcome him, but I am certain he had a hand in it."

Roland's voice interrupted their conversation, "Pearl, any instructions? This channel is getting narrow and the gator population is getting thick."

Pearl looked around and gave a frustrated groan. "We have taken a wrong turn. Have you followed any inlets since the last instructions I gave you?"

Roland chewed his lower lip. "I don't know, I've been avoiding branches and moss and cypress knees hoping I was staying on course. I figured you would say something if I needed to make a correction."

"Let's turn around Roland, and get back to some place I recognize."

Roland maneuvered the small motor boat around a cypress stump and turned to retrace the way they came. He stood for a moment, peering around a mass of hanging moss when the boat

SUPERNATURAL INTERVENTION

began to rock violently. A huge alligator glided through the water, his scaly body rubbing along side of the boat. Roland took off his wide brimmed straw hat and waved it at the creature. "Get out of here, go away," he yelled ineffectively. Everyone screamed as the gator's huge mouth opened, revealing rows of razor sharp teeth The gaping maw bit down hard and Roland fell back onto the seat of the boat."Are you okay? Did he get your hand? Lilly said as she leaned in to see if there was any damage."

"No but he got my hat."

"Better than your fingers she said as she lifted his arm and inspected his hand. "All digits are intact" she announced. "What were you thinking waving your hat in your hand at that thing?"

"I was thinking of protecting you ladies and running the scaly lizard away," Roland said

Pearl smiled at him and said, "That was very thoughtful and courageous of you Roland. If he comes around again, keep your hands in the boat, rev the engine, and speed up."

Roland could feel his face flush and hoped the waning light prevented the women from seeing the redness spreading over his face and neck. The evening star had risen and the sky darkened when they started back down the channel. A half hour passed as they threaded their way through the gathering darkness. Roland turned on the boat's spot light. It shown on the still water and trees ahead but failed to illuminate what lay beyond.

The boat's motor died. A collective gasp filled the silence. Roland pulled on the starter, trying to get the engine going. Nothing happened. "Maybe we are out of gas," he said flatly. "It doesn't make sense, but nothing works."

"Turn on the light," Kumira commanded.

Roland threw the spotlight switch back and forth. "It has lost power too," he said quietly. Pearl took command, "There are paddles in the bottom of the boat, feel around. We can paddle out of here." Heads bumped together as everyone clamored around blindly for the oars. The small boat rocked precariously, but steadied when they had paddles in hand. They paddled in sync with one another, hoping they were heading in the right direction.

An interminable amount of time passed. "I don't think we were traveling this way for so long" Roland said. "Pearl, do you sense anything familiar?"

"No, I'm not sure where we are. I'm sorry I got distracted. I was talking to Lilly, reminiscing about my brother, not paying attention to where we were heading."

They floated through the darkness, the sound of their paddle strokes blending with the call of the night birds, frogs and unknown creatures. The crescent moon, determined to share her glow, peaked from dark lacy clouds.

Pearl squinted into the murky bayou, "Making the trip on the full moon would have been easier, we would have more light."

Kumira said one word "Lougarou."

Pearl sighed, "Of course."

Suddenly, the group gave a collective moan as a glowing mist formed ahead of them.

Pearl spoke in a steady voice, "No need to fear, this mist is filled with good intentions." No sooner had she spoken than a face, followed by a whole body appeared from the wisps of fog.

Lilly cried out as she recognized her father. He stood in front of the boat. His gaze found her and he smiled. Lifting his translucent hand, he signaled them to follow. Lilly stared at her father, a million questions and declarations of love played on the end of her tongue. She called to him, but his ghostly form did not respond. The boat was gliding easily through a wide channel when Avery found Lilly's face, smiled and faded into the night. The little group drifted silently in the darkness. Pearl spotted a slight glow in the distance and encouraged everyone to row. They paddled straight towards the glowing light. Five minutes later, the glow was further away.

"Ahhh," Pearl said quietly. "Lilly hold your carving in your hand and concentrate on the distant light. Pearl stood, her talisman in one hand, the other hand braced on Lilly's shoulder and spoke clearly in a foreign tongue. "Syl Tira Peaural, Sy cla mi loov."

Pearl sat without rocking the boat, put her finger to her lips and made a quiet shushing noise. Within minutes the sound of fiddle music drifted over the dark waters. The dim light so far distant only a moment before, grew bright. The group gasped in surprise as the boat bumped against a wooden pier. Lights, music and lyrical voices greeted them. Strong hands helped them out onto the dock and welcomed them to the Faery village.

Chapter 49

BENEATH A SLIVERY MOON

The Faeries lead the way across a swaying bridge lit with glowing lanterns. Delicious aromas filled the air as the four guests were shown into a dining area filled with long tables and benches. They were invited to take a seat as the Faery clan gathered for a meal.

Lilly watched Pearl looking from face to face. A smile spread across her Aunt's face when she found the face of her mother. Lilly watched as her Aunt approach the older woman who wore a fringed shawl around her shoulders and held a long stemmed pipe in her hand. Opened arms drew Pearl into the loving embrace of her mother. Pearl motioned Lilly to join them, "I know you two have met before, but possibly, you don't remember your grand-mother, Sylvia."

An air of youth played about Sylvia's smiling eyes along with ancient wisdom. She took Lilly into her warm embrace and stepped back with tears in her eyes. "I see Avery in you," she said and hugged her once again. Tilting her head, she looked puzzled for a moment, "I don't remember your hair being red."

Lilly quickly told her she had disguised herself to avoid her former husband. Sylvia nodded, "We know about disguises here. They can be valuable. I'm sorry you had to use hair dye for your disguise. We have easier methods."

Before Lilly could ask a question, a young woman drew near, took her hand and pulled her gently. "Granny, can I introduce Lilly to everyone?"

Sylvia took a toke on her pipe and put up a hand. "Wait a minute. Lilly, this is your cousin Lotus. She is going to bring you around and introduce you to everyone.

"But," Lilly started to protest.

Aunt Pearl touched her shoulder, "Go ahead Lilly, there will be time for a visit later."

Lotus introduced Lilly to the smiling people who were her relatives. She could see a strong resemblance to her dad in many of them. Her dad had worn blue jeans and T-shirts most of the time. His relatives dressed in delicate fabrics that shimmered silver and green with the slightest movement. Glancing at their shoes Lilly smiled at the fanciful designs and bright colors encasing their feet. Her heart beat with excitement when her second sight caught the soft silvery light moving around and through her family. These beautiful people were her kin. She belonged here. The high cheekbones, pointed chins and huge liquid eyes of green, blue and gray smiled at her. *'I have found home, this is my true family.'*

A tall man stood in the center of the room and clapped once. He held his hands out for a moment and the room grew silent.

"Welcome to our sister, Pearl, our dear niece, Lilly, and her friends. Many moon cycles and much starlight has passed since we have had you in our company. Thank you for your visit and for bringing friends along. We will feast, dance, sing and celebrate. Later we will speak of mundane matters."

A young woman, holding a carafe half as tall as herself, made her way from table to table filling goblets with a strong sweet liquor. Steaming bowls of gumbo were served over mounds of rice along with crusty bread. Platters of sweet potatoes and catfish were passed around the table. Lilly thought she would burst.

After dinner, Lotus took one of Lilly's hands and one of Roland's and headed for the door. They followed the bayou faeries across swinging bridges, down a winding path to a separate island. Palmetto leaves rustled as the faeries stepped lightly through the night. They arrived at a clearing with soft tropical grass beneath their feet and a canopy of stars overhead. Clouds scuttled away quickly as a welcomed breeze drifted across the island. The sliver of a moon rose over the Cypress trees like a silver smile streaming a beam of benevolent light on the Faery kin below. Lilly smiled back at the moon and hugged the magic of the evening to herself.

Aunt Pearl called her name and waved with a silver flute. Roland and Lilly walked closer to the musicians and Pearl put the flute in her hand. Lilly thanked her, looked around and saw half the family playing musical instruments. Those who were not playing music danced, swirled, jumped and twirled with an abandon unseen in the human world.

Lilly put the flute to her lips and danced as she added her music to the jaunty tune. She spotted a young man sitting near a tree tuning a mandolin. Next to him, propped on the side of the tree were three instruments: a banjo, a fiddle and a guitar. Lilly approached him and with a lift of an eyebrow and a swiftly pointed finger acquired the guitar for Roland.

A fiddle player beckoned them and scooted over making room among the musicians. Lilly placed the flute to her lips, closed her eyes and inhaled the early spring air, pungent with the scent of the Dark Bayou. Music flowed and filled the clearing with the magical essence of life. Dancers, light on their feet, whirled in the Faery circle. Silver hair glowed in the starlight, green eyes flashed and lithe bodies danced with total abandon. The hours passed like minutes. When Lilly put the flute aside, a smiling man with silver braids tugged on her hand and led her into the dance.

Breathless from the ecstatic dance, she took a break and joined a group sitting on a log nearby. Pearl approached, sat next to Lilly and put an arm around her waist. Lilly put her head on her Aunt's shoulder and whispered, "For the first time since my childhood, I know the joy of being with my true family."

"Yes, I am experiencing that same joy. I have been embraced by my mother and my wonderful niece is back in my life."

The heavy white blossoms of the night blooming flowers gently folded their petals as the sky turned a pearlescent gray. Lilly breathed in the scent of water hyacinths pushing through masses of lily pads floating in the monochrome palette of the pre-dawn light.

SUPERNATURAL INTERVENTION

Roland joined her on the swampy shore of the island. They stood together silently watching the pink flow of the sky burst into golden splendor on the horizon. Roland relaxed into a huge yawn and Lilly joined him. With drooping eyes, they walked over the swinging bridges back to the Faery camp.

The sun was past its zenith when Lilly opened her eyes. The large window next to the bed looked out over the dark green water of the bayou. An egret perched on a low hanging branch, its long neck forming a graceful curve. Beards of gray green moss swayed gently in the breeze as the sun warmed a family of turtles strung like jade beads on a fallen log.

Roland opened his eyes and sat up taking in the peaceful view. "Hmmm, the Deep Bayou is beautiful." His hand moved up her back and slowly moved around her, gently embracing her breast. Lilly leaned back and lifted her head for a morning kiss. The Egret took flight as Lilly turned to face Roland and pulled him down with her onto the pillows.

Their love making was deep and passionate. They climaxed together reaching new heights of physical and spiritual ecstasy. Snuggling together afterwards, Roland whispered in Lilly's ear, "Do you think we've been taken by Faery magic or the simple grace of the Deep Bayou?"

Lilly smiled, "Both."

Roland ran a caressing finger along the side of her face, "I hope we take it home with us. That was amazing!"

A knock on the door broke the spell as they sat up quickly. "Breakfast meeting in a few minutes," said a deep voice.

Lilly and Roland found the rest of their group sitting at a round table near the kitchen. Grandmother Sylvia, along with two men from the Faery clan, sat with them. The men were similar in size, one had the shining green eyes resembling Lilly's father. His hair hung down his back in a thick silver braid. The other, younger man, had dark blue eyes and blond hair pulled into a knot on the top of his head. Both men wore silver seven pointed stars around their necks and one of Avery's carved animal amulets on a cord that fell over their hearts. The older man, who Lilly soon learned was called, Lance, invited them to grab a cup of coffee and join them.

They sat together sipping hot coffee. Everyone's eyes turned to Pearl, who flushed a deeper pink than usual, swallowed and explained to her kinsmen exactly why they had come to the Faery village. Kumira added what she knew of the pyramid and had several questions answered. Lilly explained the attributes of the Innana crystal, slipped it over her head and laid it in the center of the table.

Their hosts looked at one another for a moment. Sylvia spoke first, "We are aware of the pyramid and know a bit of its history. Lance and Ani," she said nodding at the two men sitting at the table with them, "will be your guides. Lance has an unfailing sense of direction and Ani feels the pull of magic stronger than anyone in our family. With their help, you will be able to find the pyramid and, hopefully a way into it."

The four friends grinned at one another and Roland spoke up, "When do we leave?"

Lance, accustomed to being in control, put his napkin on the table and stood, "Ani and I will pack our gear and we will return to New Orleans with you. From there, we can decide the most auspicious time to leave."

Sylvia spoke and the voices at the table hushed. "I have not seen my daughter and my granddaughter in many years. I ask you stay one more day, at least, so we may have a proper visit."

Pearl nodded and looked at Lilly, "We would love to stay one more day and return to spend many more when our work is done."

Sylvia smiled, "Ah, it is settled."

Rosy tones tinted the sky and a slight breeze caressed Lilly's cheek. She drank in the sight as she sat on her grandmother's porch overlooking the dark green waters of the bayou.

A stand of cattail plants swayed nearby lending their rhythmic percussion to the natural music of the bayou. Sylvia sat in her rocking chair smoking her long stemmed pipe. Concentric circles of aromatic smoke drifted out over the still green water.

As Lilly watched the smoke rings she noticed how dreamy and relaxed she was feeling. "Grannie," she said quietly, "What do the faeries do out here in the middle of the Dark bayou?"

Her grandmother chuckled, "It is not about what we do. It is about our being." Lilly looked puzzled so Grandmother Sylvia continued, "We witness the natural world and are part of natures balance. Our energy naturally sustains the water plants and the interaction between the living systems of the bayou. The Faery ken have been here for centuries assuring the egret finds a home, the ibis gets a fish, the turtles have a fine place to sun themselves and the banks provide a gathering place for the gators. We speak with the plants and creatures of the waters. Knowing their ways, we are able to protect them.

"But we ate catfish!" Lilly exclaimed.

Sylvia nodded, "Yes, some creatures have taken form in this lazy bayou with the express purpose of providing food. The fish live out their life span before they are enticed into fish nets and experience a gentle passing. We eat them with gratitude and strengthen our bond with their species."

"What do we do?" she continued repeating Lilly's question, "I would have to say we love. Our intention for beauty and balance expressed as love, permeates the area and sustains it. Without the magic of love, the world withers."

Lilly nodded as her heart opened, embracing the beauty and grace of the wild, renewing her connection to her Fae heritage and the swampy world of her childhood.

Part VI

AWAKENING

"AWAKEN FROM YOUR DREAM AND
SYNCHRONIZE WITH THE POWER TO HEAL,
STEP INTO PURPOSE AND
LIVE AS YOUR SACRED SELF."

Melinda Rodriguez

Chapter 50

T O U C H P O I N T   S O U T H

A variety of canvas bags, tents and bundles were tied to the top of Lucky's van. Everyone was eager to set off on the journey. Lilly, Roland and Aunt Pearl sat in the back seat. Lance sat up front with Lucky and Ani folded himself into the space behind the back seat. The mood was upbeat and excited. James and Jolene climbed into Kumira's luxury sedan to follow Lucky's van down the narrow highway toward the Gulf of Mexico.

From stories passed down through generations in the Faery village, Lance and Ani believed the ancient pyramid was located in the marshy area of a small island near the mouth of the river. First order of business was getting to the island.

After numerous stops along the way and questions to the friendly Cajuns in the small town of Buras, the group, heavy with supernatural talent, was directed to a little store, no more than a shack, on a side road. Lance, disguised in a fisherman's glamour, walked into the store. He came out of the store smiling and carrying a red metal gasoline can. Lucky followed Lance's directions to a small dirt road about a half a mile from the store. They turned and Kumira's car followed closely. Lucky pulled the van up and parked next to a group of palmettos. They stepped out onto the marshy earth, stretched and breathed in the briny scent of the river.

Three canoes were pulled up on the marshy ground. A large boat with an outboard motor was tethered to a tree in shallow water. Lance pointed to the motor boat. "I paid for the bigger one plus gas for the trip back." Within minutes they were heading straight across the Mississippi River.

As they grew near the island, Lucky saw a pier jutting out into the water. A green metal boat, its' engine askew, sagged in the water near the shore. "Hey, are ya'll sure this island is uninhabited?"

Lance and Ani muttered, "Don't know." The rest of the group shrugged. Lucky steered the boat along side the pier and threw a rope over one of the posts. He gave Roland a hand up out of the boat and they helped their fellow travelers onto the pier. The group stood together on the rickety boards, surveying the wide swath of tall grass before them and the jungle forest in the distance.

Lance led the way with a swing blade, cutting a path through the hip high grass. Lilly and Roland held hands and followed close behind the rest of the crew. The men had machete's in hand and small shovels strapped to their backs. They took turns hacking a path through the tall grass.

James moved ahead of the group with his swing blade. He stopped suddenly and called out, "Hey, come see this!" It was a post about six feet high with a sign nailed across the top. One end of the sign was formed in the shape of an arrow pointing towards the South. TOUCH POINT SOUTH was painted on the sign in faded red letters. "Let's see what this is," James said as he followed the direction of the arrow. Ten minutes later they came to an old, abandoned house.

"There is strong aura of magic around this place," Kumira said in a quiet voice.

James looked around with a raised eyebrow. Everyone nodded when he said, "Lets go check it out." It was obvious, by the size of the house and furnishings, a large family had once called it home. There were seven bedrooms, a huge kitchen, dining area and one large bathroom with several outhouse style circles cut in an enclosed wooden bench. The group wandered through rooms strewn with mats and pillow rotting in the dampness. Baby beds and playpens, children's toys and dolls were scattered throughout the old house.

Kumira and Jolene found a long low table in one room.

Brushing away cobwebs, they found a box of incense, candle stubs and a brass statue of the three Graces. Rubbing off dust and debris, Kumira sat the statue on its base. "This was a sacred place, a sanctuary of some kind. Where did the inhabitants go?"

"It looks like they left in a hurry," Jolene observed.

"Yes, it does. How do a group of people with kids leave an island in a hurry?"

"If the motor boat we saw at the pier belonged to them, they didn't leave by water," Jolene observed.

"We know they didn't leave in the boat," Kumira agreed. Shrugging, Jolene said,"Maybe they had another boat."

Kumira shook her head from side to side, "With a pyramid near by, there may be an inter-dimensional portal on the island. The people at Touch Point house may have left through the portal."

Lucky and James came in on the tail end of the conversation. "They aren't here now and it looks like they have been gone for a while. I'd like to come back to explore more of the island and do some sketching," Lucky said. "But for now, lets get on with the business at hand."

James addressed the group standing together on the sagging front porch, "If we get separated, if anyone gets lost, try to make it back to this house." Everyone agreed as James took Jolene's hand and lead the way.

The group walked toward the thick tangle of woods with heavy undergrowth, massive tropical plants, and cypress knees blocking their way. The going was difficult. The men used machetes to chop through curtains of thick vines, stinging plants, and huge palmettos. A half mile or so into the woods they came to a clearing, everyone stopped and looked at Lance and Ani. "Which way?"

The Fae brothers stood together and slowly turned in a complete circle, simultaneously pointing west. The group trudged through the jungle for over an hour taking circuitous routes

AWAKENING

around impenetrable areas of thick foliage. The earth beneath their feet turned into sticky dark mud the further west they walked.

They came to a sudden halt when Lance and Ani raised their arms, "Stop. We are near the pyramid. We can feel the energy." Ani pointed directly into the dark, thick, jungle growth, "That way."

Jolene quickly cut off a moan as they continued to walk through the dark, humid jungle like forest. The heat of the day was at its zenith when the group stopped, unfolded sheets of heavy plastic over the muddy ground and sat down for lunch and a short rest.

Refreshed with food and drink, the group took a collective deep breath and resumed their mission. They men hacked vines and pulled branches aside The women warned of spider webs and snakes.

Ani, in the lead stopped in his tracks and shouted, "Quick sand."

"Aw crap," Roland said explosively.

Lilly looked at him, "We can go around it."

"Yea," Roland said, "I don't like mushy ground. I draw my strength from the earth. Soggy places drain my energy." He picked up his machete and walked gingerly around the quicksand.

Ani gave a high pitched whistle. Lance raised his arm and everyone stopped for a moment. Lance signaled the group to come forward. They gathered around the two brothers and turned their eyes up expecting to see a pyramid towering through the trees. Not finding a magnificent structure before them, their eyes turned to Lance. He pointed down and they saw the small pyramid covered with green moss, barely visible in the marshy jungle.

"It's small!" Lilly exclaimed.

Lance shook his head, "No, it isn't small, its sunken into the mud. This is the top of it."

"Let's find a way in," James said with a tremor of excitement in his voice.

AWAKENING

The two Fae brothers, the Druid Priests, James and Roland, walked around the pyramid. They walked around it clockwise, counterclockwise and clockwise again. They stood in silence for long minutes at each side of the pyramid.

Within an hour they were unanimous in their opinion. James turned to the little group looking wilted as they mopped sweat off their faces and fanned themselves with leaves, "There is some leakage of energy on the North side. That is the only direction we are getting any reading on this thing,"

The digging was slow and difficult. The muddy earth continuously slid back towards the pyramid and the men found it difficult to keep their footing as they shoveled. Swarms of mosquitos gathered and hung in the air as the sun began to set. The group decided to give up for the day. They followed their path back to the old house. Lucky found a broom in the kitchen closet and went to work clearing a work space in the kitchen.

Lilly found the bathroom and decided to turn on the water faucet to the bathtub. Brown water gushed out of the faucet. Lilly let it run down the drain. Eventually, a slow trickle of clear warmish water flowed into the tub. Closing the drain, Lilly left the slowly running water and went to clean a room where the group could sleep.

Anticipating a relaxing bath and looking forward to being clean again, Lilly opened the door to the bathroom. "Oh my stars! Everyone come see this." The bath water, nearing the top of the tub, glowed an eerie florescent green in the dark room.

Quietly, Aunt Pearl advised, "We are going to have to skip our baths tonight." Laughing and shaking their heads everyone headed out of the bathroom.

Roland turned to Lilly, "Are you going to pull the bath plug or are we going to use the glowing water for a night light?"

Lilly was disappointed. She turned to James, "Why is the water glowing?"

"I'm not sure, Lilly. I would bet the tub filled with river water.

334

There are so many chemicals dumped in the Mississippi River as it flows to the Gulf of Mexico, the combination could easily become fluorescent and very toxic."

"Maybe that is why the family left. The water became too toxic to bathe in much less drink," Lucky said. Laughing nervously, the group gathered in the kitchen for sandwiches washed down with the water from their canteens. A gibbous moon was rising when everyone lay on top of their bedrolls and fell into exhausted sleep.

Chapter 51

PYRAMIDS AND PORTALS

The sun peaked over the horizon, as Jolene and James stood on the porch ready to finish the work they had come to do. Ani, Lance and Lucky came out looking refreshed from a good nights sleep. Kumira arrived with her long braid pinned in a coil on the top of her head. Roland and Lilly joined them, their faces glowing with excitement.

As the men excavated, the women went to work clearing the top of the pyramid. When the vines, moss and tenacious foliage were pulled away, the crystal capstone of the pyramid reflected the morning sun.

Lilly stepped back, "It's a crystal! The capstone is a crystal!"

Kumira stood beside her, "This is a very good sign. The pyramid is powerful. Now that the capstone has been revealed, the sunlight can activate whatever ancient magic lies within."

Around noon Ani called Kumira to the north side of the pyramid. She came forward and inspected the portion they had cleared. With a quiet whoosh of air, Kumira was gone. The Atlantean priest stood in the mud leaning on his staff. His ancient eyes fixed on the pyramid.

The priest spoke indecipherable words in a commanding voice. He ran his hand around an invisible seam on the side of the pyramid. There was a clunk and the stone moved slightly. Lance turned to grab a tool. Using a metal bar, he forced the stone to open so everyone could slip inside the cool dry interior of the pyramid.

With flashlights on, they took a few tentative steps inside. Lilly looked around for the Atlantian priest, but saw Kumira, her eyes huge as she peered pass the entrance. Turning her focus back to the pyramid she shone her light on the smooth stone of the

336

floor and walls.

The group moved toward an arched opening beyond the entrance and stopped. Lucky made eye contact with each of them, "Shall we go on?"

There was a moment of hesitation. Lilly stepped forward, "Of course we shall." Stepping through the archway she entered total darkness. Pinpoints of light from flashlights suddenly dimmer, pointed at the walls, ceiling and floor. All eight flashlights landed on a ledge on the far side of the room. The group neared the ledge, their footsteps echoing off the stone walls.

"Let's turn off our lights," Lilly suggested. The group huddled together in the dark. When their eyes adjusted they saw a blue light pulsing below the ledge.

The group stepped closer and peered into a swirling pool of color. They watched as the shimmering pool took on form and substance. Lilly saw jeweled peacock feathers with glowing golden eyes. Lime green plumes, interspersed between the peacock feathers, undulated with energy. The feathers swelled slightly as they formed a mandala of brilliant color and texture. Concentric circles of shimmering gold formed a golden spiral.

Lilly leaned over the ledge, awed by the beauty of the bright colors. She stood mesmerized staring into the mandala as the golden spiral began to move. She heard Roland say something, turned her head to look at him, lost her balance and catapulted over the ledge into the swirling pool of jewel encrusted feathers.

Like Alice down the rabbit hole, Lilly fell for so long she could no longer tell if she was moving up or down. She spiraled through dimensions of sound and color, spitting bits of feather off her tongue. When the spiraling stopped she was floating, arms stretched out from her sides, legs out behind her and eyes slightly bulged.

After an eternity, or maybe only a moment, she was hovering over an enormous collection of glittering gemstones. Poised in mid-air she watched the dazzling stones form a geometric kaleidoscope. Entranced by the glowing gems, myriad textures, and the cascading sound of bells, Lilly put her hand out and touched a glowing green stone. Her fingers had barely touched the surface of the emerald when she slipped through the kaleidoscope and fell into a sarcophagus. Holding her hand over the dull priestess crystal around her neck, her mind filled with a silent scream for a mere second before darkness welcomed her.

In the darkness there was peace. Time stopped as her consciousness stirred and centered on a point of light in the distance. The light grew closer and revealed two women sitting together in the twilight watching stars appear in the darkening sky. The older woman removed a thick gold chain from around her neck and placed it over the young woman's head. A flash of violet light illuminated the night followed by a glowing red knife piercing the older woman's heart.

The young woman caught sight of the dark clothed unholy monks and the wickedly sharp knives they wielded. The knives, fueled by the monks desire for power, glowed blood red. With adrenalin rushing through her body, the girl ran for the shelter of a near by cave. Glowing red daggers whooshed by her as heavy footsteps grew closer. She weaved as she ran, avoiding the daggers. She felt her lungs would burst and her legs collapse before she made it to safety. The world moved in slow motion as she entered the cave and ran through a labyrinth of tunnels. Exhausted by terror and hours of evading her pursuers, she collapsed.

The warrior monks had crept through the trees ready to invade the temple of the vestal virgins in their sanctuary by the sea when a violet light flashed on a nearby ridge. The dark clothed monks grinned at one another when they spotted the two helpless women sitting on a ridge, a violet light glowing between them. They had fallen upon the girl and her mentor determined to capture the powerful stone. Stories and legends of the violet stone had filled them with fear and longing throughout their lives. They had seen the priestess pass the violet stone to the young girl, they knew it was real and within their reach. Failing to catch the young woman running into the cave with the violet fire, the monks, their blood boiling in anger and crazed with frustration, turned slashing and screaming at one another. Their blood lust sated, the survivors began to move as one through the countryside.

The young priestess opened her eyes to total darkness. She sat up and, as her eyes adjusted, she saw the darkness was broken by the dim violet light of the crystal around her neck. Taking the crystal from under her tunic, she held it up and looked at her surroundings. She stood and began to walk. The tunnel narrowed and she crawled on her belly. Twisting and turning, she propelled herself forward with her feet. Her eyes found a glimmer of light and she surged forward with renewed strength. A babe struggling through the birth canal of the stone cave, she labored toward the light. She arrived at the end of her struggle to find the opening covered by bushes and thorny vines. Placing the Priestess crystal beneath her tunic, she squeezed through the bushes, and fell onto the beach awash in the light of dawn.

Unsure of the power of the crystal or how to use it, she struggled with paralyzing fear. No sooner had she been named keeper of the stone, than her mentor was murdered. Her head spun with a thousand questions she feared would never be answered. Free of the mountain caves, she forced her body forward. Keeping to the sparse woods alongside the road she approached villages warning of the band of warrior monks stealing through the land.

After days of begging food and sleeping under bushes, she entered the gates of a city unknown to her. The thrumming energy of the crystal and its violet light lead her to the center of the city to the temple of the Goddess. She sought the high priestess of the temple and told her of the monks and their knives.

The priestess nodded wisely, "They carry great fear and misdirected anger. They have been taught corrupted stories and mis-information which darkened their souls. We will set protective wards and make preparations."

Safe within the temple, the young crystal bearer relaxed into deep meditation. Recovering from fatigue and fear, she was able to hear the message the crystal whispered and absorb the power it offered.

She came out of her meditation filled with profound relief. She hurried to find the high priestess. Although she was young and inexperienced, she spoke with the authority of the violet flame. "I have received valuable information from the higher dimensions.

The high priestess nodded, "Tell me child."

Taking a breath, she began, "The greatest gifts of the crystal is the transmutation of negative energy into compassion and understanding. We have nothing to fear from dark monks with shining knives. It is they who fear what they do not know yet long for despite themselves. We must offer them the gift of true vision through the crystal of the violet flame."

Gathering the priestesses, initiates and servants, the young woman spearheaded a procession. She held the crystal aloft, its violet light illuminating the way as they proceeded onto the stone steps of the temple. The monks had arrived and surrounded the Temple of the Goddess. They stood, hands on their weapons ready to surge forward.

With the Jewel of the violet flame held high, the young priestess spoke so all could hear, "You are gifted with true vision, true knowing and true forgiveness." Rays of violet light spread across the steps and the grounds surrounding the temple.

The surging monks dropped their knives on the ground as the violet rays awakened their third eye. Their inner vision expanded, encompassing the oneness of all. After moments spent in stunned silence, the clouded vision of their third eyes cleared and compassion stirred in their hearts.

Weeping, many of the monks fell to their knees. A few, turned and ran away in fear. The young priestess spoke into the silence,

340

"You have received the awakening of the violet flame. Do not squander it. Nurture your new awareness. Keep you hearts open. A new life is possible for you."

Lilly, lying motionless in the sarcophagus, watched with her inner eye as her consciousness floated through multiple dimensions expanding her third eye and crown chakra. Suspended in a timeless void, her vision opened onto magical realms. Healing vibrations pulsed within the strands of her DNA.

When she became aware of the satin pillow beneath her head, her eyelids fluttered then flew open. Darkness was dispelled, beams of sunlight fractured into a shower of rainbows pouring through the crystal cap of the pyramid. Her hands found the sacred stone around her neck and pressed it to her heart. Breathing deeply, she trembled as higher frequencies entered through her crown chakra and aligned through her body. The ring of crystal bells, drew her out of the sarcophagus. The air itself emanated the colors of the rainbow. She spun around in amazement, drinking in the power and beauty floating through the air.

She moved to the center of the room staring at the intricately carved walls slanting up to the crystal capstone. She recognized the form of her protector, Quetzalcoatl, among the carvings as she tilted her head back and stared into the light of the crystal capstone above. The warmth between her breast increased as the Inanna Crystal vibrated with new urgency.

Pulling the gold chain up she took the crystal in her hand and held it over her head. The light from above was blinding. Rainbow colors deepened into vibrant hues swirling through the room. The sound of bells, gongs and chimes was almost deafening. The vibrations shook her body. Sweat poured into her eyes, and ran in rivulets between her breasts.

The Priestess crystal grew so warm she was afraid she might drop it. The second she thought she couldn't hold it any longer, everything stopped. The rainbow light was replaced with a violet

AWAKENING

glow. The sacred tone of love filled the air.

"Thank you," she said aloud, "thank you, thank you, thank you!"

She stood beneath the crystal capstone, breathing in the sacredness of the moment. Turning slowly, she felt the call of her friends and lover. Her eyes searched for a way out. The kaleidoscope portal had disappeared. Peering through the violet air, she saw a door. It was huge, twenty feet high carved of lapis lazuli with gold hinges and hardware. "I hope I can open it," she thought to herself. Her hand only touched the golden door knob and the heavy stone portal opened.

Lilly entered a wide corridor with hieroglyphs carved into the stones. Every few feet a statue of some ancient deity stood. She walked to the end of the corridor and found a solid stone wall. Turning back Lilly's eyes roved over the hieroglyphs looking for a line or crevice that might signify an opening, a way out.

'*There! Something looks unusual,*' she thought stepping up to a barely visible crack. She ran her hands over the symbols on either side of the thin crevice. Nothing happened. She pushed on the stone wall straining her shoulder, still nothing moved. Holding the glowing crystal in front of her, she scanned the crevice with the violet light. The stone moved slightly. Running the tip of the crystal along the slight opening, she pushed gently with one hand. The door swung open. Kumira stood on the other side, smiling. She took Lilly's hand and they followed the sound of voices to the entry to the pyramid. Aunt Pearl stood with her friends with worried looks lining their faces. At the sound of footsteps, the group looked up as one. Tight faces filled with relief as they smiled with joy and surprise. Lilly stood in Roland's embrace glowing with the newly awakened violet light.

After drinking in the love of her friends she looked into their eyes as she spoke, "Our mission has been accomplished. The crystal has been awakened and attuned to a higher vibration. The right ingredient for the reawakening was present! The ingredient was my buried memory of the deeper message of the crystal. When it was created it may have been to power advanced technology through the nervous system of its owner. That purpose is no longer primary. Over time, the Inanna Crystal has been recalibrating to the vibration of the new awareness rising in the world. Merlin deciphered the message and shared it with those who could hear the truth thousands of years ago. The crystal's purpose is not about power over anything, it is about the power of Love. We are standing on the precipice of awakening to a new way of being. Love is the key to creating a world of Peace, acceptance, creative thought, and compassion.

"The old paradigm is slowly eroding. The pendulum of consciousness will swing wildly. Those indoctrinated by restrictive religious propaganda and outmoded social mores will struggle to maintain their hold on a world evolving out of their control. It will not be an easy ride. Society, politics, and religion will cling tightly to the old ways causing imbalance and strife. The shadow, those dark aspects of ourselves, our country and our world will rise to be examined. Darkness will seek to prevail and over ride messages of love, empathy and compassion.

"We are the pioneers, the light bearers of the coming age. In the decades ahead the thought patterns of previous centuries will no longer serve us. Fear, resentment, revenge, control and bigotry hinder the evolution of the peoples of the earth. The violet flame within the crystal is not for me alone. It is an energy to share during the coming decades of turmoil and change."

Her lover and her friends stood back for a moment looking at her in amazement. An invisible fog, lifted from their eyes. Ancient awarenesses buried deep in their hearts, awakened. A new vision was born.

Roland ran his hands through the silver white curls on Lilly's head. "Your red hair is gone," he said.

Lilly put her hand to her hair. "I am aligned with my true self, I'm no longer afraid."

Weariness overcame her and she lay with her head in Roland's lap on the drive back to New Orleans. Arriving home, she took time for a bath before joining her friends in Jolene's apartment.

Everyone was gathered in the living room discussing their experiences on the journey. Those members of the coven who had not traveled with them listened intently. The room fell silent when Lilly entered. Everyone spoke at once, questioning her, welcoming her and exclaiming over her adventure.

"Wait, wait a minute," Lilly said with good humor. "Give me a minute and I will tell you all about it. Those of you who have heard it before will benefit from hearing the message again."

An hour later she fell silent. She looked around the room, making eye contact with each of the magical beings she had come to know and love.

Taking a breath, she continued, "Jolene told me, soon after I arrived at Panthea's the day would come when I would forgive my abusive stepfather, my abusive husband and myself for allowing the abuse. I did not believe her. Now, I see how everything unfolded perfectly. I agreed to marry Alex. His energy was familiar. It was the same seething rage below the surface that my stepfather carried. My abusive marriage did not break me. It forced me to seek my own power. My search lead me to the teaching and support of friends, to the realization of my true self and my heritage. Even the horror of my poisoning and abduction by Regina has served a higher purpose in my life. If she had not taken the crystal, if the violet light had not faded, we would not be sitting here having this conversation. My Aunt Pearl would not have arrived to guide me to my family in the Dark Bayou.

"I lost myself in the drama of my life, as we all do. As our consciousness evolves, we can remain awake and present in real time. Our third eye opens allowing us to see the bigger picture, including the destructive patterns as they are manifested. When we become aware of our part in the lessons we are learning, the agreements made through time, and in alternate dimensions, it is easier to forgive all perceived wrongs and know everyone is playing their part in our agreed upon earthly drama.

"The light and energy of the crystal has been recalibrated to a higher level. I have awakened to it. Right now I am free from the pain of the past. It is the responsibility of each of us to remind one another, gently, when we fall into unconsciousness and close our hearts. The violet light has the power to open the heart and mind, illuminating the path to our greatest good. In a state of openness and greater vision, we allow ourselves to follow the guidance of our higher selves. All of us sitting here and those who follow us through time must be the way showers. The time has arrived for the awakening of the people of the Earth. It is not my work alone. Everyone may shine the light from within their hearts and share the wisdom of compassion. Embody this message, live it so the people of the earth may evolve into their higher aspect."

Madeline sighed and said in a reticent voice, "But Lilly, you have the crystal. How are we to access the wisdom and vision of the violet light and experience this wondrous awakening?"

Lilly held the crystal in front of her for all to see. "It is not about the guardianship of the crystal, it is the willingness to attune to the frequency of Love and allow it to be your guiding light. This means we must let go of manipulations, judgements, fears, whatever keeps us from staying in the frequency of Love and acceptance. The violet flame is a cosmic force, hold it in your heart. Allow the vision of it to penetrate your third eye and look on the world through the lens of Love."

AWAKENING

Chapter 52

SPRING EQUINOX

....

THE CIRCLE IN THE SQUARE

*J*ackson square glowed with color. The crepe myrtle trees dazzled the eye with puffs of frilly purple. Azalea bushes flamed in shades of bright pink. Creamy magnolias filled the air with the sweet scent of spring.

The strum of a mandolin laced the air with expectation. Silvery flute notes cascaded through the crowd drawing them closer to the brightly garbed musicians gathered in the center of the Square. Lucky's violin gave wings to a lilting tune while Forest grounded the music on his drum.

From around the corner of the Presbyter, a group of fair haired dancers, leaping and twirling paraded into the square. The sound of tiny bells cascaded through the air as they formed a circle, dancing and prancing around the musicians.

Lilly spotted Aunt Pearl among the Faery dancers, holding a bright pink scarf aloft floating on the breeze. Jolene and James danced to the Celtic tune as Claude and Madeline twirled together. Sabine, her beautiful smile lighting up the day, held young Ivan in her arms as she swayed to the jaunty rhythm. Roland's voice rose adding lyrics to the music:

"You are the magical, mystical multifaceted ones,
True windows to the light.
You can write your own story, dream your own glory,
Shine on, oh so bright.
Arise all lovers, step into your power, embracing your life.

This is your finest hour, rise and live again, open up your gates.
Step into the stream of love, it never is to late."

The ecstatic chant of OOOOO,EEEEE,AAAHHH could be heard above the music, announcing the arrival of Kumira and the Order of Interplanetary Adepts.

A gentle vibration of the ground announced the arrival of Alustra, Shemo and the Vodou drummers and choir.

The music, dance and voices raised in song, created a vortex of Love illuminated by the violet light of the Inanna Jewel. The streets of the French Quarter were deserted as everyone was drawn to the circle of magic shining in the center of the Square.

From high atop the spire of the Cathedral, a raven watched the colorful milieu below. Freed from the curse which had held him in thrall to the witch, Regina, he basked in his reclaimed power. Taking flight, he road the air currents over the river. Turning his head to the side, the raven gave an ecstatic cry as he flew towards the sun, leaving the crescent city to the musicians, mambos, faeries and witches.

Hannah Desmond spent most of her life in New Orleans and part of her adult life in the French Quarter. She was in San Francisco for the summer of love and it was there that she immersed herself in alternate realities and the practice of magic.

In the early 80's she was ordained a priestess in the Fellowship of Isis, an international temple religion honoring the Goddess of 10,000 names.

In the 1990's Hannah started a tour company in the French Quarter, Crescent Star Tours. Her tours included ghost stories, vodou stories, and stories of the magical underpinnings of New Orleans.

In the *Jewel of Inanna,* Hannah draws from her extensive metaphysical studies and occult practices to create a cast of characters who surpass their humanness and live from the heart of their magical being. *Jewel of Inanna* is a fun romp through the supernatural world, a love story, a story of betrayal and, ultimately, a story of awakening.

Hannah lives in Asheville NC where she continues to write fiction and run Heart Light Weddings, offering her services as an officiant, minister and priestess to all couples wishing to form a loving committed union.

A Note from Hannah Desmond

Dear Reader,

Thank you for reading *The Jewel of Inanna.* I hope it transported you to the free spirited and magical days in the New Orleans French Quarter of the 1970's. This was a fun book to write as it brought me back to my days living in the 1970's French Quarter.

The *Jewel of Inanna* is book one in *The Perils of a Pagan Priestess* series.

If you enjoyed *The Jewel of Inanna*, I'd appreciate it if you leave a review on Amazon. A few sentences can make a big difference! Reviews are so important; the more positive reviews a book has, the more promotion it gains through Amazon and other outlets. More positive reviews let other readers know that this is a book they will enjoy.

I would also like to invite you to join my mailing list to stay up to date on my new releases, special sales and book signing events. I send out an email about once a month, at the most so you won't be bombarded with emails from me.

You can sign up here: Hannah@HannahDesmond.com

With Gratitude,
Hannah Desmond

Made in the USA
Lexington, KY
20 June 2018